Phantom Studies

Deathwalker,
Book 1

Brad Younie

Book design by Brad Younie
Cover Art by Jamie Noble Frier
Interior Art by Peter F. Daigle

ISBN 978-1-7333715-3-7 (paperback)
ISBN 978-1-7333715-5-1 (hardcover)
ISBN 978-1-7333715-8-2 (ebook)

www.bradyounie.com

1

Professor Harrison was one of those teachers who loved lecturing to his students whenever he could. His being dead meant his information was absurdly outdated. He was a Haunt —a term I coined for a ghost trapped in one place, forever doomed to wander its halls. The teacher haunted Grendel Hall, the Anthropology building of Boston's Brent College, where I had just started attending. At least this Haunt had come to grips with his ghostly nature and no longer appeared like a corpse. He looked alive, and it had taken me a minute to realize he was a spirit. The apparition resembled a stuffy professor from the Victorian era with his tweed jacket and the pipe he removed from his pale lips to blow smoke that drifted a foot above his head, only to vanish like the illusion it was. He stood behind a desk and rambled on to me about his time as an archaeologist in Egypt.

". . . It was an age of discovery. I was elsewhere, uncovering yet another looted tomb in The Valley of the Kings when Howard Carter made his great find. Ah, he was so lucky . . . But my finds were not inconsequential. In fact, I discovered a—"

Okay. So, he was from the twenties or thirties. It wasn't always easy to tell.

"I'm sorry, Professor, but I am in a hurry. Can you please—"

"I beg your pardon?" The ghost looked at me in astonishment, as though I had done something extraordinary. Something unique. I had, but I already knew that. "You see me? And you *hear* me?"

My eyes rolled at that. This revelation always came as a shock to the dead. I once wondered at that, but I got used to it. That he had been lecturing to me under the belief that I didn't know he was there said some interesting things about his mental state.

"Yes. It's a gift, sort of. But I need your help—"

"Yet you are alive. Tell me, how can you do this?"

"It happens every night, and I can't stop it. Now, if you would—"

"Why, this is amazing! Truly astounding! That a living and breathing person, and a student no less, would be here speaking to me, why—"

"I'm *trying* to speak to you, but you keep cutting me off. If you'll give me a chance, I do need your help."

The expression on Professor Harrison's face switched from one of joy to frustration, then to annoyance, before settling on the creased brow of caring.

"Oh! Of course! Don't let it be said that I wouldn't assist a student in need. What is your dilemma, my dear?"

"My friends and I are trapped in the building. Grendel Hall closes at nine o'clock sharp, and it's now ten past."

"You should have paid more attention to the time," the professor said. Apparently, teachers hadn't evolved much over the decades.

"I know. We were studying and got carried away."

"Ah. And what were you studying?"

"Anthropology."

"Excellent!" A puff of ghost-smoke drifted from his mouth to vanish above his head. "Another scholar. I would love to have a long conversation with you. I am sure I have missed many significant discoveries in my time stuck in this building."

"That would be great, but first, I have to get out of here."

"Yes! There is only one way. You must find Mr. MacNair. He is the custodian of this place of learning. He would have gone to fetch his mop and bucket. Now, you said you are here with friends?"

I nodded. "Three of them. We all went looking for help."

"And I suppose none of them can see spirits?" His voice had lost its lofty tone and assumed one of confidence.

I frowned as a thought crept into my mind.

"How much did they see?" I mouthed, not yet willing to face them.

"Too much, I am afraid." He didn't whisper. There was no

need. I sensed a touch of understanding in his voice. And pity, perhaps.

I bit my lip. "Thank you," I said silently and then turned around to face my study group.

The three of them stood inside the doorway. Jenna Rand, my roommate. Beside her were Scott and Julie, other students in my Archeology class. I didn't know them as well as I did Jenna, except that Scott was friendly with all of us, and it made Julie jealous. Because the sun had gone down, they looked dim, with all the colors of their clothing and skin muted, like everything else in the world. Even Jenna's bright unicorn shirt seemed drab.

It was a part of my condition. Every night from sunset to sunrise, I crossed into the Ghost World. At least partway into it. The place that spirits of the dead inhabit becomes solid to me, while that of the living grows less so.

My companions stared at me as though I had sprouted five heads from my neck. I had told Jenna about my gift, but even she goggled at me, dumbfounded.

"Well," I said with a shrug. "What can I say? I'm weird." Scott and Julie left the room without a word. He shook his head, having made his own judgment, while she giggled.

Professor Harrison called to me as I crossed to the doorway. "Please return to visit me some time. I would dearly love the conversation." When I flashed him a quick smile and nod, he added, "Mr. MacNair is down the hall to your left."

"This way, guys," I said and turned in the direction my new dead friend had recommended.

Jenna fell into step beside me. "We'll talk later," she said.

The others exchanged glances, then followed behind. Julie whispered something to Scott, and though I couldn't make out her words, I knew exactly what she told him.

Down a secondary hallway, I spied the custodian. He was short but stocky with a muscular build. One that was used to hard work. He wore overalls and carried a mop and bucket-on-wheels setup. But I nudged Jenna and made sure she saw him, too, before I spoke.

"Mr. MacNair!" I called. He looked up, startled.

"What are you all doing here?" the man said.

"We lost track of time while studying," Jenna replied.

"Now we're locked in," I added.

"Well. I guess I can't be mad since you were *doing* school-work. What was it?"

"An essay," I said. "For Professor Landry's class."

The man chuckled. "He does that every year. I should learn to expect this."

He leaned his mop against a wall and marched by on his way to the front door.

"You've been working here a long time?" I asked. Being friendly to the guy with the keys was a smart plan.

"The past ten years. Oh, it's not bad," he said when Scott and Julie cast him disgusted looks. "It pays well enough, and the work's easy. And I've got the run of this place every night."

"Sounds like a good deal," I said. "I'm Lexi, by the way. Lexi Downs."

"The name's Tavin MacNair. But my friends call me Mack."

"Well, Mack, I'm glad we found you. We didn't want to get stuck in here overnight."

"Ha! I would have heard you before too long."

He stopped at the entrance and drew out his keys. Once inserted into the lock, he gave it a turn and the mechanism made a reassuring click. The custodian pulled the door open, and the night air blew in cool and fresh.

"Thank you, Mack," I said after Scott and Julie stepped outside.

"We appreciate this," Jenna added.

"Don't mention it."

The walk back to Wembley Hall, our dorm, was uneventful from a spectral perspective. Sure, the moon looked pale and didn't have the glow that normal people said it had. The grass shuddered in the breeze coming in from Boston Harbor, and I found myself on edge as we strolled along the paved walkway to the tall, well-lit building that housed our room. We passed a wooden sign that read "Brent College" in big colorful letters, followed by names of campus buildings and the directions in which they lay. It was dimmer than most things in the Quad. Probably because it was new. The older something was, the more detail it had at after dark. Grendel Hall, the place we had left, was the most detailed structure on campus through my weird night vision, so it must have been quite old and changed little. But at least no more apparitions bothered us on the way.

I had to explain things to Jenna once again. She insisted she believed me, but I had my doubts. Normal people don't believe in ghosts. Even those who say they do get skeptical when others tell their stories.

But I was okay with it, as long as my oddities didn't bother my new best friend.

2

Tom Prichard was a living stereotype. His face had that neo-Neanderthal look with its prominent, bony forehead and powerful jaw topped with a fuzz of blond hair in a close-cropped military cut. The blue eyes would have been attractive if there were any intelligence behind them, but he fit the look too much. The athlete's head sat on a thick neck supported by broad shoulders hidden under a New England Patriots T-shirt. Yup, Tom played the part of the big dumb jock like it was the role he was made for. Now, I don't have a problem with guys like him. They usually have a problem with me. It was every day of my life in high school.

"I know you," he said. It was before class in a huge lecture hall with elevated rows and built-in seats like a movie theater. He had turned around to jeer at me. Jeering was Prichard's native language.

"Really?" I said, not trying to hide my rolling eyes.

Prichard failed to notice and continued on as though I had asked him to. "Yeah, you're the ghost girl. Everyone's been talking about you. They say you see ghosts and shit." At that, several of the students seated around us turned their heads our way. The professor hadn't entered the room yet, so they needed something to watch.

Yup. A real brainiac, this one. I tried to keep a low profile when it came to my condition, and I didn't take well to ridicule. "Well, I certainly see shit," I said, my brown eyes meeting his blue. The brown won, and he shifted his gaze downward. I could consider that a win, since his gaze now locked on my chest.

He frowned. "But is it true? Can you see ghosts?"

I crossed my arms over my chest, and he shook his head, momentarily disoriented.

Half a dozen sets of eyes were on me now, and I didn't want to answer that in front of them. "Why do you ask?" I said instead.

"They say there's a ghost in my dorm. You could find out if it's true."

"Why would you want me to do that?"

"Oh my god!" gasped a girl who was sitting next to Prichard. "She thinks she *can!*"

I didn't respond to her. In fact, I pretended she hadn't even spoken. If I tried to deny it, I would be both lying and making it worse. If I agreed, it would still make it worse. It was a catch-22 I had gotten used to and learned that silence was the best response.

Prichard laughed as though the girl had said something funny. There was nothing humorous about her.

"It'd be pretty cool, though, don't you think?" he said, sobering a little. "I mean, you come to the dorm and do your stuff and talk to the ghost and shit."

"Yeah, we could make it a party! A ghost party!" This new bit of witticism came from the dope to my right, and it seemed to spark a lot of interest among everyone. More people turned around at the announcement of a party.

"Hey!" Prichard said, shushing the onlookers with his booming voice. "So, what do you think? Will you do it?" He wasn't smiling when he said it. In fact, his expression held a hint of apprehension. Just a hint. That made me wonder what his intentions were, but I still knew what my response had to be.

"Let me get this straight," I said, in my most intelligent, businesslike tone. "You want me to come to your dorm with everyone around and tell you if there's a ghost in the building. If I say there is, everyone will make fun of me. If I say there isn't, everyone will say I'm a fraud. Either way, I'm a joke, all for your personal enjoyment. Does that cover it?" My tone might have grown darker as I went because the conversation pissed me off.

There was a murmur of talk among those who had hoped for a party. They were annoyed that there wouldn't be one after all. Tom Prichard, however, continued to regard me, his smile still gone and disappointment painted all over his face.

A door opened down beyond the seats, and a tall woman entered. She wore dark blue slacks and a plaid shirt. Her long, graying hair was partially tied in a bun, with the rest falling down to her shoulders.

The students all turned to face forward, and the talking ceased. Prichard's gaze lingered on me for a second or two, and then he settled in his seat as well.

Professor Porter led the class in a contrast between the author we had read last week and the one we were reading this week. She tried to make it a spirited debate but only got a few students interested. We were only two weeks into our first class beyond high school and weren't ready for anything in-depth. I would have joined in, but it was nice not having everyone's eyes on me for a change. It left me alone with my thoughts.

The story of my talk with Professor Harrison had spread. I'm not sure how it had, since it just happened, and Scott and Julie might not even have understood what I was doing. Maybe Prichard knew one of them. Whatever the case, it was still bound to happen. It was impossible for me to ignore ghosts that didn't want to be ignored. And that meant people were going to see me interact with them. It had happened often since I was little, and so everyone in school knew about it. It was only week two of the semester. I had hoped for a little break before it happened here. Yet here we were, and everyone knew.

Hence, Ghost Girl. Not the worst nickname ever. It was better than Loony Lexi, like I had been in middle school, or Alexandria, Queen of the Dead, as some people called me in high school. I guess I could live with Ghost Girl. To be honest, I was lucky to last as long as I did at Boston's Brent College without a nickname.

I forced myself to take my time leaving lecture hall when the class ended. I had no interest in bringing attention to myself in front of any would-be bullies. Instead, I gathered up my book and papers and stuffed them into my backpack. Then I hefted it and filed out of the room through one of the back doors. My classmates had forgotten about the pre-class fun and left me alone. I escaped the crowd by passing the stairs that everyone took to the bottom floor and outside. With the hallway empty, I continued toward the library.

Professor Harrison, my new ghost friend, had taught here in the 1920s, so I thought I'd try to look him up. After all, it's useful to know who you're talking to. Of course, I had no chance of sending him along to the afterlife, since I've never been able to do that, and he seemed to have no interest in such things. This was for idle curiosity.

"Hey! Ghost Girl! Wait up!" Tom Prichard's voice carried down the nearly empty hall to strike my back, making my shoulders cringe.

I kept walking.

First, his panting breath reached me, and then he appeared and fell into step beside me.

"Hi!" He grinned at me, and it looked like he was trying to be friendly. Odd.

"I have a name, you know."

"Yeah." He looked away now, frowning as he walked next to me. "But I don't know it."

I wasn't going to offer any help. If he wanted my name, he'd have to ask. "What do you want?"

"Your name." It wasn't what he wanted, but I'd give him a brownie point for it.

"Lexi. Lexi Downs. Now, what do you really want?"

He repeated my name soundlessly, his lips moving to form each syllable. Then his face twisted nervously, as though screwing himself up for something.

"Look, I didn't mean for things to get out of hand like that." The words burst out of him in an awkward string that threatened to break apart at any moment. It wasn't like the stereotyped jock-man I had met in the lecture hall. All right, color me curious. "But I *was serious back there.* I want you to look for the ghost in Fenway Hall, my dorm."

"You're talking like you're serious." I kept my tone even, with a hint of skepticism. I didn't look at him but kept walking. The classrooms passed by as the library at the end of the hallway drew nearer.

"I *am* serious." His tone matched his words. That surprised me.

Stopping in my tracks, I turned to face the guy. Tom Prichard was more intimidating when standing beside me than he was when sitting one level below me in the classroom. He towered over me, at least six inches higher than my five-foot-five body, his broad shoulders adding to the young man's frame. This was a guy built to carry a ball through crowds of angry men, and I realized he was not someone to get on the wrong side of.

Yet his face lacked the hardness so typical on the gridiron.

What met my gaze as I lifted my head to regard him was uncertainty and something else. Was it fear?

My facade softened at that moment as understanding sank in.

"Have you seen a ghost, Tom?" I whispered it. I didn't want anyone else to hear it.

He looked around, first one way and then the other. Then he spoke in an equally subdued tone, "Let's sit somewhere."

With a single nod, I led him into the library and to a small table in a discreet corner. It was noon, and most people were in class or at lunch, so the place was practically deserted. When we were seated, he took a moment to collect his thoughts before speaking.

"I don't see it, but I know it's there." Simple. To the point.

"How so?" I asked.

"I see things, like something moving at the corner of my sight, but when I look, there's nothing there. And I can feel it."

He shivered then, and tears welled in his eyes. "Have you ever had someone leaning over your shoulder and whispering into your ear? It's like that, except you can't see or touch him and the whisper is only in your head. Everywhere I go in the whole damn dorm, it's the same thing. I can't sleep and I can't concentrate. I have to do my all my homework in another building. I'm never alone there. It follows me."

"You said it whispers to you. Can you hear it?" That is an exceptional feat in itself. Either he has some sensitivity to spirits, or the ghost is strong.

Tom shook his head. "I hear, or think I hear, whispering in one ear. But I can't make it out. No words, just a hint of it." He crossed his arms over his chest and cast a nervous glance over his right shoulder.

Okay. That was more normal. His descriptions were typical of a haunting, but this ghost had stepped things up. Anyone would be freaked out if they had whispering in their ears all the time and couldn't escape it.

"Do you know if anyone else has felt it, too?" I kept my voice calm and professional, like a cop interviewing a witness.

He shook his head slowly. "Only me. But I'm not crazy, Lexi. I know it's there."

"Have you felt it during the day?"

"All the time."

"Have you felt it outside the dorm?"

"No. Can you get rid of it?"

I raised an eyebrow at that. "I'll confess. I *can* see ghosts. In fact, I can interact with them."

"Like when you talked to one in Grendel Hall," he cut in.

"Yes, like that. But Tom, I don't think I can get rid of any. I mean, some come looking for closure. In theory, if I can provide that closure, the ghost will move on and go away. But I've never done it."

"Can you try?" His watery eyes pleaded with me. My defenses deflated within me. Damn, the big jock got to me.

"I can't guarantee anything," I said. "But I'll try. And Tom," I added, meeting his wet eyes with my hard ones. "If I show up and there's a bunch of people there to give me shit, I will bring you down. You might not believe I can, but you would be surprised what I can manage."

Prichard shook his head vigorously. "No. This isn't a prank. I'm totally serious."

"For your sake, you'd better be."

3

Jenna Rand showed up at my table as Tom Prichard ambled away.

"What was that about?" My roommate glanced back at the departing jock, the guy's blue jeans just tight enough to show off his athletic butt. I had to admit, for a human ape, he looked real good.

"A surprisingly personal conversation," I said and rose to search for information on the school. My roommate followed in my wake. Her curiosity piqued.

Jenna was not like me at all. Where I was cynical and abrasive—yeah, I've been told that—Jenna was bright and cheerful. She was one of those people you don't want to deal with in the morning until you've had a cup of coffee. I swear, she was a walking flower garden. Not many people could handle her, and I was usually the type who couldn't. But somehow she got past my defenses. I liked her, and I didn't know why. It wasn't her cheerful demeanor. It wasn't her love of pop music. My black Slipknot T-shirt attested to that. It could have been that when I told her about my ghostly condition, she accepted it, even though she clearly didn't believe in it. Yeah. That had to be it.

"Personal, eh? What about?" Her grin betrayed her need for juicy gossip.

"Do you even know what 'personal' means?" I asked.

Jenna gasped. "He asked you out!"

"He did not." My tone remained calm, even though I wanted to throw the words like hot coals. Casual disinterest is far more effective at convincing someone you aren't attracted to a person.

"Okay, but I'm still interested. What did you talk about?"

That raised an eyebrow. "Just *okay?*"

"He's not your type. Then what could it be?" Jenna begged as the two of us strode down a little-used aisle of bookshelves. "I won't stop bothering you until you tell me."

Ugh. "Do you promise not to tell anyone? Oh, of course, you can't. That's what gossip's for, isn't it? Telling people?"

Jenna looked affronted. "Hey! I don't gossip. This is just curiosity. I want to know why that guy, who's not your type, wanted to talk to you."

"Why?"

"Because you're my friend and roommate. There's a code, you know. Roommates have each other's back. You've been burying yourself in your studies since the semester started last week. You need to get out and have some fun."

That earned her a chuckle. "Okay, I'll tell you. But keep it between us. Tom's pretty upset about this."

She raised her hand like she was about to take the stand. "I promise."

I told her about the conversation with Prichard. She kept quiet throughout, then considered me for a moment. I guessed what thoughts were bouncing around in her head, but I gave her the time to work it out. She knew what I could do. That is, she knew what I *believed* I could do. Was she convinced? Of course not. How could she be?

"That's not what I meant by having fun."

"It's kind of close, don't you think?"

"In a twisted, demented sort of way."

"I'll take that," I said.

"You're hopeless." She grinned. "Are you really going to do it? The ghost thing, that is?"

"Sure."

"And you think you can help him?"

"I don't know. Maybe. I can talk to ghosts. Maybe I can convince it to leave Tom alone. It's worth a try, right?"

There was a pause, and I knew what was coming. Jenna would handle it more gently than anyone else would, but it still had to happen.

"Now, I'm not trying to be a jerk or anything," she began, "but can you *really* talk to ghosts? As a scientist, I've never believed in spirits. I wouldn't have thought you would, either."

"Seeing one almost every night since I was little made it

hard to disbelieve. I don't want spirits to be real, and I don't want to see them, but I can't help it."

"Is it dangerous?" I liked how Jenna accepted what I said without argument. Maybe that was why we were good friends.

"Yes. But it's hard for Tom to sleep at night with this happening, so I'll do it."

"For someone you don't know. Someone you don't even like?"

"I have to live with ghosts. He doesn't. I can't fix my life, but if I can fix his, I will."

Jenna shrugged. "I don't know what to say. It sure isn't the Friday night I would have recommended."

I stopped looking for information about Professor Harrison and, instead, sat at a table doing Anthropology homework with Jenna. The nice thing about my roommate was that she never prodded too much, so she finally let the Tom Prichard subject go. Her persistence about my meeting with Prichard was a little out of character. But to be fair, she expected the topic to be light and harmless.

Eventually, we packed up our things and went off to class. We both had Astronomy next, but I planned to return to the library after class. She would go back to our room.

Thoughts about the morning's events whirled through my mind during class, and I paid little attention to the lecture. Why had I agreed to look for Prichard's ghost? I hated most ghosts and avoided them whenever I could, which rarely happened. Every night when the sun went down, they'd be there, walking around and acting like living people. And I could touch them and talk to them as though they were alive.

The problem was, *they* could touch me.

When I was young, my parents went on a rampage at my school, trying to find out who was bullying me, giving me bruises, scratches, and cuts every day. They even threatened to sue the school for allowing it to happen. It wasn't until I assured them it didn't happen at school that they backed down.

I never could tell them it happened at night in my own home. The Ghost World was a secret I kept from my parents. Some people couldn't accept fringe concepts no matter how much evidence they saw. That was my parents. If I told them, they would have put me in therapy.

Anyway, some ghosts were friendly, like Professor Harrison. Others, well, let's say that dying doesn't do much good to your disposition. Some ghosts would get mad when I refused to help them. Some didn't need a reason. They all hated it when I screamed. It didn't take long for me to learn not to do that.

Now this jock wanted me to go hunting for a ghost that's been haunting him, and I said I would. Why did I agree to do something so stupid and so dangerous?

Because he was scared.

Well, I thought, *I made the promise, so there's no going back.*

After class, I returned to the library and did some research on the school's history. Tom had said he lived in Fenway Hall. It might give me an advantage if I could find out about any deaths in the dorm.

Fenway Hall was a recent name, and there were no deaths associated with it during the ten years it had that name. Before then, it was Bueller Hall, and it was one of the oldest dorms on campus. Between books on the school and the internet, I dis-covered three deaths in the building. One was of a janitor who committed suicide in the basement in 1946. Another was a vic-tim of bullying. The boy had been locked in a small closet and left there for hours. He had a seizure and died while trapped. That was back in the early fifties. The third was a drug overdose ten years ago. Another boy, this time at a party. Everyone thought he was sleeping. They found his body the next morn-ing.

Okay, so I could rule out the suicide. Suicide victims often kept to themselves in the Ghost World. At least, all those I've met did. That left the overdose and the bully victim. Overdoses cause scared or confused ghosts. They're creepy as hell, and they're sad to deal with, but they wouldn't go around pestering a single living person. Especially a recent death like his. Yeah, ten years is nothing to ghosts.

No, my money was on the bully victim. Hell, Prichard looked like a bully, if they had a look. So, the spirit might be trying to haunt him.

According to my research, they never caught the guy who did it. So, I could find the ghost, talk to him, and tell him I'd expose the real perpetrators if he'd agree to leave Tom alone.

With a plan in mind, I stacked up the books I had brought to my table and put them back on the shelves. The plan sucked, but it was the only one I could come up with.

"What was that monster that bursts from the ground? You know, the one that's all armored?" The voice came from the other side of the bookshelf. It was male and sounded young.

"Ankheg," said another voice, this one sounding older.

"Not that one. There's another. It's armored."

"Search me. I don't have my Monster Manual."

"I'll look it up online," said the first voice.

"Bulette," I said, loud enough for them to hear.

Silence followed, and I looked at the spine of the next book I was going to put away.

Suddenly, books were being pulled away at head level, and I found myself staring through a makeshift hole at a guy. He had a narrow face and a mop of dirty-blond hair with tight curls that would scare away any comb. Add the hazel eyes that gazed at me with a look of wonder, and I would have bet money he was sixteen, if we weren't at college. I guessed he was a young-looking freshman. The kid was taller than me but hunched down to fit his head to the gap in the books.

"What did you say?" he asked.

"You asked about a monster. I said it's called a Bulette."

"You're right."

"Of course I am. I wouldn't have said it if I didn't know."

"How do you know about the Bulette?"

"My mom bought me one as a pet."

"You play?" He sounded as dumbstruck as he looked.

"Wow! Your brilliance astounds me."

He frowned at that. "I'm sorry. You don't look like some-one who plays role-playing games."

"Because I'm a girl?" Great. Sexism even among nerds.

"No." He sounded affronted by my remark. "Because you don't *look* like someone who plays."

I rolled my eyes. "You're not hitting on me, are you?" I could tell he wasn't, but what the hell. It was fun making him squirm.

"No! Of course not. It's just that, well, it's not the most popular kind of game, you know."

"It's more popular than it used to be." The gamer with the deeper voice was walking down the aisle toward me.

"I'm Rocks, and that's Ben. He's not good at talking to girls, but he's good people."

"Hey!" said Ben.

That made me smile. "Lexi Downs."

"Hi, Lexi. So, you're into role-playing games? Tabletop ones, not computer?"

"Sure am, but I haven't played in a while."

"We've got room for another player," Rocks said.

Jenna had told me only an hour before to find a way to have fun, and now I was being invited into a gaming group.

"We need a healer!" said Ben through the gap in the books.

"Okay," I said. "I'll give it a try. But I won't be the healer."

4

A raw breeze blew in from Boston Harbor and sent a shiver up my spine. Of course, it was a warm September evening for everyone not in the Ghost World. It was all a matter of perspective, and I enjoyed the comparatively comfortable walk across campus to Fenway Hall. I dressed the part for ghost hunting, with my new Brent College sweatpants, sneakers, and a tank top that read, "Strength Save" with a twenty-sided die resting on "1." Not what Egon would wear to bust a ghost, but it was the right gear for me.

Prichard opened the door like a good boy when I arrived at his building, and I stepped inside. He might have come to me for a legitimate reason, but his initial introduction still pissed me off. There was no crowd. The few people who wandered about in the lobby paid us no heed. *So, he came through on his part of the bargain. Good for him.*

Tom frowned at me. "That's what you're wearing?"

"Is there a dress code?" I asked, casting a once-over of his shorts and Patriots shirt.

"No. I just thought you'd wear something more . . ."

"Ghost hunters have no uniforms, Tom."

"Okay. What do we do now?"

"I guess go about your business. You said the ghost follows you, but nobody's with us right now. Hang out wherever you would, and do whatever you would normally do. Only not in your room. I'll follow from a distance, in case it won't manifest if I'm with you."

"Right. So, I'll go now?"

"Yup. Where do you plan to be, in case we get separated?"

"There's a common room on the tenth floor. It's got a TV and some tables and shit. I'll go there."

I nodded. "Does the ghost bother you there?"

"All the time. I'm surprised it's not with me now."

"Good. I'll see you there. Don't act like you see me. And don't show interest if anyone talks to me. The ghost can't know I'm with you."

Tom shrugged. "Okay. See you there."

And with that, he ambled down the hall toward the elevators. About thirty seconds later, I followed. I rode the elevator after him to the tenth floor. A couple got on with me. The guy glanced at me and smiled, and I returned it politely. The girl shot me a jealous look and hung all over her boyfriend. Some people couldn't leave their high school insecurities behind.

Five people were congregated in the common room when I entered. Two guys sat at a table, doing homework. They wore casual clothes appropriate for the time period. That was important, as I assumed the ghost died in the fifties. A girl was curled up on a cushioned chair by the TV, dressed in pajamas and a long T-shirt with a big illustrated cat on it.

Tom sat on the couch, watching television. Another jock leaned against the sofa and chatted with him. Like Tom, he was tall and brawny and wore a sports jersey. His curly blond hair stood out in contrast to Tom's buzz cut. The three by the TV glanced up when I entered; the girl afforded me only the slightest look before returning to her show. Tom tore his eyes away from me a little too obviously, while the last looked me up and down with a grin. The guy then turned his attention back to the show, now and then making an obnoxious comment about the program. Tom kept quiet, his eyes riveted to the screen. At least he wasn't looking at me.

So far, no good, I thought. No scrawny bully victim, and no one that resembled an extra on the set of *Back to the Future*.

I took a seat at an unoccupied table across the room from Tom, pulled out my phone, and checked my various social media accounts as I waited for things to happen.

Ordinarily, I'd wander the halls looking for the ghosts. But because I wanted a specific one that followed Tom around, watching him seemed the best option.

Ghosts didn't look like wispy vapors to me, or mists, or anything like that. Some might not look fully there, like they're missing parts of them. I call those Shadows. But they also seem to have less effect on the living world. My culprit would look solid. At least most of the time. It might appear as it did when it died, like a walking corpse that would look at me with too much intelligence for my taste. These were the ones that hadn't gotten used to their new lives as ghosts. They often came to me looking for closure. Those who had come to grips with their lot in un-life looked like they did when they were alive. Professor Harrison was one. Tom's ghost was most likely a Haunt because it never followed him out of the building. It wasn't likely to be a Shadow, as Tom wouldn't have noticed it. His ghost friend could appear dead or alive but would be solid and real-looking.

You might think it would be easy to tell a ghost when I saw one, but you'd be wrong. Sure, at night they appear to me with more detail than the living people and things around them, but that's not always obvious. In the dim, fluorescent lighting, everyone in this room would seem pale, even a ghost.

Ten minutes went by, and nothing changed. Nobody came in, and no one left the room. The jock kept talking to Tom, who tried hard to ignore him. Tom kept his eyes locked on the screen, determined not to take notice of anything around him. I had told him to act normal, and this was not normal, but I couldn't tell him. Then again, I didn't know the guy. Maybe this was his usual shtick.

A half hour passed and still nothing happened. Tom pulled out his phone and started tapping. The guy with him leaned over the couch to see Prichard's screen.

My phone beeped. It was Tom. The message read: "Well?"

I frowned. "Well, what?" These things take time, after all.

Another beep. "Are you going to do something, or what?"

Okay, Tom annoyed me. "Maybe if you send your friend away, the ghost might show up."

There was a pause. "What friend?"

I gasped. *Shit!* My head swiveled to regard Prichard's buddy with more interest.

The kid half sat on the arm of the couch and stared down at Tom's phone.

"Who's the chick?" he said. Tom's eyes remained fixed on his phone, and he didn't even flinch when the guy spoke.

But that wasn't the only thing wrong with this friend of his. The football jersey was for a team I had never heard of. Now that would be no surprise. But the shirt represented our home team, and any New Englanders would know our team was the Patriots. This football jersey had "Boston Yanks" emblazoned on it. But the icing on the cake was his hair. He had nice, tight blond curls. Curls that should wobble some in the breeze caused by an overhead vent. Tom's straight bangs moved in the light wind.

Things like wind didn't cross over into the Ghost World, so they didn't affect ghosts.

I sent Tom a text. I had to be careful not to tip the ghost off, who was looking over Tom's shoulder. "Go for a walk. A lonely hallway, maybe."

"Oooh! Look at that! She wants to meet up with you. You've got it made in the shade!"

Tom's eyes strayed to his phone, then without a word, he stood and strode from the room like a man on a mission. He should have acted more casual, but I couldn't tell him that.

Shoving my phone back in my pocket, I gave them to the count of thirty, then followed. He was already at the end of the hall and disappeared through the doorway to the stairs.

Great. I couldn't follow him. There was no way of knowing which direction he would go or how many floors he'd skip. Frustration rattled through me as I half ran down the hall to the elevators. I guess I could try one at a time until I found them.

My pocket beeped.

I drew out my phone and checked my messages. It was Tom. "Eleventh floor."

"Good boy," I muttered and jumped into the elevator.

Tom's voice drifted to me from a short way down the hall when I emerged on the eleventh floor. A girl in white pajamas covered in a million red hearts stood there talking to him. She played with her hair as she spoke to him.

Tom listened to her in a distracted sort of way. The ghost had caught his attention, but he didn't know where it was. He glanced the other way down the hall, then he turned his gaze upon me. The guy's lack of recognition impressed me. As far as anyone would know, I wasn't even there. Neither the girl nor the ghost, who stood gawking at her, glanced my way.

I walked down the hall until I was one dorm room away from them. Turning, I pretended to write on a small white-board attached to the door. Of course, I wrote nothing but watched the ghost as Tom and the girl flirted.

The apparition saw me, and for a moment, our eyes met. Then he frowned at me. *Here it comes*, I thought.

"Who the hell are you?" the ghost shouted at me. Tom and

the girl gave no reaction. The spirit could have yelled at the top of his lungs and they wouldn't have heard it.

I continued to pretend to write on the board to keep up appearances. When I replied, it was in a hushed tone, nearly a whisper, because they *could* hear me.

"I was wondering the same thing about you."

"This is my dorm. Take a powder! You're not welcome here."

I snorted. "Your dorm? Are you saying you're the only ghost in this building?"

"It's mine, so fuck off!"

"You died in the forties. Or was it the fifties?" I asked.

"I don't need to answer that. Now, get out of here!"

"I'm not dead," I said.

"The fuck you aren't."

"Do you kiss your mother with that mouth?" I taunted in my quiet voice. "Oh, that's right. You can't."

"Screw you! And I know another ghost when I see one."

"How many have you seen, since there are no others in this building?"

The ghost lunged forward at that moment and slammed me with his hands. I stumbled backward, struggling hard to stay on my feet. The message board tore from the wall and bounced around on the string tied to the pen in my hand.

A lot of ghosts have a chip on their shoulders, and I get that. They're dead, and they haven't moved on. Being trapped in a single building for eternity with no means of interacting with the living was enough to turn anyone into an asshole.

But I still didn't enjoy getting pushed around. That happened enough when I was a kid. It would not happen now.

Dropping the pen and the small whiteboard with it, I strode with purpose toward the dead student, my face set. My opponent charged me, as I expected he would, and I was ready for him. At the last second, I slid my left foot to the side, bringing my body with it. A forearm block sent his fist harmlessly beside me as he tripped on the leg that remained stretched before him. I twisted in toward him with my right hand on his wrist and my left on his shoulder. I guided his stumbling fall into the wall, which he hit with a resounding *thud.* It was a thud only I would have heard, because of his ghostliness.

I twisted his arm behind his back and held him there with his face squashed against the wall. It's funny how the dead can still feel pain in this limbo world they live in.

Now you understand why I dressed for the gym when I went ghost hunting.

Leaning forward, I whispered into his ear. "I'm alive, but I'm partway in your world. Can't explain it, it just is. Now, I'm going to let you go, and we're going to talk like civilized people. Understand?"

His head made a pathetic attempt at a nod, and I let him go, stepping back to the far wall to give us some distance. I afforded a quick glance down the hall at Tom and the girl.

The two stood there, staring at me. Both of their mouths hung open like they saw something that defied explanation, or more likely, they saw a person acting like an idiot without warning.

I shrugged and grinned stupidly. "I saw a bee." Lame, I know, but it was all I could think of on short notice. You'd think I would have a host of excuses for situations like this, but alas, no.

I picked up the message board and reattached it to the door. Then I turned and strolled down the hallway, past the ghost, who was rubbing a sore arm.

"Come on," I muttered to him as I went by, and the former person fell into step beside me.

A brief tour of the building resulted in us sitting in an unused common room on the fifth floor. I took a seat at a table and pulled out my phone to pretend to be talking on it.

"All right," I said, getting down to business. "Why have you been bothering Tom Prichard?"

His face, which had been curious, twisted in consternation. "I'm not bothering him."

"You're intentionally doing things to let him know you're there. Letting him see motion, things like that, presenting your presence. Why?"

The ghost swallowed and cast a nervous glance around, as if anyone would see him. Was he afraid to tell me?

"What's your name?" I asked.

"Dave Simons," he said with uncertainty, as though he didn't understand why I would want to know.

"I'm Lexi. You can talk to me, Dave. I'm here to help you."

"What? Like you want to help me *move on*?" Sarcasm dripped with every word. "You can't help me. I'm stuck here because I'm not meant to go anywhere else. I'm supposed to be here."

"Why? Why this dorm? You didn't die here. At least, not to my knowledge."

"Because that's my punishment."

Now it was my turn to frown. "Dave, what did you do?"

He cringed, and when he spoke, he kept his head down, avoiding my gaze. "I pranked a kid. I shut him in a storeroom. You know one of those tiny things for janitors. I was only planning on leaving him there for ten minutes, but some asshole pulled a fire alarm and I kind of forgot."

This came as no surprise. I had already read about the poor boy in the closet. But what did surprise me was there was no mention of Dave's death in the building. "I see. But how did you die here?"

"Oh, I didn't. I was hit by a car a day later while coming back from a party. I was drunk, and I fell onto the road . . ."

A frown tugged at my lips, and I eyed him with suspicion. "Then how did you get stuck here?"

The ghost shrugged. "No clue. I just woke up here. I think I'm being punished for what I did. A constant reminder, you know?"

"How long ago was that?"

"Got me. Couldn't have been long, though. I mean, look at me. I don't look dead, and I'm in good shape."

"You're always going to look that way, Dave," I said. He must be recent if he didn't know that.

"Really? That's nifty!"

"I think you died in the early 1950s, if it wasn't long after your prank." To a ghost, that *is* recent.

Dave shrugged. "I don't remember things like that."

It was time to get down to the point. "Why are you bothering Tom?"

"Is that what he calls it? I was only trying to be friends. I want him to notice me. It gets lonely here, and we've got things in common."

I had to tell him. The hard truth never goes over well, but there was no other option. "He's never going to see you, Dave. I can tell him about you and tell him you want to be friends, but he'll never see you. He can hear your voice only as a whisper and can't hear any words. You'll never be able to talk to him."

Dave sat there for a moment and stared down at his hands that lay on the table. Then, without warning, he launched himself up with unexpected ferocity, sending the chair toppling over, and stormed around the room, shouting and cursing.

I stared at the chair. Ghosts can't touch normal people, but most also can't manipulate physical objects like that. *The guy has power. A Level 4 at least. And he's upset.* A tightness in my gut warned me of the potential danger I was in, and I tried to keep it down.

"You have no idea what it's like here," he ranted, storming halfway across the room, then turning to stalk back toward me. "How could you? No living person can know the hell I live in every day!"

"I suppose you should have thought of that before stuffing the kid into the closet." My eyes closed and I cringed. I regretted those words as soon as they left my mouth, but they were out there now. I tensed, waiting for the increased tirade that was sure to follow.

The young ghost's tantrum halted at once, and he stared at me as though I had slapped him in the face.

"What did you say?" His words were quiet, yet each overflowed with a building rage. Dave Simons had killed a person, and it was accidental. But now . . .

I stood up. "Dave, you need to—"

"Do you think you're here to judge me? Is that what this is?" He walked toward me, and I backed up, moving to put a table with chairs between us. "You get to decide whether I'm *worthy* to go to Heaven or something?" He walked halfway through the table and then came to an abrupt halt.

"Well, I don't think so."

In one quick movement, he grabbed a chair and threw it at me with tremendous force. I ducked and blocked it with my left arm. Pain seared in my forearm, but that was way better than if it hit my head, which it had barely missed.

At once, the enraged ghost charged me, and I did the one thing that came into my head.

I turned and ran.

The last time he charged me, I was in control. That dynamic had changed. He was enraged and able to hurl big objects at me. And a black belt I wasn't. Master Wilder, my sensei, always said that avoiding a fight was the best martial arts maneuver you could do.

I raced from the room and zoomed down the hall, the thumping of my feet on the carpeted floor the only sound I could hear. I sped by door after door and nobody came out into the hall, though I passed three people on my way. Each one looked at me like I was crazy, but I didn't care. They could think anything they wanted as long as I got out of the building in one piece. And where was Tom? Flirting with that girl on the eleventh floor?

So, the ghost had a temper problem. I bet he had it during life, which that poor kid found out the hard way. I should have thought of that. But now I had to focus on escape.

The door to the stairs was at the end of the hall, and I knew I would have to stop running to open it. The deceased Dave Simons must have been right on my heels, so that wasn't an option. I had to turn and fight.

Timing was important. At the last second, before reaching the door, I would dive to the other side, away from the stairs, and spin around on guard. He wouldn't expect that.

Okay, now. Here we go. Three . . . two . . .

Dave's body slammed into mine, and the wall at the end of the hallway careened toward me. My forehead struck the window hard enough to whip my head back from the impact.

A flash of light filled my vision, and a world of pain shot through my head. Time got fuzzy for a moment, and I think I fell. When my mind returned, Dave was on top of me, his hands pinning my wrists to the floor.

I squirmed underneath him and twisted one wrist free. I only had a couple of seconds to decide on a target. His throat or his eyes. I knew ghosts felt pain when I doled it out; that's why I studied Kempo Karate. But did they breathe? I doubted it. At least, I doubted they *needed* to.

I shoved my thumb into his eye, pushed as hard as I could. Dave screamed in anguish and grabbed at my hand. I heard his eye make a sickening *popping* sound.

With one great effort, I spun and threw him off me. He lay curled on the ground, still screaming as he cradled his eye socket with both hands.

I stood up, got dizzy, and fell to my knees. Bile forced its way up my throat, and I had to swallow hard to push it back down.

"*You fucking bitch!*" Dave shrieked at me as he dragged himself to his knees.

And there we squared off, two injured people, one alive and one dead, both unable to stand, and both ready to fight.

"If you're being punished, like you said . . ." My words came out in heavy gasps. "This will only make it worse."

"Ha!" he snorted as he removed his right hand from his face. Blood poured from the socket as though he were alive. "It can't get any worse."

I stared at the blood that ran down his face and dripped onto the floor. It looked like actual blood. With all the scrapes I've had with ghosts in my life, this was the first time I ever did damage to one, and it surprised me it looked so—human. Though I'm sure the blood on the floor was invisible to everyone else, it made Dave Simons appear even more real. And dangerous.

"Lexi!" Tom Prichard came running down the hall toward us.

"He can't help you," Dave said. "I can kill you, and he'll just watch you die."

"Stop, Tom!" I shouted, and the confused jock skidded to a halt right behind Dave.

"Is it here?" he gasped.

I nodded slowly, and he noticed my face.

"Oh, God, did it do that?"

I gave another slow nod as I tried to stand. The world spun, and I wanted to puke all over the ghost, but I got to my feet.

Bully for me.

"I have to get out of here," I said and half walked, half fell to the door.

"Right," Tom said, all business. His mouth was set, like he was about to make the hardest play of his football career. "What can I do?"

"You don't have a gun, do you?" I was only half joking. My legs felt like jello, and my arm shook as I reached for the handle.

Dave stumbled to his feet. He had given up on stopping the blood flow. I guess he realized it wasn't making him any deader.

"That would work on a ghost?" Tom said, incredulity clouding his perfect blue eyes.

"It might, in my hands."

To my surprise and delight, Tom reached into his pocket and withdrew a knife. It was a utility knife, but a big one. He unfolded the blade, stepped forward through Dave, and handed it to me.

Oh yeah. That's right. The guy was still a ghost to everyone else.

I smiled weakly.

"Could you meet me outside to take me to the ER?"

"I could help you down the stairs."

"You'll get in the way. I can't explain right now." Behind Tom, Dave took a step toward me. He looked a lot more menacing, with a missing eye and blood trailing down his ruined face.

"No," Tom said, and his tone hardened a little, like he finally remembered he was the big tough guy. "I'm helping you."

Dave flashed a malicious grin as he took another step.

"Look, the ghost is after me, and he's going to get me if you don't let me go. You can't see or touch him, so you can't help. But I'll need that ride. It's the best help you can give. My hand worked the door handle as I talked, and it clicked open. I backed out onto the landing, the knife held in a guard position.

"Go a different way, but wait for me outside."

Tom stared at me for a moment, but his resolution ebbed as Dave passed through him. Tom nodded mutely and ran off down the hall.

I had no training with knives. They don't teach that stuff in the early ranks, and I'm only a blue belt. "Today, we'll learn blocks, stances, and knife fighting." Right.

Dave followed me onto the landing, and the door closed shut right through him. Reaching behind me with my free hand, I found the railing and began my descent.

I felt like shit, but I worked my way down while holding the knife between us. First one step, and then another, being careful to keep the blade up at all times. Dave and kept his distance. He reached up to touch his eye socket now and then, which must have still hurt, and each time it made me twitch.

A door opened onto a landing a couple of floors down, and I froze.

Living people, seeing me wielding a knife by myself, would not go over well and would undoubtedly make me vulnerable to the waiting spirit.

A couple of girls entered and started climbing. Dave, who had also stopped at the noise, now strained to look down at them. He was probably a Peeping Tom when he wasn't trying to kill me.

Luck was on my side when I heard a door open, and the excited voices went through to another floor. When the door clanged shut and silence enveloped us once more, I continued my laborious trek down the stairs.

"So, you think taking your frustration out on me is worth spending eternity alone?" I had to convince him to give this up. My knife-arm trembled with exhaustion, and I shook all over again.

He said nothing, but his face still held the rage. My handiwork on his eye couldn't have helped any.

"I'm never coming back here," I said. "You'll never have anyone to talk to again. I'm unique, and you know it. Nobody will ever be able to talk to you like I could. But your insistence on attacking me will lose you that chance forever."

"There's always Albert," he said with a shrug.

"Who?" Another step down, and my foot found the first landing. A second later, my hand that held the railing discovered its end. There were no railings on landings. Now was the time to find out if I could stand on my own. But I had to distract Dave, because he might take this opportunity to make his move.

"I'm not the only one trapped here. He doesn't get around much and almost never talks, but he's something."

I let go of the railing. My body wavered but remained standing.

"Where is he now?" The thought of another ghost coming

to his aid didn't encourage me at all.

"Probably down in the basement. He's always down there. Doesn't like people, you see. Dead or alive. But seeing as how he can't kill me, I visit him now and then."

I took a step backward and remained standing. Yippee for me! I now grabbed the next railing and put my foot on the first stair.

"Sounds like a great friend. Better than we would have been. You did the right thing to burn your bridges."

Did I ever mention that my sarcasm sometimes gets me in trouble?

With a roar of renewed rage, Dave threw himself forward at me, and I stumbled backward. My left arm, stretched at full extension, held me in place as I gripped the railing with all my strength. The knife in my right hand whipped upward, and its blade buried itself in the ghost's throat.

Here was where I would see if you could kill a ghost. An interesting concept, but one I wished I would never have to test.

The apparition grabbed my wrist and tried with all his might to force my hand and the blade backward. But he stumbled toward me, making that impossible. He landed on me with his full weight, and my arm let go. The two of us tumbled down the stairs in a mess of bodies and limbs. I let go of the knife and covered my head with my arms as best I could. When I jolted to a halt on the next landing, I lay there moaning, my head dazed and spinning.

I heard a voice speaking to me. Then I was being lifted as blackness enveloped me.

5

The first thing that told me I was alive was the pain in my head. It throbbed, sending waves of torture in my skull to break against my brain. Next came the myriad aches and pains I suffered during the fight and my fall down the stairs. Everything hurt, and the good news was that the massive headache drowned out the other pains. Small consolation, I know, but I had to grab for any I could find. And, hey! I hadn't thrown up. That was something, right?

I was in a car. The smooth cushion of leather interior cradled my body, and the frequent bumps revealed that we were driving.

We.

With painstaking slowness, I turned my head to face the driver. Tom Prichard sat in the seat beside me and steered his way through Boston's nighttime traffic to what I could only guess was a hospital.

"I don't remember leaving the stairs," I muttered, my head pounding with every word.

"You weren't there when I came around with the car, so I went looking for you. I found you in a stairwell. I think you passed out as I carried you."

"You carried me out?" I asked, incredulous.

"Well. I couldn't leave you there. It was my fault you got hurt."

"It wasn't your fault. You couldn't have known any of that would happen. Nope. It was all on the ghost. He just flipped. I don't know if he was like that when he was alive, but he's sure got a nasty temper now."

I paused, and we fell into silence for a minute. The next thing I said needed to be asked, but I almost didn't want to know.

"What did you see?"

"Only you in a heap on the stairs."

"No. I mean the whole thing. What did you see?"

Tom didn't answer right away. He kept his eyes on the road as he drove, and I saw we were making our way to Massachusetts General Hospital.

"At first, I saw you do what looked like karate on someone. Katie and I didn't see anyone. She thought you were acting weird, but I wasn't sure. It looked like you threw someone with some weight to him, not like shadowboxing. I know about fighting, and it looked like you were hitting someone real."

Another pause and I could see the gears going in his head. Whatever it was, he didn't want to say it.

"When you ran down that hall, I saw you get near the end. Something shoved you into the window. But nobody was there. There were plenty of people in the hall by then, but none near you. An invisible person pushed you, and you hit your head. Was that *my ghost*?"

"Yes," I said because I couldn't nod my head for fear it would fall off. It hurt so much.

"So, it's evil?"

"Nothing *that* bad," I said. "Just the normal, everyday kind of evil. I spoke to him. He's a jock, like you. He was trying to talk to you all this time, to be friends. Then I said the wrong thing, and he sort of flipped out. He threw a chair at me, then charged."

Tom shot me a horrified look before turning his attention back to the road. "He tried to *kill* you?" His voice growled when he said it. Another brownie point. My impression of Tom Prichard was rising by the minute. He was still not dating material, but he wasn't quite the obnoxious twit I had thought him to be.

"Tried is the operative word," I said.

"Did the knife help?"

I still didn't dare to nod. "Yup. Kept him at bay. He charged me, and I stabbed him. That's when we fell."

"Is he . . . ? You know. Did you . . . ?" He took a hand from the steering wheel to make a slashing motion across his neck.

I smirked. "Is he dead? He already was. No, I'm sure he's

still there, haunting the dorm. But I bet he's not happy. He might not like you anymore."

"I don't care." He paused, and it looked as though he were trying to screw himself up to saying something important.

"Look, I would never have asked you to do this if I thought it was dangerous. Why didn't you tell me?"

"I didn't know he was that powerful. I figured he was one of the new dead, you know, a Level 2 or 3. And he's *the* new dead. He shouldn't have been that strong. It had to be his rage issues. They made him into a Level 4."

"You've lost me with the numbers. But I didn't know it was even possible they could touch you," Tom said. "You don't see that shit on TV."

"As far as I know, I'm the only one that ghosts can do that stuff to. And trust me, I wish they couldn't."

We rode in silence for the rest of the trip and our wait in the ER. It's funny how long you have to wait when you have an emergency. After a quarter of an hour, I saw a doctor who checked me out and told me I had a mild concussion. She gave me something for my headache and a prescription for more. My nose was fine since my forehead took the brunt of the hit. I had bruises and a couple scrapes from the fall, but nothing terrible. She told me it could have been a lot worse.

Of course, she asked me many times what happened. I told her I had tripped down the stairs. She didn't believe me and seemed to assume that Tom had something to do with it. But I stuck to my story, and it seemed to convince her. Maybe my sincerity won through? All I know is that she, at last, sent me on my way with instructions to rest for the next several days.

Lucky for me, it was Friday.

Concussions suck. Even mild ones can hurt like hell. I took it easy all weekend, and Jenna quickly switched into nursemaid mode.

"I know you," she said. "You'll be getting up and trying to act like you're all better if I don't step in. The doctor gave your orders, and I'll make sure you obey them."

She refused to let me leave my room and brought me food and drink and anything else I could want. Now, at first, I was fine with that. Though I had gotten no cuts or breaks, bruises and other marks covered me, head to toe. And, of course, the enormous bruise and lump in the center of my forehead became a magnet for unwanted attention. Walking was stiff and painful at first, but it eventually got better. I found that the more I walked, the better I felt, and though it went against Jenna's rules, I convinced her with only a few threatening words.

People stared at me as I made my way, hobbling badly around the dorm. Part of it, I was sure, was because of how I looked. But the story of my strange behavior Friday night in Fenway Hall had made its way around campus. Inquisitive students stopped me every time I left my room, looking for the fresh scoop on my latest adventure. Jenna did a great job of fending them off.

"Can't you see she's hurt?" she shouted at the onlookers, and they finally backed off.

My resident assistant came to me the first evening after I came out of hiding and asked me if I was okay and if there was anything I needed to talk about. Once again, I had to explain that no living person had anything to do with my injuries except my own stupidity. Technically, I was right. I was pretty damn stupid trusting that Dead Dave wouldn't pull something like that. And I hadn't handled the situation well. It's possible that I might have set him off. It didn't excuse his actions, but he wasn't totally to blame.

My phone rang. It was Sunday afternoon, and Jenna and I were taking a walk in the Quad, the big park-like expanse of grass and walkways that many of the buildings on campus surrounded. The air was warm, and the breezes filled with an ocean smell I liked. Seagulls called in the sky, and people lounged in the grass and played Frisbee. I stopped and drew out my phone.

It was Tom Prichard.

"Hi. What's up?" That was me trying to sound casual. Not sure it worked.

"Hey. How are you feeling?"

"Like I got hit by a train. But seriously, I'm doing better. I haven't been dizzy since that night, and I'm out walking around, so that's good."

"Are you sure you're ready to do that?" he asked. "You were pretty banged up."

"You sound like my roommate. But it's good. My body needed to move around, and I wanted fresh air."

"Then you'll be in Lit tomorrow?"

"Yeah. I'll be gracing you with my presence. You can knock me down, but I always get back up."

He chuckled. "Cool. See you then. But take it easy, will

you? I want you to get better. Oh! And the ghost is gone."

"Really?" I said. "Are you sure?"

"Yeah, ever since Friday night. I've been able to sleep again. Study, too. Thanks for that. I still wish I never asked you to do it, but at least it worked."

"It makes me happy."

"So, I'll see you tomorrow."

"Yup."

The urge to vomit came over me as I put my phone back into my pocket. It wasn't because of my talk with Tom. No, the grin on Jenna's face brought back too many memories of every rom-com I had ever seen. I couldn't take it.

"Don't even start," I said.

"But it's sweet," she insisted. "He cares about you."

"He feels guilty, is what it is. According to him, it's all his fault I got hurt."

Jenna shook her head. "He likes you."

"Shut up."

One downside to "resting and recuperating," as Jenna called it, was that it left me at the mercy of my thoughts. They weren't merciful. The events of Friday night ran through my brain over and over. I kept running down that hallway. My head struck the window over and over. I fell down the stairs once, twice. Hell, I lost count. Tom's worried face as he drove me to the hospital.

Damn it! I cursed to myself Saturday evening while Jenna left me alone to work on a paper. *If I'm going to think about it, I might as well make it constructive.*

Dave Simons was dangerous. Okay. But he was still the new dead. He behaved as he had when he was alive. He exhibited no extra abilities, aside from manipulating the chair during his rage. That was impressive, but I've seen others do that. The asshole was strong but not skilled in a fight. If I had remained calm, I might have taken him down with little trouble. Though I wasn't a black belt, I was at least half way there and at the top of my class. Having plenty of opportunities to use my Kempo in real-world situations helped me progress. I had beaten up several ghosts who were more powerful than Dave. The abruptness of his attack scared the crap out of me, and I panicked. That's what went wrong.

It wouldn't happen again.

I told Tom that the ghost was still there, but he said it stopped bothering him. Good. Maybe I was successful after all.

When Monday came around, I went to my classes as usual. I couldn't cover up most of the bruises, so I didn't bother. Everyone knew about my adventure anyway, so why hide it?

Tom kept everyone from badgering me during Geometry class, which was unnecessary, but welcome. Afterward, he offered to walk me to my next class, but I insisted I was all set. He left, and I made my way across campus to Grendel Hall and Cultural Anthropology with Professor Landry.

I paused at the entrance to the Quad. The midmorning sun had dried the dew from the grass, and the cloudless sky shone bright and blue overhead. Seagulls soared on the breezes that blew in from the harbor, and I sighed appreciatively at the sensation. People played Frisbee and lounged about, while others followed the walkways to their classes. *College life. Isn't it grand?*

And as long as I stay out of Fenway Hall, I could have a good time here.

"Hi!" A guy came to a stop beside me. He was only about an inch taller than me, with straight black hair and brown eyes. He smiled, and since his expression didn't foreshadow mockery, I returned the gesture.

"I'm Kai," he said and held his hand out to me. I took it. His grip was firm, but not overly strong. Confident.

"Lexi," I said.

"Oh! I've heard about you."

My eyes rolled before I could stop them. But then again, I didn't even try. "I'm sure you have." I started walking. If he wanted to prod me for a juicy story, he would have to keep up.

"I heard you had an encounter with a ghost."

"You hear all kinds of things around here."

"Hey, I understand you don't want to make a big deal about it. I'm sure people here haven't been too nice. But I want you to know I believe you."

I halted once more and met his gaze. His eyes were friendly. Mine, I'm sure, were much colder. "Now, why would you do something stupid like that?"

The poor guy stammered a bit, as though I derailed his train of thought. Then he got a grip on himself. "I believe you because I know ghosts are real. I've seen them."

"That's nice." I started walking again. "But have you heard the stories of my encounter? I was thrown into a window, beaten up, and pushed down a staircase. I think that's the part that most people are having a problem with."

Kai grabbed my wrist and pulled me to a stop. He set his

backpack on the ground, and without a word, pulled his T-shirt up, revealing a slim, hairless chest.

Four long welts in the shape of fingernail scratches stretched from his left shoulder across his chest to stop near his belt.

He put his shirt back down and retrieved his pack.

"I got that when I was ten years old." He started walking again, and it was my turn to keep up with him.

"Does it happen to you all the time, or just the once?" I asked.

"Only once, but I have felt their presence and occasionally seen them for most of my life."

I nodded. "Misty, spectral shapes, and stuff like that."

"Yeah. It's why I'm so into ghosts. I live in Wembley Hall in room 312. Come see me sometime if you ever want to talk about it. The name is Kai Peters." He then veered away down an adjoining walkway, headed toward Gibbons Technology Center. Kai took a moment to flash a farewell smile and wave as he went. The September breeze blew a lock of hair across his face.

I watched him walk away. "I might just do that," I said to no one in particular.

6

Spending a day attending classes proved therapeutic for me. My energy level drifted back up to normal, and my joints and muscles appreciated the activity. After Anthropology class, I went to the Student Center to do some homework. The building contained various areas for students to relax. I went to the cafe in its main room. It had better food than the cafeteria, but it wasn't included on my meal card, so it wasn't free. Still, it was open during off hours, and it made a good place to sit and work.

"Um, hi," came the uneasy stammering of a male voice.

I looked up from my paper to see a young man smiling awkwardly at me. He looked vaguely familiar. I gave him a pleasant smile, giving the kid the benefit of the doubt. Something told me he wasn't here to ask about ghosts.

"Hi. What's up?"

He looked away nervously. "Um, I'm Ben. Ben Feldman. We met in the library last week." The smile that crossed his face was the kind you get when you remember a good time you had. "You knew what a Bulette was."

"Oh! Right!" I said, realization dawning on me. I pictured the kid's face framed by books on a bookshelf. "You're one of the role-playing kids. How are you doing?"

"Good," his awkwardness continued. His gaze kept wanting to drop to his feet. "Anyway, we're having game tonight. You said you'd be up to join us."

"Sure. Where will it be?"

"Strout Hall. Second floor. B Wing common room. Eight o'clock."

"I'll be there."

"Great!" The smile he beamed at me was genuine and huge, yet he turned and retreated like he thought I might bite him.

It was 7:30 p.m. when I left my room for the evening. It had been almost a year since I had played Dungeons & Dragons, and I was excited to get back into it. My backpack contained my rule books and a folder of characters, as well as some blank character sheets. A composition book was there for note-taking, and of course, I had my dice bag. I didn't collect them like most gamers did. I had a lot more than I needed, but I only bought dice if a set called out to me. Totally normal, right?

The florescent lights cast a dull glow throughout the hallway, as it always did for me at night. And, of course, The Door was there.

It stood in the wall where no door should have been and resembled no door that had existed in this century. Oversized, it rose almost to the ceiling and was wide enough to make me feel small by comparison. The long planks of dark oak were held together not by nails but by wide bracers of cast iron that were riveted to it at key places. It resembled a door that I would encounter in a D&D game. And it would be one of those doors that foreboded danger.

I had seen it before. This portal did not exist in reality. It wasn't in the wall on the sixth floor of Wembley Hall. It was in my mind. No. Not in my mind. In the Ghost World. I saw it every night, but it was always in the background; there, but not there. Like a feeling in my mind. And it followed me around. I expected to pass it several times on my way to the game. Over the years, I wondered whether ghosts could see it, or if it was for my eyes only. I never had the chance to find out.

This time, it stood front and center, and I would have to pass right by it to reach the elevators. It wasn't the first time it forced itself on me. I saw it one evening about six years ago, then witnessed a bus crash. Five people died that night. Another time, it was right before I had a run-in with my first big Level 4 Specter, almost the most dangerous on my level system of one to five. This ghost chased me to The Door, and I damn near opened it to get away. To my relief, the ghost only shouted at me, and my screams brought my parents, who scared the ghost away without knowing it was there.

Each time, The Door was like an omen of impending danger, appearing only when something bad was about to happen that I couldn't avoid. I had to steel myself and be ready for whatever came my way.

I shook my head at it. "You want me to open you," I muttered. "But not tonight. Hopefully, not *ever*."

Without another glance at it, I went past and proceeded to the elevators.

A raw wind blew across the courtyard, and I shivered. September in Boston was still warm, but as everything in the Ghost World was visually dimmer, the temperature was always colder. Summer nights were supposed to be beautiful and romantic, but I found them harsh and creepy.

The path from Wembley Hall to Strout Hall, where the group was meeting, crossed much of the college's campus, including the Quad. During the day, it was filled with students playing Frisbee or lounging about. A few people were out when I left the safety of the dorm but were moving briskly to their destinations and had cleared out of the small park by the time I entered.

I strolled in a straight line between the two dorms, leaving the walkways and forging out across the grass. My feet reveled in the turf's softness. Gulls called overhead, and I smiled up at them. My home was too far inland for seagulls, so they added an exotic touch to the place. *One day soon*, I thought as I walked. *I'll grab Jenna and head to the harbor.* I loved the ocean, the ships, and boats, and longed to visit them. *We should have time this weekend to . . .*

A sound made me stop in my tracks. It wasn't only the thumping of footfalls on the grass to my right. It was the inhuman growl that accompanied it.

There were no wolves in Boston, of course. Coyotes? I doubted they'd roam this far into the city. A dog, maybe even a rabid one. That was the most likely possibility.

I panned my gaze slowly around the area, trying to look casual but scanning the darkness for any shape that would betray the animal that made it. Streetlights lined the walkways, illuminating the paths in their warm glow. But I hadn't taken the paved footpaths, and apparently neither had my stalker. I continued to scan the area, desperate to find it before it came for me.

Why did I know it was after me? Because that was my luck; bad things always came after me. And because I had seen The Door. Animals don't become ghosts. They never stick around after death. I always figured they moved on because they never had baggage like we do. All signs pointed to a ghost, but the growl made me wonder.

Something stepped away from a tree about twenty feet to my right, and I was less than surprised to see it standing on two feet. A man eyed me from his position by the tree and then stalked toward me, tensed for a sudden spring.

It's a ghost, or I'm an idiot, I thought. A shiver ran up my spine and my heart beat wildly. I started walking again, and I continued across the grass as quickly as I could while trying to appear calm. Some spirits lose interest if you ignore them. I know, just like dogs, but it's true. Not this mysterious man, though. He increased his pace and made to intercept.

One nervous glance around the park showed we were alone. That was strange at this hour, but not unheard of. Apparently, everyone was where they planned to be. Few people hung out in the Quad after dark. Boston's a great city, but it's a city nonetheless, with no place to hang out alone at night.

I had to run. I knew it, and my pursuer knew it. It was all a matter of when I'd bolt, but it seemed ready for that eventuality. There was an anticipation in its movements that told me it was ready to give chase. Of course, I could turn and fight. I was a good martial artist, but I was no expert, and something about this ghost gave me the willies. Sure, if I had turned and fought Dave Simons, things would have undoubtedly gone better for me. But he was the ghost of a common college jock, and he behaved like that after death. If I had put any real thought into him before going there, I could have handled him.

But this was something different. It was a ghost of at least Level 4, and it scared the crap out of me. Nope. There was no sense in risking it.

Still, running wasn't any likelier to work, and I didn't relish putting my back to an attacker for a second time. The first time didn't go over so well.

I came to a stop, slipping the pack from my back and letting it fall to the ground by my feet.

My pursuer halted as well. It stood only fifteen feet from me, and shadow still obscured its features. *Was that normal?*, I thought, gauging his distance from each of the streetlights that lined the walkways. It could be normal, since he was on the grass and not directly in the sphere of any light. Of course, most people wouldn't take the time to analyze the situation, but when you'd grown up dealing with both the living and the dead, identification was essential.

He was a ghost. He had to be. And I think it was a "he." His head had what looked to be a top hat. Maybe that's what scared me. Even though I couldn't make out any details, he reminded me vaguely of Jack the Ripper, as shown in a bunch of B movies.

The intruder remained in his position and studied me with eyes I couldn't see, but that gave me the chance to look him over. The stalker was tall, at least six feet in height, but probably taller. He wore a top hat, or whatever it was. His general shape implied a suit coat and slacks. The ghost of a nineteenth century aristocrat, perhaps? But a ghost like that wasn't likely to stalk me with malicious intent. Again, Haunts often behaved like they did in life. This one acted like, well, a killer.

The figure suddenly hunched forward, as though preparing to launch himself at me, and I slid my foot back and sank into a strong fighting stance, lifting my hands up into position. Alive or dead, this guy wouldn't get me without a fight.

A shrill laugh shot through the dimly lit park, and my would-be attacker spun around in sudden alarm, toward the sound. Somewhere on the sidewalk beyond the Quad where the campus ended, a woman was cracking up at some joke I hadn't heard.

With a hiss, my stalker ran off like a rocket in the road's direction. I grabbed my bag and ran toward my friends' dorm as quickly as I could.

It was a ghost, so the innocent woman wasn't in danger. Only I was. *He is a ghost, right?* The thought ran through my brain as I ran. *Of course it is,* I consoled myself. *It was shadowy, creepy, and dressed out of time.* And I saw The Door. Clearly, this was why, and that meant it was a Ghost World confrontation. I wouldn't hang around to give it the chance to return.

It was the right thing to do, *wasn't it?*

The door to the room beyond blocked my way like a guardian, telling me to turn and run away. "You don't want to be here, Lexi," the door said to me in its silent voice.

"But I do!" I said in my less silent one. "You're just a door. Just a normal door!"

The door remained still, obstinate in its intention to bar my way.

"I want to do this, and nothing is going to stop me." My mind made up, I grasped the cold metal knob and pulled open the door.

The kids in the small room beyond turned to stare at me, their chessboards ignored for the moment. The teacher in the classroom smiled and waved me in.

"Welcome to Chess Club, Lexi!"

The first snicker happened then. Another followed at once, and then a third.

"Hey, look! It's Loony Lexi!" came a nasty voice from one kid.

"There're no ghosts here, Loony! Go away!" came a second.

The room then erupted with insults, all aimed at me with the same horrible theme.

"Are you okay?"

The words cut through the shouts of the middle school brats and the calls of the teacher for order, and I gave my head a violent shake. The door that had been only trying to help vanished and the open entrance to a dorm common room smiled at me in welcome.

A girl stood beside me with short black hair and an expression too old for middle school. Care etched her face, and the last vestiges of the old memory vanished. I was in college, a place where most people didn't know me. I wasn't Loony Lexi anymore, and I was too old to worry about names.

I nodded and drew a deep breath. That helped. My heart slowed a pace, and the shaking that the girl had noticed abated. "Yeah. I-I'm meeting with a bunch of gamers, and I'm a little nervous." It was a lie, but as lies go, it was a reasonable one.

"Oh," she said with a chuckle. "You've got nothing to worry about with them. They're harmless. And you're dressed right." She glanced at my oversized navy-blue T-shirt that had "+2 Shirt of Modesty" in big fantasy letters.

Some of my nerves eased out of me with the grin I flashed her. "Thanks. I'll be fine now."

"Okay, have fun storming the castle!" The girl continued down the hallway.

The smile faltered.

Come on now, Lexi, I scolded myself. *It's just a group of gaming nerds, and they already accepted you. Dave Simons isn't here.* Of course, there could be another ghost worse than him, but I tried not to dwell on that.

The sound of role-play talk drifted to me as I took my first tentative steps into the room. I heard words like "casting" and "experience," and I got the feeling they were tallying up experience points from their last session. That familiar activity filled me with confidence, and I increased my pace since I could follow the voices to the group. It's funny how nerd talk could make me feel safe when they were the last people I would turn to when in physical danger.

I turned the corner into the common room and stopped dead in my tracks.

This room was nothing like the small one of Fenway Hall, which was much like the one in my dorm. This one showed off the young age of the building. Tables filled the open area of the spacious room. Stacks of board games, books, and anything else a student could want when relaxing covered the counters that lined the walls. Of course, the place was still lit by ugly florescent bulbs, which made the already Ghost-World-dimmed atmosphere even paler. But it was still an enormous improvement to my dorm.

"Lexi!"

Ben waved to me from a collection of tables they had pulled together. I noticed Rocks smile in my direction. Three other students sat with them, and they turned their heads toward me as I stood there. Two of them cast friendly looks while the third frowned.

Okay. It was too late to run away. My hesitation was from fear. The chaos of social activity made me uneasy. I could be social, but I liked to keep it down to small groups. Twos and threes. My last gaming group had four people, and I had grown up with all of them. Five strangers now stared at me from across the room, and that put me on edge. But I had agreed to come, and I didn't relish walking back across the grounds so soon after my earlier fright.

I smiled my greeting and marched to the tables. Ben motioned to a chair beside him, and I took it, sliding the bag from my back and resting it on my lap.

"Hi," I said.

"Everyone, this is Lexi," said Rocks to the group. Then he motioned to the guy on my left. "Okay, starting here, we've got Tony," and the kid beside me nodded. "And Logan," who glowered at me. "You know me," Rocks said. He nodded toward the guy behind the Dungeon Master's screen. "Here's our illustrious DM, Diego." Diego tilted his head in a little bow. "And finally, we have Ben, but you already know him." I glanced at the tall, skinny kid, who sat on my right and gave him a friendly smile. His face went red, and he forced a weak grin.

"Welcome to the Dungeon Crawlers!" cried Diego with a flourish.

"Dungeon Crawlers?" I repeated with a chuckle.

"Yeah," said Tony. "It's what we call ourselves. We *had* to have a name."

"I like it," I said.

"Now, what happened to you?" Rocks said, his face creased with concern.

Oh, yeah. My bruises.

"Someone didn't think girls knew how to fight back. I taught him." I tried to make it a casual statement and opened my bag to pull out my dice and pencils. When I looked back at the table, everyone was staring at me in stunned silence.

"What? A guy attacked me, and I beat him up. I'm fine."

"No offense," said Rocks. I learned a long time ago that when someone says that phrase, an offense will inevitably follow. "But everybody always knows when there's a fight on campus. And I haven't heard of one."

I know it's a stereotype that people who play role-playing games all have social issues, but this was college. There'd be one in *every* group, RPGs notwithstanding.

"Unless it happened in some private place," said Ben. "Or off campus. She didn't say it happened here."

This didn't satisfy Rocks. "That's a nasty bruise. I would have guessed you had a concussion, and an ambulance would have picked you up for that. I never heard about that, either."

"A friend drove me to the hospital," I said. This annoyed me. The last thing I wanted to discuss was my altercation with Dave Simons. I held up a blank character sheet. "Character gen, anyone?"

"So, you got hurt *bad*?" Ben asked. Now he looked worried.

Great.

"All right, all right. I guess we'll never get to gaming if I don't clear the air on my very personal, humiliating, and painful attack."

I paused, and everyone fell silent, and there were more than a few sorry looks. They'd drop it if I told them to, but I knew it would stay on everyone's mind the whole evening.

"You don't have to say anything," said Rocks, casting me an apologetic look. "I'm sorry."

"No. I do. Last Friday, an angry person attacked me in Fenway Hall. Like an idiot, I ran, and that gave him the upper hand. When I *did* fight him, I ended it. He won't be bothering me again."

"I live in Fenway," said Diego from behind the Dungeon Master's screen. He looked out at me over the big cardboard barrier. "There were no fights like that—*wait a minute!* You were the one who got beaten up by herself. People said you raced down the hallway and threw yourself into a window."

"They didn't see the guy who was after me."

"Because he wasn't there. I saw the video Jared Smart took with his phone."

"He didn't make it in the picture," I said.

"Why not?"

"Because he's dead," I replied before I could stop myself, then winced.

That did it. Another silence fell, this one heavier than before.

"Dead?" Rocks said, incredulous.

I gave him a slow nod, the cringe on my face telegraphing my reluctance to admit what I had just said.

"Are you saying," Ben began, "that you were attacked . . . by a *ghost?*"

Here it was. I now had to say it, and it would end any chance of ever playing a friendly game with these guys. It was a shame, too, because I was looking forward to it, even though they all should have kept their mouths shut and not given me the third degree.

The character sheet crumpled in my hand as I screwed myself up to say the words. "Yes. I can see ghosts, and they can see me and touch me, as if they were alive."

A moment passed as the implications of my admission sank into their brains. Then, all at once, they began talking.

"That's awesome!" said Ben.

"Very cool," said Rocks.

"I knew it!" shouted the DM.

"Of course, that makes sense," said Tony. He cast a knowing look at Logan, and they shared a secret smile.

"No, it doesn't!" I couldn't help saying the words, and they all looked at me like I was nuts. "How can you all accept my answer that a ghost attacked me? Nobody would believe that!" These guys were a mystery to me. First, they interrogated me like I had done something wrong, and then they said "okay" as soon as I threw in the ghost card. It was insane.

"My house is haunted," Rocks said.

"Mine too," said Tony.

"Nobody would give an excuse like that if it weren't real," said Ben.

"And I saw the video," said Diego. "That's the only thing that can explain what I saw."

What could I say? They all seemed to take me at my word and were ready to move on. That is, except for the guy who had frowned at me when I first came in. Logan. He kept quiet throughout the entire conversation.

"Okay," I said with a shrug. "Should we game? Do I need to create a character, or can I use an existing one?"

"We all made new characters at the start of the semester," said Diego. "We're only a couple of weeks in. You can make one."

At that point, the game began, and they all talked and gave plenty of advice on character creation. I appreciated some, but most was unnecessary. I was no newbie.

We started the story once I made my character. I was to play a Human Monk. They fit me into the story, and things went well. That is, things kind of went well. Logan kept casting me dark looks. It annoyed Rocks and Tony, though the rest didn't seem to notice. But it pissed me off. At last, I couldn't let it sit any longer.

"Do you have a problem with me?" My words were clear, direct, and loaded with accusation. They forced Logan to meet my gaze.

"Yes, I do." He didn't sound as confident as I did. Good.

"Spill it."

"Tom Prichard."

One of my eyebrows raised of its own accord. "What about him?"

"I saw you with him at the library." Groans erupted around the table. I ignored them.

"So?"

"So, I don't like him, and I don't like his friends."

"I take it he isn't nice to you?"

The groans turned to snickers.

"Yeah. You could say that."

"Look. I'm going to say this once. I don't know the guy well. He's not my type. I helped him out once because he needed it. That's it."

"I don't believe you," Logan said.

"I don't give a shit. That's all the explanation you're going to get from me, and it's more than you deserve. If I'm not wanted, I can leave."

"No!" said everyone at the table at once, save Logan.

Ben leaned over and whispered, "If you just tell him why you helped Prichard—"

"I don't have to tell him anything."

"Logan," said Diego in a placating tone. "It's obvious what she did for him. She fought the ghost in Fenway Hall, and I saw a video showing Prichard helping her up and giving her a knife." He turned to face me. "That ghost was haunting him, wasn't it?"

I didn't respond, but the frown on my face answered his question nicely.

Logan softened. "But why would you help him if you didn't know him?"

"Because nobody deserves to be haunted. And, to be fair, I didn't know he was a bully. A dumb jock, yes. A bully, no."

Everyone laughed at that, even Logan. That seemed to solve the problem, and the game, once again resumed.

We packed up at midnight. Logan and Tony lived in Strout Hall, so they went off to their rooms. Rocks, Ben, Diego, and I hiked out into the warm September air. Of course, warm for them, not for me. Still, all things considered, it wasn't that bad.

"Where are you headed?" Ben asked me.

"Wembley," I said.

"That's my stop," said Rocks.

Ben grimaced. He and Diego went off to their dorm a minute later, leaving me alone with Rocks.

I felt safer walking home with a friend. Rocks was no powerhouse by any means, but he had broad shoulders and a deep voice and didn't come across as a wimp. Still, it was having somebody with me that mattered. Safety in numbers and all that.

We started across the grass in the Quad when we noticed the emergency lights near the road. At least two police cruisers and an ambulance had parked on the side of the road near some bushes where the Quad reached the sidewalk.

My close call with the ghost brought me to a halt. Could I have been wrong? Was it possible that the creepy man with the top hat wasn't a ghost, and I had gone on my way with a dangerous man on the loose?

I turned and ran toward the lights, Rocks chasing after me.

7

Three police cruisers blocked a portion of Boylston Street, their flashing lights blinding in the dark night. Two medical vehicles were parked at the curb. A black sedan with lights inside its grill completed the scene. A knot formed in the pit of my stomach. If this was a murder and I could have prevented it, I would never forgive myself.

Yellow tape, a police officer, and a crowd of onlookers prevented me from seeing the body. But as we approached, I knew there had to be one. The cop's expression was severe and pale. *Has he seen it? Was it* that *bad?* I forced my way to the front of the throng. Nobody wanted to let me through, and I had to shove against the mass of onlookers. It's sad when people love seeing death so much they get mad when someone gets in their way.

Finally, I made it to the tape. Rocks jostled up behind me. His eyes were wide as he took in the scene.

"Excuse me," I called to the pale cop, who stood a few feet away on the inside of the police line. I had to shout like that three times before he noticed and came over.

"Please stay back, ma'am," he said when he approached me.

"Was somebody attacked?" I asked.

"This is a police investigation. Please—"

"I have information. I saw something tonight that might help."

A frown crossed the man's pallid face, and several people turned to stare at me.

"Is there someone I can talk to? Give my statement to?"

The cop nodded and called over to a man in khaki slacks with a dark gray suit jacket. Pale Cop waved him over, and the detective approached. The plainclothes guy was old, in his early forties, with short brown hair flecked with gray. Though not pale, like the cop, the detective looked beleaguered, as though he felt he was in over his head.

"What's up?" he said to the cop.

"This girl says she saw something," the uniform said.

The detective turned his frown on me, painting his disbelief in every crease of his face.

"That true?"

My nod was deliberate and confident. "That's right."

"What did you see?" Pale Cop asked. My confidence made no impression on the man.

"Do you want me to say it in front of all these people?"

He took a deep breath and let it out as he ran his fingers through his hair. Then he shrugged.

"Fine. Follow me." With that, he walked off.

"Wait here," I called to Rocks, who nodded mutely and stared around the scene.

The detective led me, not beyond the tape but to the road where the unmarked police car sat. Nobody was there.

A group of police officers and medical personnel huddled among some bushes that lined the edge of the campus Quad. I couldn't see what they were looking at.

The detective walked up to me. "Okay, what did you see?"

"At about nine o'clock tonight, I was walking across the grass, over there." I motioned toward the decorative lawn I had crossed earlier that night. "When a man came stalking toward me."

"He *stalked* toward you?"

"Yes. He was keeping in the shadows, but I could see him. I saw his profile, anyway. He was tall and dressed in black. And he wore a top hat."

The detective stared at me, as though unsure whether he could believe me.

"Would I make up something like that?"

"Did you feel you were in danger?"

"Of course. I said the man was stalking me. He was coming for me, and I had just decided to stand my ground and fight when he heard a noise from the street and ran off."

"If you thought this man was going to attack you, you should have called the police? Did you?"

I looked away from him when he said this. He had struck on the source of guilt that had been gnawing at me since I saw the police lights. If I had called it in, the person who lay dead in the bushes might have survived.

"I didn't. And that's why I'm here. I feel terrible about it, but I wasn't sure what I'd seen."

"What's not to be sure of? You said you saw him and that he was going to attack you, right?"

"Yes, but . . . well, you see . . ." I trailed off. Now we had come to the point, the one I didn't want to make because it was likely to invalidate my entire statement. But I didn't know what else to say. I had to tell him something, and I couldn't think of anything that would help. The truth wasn't likely to be any good, either, but there was nothing else to say.

"Are you withholding something from me?" The detective's frown deepened. Now I had to say it. He was expecting something, and I'm a terrible liar. I blurted it out too fast to change my mind.

"I thought he was a ghost."

There. I said it. Six lousy words that would force the conversation to take a nosedive.

The detective stood watching me. He eyed me as I looked away again. When I cast him a sidelong glance, he was frowning, but he still appeared serious. He hadn't rolled his eyes, and the intensity remained on his face.

"Why would you say something like that?" he asked, and that snapped my eyes back to him.

"What do you mean?" I said in barely a whisper.

"You didn't want to say it. And you weren't bragging when

you did. There are two types of people who claim to see a ghost: those who want to impress someone and those who actually saw one. You weren't trying to impress me."

Okay, so the guy might believe in ghosts. All the years of keeping this to myself meant that when someone took me seriously, I couldn't help talking about it. Like a floodgate flung wide open, the words would inevitably spew from my mouth in a stream laced with relief. Relief that I was not alone.

"Because I saw one. Or at least, I *thought* I had. Ghosts can't kill people. Not normal people, anyway. That's why I didn't call 911. But when I saw the police lights . . ."

"What do you think this figure was that you saw? You sound like you were sure it was a ghost."

Why was this guy treating me like I wasn't full of shit? How could he take me at my word when we were talking about killer ghosts? But whatever the case, I had opened up, and it was too late to stop. "Three hours ago, I would have bet money it was a ghost, but now I know it couldn't have been."

"Why not?"

"Because ghosts don't hurt people. It's not that they don't want to, they *can't*. Not usually."

"Not usually? But they can sometimes?"

When the person's me. Of course, I couldn't say that. Right now, he thought I was an average person who believed in ghosts. Maybe even like himself. I wouldn't push it.

"They can't kill people." I said it with as much sincerity as I could muster.

Once again, he stared at me, drilling holes into my head with his eyes.

"How do you know that?" He asked the question I was hoping not to hear.

"I . . . don't want to tell you."

"You know I'm a cop, right?"

"It's just that, well, I don't want you to ignore my statement because of my answer to this question."

He nodded as though he understood me. He couldn't.

"Don't worry. My mind is wide open."

"I doubt it, but here goes. I can see ghosts. I have all my life. They are around me so often that I've gotten to understand them and their behavior."

Then a strange thing happened. He pulled a notepad from his pocket, flipped it open to a page, and held a pen ready.

"What's your name?"

"Alexandria Downs. But I go by Lexi."

He scribbled it down. He also took my dorm address and my cell number. Then, he drew a business card from his pocket and handed it to me.

"Please call me if you have any more information, or if you see this *figure* again."

My head bobbed its affirmative, my mouth unable to create words. This detective wasn't at all what I had expected, and even when the interview had gone sideways, he still treated me with respect and understanding. He shooed me back to the crowd, where I rejoined Rocks. We turned and walked away from the scene.

"What was that all about?" Rocks asked as soon as we were away from the crowd and once more entering the grassy park.

"I think I saw the suspect," I said.

"And what happened? I heard people say someone died."

I nodded but said nothing. The detective's behavior still had me thinking. Had he already considered a ghost? That was ridiculous. Why would he?

"That means you saw the killer?" Rocks's words broke me from my thoughts.

"Yeah, I think so. I'm not sure."

"What do you mean?"

"What I saw was a ghost. When I saw the police lights, I thought I might have been wrong about that, so I gave my statement."

"But you believe it was a ghost." It wasn't a question. He knew what I was thinking.

"Yeah. It didn't look normal. I'm sure it was a Level 4 Haunt, at least."

"Level 4?" Rocks said incredulously. "There are levels?"

I chuckled. "I've built my own classifications over the years. Each type of ghost has a name because they aren't all the same. And I've come up with a level system to rate how much of a threat they are to me."

"What's a Level 4?"

"An active ghost that might hurt me."

"And a Haunt?"

"A spirit that's tied to a location and can't leave it."

"Ah, like the one people say you talked to in Grendel Hall. He must also be a Level 4 Haunt."

"Nope. Professor Harrison *is* a Haunt, but he's a Level 3. He accepts what he is and is okay with it. He acts like he's part of the staff and talks my ear off about the way the school used to be. Because he's friendly, he's at a lower risk. A three."

"So, Level 3's are harmless."

"Yeah, mainly. As harmless as any person can be. He might have a trigger. Something that sets him off. It happened with the ghost in Fenway Hall. But he was less comfortable being a ghost, and he had anger issues that put him at a Level 4. Some still cling to life. You know, like death's only a phase or something. He kept following Tom around like he wanted to be friends. But Tom couldn't hear him. He just felt his presence. Ghosts like that are often twitchy. I was careless and assumed he was a Level 3. It almost got me killed."

"Wow. That all sounds complicated. How many levels are there?"

"Five that I know of. I've only seen one through four." At the prodding look he gave me, I grinned. "Ones are the most harmless ones. Like the ones I call Echoes that keep repeating the same thing over and over, like a recording. Ones always ignore me. They are the most harmless, though they can be some of the creepiest. Level 2's are scary and look dangerous, mainly because they appear all messed up, like when they died. But they never bother me. I think they can't touch me, so the most they do is look at me."

"Okay," Rocks said. "What about Level 5?"

I stopped walking. It took Rocks two steps to realize that I had, and he came back to me. "I've never seen one, but I've heard hints of their existence."

"What are they?"

"Feral Ghosts. An apparition who has lost all sense of intelligence but still has a mind. If you'd call it that. These act more like animals, with only a hint of their human past. They don't like people."

"But ghosts can't hurt people, right?" Then his face darkened. "But you got hurt. How does that work?"

"Ghosts *can't* hurt people. At least, they shouldn't be able to. The most you can get from a ghost is a scratch or a push or something like that, and even then, that's only for people who are really sensitive. Someone like you might see a mist or a shadow, or hear a whisper, but you'd never get hurt by one."

"Then how did you get beat up?" Rocks insisted.

"Because I'm not normal. Nobody else can touch ghosts like me. It's like I'm both in their world and our world at the same time."

"And if you can touch them . . ."

"They can touch me. Yeah. Dead Dave Simons realized that, and this happened." I pointed to the mark on my forehead, which still lingered.

"What you saw tonight. It was a ghost?"

I nodded slowly. Everything about that figure screamed spirit. "Yeah. It was. I'd stake my life on it."

"Then he didn't kill anyone. He couldn't have."

"Unless I was wrong about that."

"Do you think you might be?"

"I don't know. Maybe. But why do you care so much? You don't really believe in all this. I mean, I opened up and told you because I know you won't mock me or give me shit about it. But you can't believe me."

"My house is haunted. I already told you." He said it like he was stating a fact. He also didn't look at me. Anyone who lies about this stuff will look at you. They think it makes them seem more sincere. It doesn't. Rocks said it like it was any other thing out of his mouth, and that lent credibility.

"You're certain about that."

"Yup. Saw things and heard things I couldn't explain otherwise. Convincing stuff. And you say it like it's real."

"I must admit, it's nice to have someone to talk to about this."

"Anytime, Lexi."

We split after we entered the dorm. Rocks's room was on the first floor, while mine was on the third. I took the elevator because there would be less chance of meeting a ghost there than on the sixth. Maybe it's all the electricity used, interfering with its ability to manifest. Perhaps the thing would rise and they wouldn't, and it would go right through them. Whatever the case, I'd never seen one on an elevator, so I took it.

After punching the number, I realized I still had the detective's business card. I held it up and read it.

Detective Joseph Ross, Boston Police Department.

8

A crowd of students stood in our way as Jenna and I entered the dorm lobby on our way to breakfast. Resident assistants blocked the exit, causing the traffic jam. Another handed out fliers while Bob Tierney, the first floor RA, was making an announcement to the crowd of students itching to leave.

"Nobody from the school was hurt in the attack. But because the suspect is still on the loose, the police have asked us to step up security. We're just obeying rules."

"But what if I don't have anyone to go with?" asked a student who stood alone on the fringe of the crowd.

"You'll have to tag along with another group that's leaving. Ask an RA if you can't find anyone. We don't want to make things hard, but we need to stay safe."

Vicki Hanson, the RA for my floor, came up and handed us each a flier.

"What's going on?" I asked.

"There was a murder on the edge of campus. Someone attacked a person walking down Boylston Street. The police asked us to have everyone walk in groups. Nobody should go outside alone. At least at night. It shouldn't be a problem during the day. The flier says it all."

"I guess more security makes sense," Jenna said after we got past the blockade and made our way to the cafeteria for breakfast. "I mean, a murder, right here on campus . . ."

My mind entertained only one thought: it *was* a murder, after all. Of course, I had suspected it all along, but somehow hearing that confirmation brought me back to last night and my monumental screw-up.

"Crazy, isn't it?" came a voice from beside me. Jenna and I both flashed the intruder surprised looks laced with annoyance. Kai had come up from behind and now walked beside us. At our surprise, he held up the flier. "The murder. It's crazy, right?"

"And you are?" Jenna asked. She didn't sound upset, only curious.

"Kai Peters. Lexi and I already met. I live on the third floor. I guess the killer's still out there."

"It looks that way," I said.

Jenna shifted her head from me to Kai and back to me again. She narrowed her eyes when I returned her gaze. I mouthed the word *later*, and she kept quiet.

"I'm off to the Student Center," Kai said. "Would you ladies care to join me?"

I shrugged but smiled. "Sorry. Cafeteria for us. It's closer to our class."

"Okay. Your loss." And with a quick wave, he trotted off.

"Since when are you meeting guys and not telling me?" Jenna said as soon as Kai was out of earshot.

"We barely met. But we have things in common."

"He's cute. Are you thinking of going out with him?"

I shrugged. "He's got his own interest in ghosts." I told her about our previous meeting.

To be honest, I hadn't thought about Kai since the other day. The idea of talking to someone who had also seen ghosts intrigued me. That he was cute with his deep brown eyes and infectious smile was a bonus.

I hated my neighbor's house. It wasn't the way it looked. The big split-entry home seemed as good as any other house on my street. The sky-blue paint with white trim and immaculate lawn made it the picture of suburban life. I even liked the family that lived there. We never talked or anything, but they always smiled when I walked by or played in my yard. No. I didn't hate the building or the people there. The source of my ire was something else. Something sinister.

It was *her*.

The sixteen-year-old girl burst from the front door as soon as she saw me. The door remained closed even though she had thrown her arm out to shove it open. She strode through it and across the grass on an intercept course toward me.

That day, I had lost track of time, and the sun already failed to hide the night stars when my trek down the sidewalk brought me past her home. My heart beat a quick tempo, and my feet shifted into a near trot as I tried to outrun the ghost without breaking into the frantic dash my brain screamed for. I had learned not to panic in the face of the dead, no matter how terrified I was. It made me look suspicious. It made other people think there was something wrong with me.

"Hey!" the girl shouted, but I kept walking. I figured if I ignored her, she might go away. Yeah, I was stupid back in those days. But, hey, I was only twelve.

"Hey, you! Stop! I gotta talk to you!"

My body came to a sudden halt before my mind could tell it not to. Like most kids, my parents taught me to respect my elders. Of course, that rule didn't apply in this case. But panic spread from my gut to my legs and arms and head, and I found myself frozen to the spot, as though my shoes had melted to the concrete.

I stared in mounting horror as the angry girl marched toward me.

"Why do you keep running from me?" she shouted when she came to a stop only two feet from me, on the edge of the grass. I wondered if she could step onto the sidewalk. I didn't want to find out.

"I-I don't know," I said.

"*I-I don't know!*" the girl mocked, her lips twisted in a fake pout. "You think I'm going to hurt you. You're scared of me."

I took one step away from her. The girl's hand shot out quicker than I thought an arm could and grabbed my wrist.

A gasp escaped my lips, and I started trembling.

"I'm not the one who's going to hurt you," she said. Her grip on my arm tightened, and I moaned. "I'm here to help you, so stop your whining!"

"Please, don't . . ." I know it was contrary to what the girl had said, but you can't be expected to say the right things when you're terrified. And I thought this girl meant to hurt me, no matter what she said.

"Old Man Winters." Her face contorted into a sneer as she said the name. "You talk to him. You're *friends* with him. Aren't you?"

I nodded in quick, jerky movements, not daring to leave her waiting. "He's nice to me."

"He's dead, you know."

"I know." My words came out in a near whisper. I wanted to say, "You are, too," but my mouth wouldn't let me.

"I'm dead, too." Her voice sounded resigned then. Sad. Her eyes dropped to stare at her feet. "I know that now."

Her grip on my wrist loosened, but I didn't dare pull away. Her words petrified me, yet I needed to know what she was getting at. I wasn't sure why. I just did.

The girl's eyes shot back up to mine, and I gasped once more. "He was nice to me, once. Talked to me. Told me I was sweet. He gave me gifts. Candy."

She pulled me close to her with a suddenness that drew a yelp from my lips. She dipped her face to within inches of mine. "He *killed* me. Old Man Winters did, back when he was alive. And he'll kill you the same way. Stay away from him. He's stuck in his yard. He can't get you if you stay away from his yard. The bastard will try to convince you. Tell you he likes you, but he will kill you, if you let him. Don't let him."

Though dead, the girl's eyes had the semblance of life, like the rest of her. And those eyes ran wet with tears.

"You'll stay away from him, won't you?" she asked, almost pleading.

I nodded.

"You're not just saying it? You'll do it? Leave him alone?"

"I will. I don't want to die."

The girl let my arm go. Her face cracked a slight smile. Relief softened her features.

"You better get home. Your parents will worry."

Another nod from me, and I started walking. I picked up speed as I went, but when I looked back, the girl waved to me. And I waved back.

I never visited Old Man Winters after that. The girl watched me when I went by the old man's house, which was across the street from her own. Each time, he came out to talk, but I avoided him. He seemed more frustrated than disappointed, and that made it clear the girl was right.

After a few weeks of my diligent efforts to avoid the old killer, I stopped seeing the girl. I don't know if she's still there and left me alone, or if I somehow gave her closure and she moved on. To my knowledge, ghosts don't move on. At least, I've never seen it happen. Maybe she's there after all, living her un-life content, knowing that she saved one girl from the same fate that befell her.

The grunts of chairs being pushed back from their desks tore me from my dream, and I glanced around my Sociology class, which was now emptying itself of students. After taking a moment to push that memory away, I packed my backpack and left with them.

The Principles of Archeology classroom resembled most from my high school. Rows of small desks formed neat lines in the rectangular room. Windows spaced along one wall normally filled the room with morning light, but their shades were drawn and the lights were out, casting the place into darkness. The professor's desk faced the class near the only exit. A large-screen television hung from a corner of the room, and all eyes were on it as a show about the Skara Brae site played out.

"Are you sure the detective believed you?" Jenna whispered to me as I stared at the screen. We sat in the back of the class, not because we wanted to talk but because we arrived late. I wanted to learn about Skara Brae, but Jenna was more interested in my story of last night's excitement.

"Yes," I said, keeping my eyes glued to the screen.

"You shouldn't have mentioned the ghost."

"He was interested. And it was important."

"Why? What could the police do, even if it was a ghost? And I still doubt he believed you. People can't accept stuff like that."

"You don't think I know that? Well, it's done. I told him, and we'll have to wait and see what happens."

"He won't follow the ghost angle. If a spirit was responsible, the police will never solve it."

That last statement caused the screen I stared at to blur and my mind to freeze on that one thought.

If the killer were a ghost, the police wouldn't solve it. Only I could.

Professor Landry's voice rang out as he continued his lecture and pulled my attention away from that nasty thought. It was Archeology class, and it was my favorite. I did my best to stop thinking about ghosts and to focus on, well, the dead settlement the teacher was discussing. I guess that wasn't too different after all. But it was a help, and the class flew by as I took notes on the ancient Scottish find.

When the class ended, I told Jenna to go on without me and hung back to talk to Professor Landry. He was tall and thin, and old enough to have a hint of gray in his black hair and beard. The archaeologist had a grizzled look with deeply tanned skin, rough hands that had seen more than their share of hard labor, and a wisdom in his brown eyes that hinted at experience you can't get through scholarly pursuits. This wasn't a normal teacher used to sitting behind desks and doing research. The professor Jacob Landry was a man of action. He knew his stuff.

The Indiana Jones of Brent College was packing his books and laptop into his bag as I stepped up to his desk.

"Professor Landry," I said. "May I ask you a question about the Skara Brae site?"

He paused in his work and looked up at me. "Of course, Miss Downs. Shoot."

"The show focused on the discovery of the site itself, but not much about the people. Do we know what they were like?"

Professor Landry set his bag down to afford me his full attention. "Too many of my students are interested only in the artifacts and the buildings. The things they can see and touch.

It's good to see that at least one of you shows an interest in the cultures." He took a scrap of paper and scribbled something on it, then handed it to me.

"They were a part of the Grooved Ware People. I wrote it down for you. You can look it up. They were an agricultural people who farmed the land, hunted, and fished."

"Thanks, Professor." I turned to leave and then stopped. "Do you know if they had any fascination with death? Like, did they have rituals about it?"

"Why would you want to know that?"

I shrugged and grinned. "I like the topic. I'm a horror movie buff."

He chuckled. "I like that subject, too. Digging up tombs and burial sites has a way of doing that. But we have no way of knowing, I'm afraid. We didn't find any graves near the site, nor any artifacts that would point to such a thing. I doubt they were, though."

"Thanks again," I said and headed to the door.

"Oh, and Lexi," Professor Landry called to my departing back and continued when I looked at him. "Feel free to see me if you have any more questions about a culture and their peculiar customs."

"Of course," I said and left.

Call me predictable, but part of my reasoning for studying Anthropology was to find out if anyone else ever had my abilities. It would be nice to know that it wasn't my own unique, macabre mutation. I planned to take him up on his offer. Surely a culture that revered the dead would be the most likely to have an ancient Lexi Downs running around talking to their ancestors.

9

You would think I would avoid the night. That as soon as the sun had gone, I'd take a sleeping pill and settle down for as deep a slumber as I could manage. But that never worked for me. I tried it for a while but eventually gave up. It's no fun trying to deal with an upset ghost when you're drugged and groggy. Besides, it was *my* life, and I didn't want them to control it.

That evening found me in my dorm's common room in my sweats and a T-shirt that read, "Keep staring, I need karate practice!" I went through some warm-ups and then worked a few basic moves. Since my dojo was back in New Hampshire where my home was, I had to work out more to stay in practice.

Of course, The Door was there. The big oak monstrosity that was in my head took up a section of the wall near the TV. It wanted me to open it, but as always, I ignored it. If there was one thing I'd learned in my life, it was to know danger when I saw it. And that thing radiated danger like an iceberg does cold.

My talk with Detective Ross weighed on my mind. He didn't tell me anything about the crime, but his interest in my statement told me something. A person was murdered, and he was open to suspecting a ghost, despite how ridiculous it sounded. That meant he was desperate. There must have been problems with the crime scene that didn't add up.

I stopped practicing my blocks and performed #2 Kata, the most recent form I had learned. Katas resembled a cross between shadow-boxing and a dance. They're like both those things, but that isn't their intention. A kata is like a choreographed fight. You're supposed to imagine yourself striking and kicking multiple opponents throughout the course of the form. I found it helped me relax, so that I could focus on things I needed to work out in my head.

As I went through the practice fight, the image of Top Hat returned. I blocked a fictional punch and responded with a wrist strike that shot upward to hit his jaw. *Could that figure have been a real person?* I thought as I took a step backward and repeated the process. *He was all shadowy, not as distinct as I would have expected.* I tried to remember where the trees were in relation to the man, and if their shadows would account for the lack of detail. *He started beside a tree, but he came at me and he was still unclear.* I spun around into a cat stance, as though looking for attackers behind me, then pivoted a bit to my left, my hands still forming a claw. *Nope. It was definitely a ghost. The top hat and the lack of features made it old. Sometimes the really old ones can become less distinct, like they stopped caring about appearing real.* I threw a back kick followed by a side kick. *A Level 5 that blends into the shadows. That's about as bad as you can get.* I finished the kata with a bow.

I had never heard of a ghost that could kill a person, and that threw this one into uncharted territory. Now, some can knock a person down the stairs or something like that. At most, it could push someone or scratch them. But murder was always reserved for the living evil. *Top Hat was definitely not alive.*

Now I wasn't as confident about my killer. If it was a ghost, it didn't murder that person. Plain and simple. Then how would I find out if that figure was a spirit?

I had to talk to another one.

Grabbing my water bottle and key card from a nearby table, I drank my fill and trotted back to my room. Jenna sat at her desk in the dimly lit bedroom with her back to me and headphones over her ears. I quickly replaced my sweats with shorts, added sneakers, and grabbed a small bag containing my wallet and my phone.

"Hey, Jenna!" I called.

She jumped, then pulled her headphones off one ear. "You scared me!"

"Sorry! I'm heading out to Grendel Hall. There's something I have to look into. Thought I'd let you know."

"But I can't go with you. I have this paper to write."

"It's okay. It's not far, and I'll find people to walk with."

She looked at me for a moment as though deciding whether to trust me. At last, she let her breath out. "All right, but if you're not back in an hour, I'll come looking."

"If I'm not back by then, Grendel Hall will be closed. But thanks!"

And with that, I left the room.

The classifications I'd come up with for the different types of ghosts only covered so much. I mean, I had Echoes, Talkers, Shadows, Haunts, Specters, and Ferals. I had told Rocks about Echoes, Haunts, and Ferals. Talkers can't be seen and never touch me, but they make noise. Specters are like Haunts, but they're not trapped in a specific place. They can roam around. The level numbers I've got handle how dangerous they are. When combined, I've identified most of the spooks I've seen in my life. But now and then, there's one that stumps me.

Professor Harrison was old in our reckoning. Yet as ghosts went, he was still pretty young. He died only a hundred years ago, and that was nothing, spectrally speaking. He was solid to me and would look like an average teacher if average teachers wore stuffy tweed jackets that covered white shirts with stiff collars. The prof was a Level 3 Haunt. He *could* hurt me if he tried, but he wouldn't want to. He had accepted his lot in the afterlife.

I strolled the dimly lit passages of Grendel Hall and looked around for my dead friend. This was risky since I didn't know how many spooks haunted the place. Still, I wasn't too concerned. I figured the professor would be less relaxed if anything dangerous lived here.

"Ah! Miss Downs!" the old teacher said as he walked through a wall and almost collided with me. I always thought it was funny that a ghost could pass through a solid wall yet bounce off me.

"Professor Harrison!" I called, glad to have made contact after ten minutes of wandering the halls. "I've been looking for you."

"That is wonderful, dear girl. I would be delighted to continue our discussion on Third Dynasty—"

"I'm sorry, Professor, but I need to change the subject."

"Of course! What would you like to discuss?"

"I want to talk to you about, well, ghosts."

The deceased man's delighted smile vanished at once. "Ah. I see. I must say it is not a topic I prefer discussing."

"It's important, Professor. I wouldn't bring it up to you if I had any alternative."

My pleading face must have been more convincing than my words because he took a long breath and nodded. I like how some ghosts cling to physical activities they no longer need, like sighing. Those who give it up are the ones I worry about.

"Very well. Follow me." And he turned on his heels and vanished back through the wall.

I stood there, staring at the barrier for a moment. *Nice joke, Prof. Good one.* Then I went a few paces down the hall and entered the room through its door.

The professor sat on the teacher's desk of a small classroom, and I wondered, for a moment, if that had been his when he was alive. His smile vanished, but he still looked friendly. I joined him by sitting on a front-row desk.

"Now, how may I help you, Miss Downs?" Professor Harrison asked as a teacher would to a student.

Now that it had come to it, I wasn't sure how to proceed. Just because the prof was a ghost, it didn't mean he knew all about them. But I had to try, and the direct approach made the most sense to me.

"Do you know of any other ghosts here on the school's campus?"

Professor Harrison rolled his eyes.

"Do you know all the living people on campus? I am just one spirit here. There are others, but I have never taken a census."

"I understand that," I said. "But I thought you might know of some. Or at least one."

"There is a particular spirit you are interested in?" He sounded intrigued now, though he spoke with care as though the conversation might still go awry.

"Yes. It's outside, haunting the Quad. It's old. At least, I think it is."

"*How* old is this spirit? Before my time?"

"I think so. He wore a top hat."

He chuckled. "Men wore top hats in my day. *I* wore one if you can believe it."

"Okay," I said. "You got me with that. But there seemed to be something wrong with it."

"In what way?"

"It was all shadows. I couldn't see its face, even though

there was enough light in the Quad. I only saw its shape, including what would be a coat or a cloak and his top hat."

"I would guess that some spirits only manifest that way," the professor said.

"And it growled at me."

That earned me raised eyebrows. "Growled? Are you certain about that?"

"Absolutely."

"Hmm. That is troubling. Though I am trapped in this building, some are not. I have a rapport with them. I will talk to my friends and see what I can learn about your top-hatted spirit with the growl. Come visit me tomorrow night, and I might have answers for you. Until then, go to the library and research the school's historical records. There might be a mention of such a death on campus."

"Are you giving me homework, Professor?" I asked with a wry grin.

"Of course! I *am* the professor, and you *are* the student."

"Good point. I'll check it out."

"And Miss Downs," he added, as I slid off the small table. "I would recommend not confronting it."

"I don't have a death wish." I flashed him a quick grin.

"I'm talking about emotional trauma, of course. Ghosts cannot hurt the living."

"Professor, I'm not a normal living person."

"Yes," the ghost teacher said. "There is something different about you. I was certain you were deceased, like me, when we first met. It surprised me to learn differently."

"I get that a lot."

"Have you ever tried to solve the mystery of what you are?"

"Nope, and I don't care. I just live with it."

"I am curious, however. I might have questions for you at some point." Apparently, death didn't curb his scholarly interests.

"Thanks for the warning," I said with a wink. "I'll be back tomorrow night for your answer." It was almost nine, and the building would be closed soon, so I ran back to the entrance. Mack was preparing to lock the place up.

"Running late again, I see," he said, but he smiled as he opened the door for me.

This gave me the chance to catch my breath. "Sorry, Mr. MacNair."

"Call me Mack."

"Okay, Mack. I'll try not to make a habit of it."

"No worries. Just try to be in my sight before nine, and you'll be okay."

"Thanks!"

I went out into the night. The giant oak door shut behind me with a solid *thud*, and I could hear the locks click into place.

I shivered against the cold air that blew around me as I walked through the damp grass on my way back to my dorm. Though night had settled on the city, the campus was still alive. Several students went here and there across the expanse, all of them on their way to their own destinations. And all of them went in pairs or groups, as the school now required. Another chill cut through me, and I wrapped my hands around my chest to keep them warm.

Then I stopped.

It wasn't this cold when I went to see Professor Harrison, yet there I shivered in the late summer air. The ordinary rawness of the Ghost World didn't bother me, but this did. I cast my eyes around the Quad and frowned at a mist that drifted in from all directions, blanketing the ground in an eerie fog.

Was this a real mist that affected everyone, or was it a feature of the Ghost World that only I could witness? It was tough to tell sometimes. I looked up and saw a clear starlit night, with no clouds to signify bad weather. And the cold wasn't coming in off the shore, as it should have. The ocean breezes also had no effect on it; the mist moved of its own accord.

No, this was a ghost fog. And that meant some big spectral event was happening. And then I remembered my sight of The Door.

Not again!

I ran across the quiet park, through the damp grass, heading straight for the street.

The screams began as I neared the scene of the last attack. The police had cordoned off an area of grass from the street to the bushes that marked the end of the Quad. My end of it was broken. The yellow police tape now fluttered in the harbor wind.

I charged through the tape and dashed straight for the dark shape that hunched low over a crumpled form. The screaming had stopped.

The apparition's head spun toward me, its top hat still affixed to its head. But that was the only detail I could take in as the full force of my wild charge plowed into it.

The ghost toppled to one side, and I fell over it and crashed face first onto the grass. I rolled several feet away and hopped back up to stand before it. I had achieved my goal because the ghost was no longer interested in the body on the ground. Of course, it now had eyes only for me. I spit grass and dirt from my mouth and sank into a guard position.

The apparition, which it was, wore shadows like a cloak about it. Though the area was well lit with streetlights, the humanoid figure stood before me with the darkness rippling like a disturbed fog around its form. I couldn't tell any features of its body, aside from its height of about six and a half feet and the hint of a tuxedo, complete with bow tie below its neck.

Its head, however, was clear to me.

The face had two eyes, a single nose, two ears, and a mouth. But to say it looked human would be a lie. The black pupils of its eyes floated in separate seas of a red so intense they shone with their own eerie light. Its skin, though hinting at a human color, was gray from the tendrils of night that swirled around its body. The mouth stretched wide in an evil grin, and a single row of dagger-like teeth flashed at me, their whiteness concealed under a coat of dripping blood.

Now, just because it didn't look human doesn't mean it never was. Some ghosts, especially the ancient ones, can change their appearance to suit their mood. Right now, this one's mood was quite clear to me.

It wanted to rip me apart.

Okay, so charging straight into it might not have been my best plan ever, but now I had to live with it. And I intended to live.

So, I did two things. First, I lowered myself into a strong, fighting stance, remembering everything they had taught me in Karate class.

Then I screamed.

Chuck Norris wouldn't have done it, but I had my reasons. It forced my opponent into acting early, without planning its attack.

The abomination from Hell lunged. Its arms appeared from the swirling mist and reached for me, its bony fingers like claws.

I could have closed with the thing and fought it, but I didn't have the guts for that. At the last possible second, I stepped to one side. With a graceful swing of my arms, I nudged its reaching arm past me while I pushed on its shoulder in the direction it was already going.

The apparition shot past me and then stumbled over the sidewalk and into the street, its own charging momentum taking it away from me.

With a sickening *thump* and the screech of brakes, a car hit the monster. But instead of rolling onto the hood, the shadows engulfed it as though splashed by black paint, and then it vanished.

At once, the unnatural cold that clung to the place dissipated, and the mist parted. I ran back to the body that lay in the grass in the center of the old crime scene and knelt in the grass to help.

A terror that I had never experienced before surged through me. A fit of shaking overwhelmed my body, followed by nausea. I turned away and threw up; the image of what I saw burned into my mind.

The face of a woman had stared up at me with wide, unblinking eyes. A bite had been taken from her exposed neck. A bite that had removed almost everything, leaving a ragged mess of blood, muscle, and a hint of bone.

10

I don't know how long I waited for the police to arrive. I didn't even call them. Everything was a blur. People came and crowded around. They talked to me and helped me to a curb where I could sit. Someone even sat next to me for a while, but I was numb to it all.

That creature was a ghost. It should not have been visible to anyone but me. It should not have been able to *kill* anyone but me. I wasn't quick enough to help that person. No matter what I did, and how cool my ability was, it never made a difference. That ghost wasn't gone. I didn't save the woman. And more people will die because my condition doesn't help.

The sound of sirens broke through my malaise, and the details of the world took shape around me. I sat alone on the curb while several people had formed a semi-circle around the body and kept back a growing crowd of onlookers.

The car that hit the ghost was now parked at the side of the road, a stone's throw from me. The man who must have been the driver was deep in conversation with a couple of college students who had apparently witnessed the accident.

There was no sign of the ghost.

Several police cruisers converged on the site, two of them pulling onto the sidewalk. Uniformed cops came out and immediately began dealing with the crowd. Another car came to a halt in front of me. It was a late model Impala that looked like it had gotten a lot of mileage in a short time. The familiar form of Detective Ross exited the vehicle and came around to the sidewalk. He saw me right away.

"Why am I not surprised to see you here?" he said.

I afforded him a slight grunt, but his words did their job, and I managed a weak smile.

He glanced over at the fresh crime scene that sat amid the old crime scene.

"Another body over there? Like the last one?"

"I never saw the last one," I said.

"Good for you."

"I threw up." I motioned toward the corpse in the grass.

"Then it's like the last one. I have to check it out and talk to the men. But I'll be back, so please stay put."

I nodded and let him walk away.

My mind came back into full consciousness then. The brief talk with the detective helped, and I could think more clearly.

Standing, I paced on the sidewalk and noticed that the police had taped up the area around me and the crime scene. A crowd had formed, and some stared at me, as though wondering why I was there.

I turned my back on them and paced down the pavement. That creature was a ghost. It had to be. But it touched that woman and that car. Ghosts can't do that.

This one had.

What was it? A new type of ghost? One I had never heard of before? A shiver ran through my body, and I swallowed to prevent any more bile from rising in my throat. Could the victim see the ghost? Did the driver? He felt it, but did he *see* it?

I went over to the driver, who now stood in silence waiting to tell his story to the cops. Right now, they were with the body.

"Excuse me," I said.

The man spun around, surprised. "Hey! You were here. You saw it happen."

I nodded. "I'd like to ask you a question. Did you *see* the person you hit?"

He frowned. "Are you suggesting I wasn't paying attention?"

"No! Of course not. He ran into the road too fast for you to stop. It wasn't your fault. It's just . . . well, what did he look like?"

The man calmed at once, then grimaced. "You know, I can't say. I saw something shoot out into the road, but to be honest, I couldn't see it well. It was like a shadow. I guess the light wasn't good."

"I think that was it," I lied. "Nothing else makes sense."

"I know, right?"

"Thanks." I turned to see Detective Ross walking determinedly over to me.

"Okay, Miss Downs, your turn. Let's talk over there." I followed him to a spot far from both the street and the body. The Door was there, not in any wall but by itself, looking even more out-of-place than usual. Of course, the detective didn't notice it.

"Tell me what you saw this time."

I met the detective's face, my eyes grabbing his. "How open are you? We talked about ghosts last time, and you acted like you believed me. If I talk about ghosts now, would you take me seriously, or take me for a loony?"

"I guess it would depend on how loony it sounds," he said.

Fair enough, I thought. "Then I saw a man in a black suit and top hat hunched over the woman. I knocked him over. He attacked me, and I sent him reeling into the street, where a car hit him. It was all self-defense."

He continued to meet my gaze.

"Your story's missing a lot of details."

"That's the non-loony version," I said. "You're not ready for the complete one."

His eyes never left my face as they roved around my hardened features. His gaze then broke off to make a circuit of the area. We were alone in our corner.

"All right, I'm not like your normal cop. I've seen things. I've dealt with . . . horrors that even *you* wouldn't believe. I've fought them. You can tell me, and I will take everything you say at your word. But it'll be off the record, since my boss enjoys not thinking of me as crazy, and I'd like it to stay that way."

A slight grin cracked my serious countenance, and I nodded my agreement. "Okay, then. You get the full story, unabridged. I have a special ability." I filled him in on that, giving my now standard description. Then I told him what happened, leaving nothing out. I explained that I study a martial art, and that I intentionally sent the ghost into the street under the assumption that it couldn't die and nobody would see it. When I finished, Detective Ross stood there for a moment, deep in thought. He looked over at the crime scene. Paramedics were there now. They wouldn't be able to help.

"You're saying ghosts can do *that* to a living person?" He motioned with a tip of his head toward the body in the grass.

"That's just it. They can't. Strong ones can move objects, though usually not far and only small stuff. But none of them can kill a person. It can't be done."

"Yet you're saying a ghost did it. A ghost killed that lady over there. And the man three nights ago. How can one kill a person when you say it can't?"

"I don't know. It doesn't make sense. I've never heard of anything like this, and I've certainly never seen it before. To be honest, it scares the shit out of me."

He raised an eyebrow at that. "And ghosts don't usually scare you?"

The curt shake of my head showed that the question didn't deserve a spoken answer.

"Then you're tougher than you look. If I could see ghosts all the time, I'd be terrified of them, especially if they could hurt me."

"After eighteen years of sharing their world, you kind of get used to it. At least a little."

"Right." Detective Ross paused for a moment, then said the question he had to ask: "How would I go about stopping a ghost like this?"

My gaze went back to his face, and I looked him right in the eyes. "I don't think you can."

"Okay, I think it's time that you tell me . . ."

The detective went on, but I was no longer aware of what he said. My gaze had panned over the crime scene as we spoke and had stopped on a person I hadn't noticed before. A woman of about thirty years of age stood by the group of medics who examined the corpse. Her hair was blond and disheveled, with bits of grass in it. Blood plastered the jogging outfit she wore, but thankfully, her neck remained intact.

I had crossed half the distance toward her before I realized I had left Detective Ross behind. That didn't change my course of action. I walked right up to the ghost and tapped her on the shoulder. She jumped, then turned to face me, her expression a mix of terror and confusion.

"Hi," I said. It was important to not be too pushy, because it could scare her off. But I had questions that needed answers. "I know this is all crazy, but I have some questions to ask you. When I'm done, I'd be happy to answer any you might have about your current situation."

"Y-you can hear me," she said, surprised. "Nobody else can."

"I know. Please, can you tell me what happened to you?"

Her head bobbed around like it was trying to follow an elusive fly, but she was only trying to figure out what was going on. "I don't know. I don't know what happened to me. Am I . . ."

I glanced around, up Boylston Street where the woman must have come from, then back to her standing there in her jogging clothes.

"Look at me." She turned her head back to me, but the panic had risen in her. It was now right behind her eyes. I didn't have much time.

"You were out for a run. You were running down Boylston Street, near Brent College, when something happened. Please tell me what you saw."

My reciting of normal events that she did when she was alive helped her panic to recede slightly, and she considered my question. Slowly, she nodded and then spoke, her voice broken and shaky.

"Someone grabbed me. He came out of the dark and pulled me in. I tried to fight him. I tried to scream, but he was too fast, too strong."

Once again, her eyes widened, and she started breathing fast. She was going to lose it!

"Okay! Okay! Calm down." I pulled her to me and hugged her. She resisted at first, then melted in my arms. I held her there for a minute and then asked my question.

"Did you see his face? Can you tell me what he looked like?"

"I-I didn't get a good look. There were too many shadows."

"His face was close to yours. You should have been able to

see. What color were his eyes?"

Her head shook slowly back and forth as she thought about her killer. "He had no face. It was all black. It was as though he wasn't even real."

"I see." That wasn't what I saw, but now both witnesses, who were alive when they encountered it, had seen no details of the ghost. It wasn't as solid as it was to me. But it was real enough to kill this woman and hit that car.

"I'm dead, aren't I?" The ghost's voice was small and scared, but calm.

I nodded and would have said more, but someone put a hand on my shoulder.

"Miss Downs." It was Detective Ross. I turned to find the man watching me with great interest. "I have to get back to work, but I'd like to meet with you soon to talk about this. You still have my card? Good. Call me tomorrow when you can."

I nodded my agreement, then looked back at the ghost. But she had gone. The spirit had vanished. Would she return as a ghost, or had she passed on to what lay beyond? I didn't know. I hoped she had. Whatever awaited us there, it must be better than this limbo of the forgotten.

"Hey, Ghost Girl," a voice called out to me. A girl sitting one row in front of me in Literature class shifted around to mock me. "I hear you were at the scene of the crime last night by the Quad. Did you tell them that a ghost did it? Or did you want to make contact with the new victim?"

Everyone around her laughed. I laughed, too, dry and mirthless. Tom Prichard, however, did not. He stood up to his full girth, which was big and mostly muscle, and glared at her. "Leave her alone, bitch."

She stared agog at Tom for a moment and then whipped her head away from us. Everyone else quieted down. Tom cast his glare around the place, then nodded his satisfaction. "Good," he said and sat down.

"You don't have to do that for me," I whispered. "I'm a big girl."

"Yes, I do," he replied.

The teacher began her lecture and saved us from any more unnecessary talk. But when all was over, he waited for me to leave the hall.

"How are you feeling?" he asked, slipping into step beside me.

"I'm fine."

"You've been avoiding me," he said.

"I've been answering your calls."

"But you hardly say anything. It's like you don't want to talk to me."

"Look, Tom. I appreciate that you feel indebted to me for helping you out, but you aren't. Don't feel like you owe me anything. I would have done that for anyone."

"I know. It's just that, well, I want to be friends. I didn't treat you that good at first, and I want to make up for it. Besides, I like you. You've got balls, so to speak."

I chuckled at that. "I can't be friends with you if you still go around treating people like shit. Turn over a new leaf, and then maybe."

"Who do I treat like shit?"

"Logan Reyes, for one."

Tom winced. "You know that guy?"

"Yeah. A friend of a friend. But I don't like bullies."

"You can tell *him* that. I'll leave him alone when he stops yelling shit at my friends and me. You know, like 'big hairy ape' and shit like that."

"He does that? I'll tell him to stop teasing you, then."

"So, are we good?"

"Yeah. As long as I don't see you torturing people smaller than you."

"Great! Oh, by the way, that ghost is back again. All the time, like before. But I don't want you to do anything about it. I can handle it."

I stopped walking and gaped at Tom as he came back to me. The ghost was back. After all I went through, Dave Simons was haunting him again. All my life, I had run from them and even fought them off, but never once had I ever done anything to get rid of them.

Maybe it was time I did.

School is hard. It's even harder when you have dangerous monsters on the loose, and only you can stop them.

Only me.

Was that true? Could it all be up to me? Detective Ross couldn't find Top Hat. It would be invisible to living people during the day. And was it *always* visible to them at night, or did it only appear when it attacked? I didn't know, and I honestly didn't have time to figure it out. I had school. And I had Dave Simons.

Dave was a ghost. An ordinary ghost, not a monster like Top Hat. And I couldn't get rid of him. How could I even think of stopping the killer ghost if I couldn't take care of a Level 4 Haunt? One that had pissed me off. I had to figure out how to manage that.

Modern-day ghost hunters don't catch their prey. They look for evidence. If I was to start getting rid of ghosts, I had to see if anyone in the past knew how to do it.

Professor Landry, my Archeology professor, had told me to see him if I had questions about ancient cultures. Most teachers liked to talk shop, and he was no exception. It was time to pay him a visit and see what he knew.

It was a blustery Wednesday in the Quad, where dark clouds loomed overhead, and the leaves on the trees had flipped over, warning of impending rain. I ignored all the signs and made my way across to Grendel Hall. The old Anthropology building was becoming my second home, since I spent so much time there working on the subjects I loved. It was also the oldest-looking building on campus, and its big oak front doors opened ominously with the wind and clouds at my back. Honestly, it looked like a scene from *The Omen* or something.

I wandered the old, dimly lit corridors in search of Professor Landry's office. A successful bit of hunting and asking directions led me to a large room in the basement. I could hear movement and the professor's voice as I approached. I stopped at the open door and peeked in.

Less of an office and more of a lab of ancient artifacts filled the room. Long tables ran the length of the space with others near the edges, giving only enough room to squeeze yourself down. Shelves with protective glass doors decorated the walls. Professor Landry stood in one corner. He was organizing a group of relics and talking to himself.

"I've got to change the lock tonight," he said, frustration tinting his words.

"Was there a break-in?" I asked.

The professor jumped and spun around, almost dropping the ceremonial mask he held. He relaxed noticeably at the sight of my face. He turned back to the table and continued his work.

"Lexi, what are you doing down here?"

I entered the room and walked along the line of tables to stand a few feet from him. "You said I could find you if I ever wanted to talk shop."

"Oh, right. You were interested in death cults." He paused, then cast me a sidelong glance. A hint of a grin tugged the corner of his mouth. "Say, you haven't come down here within the past week, have you?"

"Um. No. This is my first time in the dungeons."

The grin won out, and his face brightened, shoving his beard aside to reveal white teeth. "Someone came rummaging through my Native American section. I think I'm missing a few items having to do with a possible death cult."

"Hey, it wasn't me. That was just a passing fling."

"I know you didn't do it," Professor Landry said with a chuckle. "I was having fun. But it still annoys me. It happens every year, you know. Someone always gets in here and causes havoc. Anyway, what did you want to talk about?"

"Do you know of any cultures that put a lot of effort into

banishing unwanted spirits?"

"Ah, so now you've switched from people who revered the dead to those who feared them. You pulled a one-eighty on me."

"Yeah. I kinda did. But this is important."

"Do you have a spirit you want to get rid of?"

"Maybe. Do you have a ritual or something that I can use to banish a ghost?"

"Take a look around you. This room is a veritable repository of strange things like that. But finding one would be time-consuming. And I'd want help."

"Tell me when," I said.

Professor Landry stopped straightening out his artifacts and regarded me curiously. "You're serious about this."

"I am, and I have my reasons. Please, don't read too much into it and trust that I know what I'm doing."

"I've heard rumors about you and ghosts. I tend not to believe in that kind of thing, but I have an open mind. Still, as a professor at this institution, I can't offer my time for any old thing. Sell me. Show me its academic worth."

I drew in a long breath as I collected my thoughts and formed the statement that was most likely to work with him. Then I slowly let it out.

"In science, we're supposed to accept facts as truth and to challenge theories with the scientific method to prove whether they are fact or false."

"That's right, but—"

I held up my finger. I wasn't done yet.

"Though ghosts haven't been proven to be impossible, the

current evidence considers them *improbable*. Therefore, I should focus on things more sensible. But I have my reasons to focus on this, and I don't have time for someone to tell me that what I have experienced is wrong, when he doesn't know what my experiences were."

"Fine. You sold me on it. Sometimes, you've got to pick the subjects your heart points you to. Are you considering using this ritual in a scientific experiment? What kind of controls will you have? What do you plan to record?"

"I suppose that depends on the nature of the ritual."

"Okay, I think I can dredge up something you can use, but it will take some effort. Are you willing to help with the research? That is, as long as you have time after all your studies."

"Of course, I'd be happy to help."

"Good. I was going to be here tomorrow night at five to clean up this mess. Show up around then, and we can work on finding you a ritual. And be ready to go through a lot of books."

I was still saying my farewell to Professor Landry when I walked out into the hallway and nearly ran into Mack.

"Sorry!" I exclaimed, and the janitor jumped in surprise when I skidded to a halt. "I should be more careful!"

"Oh, it's you! Ms. Downs, right?"

He remembered my name. "Call me Lexi."

I fell into step beside him as we walked toward the entrance.

"I see you were working in the artifact room. It must be full of wondrous items." He held a tone of casual curiosity, but I detected a hint of genuine interest hidden in his words.

"I would think you'd know. You clean the entire building."

"All but that room, that is. The artifacts in there belong to Professor Landry, not the school, so he has the only key."

"Ah." It made sense, since the room was dusty and all the tables piled with all kinds of ancient stuff. It couldn't have had a proper cleaning in years. "I'm sure it's for the best. That room's full of breakable stuff. You wouldn't want to knock anything over in there."

"I suppose you're right," he said as we approached the door. "But I'd still like a look inside. You see, I was an Anthropology student once myself."

"Really? What happened?"

"Now *that* would be a story for another time. Let's just say that things happened, and it was decided that anthropology wasn't for me after all."

"That's a shame!" I wondered what could have driven him away from his dream, but I didn't dare ask. It was likely a sore subject.

"Nah. I still got to travel the world before settling down to this quiet job. My life turned out to be as full as I could want it to be."

"That's good." But I couldn't help notice the regret in his tone. Or was it bitterness?

We stopped at the door.

"It's daytime," he said with a wink. "You don't have to leave on my account."

That earned him a grin. "Yeah, but I've got things to do."

"Then I won't stop you. Have a good day, Lexi." He opened the door and bowed like a gentleman.

11

Cold wind and a spattering of rain hit me when I emerged from Grendel Hall. My dorm, where I had planned to eat lunch, was a considerable walk across the open, and now rain-soaked, expanse of the Quad. That left the cafeteria and the Student Center. Though the former was closer, I hated the noise and size of it, so I opted for the latter. It had a nice little cafe with cozy tables I could work on as I ate. I set off down the walkway that lined the edge of the old Anthro building. Though technically part of the Quad, the path ran close to the buildings, which offered at least marginal protection from the rain.

I took a nervous glance out over the grass as I hurried

along. There were no shadows in sight. And, though the clouds darkened the place, it was still daytime. Even so, I had to pause. The far corner by Boylston Street dragged my attention to it against my will. Two people murdered. Two people killed by a ghost. Detective Ross said to call him, but I wasn't ready to deal with that. And I had a date with a friendly ghost that might give me more information. My eyes, soaked by more than the rain, blinked, and my body found the ability to move.

The cafe was not as busy as I had expected, probably because of the rain. But I was all the happier as I stood through the short line and ordered my chicken tenders with fries. Then, I set up at a table with my Calculus book out and started on my homework.

I hadn't gotten far, in both lunch and work, when someone pulled up a chair and joined me.

"Keeping busy, I see," said Kai Peters. His hair hung flat from the rain, but he combed it back from his face. One drop of water dangled from the end of his nose, and it was too cute not to grin.

"Staying dry. It's raining hard now, I take it."

"It hit when I was almost here. They say you get less wet if you walk in the rain, but in a downpour, you're just screwed."

He hefted his backpack onto his lap. "Mind if I join you?"

"Not at all." I motioned toward the second half of the big, round table. I might prefer to work alone, but I was okay with Kai joining me. It surprised me, but I paid it no mind.

He moved to the chair opposite me and set up. "To work, I guess."

"It's why you came here, isn't it?"

"Until I saw you. Now Sociology doesn't seem too important."

"Aw, aren't you sweet," I mocked, but my burning cheeks gave me away.

He had a grin that held nothing back. Wide and toothy, it conveyed his happiness with more sincerity than most people I knew. Only Jenna was able to top him with cheer.

We spent the next hour working on homework and chatting about random things. He bought food, and we got into a game of tossing fries across the table to each other's mouths. Kai never mentioned ghosts at all, and neither did I. We had passed an important hurdle with that. Until then, I feared that our relationship began and ended with our shared paranormal experiences. I was ecstatic to discover differently.

In fact, I wasn't approached, mocked, laughed at, or even looked at the entire time. Apparently, my reputation didn't go far, and my anonymity among the vast majority of the school's population made working in public workable.

"I must beg your leave, madame," Kai said with a bow.

"For what, kind sir?" I asked, continuing his charade.

"To leave, I suppose. I have a prior engagement that does not appreciate tardiness."

I laughed at that. "Then your leave is granted."

He stepped over to me, and I rose to meet him. Our faces were close, our lips only inches apart. Would he kiss me in the middle of the cafe?

He stepped back, and his face betrayed the same thought that had run through my head.

"Until we meet again," I said.

"Of course." He bowed, then grabbed his backpack and left the room.

Now, people were staring at me, but their looks showed no mockery at all.

An hour later, I packed up and headed back to the dorm. But first, I pulled out my phone and stared at its blank screen. I had to call the detective. "Better get it over with," I muttered and pulled out his business card.

"Hello, Detective Ross," I said and tried to cradle the phone between my shoulder and head as I stuffed my books into my bag. "This is Lexi Downs."

"Good. Thanks for calling. I'd like to meet with you to discuss your unique perspective on my case." His tone was all business, his gruff voice coming across like a cop in an old black and white movie.

"Okay, when and where?"

"How about five at the Stuart Street Diner?"

"Isn't that a bit cliché?" I said.

"Shut up. I like the coffee. So, is that good?"

"It'll be fine," I said with a chuckle.

"Be careful when you come. Don't go near the crime scene, even though we have cops patrolling." These last sentences were the only ones that conveyed any emotion beyond annoyance. Was it concern? *Aw, that's sweet.*

"Don't worry, I don't want to. That would be the long way, anyway."

"Good." He hung up. Another cliché. Do all police detectives get their training from TV procedurals?

Stuart Street ran parallel to Boylston, and Brent College was sandwiched between the two. The diner was a five-minute walk down one side street, then around the corner and another minute or two down Stuart. The rain hadn't stopped by then, but it had diminished into a constant mist that blew at an angle with the ocean wind. I wore a jacket and carried an umbrella to combat the Boston weather.

The Stuart Street Diner was a typical New England dive. Though not built from a train car, the building was narrow and long and hinted at that classic train-car shape. A counter ran along one side of the place with stools occupied by a handful of people, all of which were dressed blue collar. Not a single college student could be seen in the joint, a thought I was painfully aware of as I walked down the aisle looking for the detective. His head gave a grim nod from a table in the far corner. I made it a point to be a few minutes late to ensure that I wouldn't be sitting there alone. Looking around at all the sullen faces, I was glad I had.

I hung my jacket and umbrella from a metal hook at the end of the bench seat and slid into place opposite Ross. I flashed the man a pleasant smile to offset his dour frown.

He looked tired, and while he didn't wear a hat, his hair was dry, implying that he had one somewhere. He had piled his trench coat unceremoniously beside him. The gray suit was clean and in good shape, but he wore it like he hated it. The loosened navy blue tie hung crooked against his shirt. He picked up the menu and stared at it as though he hadn't noticed me arrive.

"You want something?" he said, motioning with a slight

head-tilt toward the other menus standing on a tray at the end of the table by the window.

"Coffee sounds great. I've got a long night."

He nodded and flagged the server, who came over a moment later.

"What do you want tonight, Joe?" she said. *He's a regular,* I thought. *How sweet.*

"Just coffee. Black. How do you want yours?" He glanced at me.

"Cream. Sugar."

"Gotcha!" The lady smiled and bustled off.

"So," Detective Ross began, putting the menu back in its place. "Tell me all about your special ghost abilities."

"To be honest, I'm not sure I want to. I mean, it never goes over well, and I can't prove any of it."

"You'll find me more likely to believe you than anyone else in Boston."

I didn't think he would give me a choice at this point. If I wanted to help solve this case, I had to open up. "Okay. At night, between sundown and sunrise, ghosts become visible to me. But more than that. They're solid to me, like living people. I can understand them and talk to them. And . . . they can touch me."

"Let me get this straight. Once the sun goes down, the population of the city suddenly doubles?"

I nodded. "I don't know if I see *every* ghost that exists, but I meet an awful lot of them. Most walk around doing what they did when they were alive. A few have intelligence and awareness, and those are the ones I can interact with."

"Now, when they're solid for you, are they see-through for everyone else?"

"That's right. You would see only the living while I see those plus the dead. The ghosts would walk right by you, and you wouldn't even know it. Hell, some might walk *through* you."

"But they'll bump into you."

"Yup. Some think I'm dead, too."

"Do *you?*"

I thought about that question for a moment. After all, it's one I've spent a long time considering. "I've had this since I was little, and I've grown physically and mentally. I eat, go to the bathroom, get hurt. Ghosts don't do any of that."

"Good. I didn't want to have to convince you that you're alive."

The server arrived and delivered our coffee. I had to admit it smelled delicious.

"Now, about this killer ghost . . ." He raised his cup to his mouth and blew the steam, then set it back down. I let mine sit.

"I call him Top Hat because I don't know his name. He's a Haunt, stuck in one area. In the Quad or near it. He dresses old, like early nineteen hundreds old, with a top hat. But he's not fully formed. It's as though he embodies the shadows in the place. His face was solid enough when he killed that woman." I shivered at the thought, then lifted the mug and held it between my two hands. "But the rest of him was a mass of swirling darkness."

"Can you describe his features? We might trace back and

identify him."

I snorted. "That's the problem with Top Hat. He's not a normal ghost. His face didn't look human. He had a big mouth with lots of sharp teeth." I chose not to mention the blood dripping from them. "And when I first saw him, he was stalking me, from shadow to shadow, until he crept across the grass toward me. And he *growled*. You know, like an animal."

I gasped at my sudden realization. "A Level 5." That came out in a near whisper.

The detective frowned. "A what?"

"I've come up with classifications for the ghosts I've seen, based on their behavior. I've never encountered a Level 5 before, but a couple Haunts have told me they exist. It's a feral spirit, one who lost all of its humanity and became a monster. Other ghosts fear it."

"How does one become feral?" the detective asked.

"I don't know. They're rare. This is my first. All of my experience says it shouldn't happen, but it does."

"This is a one-off? A single ghost that goes crazy and kills people?"

"Yeah. *No.* I mean . . ." I shook my head, then took a breath to calm myself. "Ghosts can't kill anyone. I've witnessed powerful spirits that can manipulate objects in the real world. And I mean *horribly* powerful. Ghosts that terrify me and chill my blood. But they can only move small objects around. They can't even do more than scratch a person, and that person has to be at least a little sensitive to them."

"But two nights ago, you said this ghost killed those people."

"I know. It did that. Without a doubt."

"That doesn't jibe with what you just said."

"You're right. But it happened anyway. We're in unexplored territory, Detective. This is something I've never seen before and have only heard of through the nightmares of other ghosts. And I don't think they thought Ferals could kill the living."

Detective Ross took a sip from his cup. He savored it before letting it go down, then leveled me with his gaze. His eyes were tired, as though he had seen far too much death for his own good. I bet he had.

"Here's my question: how do we stop it?"

I followed his example and sipped my coffee. It was delicious, which surprised me considering how cheap the diner looked. "I'm working on that."

"What do you mean, you're working on it?"

"Just that. I'm following a lead. An anthropological one. It's my major. Some cultures revered the dead, and some feared it. I'm looking for a ritual intended to banish evil spirits."

"That sounds hokey to me."

"You got a better idea?"

"Is there something that hurts them? Iron hurts fairies, so what about ghosts?"

The look I gave him spoke volumes about that last remark.

"In folklore!" he said, though I wasn't sure I believed that. There was more to this guy than he let on. "What do you think? Could iron hurt ghosts? Or holy water, maybe? We've got to have a weapon, because even if your ritual works, we might need to force it into a circle, right?"

Okay, the thing that had been bothering me about this

man had reached the tipping point at last. His reference to fairies was only part of what bothered me. He sounded like he bought into all of that, which made me the sanest of us both.

I leaned forward, and my face grew hard. "Okay, Detective Ross, spill it."

He looked affronted. "What did you say?"

"You had me tell my whole crazy story about ghosts. Now you tell me yours. Why do you believe me so readily? How do you know about fairies and iron? Hell, why do you *believe* in them? And why are you talking about rituals of banishment like you assume they're real? I know why I am. I need to understand why you are."

The urge to hit me in the face passed over Ross's own, then a look of confusion replaced it before settling on a blank stare. "I'm a cop with a tough case. I have to consider every avenue."

"Yup," I said, setting down my cup and standing. I grabbed my umbrella and coat. "Goodbye, Detective Ross."

He watched me in muted surprise as I collected my things and then burst into life as I took my first step away.

"Wait!"

I did as he wished but continued to show him my back.

"I'll tell you." It was a simple sentence, spoken in a diminished tone that held a lot of emotion. Desperation. Defeat. Those were the strongest, but rage simmered underneath.

I turned around and hung my stuff up again. Then I sat back down and sipped the coffee.

"I'm glad," I said. "This is good Joe."

"Good Joe?"

I shrugged. "Seemed appropriate, given the situation. You

must admit, this all seems rather noir."

"Whatever."

We both drank in silence for a minute. This time, I waited for the detective to start "spilling the beans," as they say. At last, he set his mug down.

"I've been a cop for a long time. We all see our share of crazy shit. Most of us gloss over what we see and rationalize it into something we can explain. It's the best way to keep your job and your sanity. Some of us have seen some shit that you, with all your ghosts, wouldn't believe. And I didn't have the luxury of pretending it wasn't real. Of course, I knew better than to report it for what it was. You can't report something like, 'woman was hacked to near death by a pint-sized goblin wearing a cap colored red with human blood,' unless you have evidence. And when you deal with shit like this, the evidence has an inconvenient way of disappearing.

"So, when you come talking to me about ghosts you can touch and special whacked-out ones that can kill people, well, I have to listen to you, because nobody else will. And you might be right. So, I ask you again, is there something we can use to fight the damn things?"

Now it was my turn to sit in stunned silence. I didn't expect an explanation like that. Hell, I didn't expect an explanation that sounded genuine, but this one had that all over it. What could I even say in response? Ignore it and answer his question, I decided.

"I don't know. I never thought about it that way. I study martial arts so that I can hold them off and send them running. When I hit them, they feel the pain. When anyone else does, they don't even notice it. Now, I hurt one in Fenway Hall a week ago, and I've been wondering what he's like now. It was the first time I did actual damage to a ghost, like making him bleed. I'd like to know if he still has the wounds."

"Wait a minute! Ghosts bleed?"

"I'm sure it's for show, or ectoplasm, or something. It *looked* like he was bleeding, and he seemed to think he was. But I kind of popped his eye out and stabbed him in the throat."

"You stabbed a man in the throat?"

"A ghost. Just a ghost. He was already dead. I didn't make him deader. But yeah. I stabbed him."

"And it didn't get rid of the ghost?" His face held a smug I-told-you-so look I found annoying.

"I passed out right after, and someone got me out of there. But I hear he's back to bothering the student who told me about it."

"That knife, was it a regular one?"

"Yeah, a big utility knife."

Ross nodded. "Steel blade. We should try iron. That works on other supernatural bad guys. Might work on ghosts."

"I'd prefer the ritual way," I said. "Seems less violent."

"Sure, but you might need something to get the ghost to do what you want or get it where it needs to be. That's where the weapons come in."

"You seem pretty stuck on them," I said.

"You're telling me I'm trying to fight a monster I can't touch, but it can kill me. So yeah, I want a weapon."

"Top Hat was solid to everyone when it attacked. It killed its victim by tearing her apart, and it got hit by that car. It vanished after that, but for a short time, it was solid."

"But not destroyed."

I drained my mug. "I don't think so."

"Then, you get my point."

"All right. I'll do some research and see what I can find. But we can't prove anything until they're used against a ghost."

"You say you see them every night."

"Are you suggesting that I attack a ghost at random, just to see what it does?"

"Why not? They're already dead."

"But they still have a mind and personality. And feelings."

"You said some don't. Some relive their past lives. Pick one of those."

I sat in silence for a moment. Ross had made a good point, but I still wasn't about to attack anything unprovoked. At last, I nodded.

"Okay. I'll see what I can do." Arguing with the man would get me nowhere, and maybe I'd find a ghost that *would* provoke me.

"Good." He stood up and pulled a hat from beside him on the seat and donned his coat. "Let me know if you learn anything. And don't go out in that Quad at night."

He strode away down the aisle before I could tell him not to treat me like a kid. I don't think I would have said that, even though I thought about it. But it was rude of him to not give me the chance.

Anti-ghost weaponry. That was my next project. As much as I wanted to give those spiritual bastards hell, I wasn't looking forward to the job.

12

It turned out that researching ghost weapons wasn't that hard. There's plenty of folkloric evidence that iron repels evil spirits. An iron knife, or more easily, an iron crowbar, could be useful. Also, salt is said to disrupt their presence in our world. Granted, I got that one from a TV show. But hey, they get stuff like that from some source, and it might be legit. I figured that making a few homemade salt bombs would be easy to do and could be useful. What's the worst that could happen? I throw it; it fails to work; I beat the ghost in the head with the crowbar. A trip to an auto parts store should do the trick.

In the meantime, I had a date with a dead professor.

The rain had stopped by the time I entered the Quad at

eight, but the grass was so wet that I followed the concrete walkways around the edge until I reached Grendel Hall. And yes, I avoided the far end of the park. And also, yes, I kept my eyes wide open the whole time. You would think I would be a stickler for following the go-in-groups rule the school was touting, but hey, I guess I'm a rebel.

Grendel Hall sat dark and lonely, with only a handful of lights showing in the windows. I entered and wandered the halls on my search for Professor Harrison. I made for the room we had talked in before, and that was where I found him. He stood by the whiteboard of the empty classroom, staring up at the writing still left on it.

"Is this true?" he said as I entered. "Did dinosaurs have feathers?"

"It's a whole new world, Professor. They say that birds *are* dinosaurs."

"Amazing! Truly amazing." He turned to face me and smiled.

"What have you got for me?" I asked.

"Straight down to business. I like that. I would have enjoyed having you in my class. My friend came by last night and we had a talk about the spirit that's haunting the Quad. She says his name is Luther Randolf, and he was a wealthy man back in the day. He owned a mansion here in Boston and was well-to-do."

"How far back was 'the day'?" I asked.

"That would be the turn of the century. I suppose that term is outdated since there has been another. The early 1900s. She did not know precisely."

"And why is he haunting the Quad?"

"Because, my dear, he was murdered right there on campus. Of course, it wasn't a college back then. He and his wife were walking home from the theater one night, when they were waylaid by ruffians and slain."

"Is his wife around here?"

"Oh no. She never tarried. That left Luther irritable."

"But not a killer," I said.

"That's right. The last time she saw him, he was wandering around the Quad like he always did, and they chatted."

"When was that?"

"Right before the semester began. He has been out of touch since then."

"His current behavior is recent."

"It would appear so. But that's all she told me. I hope it's enough."

"I think so," I said. This news gave me plenty to think about.

"Thank you, Professor. You are always a great help."

"Miss Downs," the ghostly teacher said, as I turned to leave.

I paused at the door and regarded him. He stood by the desk and looked around awkwardly, reluctant to meet my gaze. He absently tried to pick up a pen, but his hand went through it.

"Is there something wrong, Professor?" I asked.

"This spirit. What you described should not exist. That makes it dangerous and unpredictable."

"I know. It's dangerous. It's killed two people already."

"That's not what I mean. You should put thought to *how* this spirit came to be this way. If a normal spirit can be turned into a monster, well . . ." He broke off and looked around the room as though for help. "Miss Downs, *I* am a normal spirit. If it could happen to Luther, then I could be next. I don't want to become a monster. I'm afraid I might end up hurting you."

My jaw dropped open as I stared at him from the doorway. That had never occurred to me before. And I could see what was eating at him. He was stuck there on campus. There was no running and hiding for him. All he could do was stay and wait for the same thing to happen to him. How can you stay sane through such a thing?

"Oh, I'm so sorry, Professor. But I'm working on it. I'm looking for a ritual or something that can put Luther back to the way he was. There must be a way, and if there is, I'll find it."

He flashed me a weak smile. "Thank you. But be careful. I'm more concerned about your safety than my own. And try to find out what is causing this. I believe that's of the utmost importance."

An icy breeze met me on the concrete stoop, causing the leaves to rustle among the trees of the Quad. Somewhere, beyond the rain-soaked clouds, the moon rose uselessly into the sky. The crisscross pattern of concrete walkways cut the expanses of lawn into sections before me, with tall lights illuminating the paths in small circles of pretend safety. Small trees also decorated the walkways. People were out, walking this way and that, but they all moved in groups, and all stayed near the safety of the buildings.

All except one man who walked stupidly down a path through the center of the park, talking on his phone.

What an idiot! I thought and descended the steps to the paved walkway. As my foot touched the tar, the door behind me opened. I looked back to see two students emerge. But that's not what made me gasp.

The Door stood beside Grendel Hall's big double door and was even more imposing than the old building's oak portal. *Why is The Door here?* I asked myself, but I knew the answer.

Glancing around, I found the lone kid walking through the Quad. A shadow by a tree stretched far longer than it should have, especially in the darkness of night. Was it Top Hat? If it was, it was stalking Mr. Oblivious out there.

Oh, not again.

Right now, the shadow was stalking, following the man. The idiot had recently entered the Quad, so the attacking ghost would probably wait until he was closer to the hedge along the far side. I had time.

At once, I sprinted to the nearest tree out on the field. My plan was to sneak up on Top Hat and catch him from behind.

I reached the tree and saw Top Hat drift to another. It moved slowly, so that its shadowy form would blend with the general darkness of the grounds. That gave me more time.

I bolted to the next tree, then quickly went to another. I was gaining on it, and it still didn't see me. Two more sprints like that, and I was now positioned one hiding place behind Top Hat, which was about to spring at the walking target. The guy was still on his phone and chatting loudly about some party Friday night.

We were all nearing the bushes now, and Top Hat made its move. It went faster this time because it was on the attack. But I was quicker still, and it paused as the thudding of my sneakers reached its ghostly senses. It spun around to face me as I struck it.

This time, I didn't plow into it. Instead, I ran past him and swept his neck with my outstretched arm. My limb struck a solid neck, and the apparition fell over into a heap on the ground.

"What the hell?" shouted Clueless Man as he whirled around to see me squaring off with a man of shadows, who was now on its hands and knees, trying to get up. I threw a front ball kick to Top Hat's head. I was hoping to make that hat go flying, but it didn't. Still, my kick was textbook perfect, and its head lurched to one side as the monster fell over again.

"Oh, my god! What is that!" the guy cried, finally aware of what was going on around him.

"Run!" I shouted at him as I landed an axe kick onto the monster's back. The guy finally got a clue and fled.

But the ghost was ready for me this time. It rolled toward me and, before I could get my foot back onto the ground, it knocked my other leg out of place.

I fell backward onto my butt, yet I didn't lie there. If there was one thing my Kempo class drilled into me, it was knowing how to fall. As soon as my ass struck the pavement, I rolled quickly to one side and was back on my feet in an instant.

So was Top Hat, though, and its face had opened up to reveal those nasty sharp teeth. Thanks to me, they didn't drip blood yet.

Yet.

It lunged forward, its arms outstretched to grab me by the shoulders while its maw went straight for my face.

I leaned to one side, my left hand guiding its arm past me and my right fist embedded into its solar plexus. My strike had enough force to drop any real man. But this was no man. Or it wasn't real. Or something like that.

Top Hat remained standing and struck me hard in the face with its right arm, sending me sprawling on the ground.

Great. My left hand was there on guard, but I hadn't expected its attack, and so it had plowed right through my weak defense and got me.

I rolled over and tried to stand up, but it leaped on top of me. It threw me over onto my back and pinned my shoulders to the ground with its hands. This took most of the freedom away from my upper arms, so I couldn't struggle against its grip.

It opened its mouth to bite my face off, the huge maw twisting its normally human-looking face into a grotesque mess. But it was the eyes that sent a chill up my spine. Even the Echoes show something in their eyes; some vestige of humanity that had not quite left them. Yet Top Hat's eyes were empty black orbs, devoid of everything. No emotion. No intelligence. Nothing.

I had to stop it, to escape somehow, and there was only one way I could think of. When I was a little girl, I had gotten good at squirming my way out of tight spaces. Literally. It was like I was covered in grease. I squirmed, and I got away. It was a skill

I used a lot against ghosts, but I left it behind when I learned martial arts.

I channeled my inner child with all the gusto I could muster. My body became almost fluid as I twisted and pulled and pushed and spun every part of myself that could move. The monster had tensed for lunging its toothy jaw at my face when its body suddenly slid off mine, its legs falling off my own. Its grip loosened slightly on my shoulders.

That was enough.

With a sudden twist, I dislodged the creature's body from me, and it rolled to one side. I leaped to my feet and threw a front ball kick to the side of its head, followed by an axe kick to its solar plexus. The head snapped to one side but failed to break its neck. The second kick did nothing to it. I guess the ghost didn't need to breathe. That would have left a person in terrible pain and gasping for air.

I stepped back and waited for the monster to stand. I had every intention of kicking its arms out from under it when it did.

Sirens rent the night, and I glanced up for only a moment. A fire truck raced by after some other emergency. Then there was a rush of shadows, and Top Hat had vanished.

I stood there in the middle of the Quad, my heart racing and my breath coming in quick gasps. I panned my gaze around the place and saw that I wasn't the only person ignoring the safety rules. At least three students walked the paths of the Quad on their way across campus. They all kept near the buildings, but they still made themselves vulnerable.

Detective Ross was right. We needed a weapon, and we

needed one now.

Kai texted me during Sociology class. He wanted to get together to talk about ghosts. I agreed to meet him in his room. I had an hour break, so I went back to my room, dropped off my bag, and went down to Room 312. His door opened only a few seconds after I knocked. Kai stood there in full college attire: T-shirt, jeans, and sneakers. He grinned at me.

"Hi. I'm not quite ready. I have a few more sentences to write. Come on in." He left the doorway and went to his desk where his computer sat running. An essay showed on the screen, and he went to work on it.

My plan was to wait in the doorway. I might have been brave with ghosts, but with real people, I erred on the side of caution. I stood in the open doorway and glanced around his room. Two things came ready to my mind. He lived alone. The bunk bed against the right-hand wall had a used-looking bottom bunk and a top one that served as storage for books, bags, and anything else he wanted out of the way. The second thing I noticed was his obsession with the occult. Posters sporting pentagrams and other ritual symbols hung on the walls. Even a picture of Aleister Crowley stared at me from above his desk. Ghosts shared the spotlight, though, with lots of photos of apparitions and such dotting the spaces between the posters.

Kai left his computer and came over. Upon seeing me staring at his decor, he chuckled. "I know, it's all creepy. But when you've been haunted by ghosts all your life, it has a way of making an impact."

That statement pulled my attention from the macabre decorations. "All your life? That's right. You said something like that."

"Let's go," Kai said, and closed the door to his room. We made our way, side by side down the hall to the nearest common room.

This was a duplicate of the one on my floor. Semi-spacious with several round tables lined with chairs for people to study, it also had a counter along one wall that was bare of objects. A nook in one corner had a sofa and several miscellaneous chairs, all pointing at a TV. Three people were there watching some show with the volume turned down. Two of the tables were occupied, and we took one in a corner far from the television and the door.

"It looks like you're as interested in ghosts as I am," I said, getting the conversation going. "Except, I'll admit, I don't hang posters and pictures of them all over my walls."

Kai chuckled. "I'll bet your roommate's glad for that."

"Yeah, what happened to yours?"

"He didn't like me, so he found someone who had lost a roommate and moved in with him. To pay the extra fee for having the room to myself, I work at the front door some nights. I sign people in and out."

"That sounds worth it."

He shrugged. "I get a lot of homework done when I'm working there."

"I'd love to hear your story," I said. "In what way have you been haunted by ghosts?"

Kai glanced around the room to ensure no one was listening. "I'm clairvoyant. It means I can sense ghosts in a building.

I can see them sometimes, better than anyone else could, anyway. And sometimes they come to me."

"You see ghosts? Are they detailed? How often do you see them?" I was so thunderstruck by his story that I couldn't help firing off the questions that thrust their way into my head.

He smiled, and it looked like a lot of tension drained out of him. "That's a way better reaction that I usually get. But, yeah. I see ghosts. Not all the time, and they're always kind of misty, like you see in pictures. I don't see them often, but when I do, I know it won't be good."

"And that's when you got your scratches? When they came to you?"

He nodded. "According to what you read in books or see on TV, the ghosts want something from a clairvoyant. Like, they want closure or something. You know, something I can give them. But sometimes they come to me only because I can see them. A few come just to torture me. To hurt me."

He forced a grin to dispel the dark expression that had descended on his face as he spoke. "So, what about you? What's your story?"

"Well," I said. It's always hard telling people about this because it's so difficult to believe. But Kai seemed more accepting than most people, given his experiences. I told him about what I can do, except I didn't mention the part about being able to touch them. That was the hard pill to swallow, and I didn't want to push him away. Besides, it would sound like I was trying to one-up him. "I could walk down the street at night and see a handful of people, and one or two of them might be dead. They look real to me."

"Wow. That's worse than me. I doubt I see them all. And I don't see them all the time."

"I'm surprised you believe me. Nobody ever does, so I keep it to myself." *Until this crazy semester,* I thought.

"Nobody believes me, and yet I have the scars to prove it. But tell me, Lexi, do you consider your ability a gift or a curse?"

I paused for a moment, pondering his question. That was something I never considered before. I always told the people I confided in that I would give up the ability if I could. But was it a curse?

"I think it's neither of those things. It's part of me. I wouldn't be the person I am without it. I'm not sure I'd want to keep it if I could get rid of it. But you know? Maybe I would."

"Exactly! It's what makes us unique. Special. Have you ever thought about learning more about that world? You know, figuring out how it works and what you can do with the ghosts?"

Another good question. "Right now, I need a way to fight them. There's that."

"Of course you would. I do. Have you made any progress? In trying to fight them, that is?"

"Not really." I didn't mention my martial arts training. It wasn't the type of fighting I meant. And it wouldn't make sense to him, since I never mentioned the touching part. Besides, karate has had a way of scaring away the guys. You'd be surprised at how many men don't like being weaker than their girlfriends. "Just a little research."

"What did you find?"

"According to folklore, iron hurts them a lot. Salt can cause apparitions to disperse."

Kai nodded. "An iron weapon and some kind of salt bomb? I bet we could fashion something like that. I could rig some clumps of salt in a wrapper that would shatter when it hits anything. Throw it at the wall or ceiling above it and it'll rain salt."

"And for iron weapons?" I asked. "This is the harder thing, since you don't see many objects made of iron anymore."

"Chains, maybe. An old skillet or pan. Or a fireplace poker! Yeah, those are made of cast iron. And they'd make a good weapon."

"Cool," I said. "All I could think of were crowbars and train track spikes."

"Hmm," he said, thinking. "We'd have to buy a crowbar, but that could work, although most of them aren't iron these days. The spikes are a good idea, though. You can find them lying along the subway tracks. Not tons, but I should be able to scrape up a few."

I hadn't planned to mention the spikes it just popped out. Now I'm glad it did.

Kai let out a breath. "If only there was a place where we could test this stuff out. You don't know of a ghost you'd like to stick with a poker, do you? One on campus, perhaps?"

Of course, two came to mind. One was too dangerous to test with. The other was an ass, but I didn't want to provoke him. It didn't seem right.

"Not really."

"Hmm," he said, thinking. "I know of a place. Not on campus, but not far away, either. Would you be up for a little adventure?"

"When?"

"Tonight."

"It's a date!"

He grinned, and that made me grin, too.

It was five o'clock, and Professor Landry and I were hard at work in his relic room, going through book after book of details about ancient cultures. He had finished putting it back in order, but it still had a wild, disorganized look. He showed me around when I first arrived, and I discovered it was far less unruly than I'd thought. What I had taken for clutter was a simple overabundance of items. This was a room overfull with artifacts. But he had them all neatly sectioned by location and culture.

The professor stood at one end of the room and pored through a stack of books on the folklore of the British Isles. I sat in a tall barstool-like chair at a table at the other end, with a pile of books about Mesopotamia. He told me I wasn't likely to find anything in the annals of ancient Sumer and Babylon, but I was tired of looking at hieroglyphs and needed a break. Besides, the really old civilizations called to me.

"I've found some things," Professor Landry said with a yawn. "But they aren't banishing rituals. More like tips for warding them off."

"After a while, cuneiform letters all look alike." My yawn followed his, and it made me realize how tired I was. I glanced at my watch. 7:22 p.m. We had been at this for over two hours.

"You're not trying to read it, are you?" he asked.

"No. There are transcripts. But I like to look at the samples of text. I'd love to learn it sometime."

"I still think you're going down a dead end with that one. You should jump further ahead in time, like Egyptian or Greek."

"I know. I'll stop after I finish . . ."

My eyes fell onto a photograph of a tablet dominated by the angular writing of the Sumerians, but with a picture etched into the stone. It depicted a man with his arms raised, facing what looked like a fire or a pyre. A word that I had already taken to mean "dead," or "the dead," was written in several places in the text around the picture.

"Hang on," I said. "I think I might have found something."

My teacher set his book down and joined me in my corner. "What is it?"

"I'm not certain, but it looks like a ritual, and it talks about the dead a lot."

He took the translation and studied it for a few minutes. Then he began mumbling to himself as his eyes went from the transcription to the picture and back.

"Well, I'll be," he said at last. "I think you're right. This could be what you were looking for."

"But can we translate it into a working ritual?" I asked.

He stared at it for another moment and then nodded. "I think it's a bit much, even for you, Lexi," he said. "But I can do it. It'll take a little time, but I love a challenge. Give me a few days."

Good, I thought as I left the building and made my way back to my dorm. *Now all I need is a weapon so the detective can help.*

I had a nice, Doorless walk back to my room, and it made the stroll enjoyable. If Top Hat tried anything then, I would have been at its mercy.

13

Kai knocked on my door at 8:00 p.m. sharp. His bright smile greeted me when I opened the door, and I hesitated before returning it, because of his outfit. He wore all dark clothes, with black jeans and a black trench coat hanging open to reveal a Metallica T-shirt. In contrast, I dressed for a night at the gym, with light gray sweats, a white T-shirt, and sneakers. My black hair bounced behind my head in a ponytail.

"Is the haunting at a goth party?" I asked, a wry grin playing at the corner of my mouth.

"I was going for style. You know, Matrix-like."

"Yeah, the ghosts will quake in their boots from all that bad-assery."

"And what about you? It's not a haunted gym."

"That's good. I don't relish fighting a bunch of dead body-builders. But this is how I dress when I hunt ghosts. It lets me be limber."

"I see, and the Snow Queen color scheme?"

"Won't it be dark there? I figure we should make it easy for us to see each other."

"Oh. That makes sense. Touché."

I left my room and shut the door. I slung the bag I carried onto my back. Kai had one of those bags that looked like a cross between a backpack and rolling luggage. It had wheels and an extendable handle. He rolled it along beside him as we walked.

"Packing a lot of gear?" I asked as we strolled down the hall to the elevator.

"Iron's heavy. Now, if you found a more convenient weapon material, that would have saved me a lot of trouble."

"Still, it seems like you're more prepared than I am. All I've got is an iron crowbar and some salt. And a flashlight, of course."

"I've got the flashlight, too. One I can strap to my head. But I've also got a string of iron chains, three railroad spikes, a fireplace poker, and salt."

I stopped in front of the elevator door and shot him a crazy look. "Where did you get all that?"

Kai shrugged as he pressed the button. The muffled whirring of the motor came to life at once.

"My family lives in Boston. I grew up here. Most of the stuff came from home. I had to go scrounging along the subway tracks for the train spikes."

"You went down in a subway tunnel to find three spikes?"

"No. The trains go above ground in places. You've got to know where to look. And I wanted more than three."

"I'm impressed," I said.

A bell rang, and the door slid open. Kai grinned at my comment and entered.

The haunted house was a fifteen-minute walk from campus. The sun, which had already been long hidden behind the tall buildings of Boston, dipped below the horizon as we strolled down Boylston Street. Of course, I couldn't see the sunset with all the tall buildings around us, but I felt it. The paranormal switchover stole upon me, bringing an uncanny chill and dimness to everything as the shadows stretched out toward us. My surroundings took on a surreal appearance, with modern buildings fading into relative obscurity, while older places stuck out in stark contrast. Most of the place, however, fit somewhere in the middle, semi-dim and bland.

People crowded the sidewalk, bustling back and forth as they journeyed home from work. I tried not to focus on them much, since I didn't want an encounter with a random spirit. Kai led me off the busy street shortly after sunset, and we strolled down a series of back roads. These put me on edge for a different reason. We passed a small group of men dressed in jeans that hung a bit too low and hoodies that obscured their faces. One, who wore a T-shirt and no sweatshirt, was covered in tattoos. He glared at us as we passed by.

"Sorry," Kai whispered to me. "Abandoned houses don't come in comfortable neighborhoods."

"Yeah, I guess not." Maybe clothes that stood out were a bad idea.

The old, seedy-looking businesses soon gave way to older, more decrepit residences. We hurried past them, as more people we didn't want to meet stared at us like resting lions at passing prey. At least two of them were ghosts, and I tried my best to pretend not to notice them.

At last, we arrived at our destination. The exterior of the house didn't disappoint. It had once been a multi-family residence, but I doubted anyone had lived there in decades. The paint had long since peeled off, now only showing sparse remnants of the gray it used to sport. A wide front porch had given families enjoyable summers once upon a time, but now it was a sagging mess. Its roof, though still intact, threatened to fall in at the slightest touch, yet somehow survived the unpredictable Boston weather. Plywood planks covered all the ground-floor windows. Those on the second were still intact, but some lacked their panes. Grass grew tall and brown on the five-foot-deep yard split down the middle by a cracked and uneven concrete walkway.

"You are not serious," I said as we stood at the start of that path. As I looked up at the second floor, a face stared back at me from a window, its pale features framed by limp, black hair that blended with the surrounding darkness. Its eyes looked like pools of shadow amid the white of its skin.

Great. A ghost that made no attempt at looking alive. I hated those.

"Of course I am," Kai said. His voice had lost its earlier joviality, but his eyes sparkled with anticipation.

"It's haunted," I said.

"I know."

Kai's whole body shook with a mixture of excitement and terror. This was personal for him.

"Okay, it's time you tell me about this place."

"I don't know its history. When I was a kid, my friends and I used to come here. We dared each other to go inside, but none of us had the guts to do it. One day, we convinced Jeff. He was a new friend and wanted to fit in." He held up a defensive hand at my reproachful glare. "I was against it and told them we shouldn't. Of course, I couldn't explain why because they'd laugh at me. So, I didn't protest hard and eventually went along with it. Anyway, about five minutes after he climbed in, we heard him scream. Then we heard noises, like running or falling. When everything got quiet, we tried to decide what to do."

"What happened?"

"I climbed in after him. Nobody else dared. I found Jeff at the bottom of the stairs, all curled up."

"He fell down the stairs?"

"Something *pushed him*. He had scratches all over him, like from fingers. His arm had broken, and he had a lot of bruises. I went upstairs to find out what hurt him and found a ghost at the top. It was all misty, but I think it might have been a little girl dressed in white. I'll never forget what I saw."

"What happened with the girl?"

"I ran. It must have come up behind me because when I turned to go down the stairs, it raked its nails on my back. Damn! They felt like claws. It pushed me, too, but I caught the railing and didn't fall. I grabbed my friend, and we got the hell out."

He turned his back to me and lifted his shirt. Bit by bit, he'd been giving me a tour of his body. But I understood why when I saw it. Four long marks marred his back. They looked vicious, deep, and violent. He pulled his shirt back down.

"My battle scars," he said with some pride. "My clairvoyance grew strong after that."

"And you want us to go in there," I said. This was madness. He just described a Level 5 apparition. A powerful one, if he could see it. A feral ghost. The most dangerous kind. I'd never met one, probably because I avoided places like this.

"We need to test these weapons on a ghost you don't care about. I don't think either of us would mind hurting the little girl that attacked my friend."

"You want me to hit a little girl with an iron crowbar?" This was a conversation we should have had back on campus. My confidence in this excursion slipped a little.

"It's a ghost. And it's all a bunch of mist."

"It'll look like a little girl to me."

That didn't deter him. Maybe he didn't believe me after all. "It's a *monster*. Shall I show my scars again?"

"No. But I don't know if I can hit a ghost that looks like a child."

He sighed then. It was full of frustration with a hint of understanding. "We can go in and see what happens. But when you see it, I bet you'll change your mind. You're still up for this, right?"

"It's just I've never met a Level 5 before." I wondered if this feral ghost was anything like Top Hat. Was he typical of Level 5s?

"A what?"

I shifted the pack decisively on my back. "Level 5. It's what I call the most dangerous types of ghosts."

"You've got a scale for them?"

"We'll go over it another time. Let's get down to business."

With a quick glance at Kai, I strode down the cracked walk to the porch stairs. But when the first step groaned under my weight, I paused.

"I think the house has gotten weaker since you were here last."

Kai frowned as he came up behind me. "Yeah. If the place turns out to be unstable, we should leave. Fighting the ghost is one thing; fighting the house is another."

"We might end up fighting both."

"We can try finding the sturdiest section and stay there."

"I saw the ghost in the window. It's upstairs."

"Upstairs?" Now the ever-confident Kai showed his nerves. The sudden reaction, and the wideness of his eyes, were unmistakable. But he recovered quickly. With a grunt, he hefted the heavy wheeled bag. "Let's go."

He shouldered past me and started up the stairs. It was his gig, so I didn't mind. The stairs held despite their protests, and I joined him on the surprisingly stable porch. They sure didn't make them like that anymore. Kai tried the door but found it locked or rusted in place.

"No problem," he said. "May I borrow your crowbar, madam?" he added with a flourish.

I grinned but pulled the tool from my bag and handed it over.

We made quick work of the boards covering the window to the left of the door. He pried each board up, and then we both manhandled them off. The plywood came away with ease. Sticking his head through the hole, he looked around before handing back the crowbar.

"It looks good in there. A lot safer than it seems from outside. I don't think we'll have to worry about the floor giving way."

"All right," I said. "I'll go in first. I can see the ghosts better than you."

He cast me a sideways glance that said "Damn, she's tough!" My cheeks grew hot, and I grinned despite myself.

"Trust me," I said.

He shrugged and stepped back, away from the open window. "Ladies first, then. But I'll be right behind you, in case you need help."

I pulled off my backpack, then I, too, glanced around the place through the window. It was everything you would expect from an old, abandoned, haunted house. The musty smell of decay permeated the air, but it didn't reek of death. Only dust, mold, and decades of neglect. I panned my flashlight around. The beam touched peeled wallpaper, a rotten sofa, dust-covered chairs, and other furniture that time had forgotten. But no ghosts met me as I scanned the old living room. An entryway with no door stood in the center of the wall to the left, on the far side of the room. The hint of a staircase peeked through it.

Okay. I knew where the little girl would come from.

Ghosts never just float down from one floor to the other. It's weird, but true. They'll walk through walls, but they'll take the stairs when they can. To be fair, though, most ghosts walk through doorways. They only use walls if all the doors are closed.

Of course, this was supposedly a Level 5 Haunt. So, I didn't know how it would behave, though I guessed it would still take the stairs to come and get us.

With a last breath of fresh air, I climbed through the window. I had to duck my head almost to my chest, but there was no way I would go through face first. First, one leg went through, then my head. I pulled my other leg through once I felt a sturdy floor under me.

Once in, I walked around the room to test the strength of the floor before telling Kai it was safe to enter. Of course, the place creaked and groaned almost constantly as I moved about, but it all seemed strong enough.

As soon as Kai had climbed through, he found a place near the center of the room and set his bag down.

"What do you think of it?" he asked, his voice cheery.

"Oh, it's beautiful," I said with a grin. "Did you notice there are no beer cans, magazines, or anything to show that anyone has been in here since it was abandoned?"

"I don't think anyone has, except for stupid kids like my friends and me. Nobody would want to party in here. Would you?"

"Nope."

"Exactly! This place *feels* creepy. It's in the air, like the whole place has an evil vibe."

"I don't see any ghosts here yet, aside from the one upstairs I saw through the window."

"Then let's get to work," he said.

With me keeping watch, Kai opened his bag and pulled out a length of iron chains.

"What do you plan to do with that?" I asked.

He smiled and laid them out on the floor until he had made a circle about four feet in diameter.

"You were carrying all that chain with you? It must weigh a ton!"

"Why do you think I have a rolling bag?" He stood back to inspect his handiwork, the headlamp he had donned before climbing through the window following his gaze to trace the outline of his circle. "Looks good," he said at last.

"What's it for?"

"To see if a ghost can cross an iron line. Wouldn't it be good to have a nice safe place to hide if the ghosts get too bad?"

"I guess, but you know they don't have to touch the ground to move." It's true. Though most usually walk around as though they're alive, and thus touch the ground, they don't have to. And the ones who are comfortable in their death often don't. And even Dave Simons could jump over a chain.

"This is to find out if they're so afraid of iron that they won't go near it. This whole excursion is an experiment, after all."

"You're right. It is. Okay, so now we're in the house, and we've set up our safety circle. Now, how do we get the ghost to come downstairs?"

"It won't like us. It'll want to hurt us. So, just being here might be enough."

"According to your story, the ghost never came downstairs. After pushing your friend down them, it stopped attacking him. And I saw it at an upstairs window."

At that moment, footsteps sounded on the floor above us. No dust fell from the ceiling, which would have happened if a real person was up there.

Kai gasped and stared at the ceiling.

"You heard it too," I whispered. He nodded.

This was a strong apparition. Either that, or Kai's sensitivity was keener than I'd thought.

"All right," I said in a hushed tone. "I'll go upstairs and try to lure it down."

"No!" Kai grabbed my arm after I took one step away. "She'll attack you, and you won't be able to stop it. I should go."

Now I frowned. Overall, I'm not against chivalry. It can be sweet for a guy to care enough about me to want to treat me like I'm special. So, he can open doors for me and pull out my chair and stuff like that. But when a guy pulls shit like this, it's just demeaning.

With a quick twist of the wrist, I made him let go. One second, he held my arm, and the next, his hand was empty. It wasn't aggressive, only assertive.

"Tell me why you're more qualified to go up there than me, and I don't want any of that *you're the man* shit."

"Hey! No. It's not that." He sounded both surprised and scared, like he feared he lost his chance with me. He might have. It all depended on what came out of his mouth next. "It's just that I'm sensitive. I can feel them sometimes. I've seen this ghost, so I'd have more of a chance."

"And you thought I was lying when I told you about my abilities?"

"No! It's just, well, I talked you into coming. If you get hurt here, it's on me."

"I make my own choices. If I get hurt, it's either my fault or the ghost's."

"Look, have you ever done something that ended up with someone getting hurt, and even though it wasn't technically your fault, you felt like shit afterward?"

A certain shadow with a top hat came to mind. He had made a good point. Rock-solid, in fact. He had let his friend go in here when he knew he shouldn't have. And I understood that. My damaged ego stopped throbbing, and I let out a long breath.

"You're right," I said. "But the fact remains that I'm the best one to do this. I can see more ghosts than you can, and more clearly. I'll be careful with the flooring and won't stray far from the stairs. And when I find the ghost, I'll keep my distance and lead it to us. Besides"—I held up my crowbar—"I'm armed."

"We can go together," he said, but I could hear him weakening.

"The stairs might not support us both. It's got to be one at a time."

"I'm coming to the bottom of the stairs at least."

I nodded, and we made our careful way across the room. Each step caused the floor to creak, but the boards held firm. With my flashlight before me in my left hand and the crowbar in my right, I approached the doorway to the stairs. A narrow hallway ran in both directions, with the staircase forming its other wall, the steps and railing visible through the opening where I stood. To the right, the passage ran a short way to a bathroom. To the left, it ran to the front of the house, where a landing gave access to the stairs. I took slow, deliberate steps down the hall toward the landing, shining the light up to the one above. There were no ghosts, but the staircase itself gave me doubts. Like all the wood in this forsaken place, the paint had peeled on some steps and had cracked with age.

When I reached the landing, I knelt and examined the floor at the foot of the stairs. This was where Kai had found his friend. The glow of the flashlight revealed a few dark splotches on the steps and railing that looked a little too much like old, dried blood. *Great,* I thought. *Either Kai's friend got more hurt than I had thought, or he wasn't the only person to get pushed.*

"Okay, you wait here," I said.

Standing, I pointed the light to the second-floor landing. It ended in a corner that opened to the right. It was in that room beyond where I saw the ghost in the window. With no-body, living or dead, in sight, I started up the stairs, taking it one slow step at a time.

One step. Two steps. The railing wobbled when I held it, and I let go, thinking it was going to fall apart as I climbed.

Three steps. Four steps. The wood made a loud *crack* under my foot but remained intact. It was solid before I stepped on it. Now a long split ran most of its length. My head also rose above the ceiling to gaze out through a railing onto the second floor. Another hallway identical to the one downstairs ran beside this staircase on the other side of the railing. To get to the window where I saw the girl, I had to continue up to the landing, then turn around and go down this passage to the other end above where Kai stood on the first floor. This new hallway looked as bad as the one below it, but the floor was intact.

"Everything good?" Kai said from the bottom landing. "Don't fall through!"

"That's the plan," I replied and grimaced because I wasn't sure I could prevent it.

Five steps. Six steps. I was halfway, and the lack of a useful railing became a problem when the wood of the step wobbled. Taking my foot off it, I stood on the fifth step and considered my options. I could call to the ghost from where I was and hope she came, though I doubted she would. Or I could skip the stair and hope the seventh would hold my weight as I took an awkwardly big step up. I decided on the latter and reached out with my right foot and tried it. I needed to put all my weight on the new step. It was all or nothing. I pushed down on it and shifted all my weight to that leg. The step groaned but held firm. I lifted my left foot and eased onto the next step.

Eight steps. Nine steps. These were fine and raised my spirits some.

Ten steps. Eleven steps. Twelve. I was on the landing in the corner, and the breath I had unwittingly held blew out in relief. The hallway ran parallel to the stairs and was above the hall downstairs. It ended at the window. I still couldn't see the ghost girl there, but another staircase rising to the attic above the first prevented me from seeing that entire area. My goal was the window. I would not go to the attic.

The Door was against the wall halfway to the landing. "I'm not opening you," I mouthed at it. It pretended not to notice me.

"I don't see her," I called down. "I'll have to move around."

"Okay!" he said. "But be careful." The concern in his tone sounded genuine. *Aw.* Somehow, it made me smile despite the dangerous position I was in.

Once again, I placed one foot before the other and eased myself down the hall toward the window at the front of the building. The stairs descended beside me, and another rose above them to the third floor. *Creak, creak.* Each board made a noise under my weight, more so than on the first floor, but it all held firm. I passed The Door, and the half-concealed landing came into view.

This was where I had seen the little girl. She was still there, on her knees at the foot of the attic stairs. The child held a doll in her hand, which she bobbed up and down like it was trying to climb the steps. She smiled at it. Her hair was long and black and messy. She looked thin, dreadfully thin. The dress she wore had once been white with little hearts on it, but it had become gray from years of neglect. A ghost's clothes don't get dirty in the Ghost World. This was what she looked like when she was alive. Her face was as dirty as her dress, and I knew her short life had been a hard one.

I stopped about three feet from her and smiled.

"Hello there."

She turned her face toward me, and now I could see that the dark patches that had been her eyes were only a trick of the shadows. They were quite visible now. They were the eyes of a child. But her face was deathly pale under the dirt and grime. That part was true. She didn't smile, but she also didn't look angry.

"Hello," she said and turned back to her doll.

"What's your name?" I asked.

"Abby."

"What's your doll's name?"

"Dolly. She's my friend."

"I can see that. Can you tell me why you are still here?"

"This is my home."

Something was wrong. This little girl didn't look or sound like the monster that could have scratched Kai or pushed his friend. This girl was a Level 3. An old one, sure, but just that. She wasn't angry and seemed content with playing like she always had. I thought about it. The landing. The dried blood. The scars on Kai's back. I gasped.

His scars were too big to be from a little girl. *There was another ghost in here!*

14

I whirled around as a shape rushed up the hallway at me. My martial arts training kicked into autopilot, and I ducked to one side, then swung my arms in an arc that both blocked its attack and used its own momentum to send it flying past me into the window. I spun around as I did this and witnessed the ghost smack the glass almost identically to how I did in Fenway Hall. I suspected the ghost was far less bothered by this turn of events, though.

It faced me, and our eyes met. It was once a woman. Her knotted and unkempt black hair hung down off her head like weeds from a zombie that rose from a swamp. In fact, it looked so much like a typical evil ghost from the movies that someone in Hollywood must have seen an actual ghost like this. The apparition's face had the same pallor as the child, but where the girl still seemed to care a little about her appearance, this creature didn't. The monster leered at me with dead eyes. Professor Harrison, Dave Simons, and even the girl on the stairs all looked at me with eyes that showed intelligence and understanding. These were blank brown orbs, devoid of human thought.

It was a Level 5 and different from Top Hat. That ghost was something else altogether. This one was more like a normal ghost, only feral. And I had nothing but my skills and my crowbar to save my life.

But at least I changed our positions so that I now had unobstructed access to the stairs. Of course, I would have to fight my way to them. It should back off once I was going down, like it had with Kai and his friend. At least, I hoped it would.

"*Go away!*" The Feral hissed. "*This is our home!*"

That surprised me. Its eyes still registered nothing on the smarts scale, yet it was talking to me. *All right, I'll try.*

"Okay. I'll leave. Don't worry. I'll go away." I took a step backward, and the ghost hunched as though to spring, and I think it growled at me.

"Who are you talking to?" came a shout from below. "Did you find anything?"

"Um. Yeah." I used a normal speaking voice, though a little louder, so Kai could hear. "I found the little girl and her mother."

"Her *mother?*"

"And she doesn't like me."

I took another step back, and the ghost sprang into action, charging me again.

I couldn't do what I did before because that would put it between me and the stairs again. This time I stood my ground. I swung my left arm up and blocked the ghost's arms as they tried to tear my face off, the beam of the flashlight creating a chaos of illumination around the hallway. Then, I brought the crowbar down as hard as I could on the Feral's head.

The iron weapon met slight resistance and then plowed through it. It felt like I had slammed it down on a sheet of water. The ghost's face screwed itself in agony as its entire body lost all cohesion. It evaporated in front of me, turning into a dull mist that hung in the air like a fog.

Well, I'll be. The iron works!

I ran to the stairs. They were still empty of spirits, so I began the descent. I tried to go as fast as I could while still taking care. I counted them as I went, knowing that I had to skip step six. The fog appeared before me about halfway down, by the infamous dead step, and then solidified at once into the monster-woman I fought in the hallway above. It looked uninjured and glared at me with a ferocity far exceeding our first encounter. But it didn't move. It stood there scowling at me, its grimy teeth bared in a snarl, its hands held before it with fingers clenching and unclenching.

It's afraid of the crowbar, I thought. Of course, that didn't help me. I was now trapped on stairs that creaked and groaned even though I wasn't moving. The wood was old and rotten and wouldn't support my weight forever. I had to get off these stairs and soon.

"Hey, Kai! A little help here."

My friend appeared at the doorway with his bag in hand and mouth gaping.

"Is that the girl?"

I frowned. "You can't tell?"

He shook his head. "I see a cloud, Lexi." Frustration tinged his reply.

"She's solid to me, and she's not the kid. It's her mother, and she wants to kill me."

"Okay, what do I do?"

"I need her off the stairs. Iron works. It made her dissolve."

"Gotcha!" He moved to the foot of the stairs and rummaged in his bag. From it, he drew a black fire poker, then he put a foot on the first step.

"Wait!" I shouted. The ghost lunged forward, and I swung the crowbar but missed as the Feral pulled back at the last second.

"The stairs are weak. It won't hold us both. I doubt it'll hold me for long."

"Can you go back up?"

"I don't want to."

"Do you want to fall through the floor? Just saying."

"All right, I'm going." I cast a quick glance behind me and saw Abby standing at the top of the stairs. She regarded me with mild curiosity.

I returned my attention to the mother in time to force her back with my crowbar.

"I can't. The girl's at the top."

"Have you tried salt?" Kai asked.

"Not yet."

He dove again into his bag and pulled out a yellow and orange water rifle. It looked like one of those powerful ones that can shoot a twenty-foot stream. He grinned as he hefted it in front of him. It never occurred to me to make a salt water shooter. I had to admit; it was brilliant.

"You might get wet."

He fired. The water shot in a concentrated stream up the stairs until it hit the feral ghost. At that point, the solution continued through the apparition, but it reacted like it hit resistance, spreading out into a mist that rained all over me.

The mother-ghost screamed in agony, and it forced me to cover my ears at the horrible sound.

"Stop! Stop! It's hurting her! Mommy! *Mommmmmy!*"

Abby was screaming now, terrified for her poor mother. She threw herself down the stairs at me; her face contorted in rage, her arms outstretched to attack.

I spun around and waved the crowbar to force the ghostly kid back, but the bulky iron tool struck her head by accident. Once again, it felt like busting a water balloon, and her head exploded in ectoplasmic mist. My weapon hit the railing, causing the whole thing to topple over onto me.

And, because that couldn't have been bad enough, the stairs, with one final vengeful groan, collapsed.

In the movies, the hero falls through the hole and expertly grabs the edge. He swings there for a moment and then heaves himself out of the hole to safety.

Bullshit!

What really happens is you're overcome with a momentary

panic that prevents you from doing anything but scream. Which is exactly what I did. The stairs dropped out from under me, and I went with them. A second later, my mind came back to me, and I grabbed the first thing my hands could find. My fists gripped the post of the broken railing as I plummeted through the hole and came to a sudden, jarring halt. The railing, though no longer connected to anything, lay flat on the staircase, too big to go through the hole. I laughed, despite the intensity of the situation, because the one thing I trusted the least saved my life.

Then the fucking thing broke, and I fell.

I dropped over ten feet to a concrete floor. As soon as my feet touched ground, I let my legs collapse, and I put myself into a roll. Learning to fall is one of the first things you learn in Karate class. I never complained back then when everyone else wanted to learn to punch, and I wasn't complaining now. Sure, my knees hurt like hell, but my legs hadn't broken, and my ankles felt okay. I might have rolled on a pile of broken wood and rubble, but that's all minor stuff. The important thing was that I was alive and more or less intact. I pulled myself to my feet, and all my joints protested at the effort. I brushed dust and debris off me and looked around.

It was a basement; the air choked with dust and a damp, musty smell. My discarded flashlight had gone out, apparently broken in the fall. *Son of a bitch,* I thought, but I knew it could have been a lot worse.

"Lexi! Are you okay?" Kai called from somewhere up above.

"Yeah. I'm fine. I'm in the basement."

"Hold tight. I'll try to find a door."

Right. Unslinging the bag from my back, I unclipped the tiny LED light that dangled from a zipper and used it to scan the rubble for the bigger flashlight. I found it lying amid a pile of sticks. Grabbing it, I turned it off and back on, but nothing happened. Then I shook it and smacked it against my hand. It burst into light.

Now, I scanned the ground to find my crowbar, and my mouth opened in stunned shock.

The floor was littered with bones. They were everywhere. I shined the beam around the room and found I was not alone. At least a dozen people stood around the place, staring at me. All of them were children no more than ten years old. I suspected they were all dead. Each wore dirty and torn clothes. Their hair, messy, their skin filthy. Some limped with injured legs or cradled a broken arm. All of them had cuts and abrasions on their skin.

"What happened to all of you?" I asked, my voice a near whisper.

One of them, a girl of about eight in a torn-up dress that might once have been pink and pigtails that were still intact, stepped forward. "They kept us."

"Who? The mother and daughter upstairs?"

The girl nodded. Others did, too.

I looked around at the kids. They wore clothes of different styles, but most notably, of varying time periods. Some dated back to the sixties.

"They were already ghosts when they did this to you."

More nods. "Not all of us," the girl with the pigtails said.

She turned to look at the far corner of the room. The other kids followed suit. I shivered.

One child sat in the corner. He didn't look up when I shined the light at him.

"Hello," I said. "What's your name?"

He ignored me.

"His name is Barry," said Pigtails. "He doesn't talk anymore."

"Can you tell me why they did this to you all?"

"She wants friends for Abby. But Abby didn't like us. Not for long. So, she looks for more."

"I see. Are you all still trapped down here?"

They all nodded.

"Is it because of Abby's mother?"

Again, they gave the affirmative.

"Okay, my friend is going to get me out, and we will find a way to get rid of the mother. Then you can all come out."

Some of them shuffled where they stood. Pigtails cast me a weak smile. "I don't think you can, but thank you for trying."

"I will. You'll see. I'll free you."

"Lexi!" called Kai. "I found the door. It's locked. I'm going to break it down."

"Okay, I'm away from it. But be careful of the ghosts! They're worse than you think."

Kai pounded on the door. He stopped now and then, and I heard his squirt gun going off. Then, with some more bangs, the latch broke, and the door burst open. Kai stood in the doorway, his headlamp making me blink. I laughed then. He was my shining knight.

"Time to go," he said. He didn't seem to notice the others in the room.

"Gladly." I joined him at the door, and we went through. I stopped at the door and said, "I'll be back to fix this. Don't worry." And then we made our way with care to the iron ring. Kai packed up the chain while I covered with the water gun, then we left through the window. I stopped to hammer the board back into place before we left. I didn't want anyone else entering that cursed home. Kai helped me.

At last, the two of us slumped against the porch railing and let exhaustion take over. My heart, which had been pounding since I started up those wretched stairs to the second floor, began its gradual decline to a normal beat. We didn't speak for a few minutes, and I reveled in the chilly night air that blew my bangs and reminded me that not everything in this Ghost World was dead.

Kai looked at me. "What did you see down there? In the basement?"

I didn't want to talk about it. I didn't want to tell him about the bone bed and the ghosts of a dozen children who would never see their parents, never grow up.

"Lexi . . ."

I threw myself on him and hugged him hard. He returned it in kind. We embraced in silence, and it was good. Real good. His warmth spread into my body, and at that moment, I never wanted to let him go.

But I did, because all good things must inevitably come to an end.

When I pulled back, tears streamed down my face. Watery

streaks ran in the dust below his eyes as well.

We kissed then. I'm not sure why I did it. I'm not even sure *I* did it. All I knew was that I needed it. As soon as our lips met, all the pain I felt from the fight, and all the anguish that followed me from the basement vanished. It was all about Kai and me, and there was no room in my head for anything else.

As we walked down the street, I glanced back at the old house. A pale face stared out at me from the second-floor window.

15

"What happened to you?" Jenna cried the next morning when I dragged myself out of bed. The night's rest only made every muscle in my body stiff and sore. I had scratches all over me, and a few cuts. At least two rusty nails had poked through the skin, which I had to take care of when I came in last night. I must have looked terrible because my roommate stared at me as though I had become the living dead. By the way I felt, I might have.

"I went ghost hunting," I said, then stood up to gather a towel, a change of clothes, and my shower kit. I grimaced as I shambled around the small room, my muscles protesting every motion.

"You've got to stop doing that. It's going to get you killed."

I decided not to tell her what happened last night. "I know, I know. But at least I didn't go alone."

"Who'd you go with?"

"Kai Peters."

Jenna's face lit up. "From upstairs? *That* Kai Peters? He's cute!"

"I hadn't noticed." That was one of those lies intended to be seen through, and by the grin on Jenna's face, it worked like a charm.

"You'll have to tell me about it. The good parts, not the ghost parts."

"I will. But shower first."

"Of course. You're filthy."

"Thanks."

After my shower, we went to breakfast in the cafeteria. I told Jenna all the juicy details of my "date" with Kai, which wasn't much after cutting out the entire ghost house ordeal.

Jenna and I went our separate ways when we exited into the Quad. She went back to the dorm while I wandered on the dew-covered grass. It felt a lot safer in the light of day. I pulled out my phone and called Detective Ross as I wandered around the little park.

"Ross." Wow. A one-word greeting. He had that hard boiled cop thing down to a science.

"Hi, Detective. It's Lexi Downs. I looked into what we discussed, and I've come up with some options."

There was a pause. I could hear noises in the background, like he might have been in an office with other people. A moment later, the background noise vanished, and he replied in a low tone.

"This is about the weapons, right?" Another short sentence. Right to the point.

"Yes, and I found that iron and salt are good against ghosts."

"How do you know? Research?"

"Um, no. I tried it out."

Another pause, though shorter this time.

"You fought a ghost?"

"Yes. Not the one we're looking for, but one that's pretty bad. A haunted house. Whacking it with an iron crowbar made it dissolve. It reappeared shortly after, but it gave me a minute to recover. A saltwater mixture made it turn into a mist, or fog. That was also helpful. I think the water had a *lot* of salt in it."

"But it didn't kill it?"

"No. It was already dead. To get rid of a ghost for good, I think we'll need some kind of ritual to banish it. I'm working on that, too. I should have something before long."

"Good. Let me know when you have it."

He hung up. Sure, he was busy and under a lot of stress. But there was no reason why he couldn't say "Bye."

Kai and I bonded over the haunted house adventure. He met up with me after I got back to my dorm, and we went to the Student Center to do some homework. I didn't have many classes on Fridays, so I had a lot of downtime to get caught up on homework. He took my hand as we strolled through the Quad. As September wore closer to its end, I noticed the air getting colder. I wore a fleece jacket over my T-shirt. Kai, like a typical college man, pretended it wasn't cold. He wore shorts with his tee. With all the supernatural cold I deal with at night, I've never been a fan of cooler climes. I'm a wimp that way.

The Student Center wasn't busy that morning. It seemed I was one of the few people who got up early when they didn't have to. I didn't want to have any homework over the weekend. Kai and I sat at a table and spread our work out. I nursed a large cup of coffee, which helped defray the morning chill and wake me up.

We spoke little as we worked, but we did exchange glances. And sure, these glances were "meaningful" and even cute. I'll admit I *liked* him. Kai was handsome, in his own way, with his jet-black hair and piercing brown eyes. And he showed a compassion toward me I hadn't expected. It also helped that we had ghosts in common, and I could talk to him about them without doubting his sincerity. As great as the Dungeon Crawlers were, I doubted any of them *really* believed me. Rocks believed I was telling the truth, but there was no way he could believe what I've told him. I was just this nice, deluded friend of his that *thinks* she sees ghosts. But not Kai. He'd seen them. They'd hurt him. And we'd fought them together.

So, yeah. There was something brewing between Kai and myself, and it felt good.

About an hour after we had gotten to work, I noticed Ben Feldman, from the D&D group, sitting alone at a table a short distance away. I recognized him by his mop of dirty-blond curls and that boyish face. He kept sneaking peeks at us and didn't look pleased. I pretended not to notice. It was obvious he had a crush on me, and though I liked him, I didn't like him that way. And with Kai here, I didn't want to deal with any drama.

I took a sip of coffee and glanced Ben's way, then gasped when I saw him coming over. He strode with purpose, as though he had psyched himself up for this, his face set and determined.

I did the only thing I could think of. I smiled.

"Hey, Ben!" I said as he arrived at our table.

He cast a blank look at Kai and then forced a nervous grin at me. "Hi!" His voice was firm but shook a little.

"What's up?" I did a good job of keeping my good cheer, even though my stomach twisted in nervous knots. Was he going to flirt with me in front of Kai? I hoped not, but Ben wasn't known for doing the right thing in social situations.

"Not much. Um. Hey. The guys are going to Faneuil Hall tomorrow to do some shopping and sightseeing. I thought you should come, since you're in the group and all."

Okay, this surprised me. It shouldn't have, but I misunderstood Ben's intent. "You mean all of us? Rocks and everyone?"

"Yeah. It's something we do. And since you're part of the group now, I thought I should invite you, too."

"That's really nice!" I said. "I'd love to. But, um . . ." I turned toward Kai.

He shrugged, a smile I couldn't read on his face. "I've got plans with my friends tomorrow. So, you wouldn't be ditching me."

"I wouldn't have ditched you," I said with a grin, assuming he was joking.

"Of course not. Just keep an eye out for more equipment."

"Like a squirt gun?"

"Or an iron spear."

I chuckled and turned back to Ben. "I'd love to go. When and where are we meeting?"

Ben had been watching with a frown during my back and forth with Kai, but he brightened up when I spoke to him. "Don't know yet."

"Okay." I pulled out my phone. "What's your number?"

He stammered a little and then told me. I sent him a text that said, "Let me know."

His pocket made a noise, and he pulled his phone out and stared at it. Then he grinned. "I will." He retreated then, packing up the stuff at his table and hurrying from the place.

"He likes you, you know." Kai was watching me. His smile had vanished, but I detected a hint of humor in his tone.

"He's harmless."

"You're in his 'group'?"

"Dungeons & Dragons. Yup. I'm a nerd. It's official."

He grinned at that, and his old self returned. "Somehow, that fits."

My afternoon was busy with classes. But the images of what happened at that house still assaulted me. I barely heard what any of my teachers said that day. Instead, the faces of those children stared at me. I saw them with horrifying clarity when I closed my eyes, but they were also there when I looked around the room. They stood at the head of the class, superimposed beside the teacher as he rambled on about archeology. At last, the lecture was over, and everyone packed up to leave. I, too, shoved my books in my bag and made my way to the exit.

"Lexi," came Professor Landry's voice as I passed his desk.

I paused and turned to him as though I didn't know who he was.

"I did it." It was all he said, but he looked back at me as though I should be excited.

"What?" I shook my head in frustration. I knew what he said must have been important, but the children had a grip on my mind.

"The ritual," he said after the last student left the room. "I've finished it. I can make a photocopy and give it to you tonight."

That did it. The import of his words burst through my malaise, and my senses came back to me, sharp and clear. The ghostly children vanished.

"You have?" I said with mounting excitement. "That's awesome!"

"I have some work to do tonight, but if you meet me at eight in my lab in Grendel, I'll have it for you."

"Okay, I'll be there."

This wasn't as easy to pull off as I had expected. Jenna outright refused to let me leave the dorm that night. She felt I had tempted fate too many times by crossing campus after dark, and she even stood in front of the door to our room, threatening to keep me there until morning.

"Look," I said, trying hard not to let my frustration show. "I have to meet with Professor Landry. He has a paper I need."

"Why can't he give it to you during the day?"

"Because I need it now. It can't wait until Monday. I'll be safe. I'll be in Grendel Hall with him."

Jenna shook her head, crossing her arms over her chest for emphasis. "You'll have to cross the Quad first to get there, and *that's* dangerous. You know what the police said."

"Yeah, they said go in pairs."

"Then I'll go with you."

"Okay."

She did a double take. "What?"

"You can come with me. We'll go as a pair, and that should be safe enough. The police say so."

"And you're okay with it?"

"I like my independence, but I appreciate you trying to keep me safe. Let's go."

With a wide grin, she grabbed her jacket, and we went off together on our journey across campus.

Jenna breathed deep when we exited the building. Boston was only hinting at autumn by throwing a nip in the air, but that enhanced her normal cheer. "What's this paper for? Your Archeology class?"

"Sort of. Professor Landry was helping me with something; a private research project."

Jenna cast me a look of pretend scorn. "Then it *could* have waited."

"Just because it's not for school doesn't mean it's not important."

"It's about all your ghost stuff, isn't it?" Disappointment laced each word.

"I know you don't like it. It's not your *thing*."

"This has nothing to do with whether I'm into ghosts. Every time you do something about them, you get hurt. You're a good roommate. If you get sent to the hospital for the rest of the semester, who would I go to breakfast with?"

"You're a great person. Lots of people would want to be with you."

"I'm a *cheery* person. Lots of people don't like that."

"Oh, they do. They just maybe resent it a little because they're not."

"Especially at breakfast."

"Hmm. You got me there. I promise I won't get put in the hospital for the rest of the semester. I can't have your lonely breakfasts on my conscience."

"Good!" And she beamed her happy little smile that coaxed one out on my face.

Grendel Hall was still well lit when we entered and several people passed us in the hallway as we made our way to Professor Landry's lab.

"I love this place," Jenna said as she gazed around in wonder. I grinned. Even though Jenna was an Anthropology major like me and spent a lot of time here, she still found the building fascinating. Grendel Hall was one of the oldest places on campus, and it looked like those English manors that you see in Victorian-era movies. Made from granite, it had lots of wood trim around doorways and such. Though not vaulted, the ceilings were higher than normal, and the main hall that we walked down was wide, a combination that made our steps echo.

"You said it's haunted in here," she said in a near whisper.

"Are there any here now?"

"Nope. There aren't many ghosts in here. I've only met Professor Harrison, but I don't see him right now."

"Okay. Let me know if one comes around. I want to try to see it."

Professor Landry was working in the lab when we came in. He looked up from his work.

"Ah, here you are. And hello, Miss Rand." He paused and looked from Jenna to me, then he cocked an eyebrow. "I'd like to discuss this a bit, if you don't mind."

"Of course, go ahead." Then I realized what he meant. He felt awkward talking about this weird side project with Jenna there. "Don't worry about Jenna. She's in on it."

"Oh! Okay." He shrugged.

"I was making a copy of the diagrams."

The photocopier stopped churning away, and Professor Landry pulled a sheet from it. He then added it to a small stack of papers and stuffed them in a manila folder. Then he came over and handed it to me.

"Now remember, Lexi. This is something from our research, a ritual described in some Sumerian writing. There is no guarantee that this will do anything. In fact, it's my opinion that it won't. I've been on many excavations and have dug up lots of tombs and bone beds, yet the dead have never come to haunt me."

"That's because their ghosts don't hang around their bodies," I said with a wink. "But thanks for all your help. I appreciate it."

"Anytime, Lexi. As long as you use this as a *learning* tool and not as a party game."

"Don't worry," I said as I turned to leave.

"No parties for her," Jenna added as she followed me out the door. "She's too weird for that."

I almost bounced with each step as we made our way back down the hall toward the front entrance. When Jenna cast me a quizzical look, I flashed a sheepish grin. "This will be *very* useful," I said.

"Why? What is it?"

"A ritual to banish ghosts."

"Oh, not again," Jenna said, almost in a whine.

"What do you mean? I've never done a ritual before."

"This is a circular conversation." The look she leveled me with said, "Okay, you win," better than words could have. "You know I'll always be here to help you when you need me. But it kills me a little every time you get hurt. Sometimes, I don't think you put much thought into how other people feel about what you do."

I didn't know what to say. She was right; I never thought about what my actions would do to those around me. I see a ghost, and I deal with it. End of story. It never occurred to me how others would react to seeing me with cuts, scrapes, and concussions. But, to be fair, it had been a long time since I got noticeably hurt. I think the last time was when I was sixteen. And for most of my life, I had to hide all that from my family.

"Jenna, I . . ."

I stopped—both walking and talking.

"What is it?"

"Shh!" I hissed. There it was. Sobs. Sobs of misery. Someone was crying. And I know that kind of crying. It's a type that most people never hear, but I have. It comes only from seeing something that fills you with utter, gut-wrenching terror.

I ran down the hall, stopping now and then to listen before running onward. Jenna followed behind, but I didn't think she'd heard it. After all, the noise wasn't loud.

At last, I found the room and ran inside before its significance sank in.

Professor Harrison stood in the middle of his classroom, staring at something that sobbed miserably in the corner. When he recognized me, he held up his hand to stop me. I halted and turned my attention to the form huddled in the corner.

It was a ghost. A woman, wearing a dress that looked from the same period as Harrison's. She hid her face in her hands, and her sobs caused the blond bun on her head to bounce. The dress she wore billowed out from her on the floor, where she knelt.

"What's going on?" I whispered. Jenna stood in the doorway, looking around in confusion. She, of course, only saw an empty classroom.

Professor Harrison came over to me. "It was Luther. The man you asked about. She went into the Quad where he haunts to talk to him. I know little beyond that; she's quite upset. I'm afraid I have never been good at handling hysterical women."

I nodded, then approached the ghost with slow and deliberate steps. When I was about five feet from her, I knelt beside her.

"What's her name?" I whispered to Professor Harrison.

"Millicent."

"Hello, Millicent. I'm a friend of the professor's. You've been through a terrible ordeal, I can see. But I need to know what happened when you went to speak to Luther Randolf."

Either my calm voice got to her, or she was already mastering herself because she stopped crying. After a few final sobs, she sniffed and then nodded to me.

"I—I went to speak with Mr. Randolf. He's always been a friend of mine. We knew each other when we were alive."

"Oh!" I said. "That's fascinating. Please, tell me more."

"When I heard there was trouble concerning Mr. Randolf, I had to visit him. I tried for several nights, but at first, I couldn't find him. Then, tonight, I saw him standing in the park behind a tree. I beckoned to him to sit and chat with me. We do that often. We always have delightful conversation. Anyway, this time, he wouldn't come out from behind the tree. I begged him to tell me what was wrong, but he shook his head and motioned for me to leave. I was afraid for him, so I crossed the grass to the tree, and that was when . . . when he . . ."

She burst into sobs once more. I sidled closer and took her hand in mine. This calmed her.

"What happened?" I asked. "Did he speak to you?"

Millicent shook her head.

"Then what did he do?"

"He did THIS!" She suddenly bared her neck. It was a mess of torn skin, muscle, and bone. With a gasp, I jumped back, releasing her hand.

"He's a monster! A *monster*, I tell you! He is no longer the man I knew. The man I loved. Something has happened to him. He's not like this. Please, help him!"

At that point, she went into hysterics, and I couldn't calm her down, no matter how many times I promised to help. I rose and joined the professor.

"Did you hear what she said?" I asked him. "She said he's changed. That this is all new. She also said he tried to get her to leave, so some of him is still there."

Professor Harrison stared at me with fear etched across his face. "What could do this to . . . one of us? I would have said it wasn't possible."

"I don't know, but I'm going to find out."

The ghost nodded but said nothing.

"I have to go now. They're closing up soon. But I'll check in on you."

He shook his head. "No. If I turn into that monster, I don't want to be responsible for your death."

I stared at him for a grim moment. "Right. Good luck, Professor."

16

Millicent's words ran through my head the next morning. *Something has happened to him. What the hell could happen to a ghost?* What could turn a perfectly harmless spirit like Luther Randolf into the ravenous monster that killed those people? It didn't seem possible.

I took a sip of my coffee. It was lukewarm. I scowled at it.

Jenna was still asleep in our room. She always slept in on Saturdays, and I had a date with the Dungeon Crawlers this morning, so I was up. It wasn't so bad, since I couldn't sleep any longer, anyway. Sometimes, a bit of news could wear you out more than a night of hard labor, at least if you spent way too much time stewing on it, like I did.

The cafeteria was abuzz with activity, as was usual for a Saturday morning. Everyone was up and ready to enjoy their day. To be honest, I was looking forward to mine. A day off shopping in Boston sounded like just the right thing for me.

Ben called as I headed back to my room from breakfast.

"We're meeting in the Quad in ten minutes. You're still going, right? We'll be at the bench in front of Grendel."

Since the Anthropology building was halfway across the Quad on its eastern edge, it made a good place to meet up. I went to my room, grabbed a few things, and left. Jenna still dozed.

I could see Ben running around in the grass as I walked in the morning chill toward Grendel Hall. He swung an invisible sword as though fighting a mock battle. Diego sat patiently, staring at his phone. Ben stopped suddenly and flashed a sheepish grin when he saw me.

"Where are we going?" I asked.

Diego shrugged. "I figure we'll go to Boston Common first, and then to Faneuil Hall for lunch. We'll check out stores and stuff along the way."

The others showed up soon after. Logan and Tony came strolling down the walkway from Strout Hall, hand in hand. Logan looked uncharacteristically cheerful.

Rocks jogged up last. "Sorry. My roommate was being a jerk."

"Okay," said Diego. "We're all here, so let's head out!"

We walked down Boylston Street in one group, occasionally making room for people to pass by.

Rocks asked me a question about ghosts as we strolled

along, and we all got in a conversation about my ability, the dead, and the details I had told him on the night of the first attack. Of course, I insisted they shouldn't believe me, but they scoffed at that.

"Why are you so determined to convince us you're lying?" Tony said at last. A round of "yeahs" followed by the rest of the group.

"Nobody ever believes me when I tell them about what happens to me at night. They say I'm lying or crazy. But you guys just said 'Yup. That makes sense.' It *doesn't* make sense. None of what I can do should be possible. Any normal person would never believe me."

"You might not have noticed this," said Logan. "But we're not normal."

"Your entire argument," said Rocks, "is predicated on your assumption that you're the only one who knows that ghosts are real. But I've seen them. I grew up in a haunted house. My bedroom used to be the kitchen of a duplex. I'd wake up in the middle of the night to the sound of someone cooking food and humming to herself. Nobody was there, but I could hear it. Sometimes, I even saw her. She was a cold, gray fog that looked oddly human-shaped. It went around the room as though gathering ingredients and cooking."

"But that's not what I see. And then I said I can touch them and talk to them. I might as well have said I'm a vampire."

"But that's just it," said Rocks. "I always knew there must be someone out there who could see and hear more than I could. It's a theory I've had for a long time. So, when you told us about your ability, I felt validated."

This was crazy. I understood that Rocks *wanted* to believe in me. But I couldn't accept that he *did*. "And you believed me without another word. You were so suspicious of my story when I was talking about normal stuff, but when I said *ghost*, you were all like, *okay*."

"It was your delivery, Lexi," Diego said. "You were ashamed to talk about it. You weren't trying to impress us. In fact, you blurted it out and then looked surprised and pissed off at yourself when you did."

"I didn't look surprised," I said.

Everyone laughed.

"The thing is," Diego continued, "you didn't want us to know about it, and that was convincing."

"Yeah. The whole 'touching ghosts' thing threw me for a bit," said Logan. "But after I saw the video of you being attacked by an invisible asshole, I knew you were telling the truth. It wasn't modified. That kind of thing is in my major. I can tell a modified video when I see one."

"And we've all seen it now," said Ben.

"But you hadn't when we played D&D."

"Like Diego said, you were believable," said Tony.

"Okay. But it's weird how many people have been believing me at Brent."

"Like Kai?" That was Ben. Everyone cast him a surprised look.

"Who's Kai?" asked Diego.

"Is he the guy in your dorm?" Rocks asked me.

"Yeah. He's a friend. And yes, Ben, he believes me."

"I'll bet he does," Ben muttered.

"What does that mean?" His attitude toward Kai made no sense, and it pissed me off.

Ben shrugged. "It's just that . . . of course he would say that, since he wants to go out with you."

Several groans from the peanut gallery followed Ben's statement, and the rebuke I was about to sling his way suddenly stalled in my throat.

I knew Ben had a little crush on me. His awkward words when we met. Saving a seat for me at D&D. The way he acted when he invited me to today's jaunt. But I never thought it was this bad.

I decided to play it carefully and not be confrontational like I usually was.

"Kai has every right to believe me, because we went ghost hunting together." I then told them all about our adventure at the haunted house. Of course, I excluded the kiss at the end. This did a great job of changing the subject. The group exploded into an excited discussion about searching for ghosts.

"*We* should hunt one down," Rocks said. This met with unanimous approval; that is, all except for me. I wasn't sure what to think. They weren't taking the subject seriously, like Kai had. Instead, Ben was pretending to sword fight while Tony and Logan discussed the hit points of the Fenway Hall Haunt and other D&D-related statistics. Diego watched me with a curious look on his face.

"Penny for your thoughts?" he said when our eyes met.

I shook my head slowly as Ben continued to goof around. "The truth is, I need to hunt down and banish a specific ghost, and I can't do it by myself."

Everyone stopped walking at that point and turned to face me.

"For real?" asked Ben.

I nodded.

"We can help!" Logan said.

"Yeah, definitely," said Tony.

"I don't think you can," I said as carefully as I could. "You're not taking it seriously. None of you are."

The breath Rocks released echoed the frustration I knew he must be feeling. "That's because we didn't know you wanted to do it. Until this moment, it was all hypothetical."

Diego nodded his agreement. "We're serious. We can help and do everything you need us to. You only have to ask."

I stood there on the sidewalk, staring at them. People jostled around us, going this way and that.

Rocks was the first to talk. "Let's not discuss it here. We're almost at Boston Common. Let's wait until we're there. Then, we'll work it out."

Boston Common was a big grassy park smack-dab in the heart of the city. Paved walkways led through to a wide, green area. Benches lined the paths, as did decorative streetlights. Trees grew in places, providing plenty of shade. In the center, accessed by cobblestone paths, was a bandstand that looked like the fanciest gazebo I'd ever seen. The place was an oasis surrounded by traffic and skyscrapers. It was beautiful. We gathered in a circle and sat on the grass. The mid-September wind blew around us, enough to cause my hair to fly in my face, but not enough to be uncomfortable.

"First, we need to know what Haunt you're going after,"

said Rocks in an official tone.

"The Fenway Ghost?" asked Diego.

I shook my head. They said they were all serious, but they didn't know what this entailed. They didn't know what they were up against. Time to be blunt.

"You've all heard about the two killings on campus."

Silence descended on the group, and they all stared at me, some wide-eyed, others just nervous. That was a much better reaction.

"So, it *is* a Haunt after all," Rocks breathed.

"A bad one. It's the first one I've ever heard of that can touch and kill a living person."

"Sounds like you finally found your first feral apparition," Rocks said.

"I think it's more than that. Ghosts have talked about Ferals, but none have described anything like this. Others on campus are terrified of it."

"How can spirits touch people?" asked Ben.

"They shouldn't be able to," I said. "In fact, there's reason to believe that something happened to him. He was never like this. He was the harmless spirit of a Boston aristocrat from the early 1900s. Soon after the start of the semester, he transformed into a monster, and now he's killing people. He has to be stopped before anyone else dies, but it will be hard and dangerous."

"How do you do it?" asked Diego. "How can you stop a Haunt?"

"I have a ritual. It's an old one, and I can't guarantee it'll work. But we have to try. It's the only way."

"But what if we perform the ritual on this monster and it doesn't work? It'll kill one of us, right?" Ben had a way of pointing out the dangers in everything we did. It was that way in our D&D game, and he was in full form today. Of course, he was also spot-on.

"That's right," I said. "I don't want to test this ritual on him."

"How about trying it on the Fenway Ghost?" asked Diego.

Logan rounded on him. "What's your deal with the Fenway Ghost? You keep talking about it."

"It's the video. I watch it a lot, that's all."

Dave Simons. The memory of what he did to me still haunted my dreams. Could I attack him without provocation? I picked up a pebble from the ground where I sat on the grass. I looked at it for a moment as I considered that thought. Then I threw it out into the park. It bounced on the grass twice and was gone. "I don't want to do that to Dave Simons. He's got a temper, and I've got a beef with him. But he's not evil. I won't just attack a ghost for no reason."

"There's the one in the haunted house you just told us about," said Rocks.

Ugh. That place. I didn't want to go back there. I didn't want to see that evil mother and her ghostly child. Of course, I'd have to at some point. Just not now. One life-threatening adventure at a time, thank you.

"The place is too dangerous. The floors aren't stable enough. And there are two terrible Haunts there. Only the mother attacked me, but I'd bet the daughter is just as nasty."

"Then it's the Phantom of Brent Quad," Diego said.

Everyone looked at him.

"Phantom of Brent Quad?" Rocks repeated, casting his friend a quizzical look.

"What? It's gotta have a name!" Diego said.

"I call it Top Hat," I said.

Diego snorted. "That's boring."

"Too true," said Logan.

"Kinda lame," said Ben.

I turned to him. "Really? You too?"

Ben's cheeks went red. "No! It-it's not so lame. I'm sure you could do better."

"But, all jokes aside," said Diego, "the Phantom is our best option. And it's the real target, anyway."

"And we turned it down because it's too dangerous," I said.

"But either we banish something we shouldn't, or we go for the real deal. We don't have much choice."

I had to admit, Diego made a good point.

Diego continued with his plan. "We'd be doing it in the Quad, which is outside and on campus. The Phantom probably doesn't want too much attention, so we can have noisemakers, like those can air horns. If it gets too bad, we just blow them and hope it'll run away."

Another good point. Hey, maybe these guys could help me with it. The only problem was whether any of them could see ghosts.

"The plan sounds pretty good," I said. "But it would help a lot if some of you could see ghosts, at least even a little. Who's up for a ghost tour of Fenway Hall tonight?"

Four hands raised at once. Ben raised his a little slower, but he grinned with determination.

"Okay. We'll meet tonight and go in looking for Dave Simons. I don't think he's violent all the time, and if he gets that way, I'm the only one at risk, and I can handle him."

"Are you sure?" asked Rocks. "Because last time didn't go so well."

"Dave took me off guard. But I'm ready this time."

With that settled, we put the subject of ghosts aside and played tourist. We went to Faneuil Hall and had fun shopping. We ate lunch at Quincy Market and visited many of the shops in that old marketplace.

At one point, we saw Kai hanging out with several other guys. I had to admit, his friends had an unsavory look to them. It wasn't that they all wore black (which they did), or that they affected a goth or emo look (which some of them did). They looked dangerous, like people you wouldn't want to meet in a dark alley. Kai was in stark contrast to his friends, with his playful smile and bright eyes.

Ben pointed him out to the others.

"*That's* your new boyfriend?" asked Logan. "He doesn't look bad. But I don't like his taste in men."

"Good," said Tony, and the two laughed.

"He's not my boyfriend," I said.

"Could have fooled me." Ben snorted. "You two were making googly eyes at each other at the Student Center."

"Is that a technical term, Ben?" asked Rocks.

"Yes, it is," he replied, sticking his nose in the air and trying his best to look snooty.

The talk degenerated on the way home, with many conversations going at once. At some point, Rocks and I walked together while the others joked about something.

"Lexi, you've had this condition all your life, right?" Rocks asked.

I shrugged. "As far back as I can remember."

He shook his head, his brow creased. "I can't imagine how anyone could go through what you do every night as a kid and survive. It must have been brutal."

"It was."

Rocks lapsed into silence as we continued down Boylston Street toward campus. The others had grown quiet now, too. I looked around, and they were all looking at me with concerned expressions.

"You should tell us about it," said Diego.

"Yeah," said Tony. "It's therapeutic. It's always best to talk about stuff like that."

Logan grinned. "Besides, we all want to know what it was like living with it as a kid."

"We won't laugh or give you shit," said Ben.

"I know you won't." It was all I said for a minute, but then I cleared my throat.

"For a long time, I didn't know that other people couldn't see the world like I saw it. Sometimes, I'd point someone out who looked strange, and my parents thought I was playing games or seeing things. When I realized this was something special, I tried to keep it secret. I stopped going out at night. This helped, but there were always those ghosts who would come looking for me. I couldn't escape them."

"I thought ghosts are trapped in one place," said Rocks.

"Not all of them. Haunts are. But the dead come in a lot

of different flavors. I've come up with names for some of them. Specters can roam anywhere. Some want company, someone to talk to. Others are looking for closure."

"Did you help any of those?" asked Ben.

"As a kid? No way! They scared the piss out of me. And what could I do? I couldn't go wherever I wanted. I didn't help any of them. There was one I might have helped, but she was really trying to help me."

"So, they're stuck there forever?" said Ben.

"I don't know."

"Have you ever asked them?" asked Diego.

"They come to me for answers, remember?"

"True. Did you deal with any violent ones when you were little?" asked Logan.

"Oh yeah. There seems to be no lack of frustrated or angry spirits. I have some scars on my back and arms and legs. But it wasn't too bad. I got good at hiding from them. They wouldn't bother me when I slept in my parents' room. They don't always like being around the living. Except for me."

"You must have grown up in a hurry," said Rocks. He looked nervous, like he wanted to pat me on the back, but wasn't sure that he should. I hated that. Pity was one thing I didn't have time for.

"My dad tried to get me to tell him who kept hurting me. When he couldn't get a good answer from me, he signed me up for karate lessons. That turned out to be just what I needed. Discipline, meditation, and the ability to kick the ghosts' asses. I don't get hurt much anymore, and I've learned to deal with them. I can talk to them now, better than I could before. It gets me labeled with names like 'Ghost Girl' and 'weirdo,' but that's minor, all things considered. I'm fine with it."

"Always remember we're here for you," said Diego. "You're a Dungeon Crawler, and that means you're one of us. We've got your back."

I had to admit, I was glad for that.

17

Why does everyone prefer having dates at night? Is it because it's supposed to be more beautiful? Or could it be that it was more likely to end with sex? I couldn't judge on the former, and the latter was out of the question. At least for tonight.

The air was cool with a friendly breeze that traipsed across the Quad to the delight of the groups of kids who went here and there on this fine Saturday night.

That was my guess from all the happy faces around me.

I could only assume the breeze was "friendly," since *my* nighttime breezes were cold and clammy. And the effect it had on the dim, shadowy campus landscape resembled the icy hand of death as it reached across the grass that bowed, terrified, from its approach.

I'd have preferred a daytime date.

The door to Wembley Hall opened behind me and Kai stepped through, his constant grin widening in appreciation when he saw me.

"I don't think I've ever seen you in a dress before," he said as he came alongside, and we began our walk toward Boylston Street. "You look great!"

I didn't wear dresses often and saved them for special occasions. Weddings, funerals, first dates. Things like that. It was a simple dress of a not-so-dark shade of blue that hung down to my knees. I knew the air would be cold for me, but I'd look out-of-place in something warm. So, I opted for a happy medium.

"And I didn't before?" I said. No. My wit never turns off. It's my gift and my curse.

"You *know* what I mean. You look great every day. Even when you're covered in dust after falling through a ruined staircase."

"Wow. You sure know how to charm a girl."

"Hey! I try."

Kai had dressed up as well, wearing a nice jacket that was open to reveal a white shirt. Straight-leg blue jeans rounded out his ensemble.

We skirted the Quad by keeping to the edge alongside some of the other dorms to reach Boylston Street and our escape from campus. This kept us as far from the crime scene as possible. Once away from the college, Kai took over the navigation. Boston was a chaotic city, with its maze of narrow streets and tall buildings. The cars that sped incessantly down every street seemed driven with a vengeance that filled me with dread. Crossing any street looked like a death sentence. But Kai approached it all with a cool detachment that came with familiarity. He was in his element, far more so than he had been on campus. This was his home.

"Where are we going?" I asked. He never told me what restaurant he planned to take me to. I hoped it wasn't one of those "haunted" restaurants. It was the type of stunt he might pull.

"I decided not to impress you with my wealth. I figured you would see that as shallow. That, and I don't have any. There's a nice little pizza place down the road. It won't be as loud as the real busy places, so we can talk."

"It's not haunted, is it?"

He laughed. I liked his laugh. It was a weird half cackle. It was unique and sounded refreshingly honest. "Not that I know of. But I'm not as sensitive as you. After all, you saw things in the ghost house that I didn't."

"You mean in the basement?"

He nodded. We stopped, and he pressed the button for the crossing light. Then we stepped up to the curb to wait. Four other people crowded around. Two started across early, and I thought they were stupid, with the cars whizzing around like they were. But they seemed unconcerned with the danger. Bostonians are a weird bunch.

"I could hear you talking to someone, but no one was there when I opened the door."

"But you saw the . . ." I leaned closer to him with a quick

look at the two people who continued to wait with us. "The bones," I whispered.

He frowned at me. "What bones?" He didn't whisper, and I winced. But the two others hadn't seemed to notice. They were engaged in their own conversation.

"The bones. Bones and skulls were all over the floor. They were everywhere. I broke a bunch when I landed."

His head shook slowly, and I could tell he was trying to remember that horrible scene. "Nope. I saw nothing like that. It had a concrete floor, and there was lots of debris there from your fall. But I didn't see any bones. And I didn't see any ghosts, either."

My mouth opened as though to say something. But nothing came out, so I shut it. *Could it be that I imagined the bones?* I dismissed that thought right away. The child Haunts were real. There was no arguing about that. And I understood why Kai couldn't see them. The bones existed only in the Ghost World. But that was strange. I had seen nothing else there that wasn't a part of the ghost itself. Aside from The Door, of course, but that wasn't a part of the Ghost World, either. It was always like I was only partway into the Ghost World, and so I could only see and touch spirits. I never saw what they saw, even though some described surroundings that were not there in the living world. *Could some spirits project their surroundings to me?*

The walk light came on and we went across. I wanted to run because those lights never stayed on long, but Kai took his time, and I had to hold myself back for him.

I said nothing more on the subject, but he kept casting me curious glances. He wanted to keep talking about it, but I wasn't sure I was ready to tell him about my whole condition. I'd concealed that from him so far, in part, so that it wouldn't overshadow his own experiences. The last thing I wanted was to brag. But I might have to open up soon, since he kept wanting to talk about it all.

When I didn't continue the conversation, Kai changed the subject. We talked about school, our differing majors, and how our workloads were. Kai was an English major, and he told me about all the books he had to read and all the writing assignments he got. He seemed to like it, though, so I guess it was the right choice for him.

"What can you do with an English degree?" I asked as we walked down another street. A ghost looked my way, and for a moment, our eyes met. He took a step toward me, but I shook my head and cast a quick glance at Kai. The apparition got the hint and, with a frown, turned away.

"I can be a writer," he said. "I plan to write books. Mostly novels about ghosts and things like that."

"Oh, so our trip to the ghost house was research for school."

"Ha! For a book, more like. I plan to write one about that house. I've been wanting to for most of my life."

"Then I can see why you went for English."

"And what about you? You study Anthro, right?"

"How did you know that?" I asked.

"We studied together, in the Student Center. I saw one of your books."

"Oh, right!" I mentally hit myself for not glancing at any of his books then. But my mind had been occupied at the time.

"Ah! Here we are!"

We stopped in front of an old brick building. It was one of many quaint old structures you see in Boston that were over a hundred years old. They were never meant to be the strip of shops and restaurants they became. It had a single floor, and the unit we stood before held a big sign that read "Al's Pizza." It had the look of a hole-in-the-wall. We overdressed.

"It has . . . charm," I said.

His grin that erupted at my comment lit his face with a warmth that almost made me forget the nighttime chill I always felt. He opened the door and gave a curt bow.

I went through and stopped short in surprise.

The outside of this place misled me. The inside was far wider than its exterior made it appear. They'd rented two units and joined them into one restaurant. They had also decorated. The result was a warm and inviting place, with plenty of room, and even a fireplace near one corner.

A young woman came up to us. She was about our age and pretty, with long red hair tied into a ponytail that bobbed on her head. A collection of freckles dotted her face near her nose, but she was annoyingly cute. An apron with the establishment's logo on it covered her clothes. She smiled at us. No. She didn't smile. She *beamed*. At Kai, not at me. It was as though I wasn't there.

"Hi, Kai! I've got your table ready. The last party just left."

She led us to the fireplace and gave us a seat before it. She then handed us menus.

"I thought we wouldn't see you here until your first break," the girl said as she filled our glasses with water from a pitcher she had been carrying.

"My college is in town," he said.

"Oh, really? Which one?"

"Brent."

"Ah! Well, that explains it. It's right nearby. I should visit sometime."

She then took our drink orders and left.

"Sounds like you're a local celebrity," I said, taking a sip from my glass.

He shrugged. "The owners are friends of the family."

This was where we fell into the standard awkward date situation. We smiled and looked at the menus, and we talked about our pizza preferences.

"What do you want on the pie?" Kai asked as we looked over our menus. We both assumed we'd share a pizza. One more way in which we fitted together nicely.

"I like all the normal pizza veggies, but if I had my choice, it'd be peppers and onions."

"Ah! A plant eater. Well, I'm afraid I'm totally a carnivore."

"Hey!" I laughed. "I like meat. Just not on pizza, if I can help it."

"Hmm." He rubbed his chin with thumb and forefinger, as though pretending to ponder a Holmesian-level mystery. "Now, *that's* a conundrum! One pie, two topping preferences."

I shrugged. "We could go half and half."

"And that would be the pragmatic solution," he said, still trying to sound like a snooty literary investigator. "But I'm afraid I'm a romantic fool. I think we should eat from the same pizza, with the same toppings."

A grin tugged at my features, and I tried to imitate his manner. "Then how do you propose solving this riddle?"

"Through compromise, naturally. I will accept onions if you will deign to eat a meat product."

A laugh tried to force its way out, and I managed a strangled snort, like I was choking or something. "Since you are willing to oblige me, I will accept your suggestion and have pepperoni. Would that be sufficient?"

"Yes. Quite."

That was it. The two of us erupted into raucous laughter, causing people all over the restaurant to stare at us. The redheaded waitress's face now matched her hair.

Once we had gained control over ourselves, Kai closed his menu and held out his hand for mine. "Then it's time to order." I placed the menu in his waiting hand, and he set them on the edge of the table and nodded to the waitress, who still watched us, her face slowly draining of its extra color. She smiled and came over.

Kai placed the order. I wasn't sure if he was going for chivalry or to keep me from having to talk to her. The first possibility was unnecessary but appreciated. The other was vitally important. Our bitchy little waitress smiled and winked at Kai before leaving with the order.

"She thinks I'm competition," I said pleasantly as I watched her head back to work while I sat and sipped my water in comfort.

"You're not." Two simple words, and they made me spin my attention to him, everything else forgotten.

"I'm not?" I asked. I wasn't angry yet. But I was curious.

He shrugged and gave me that half smile he sometimes affected when he was being witty. "How can you be her competition when she's not even in the game?" He lifted his water glass, held it briefly up to me in salute, then took a sip. "I have no eyes for her. Only you."

I blinked. I opened my mouth to say something clever, then closed it when nothing came to me. I found myself at a complete lack of words.

He grinned. "Whew! I dodged *that* one!"

My jaw dropped as he set down the glass.

"Look." His tone was now serious. "All joking aside, I have a code. When I'm dating someone, I don't play around. I date that one person. She deserves at least that. If I were dating her, I'd do the same. But I'm not dating her, even though I've known she likes me for months. There's no one else I'd want to be with than you."

"Okay." It was lame, and it came out of my mouth several seconds too late, but it was the only thing I could think to say. Kai was one of those nice guys you always hear about. The kind that usually finishes last. Yet he somehow had two girls interested in him. My mom would call him "a keeper." She might be right.

But I wasn't quite ready to accept all that. Maybe I was a little insecure, but I wanted to know why he wouldn't be interested in such a pretty girl.

"Why *didn't* you go out with her?"

"She's not my type."

"And your type is someone . . . ghost-obsessed?"

The sigh I got in response told me I played that card a bit

too much.

"My *type* is someone I have things in common with. Some-one I can be friends with as well as be romantic with."

"Now, that was well played," I said. But I grinned. Yeah, he scored points with that one. And it wasn't like we hadn't proven our friendship.

We then dove into conversation about school. To be hon-est, I forget what we talked about. It was all so nice and normal, and it didn't feel like any first date I'd ever been on. Kai and I shared a connection that kept us at ease with each other, and so we chatted like old friends. The bitch—er, waitress—arrived with our pizza, but Kai afforded her only a side smile and con-tinued the story he was recounting to me. She put the pizza down and left in a huff.

"But I like the school," said Kai after munching a bite of pizza. "Anything to get away from home."

"You're not away from it. Don't you live in Boston?"

"That's not what I meant. I'm glad to get away from my *house*."

"Oh, that's right! The haunting. The scars. It must have been bad."

He looked up from his slice that drooped in his hand and met my gaze with an intensity that hurt my heart.

"You don't know what it's like to live in a house that attacks you every night."

I raised my slice in salute. "That was my home until I was five. Then we moved."

His grin cracked the dark expression, and he chuckled.

"That's why we're so good for each other. We have common

experiences." He took a big bite of pizza and chewed with gusto.

"I hope it's more than that."

The pizza was good. Actually, it was delicious. I almost wanted it to suck so that I wouldn't have to see that waitress again. But I guess we'd end up coming back here from time to time. Damn.

Our server traipsed over with a smile on her face, and she set the bill on the table beside Kai. Then she cleaned it while Kai put his card with the bill. The redhead balanced the plates in one hand and took the bill and card with the other.

"I'll be right back," she said, and her voice held implications she was in no position to make good on.

The two of us prepared to leave. I gathered my purse and put on my jacket. Once we were ready, my nemesis returned with the receipt.

"See you later," she crooned at Kai, then turned and bounced away, looking all too proud of herself. What had she done?

Kai stared at the bill for a moment, one eyebrow raised. Then he grinned. He picked up the pen with one hand while handing me a slip of paper with the other.

"I'll sign for it, and you can do what you want with this."

I took the slip and read it.

Call me anytime. 555-7214. Marinda.

"Hmm," I said. *That little bitch.*

I crumpled it and dropped it on the table. It bounced once, then stopped like a dead thing.

He flashed me his wry grin again and offered his arm. I

linked mine with his and we walked happily to the exit. I flashed the waitress a victorious smile as we passed her.

"Goodbye, *Marinda*," I said.

The walk home was pleasant, and when Jenna leaped from her desk to inundate me with questions about the date, I just grinned and said nothing.

18

It was nine o'clock, and the Dungeon Crawlers were already congregating outside Fenway Hall when I came running up. My date had ended a little late, but it was worth it. They all greeted me with grins and cheers. Ben frowned at the bit of makeup on my face, which didn't fit with the jeans and T-shirt I had changed into. He would have to get over it.

Because Dead Dave could never hurt a living person, there was no need for them to carry any iron weapons to defend themselves with. This was good, because we'd look pretty stupid wandering around a dorm at night with crowbars and iron chains and stuff. However, because *I* could get hurt, we carried a bag of homemade salt bombs. These were little baggies of salt that, when thrown, would explode on impact, hope-fully causing a cloud of salt to mess with Dave. That should do the trick if I had to fight him and it went sideways. I didn't think we needed them, but the others insisted. Rocks had the bag of bombs because he was the only member of the group who had seen a ghost in the past, so he might notice Dave and know where to throw. Tony grew up in a haunted house, but he said he only heard noises.

Once again, I dressed casually, only this time I wore a full T-shirt, rather than a tank top. I tied my hair in a ponytail, which I didn't like because it presented a target, but I didn't want to do anything else with it. The guys, of course, dressed normal in jeans and T-shirts.

Ben wore some strange glasses that had a lot of different lenses over one eye. "They let me see through different spectra," he said. "Maybe one of them will show the ghost." He shrugged. "It's worth a shot."

Diego grinned. "Awesome! And you're right. I'd let you roll an extra die if this was a game."

"Now, remember," I said as I stood at the front door, "we're here to see if any of you can see Dave. We won't fight him if we can help it. We just want to see him. Got it?"

"Got it," they all said at once.

"Good."

The door was open this night, and a guy sat at a table right beyond it, signing in visitors. I told him we were here to see Tom Prichard. He wrote our names down, then motioned for us to go in.

Tom strolled over to us as we left the table and entered the lobby. He offered a curt nod to the others but gave me a warm smile.

"It's good to see you, Lexi," he said. "You're looking great."

"Thanks." I smiled. After all, it was the polite thing to do when someone complimented you. There was nothing more to it, of course. Tom wasn't my type. And I sort of considered myself spoken for.

He looked around, giving the gang more than a passing glance. He frowned when he saw Logan, who was quick to return it with his own. Tom looked away suddenly and returned his attention to me.

"You're hunting the ghost again?" he asked, ignoring my friends.

"Sort of. We want to find out if any of us, other than me, can see him at all. It's an experiment of sorts."

"Okay. I should probably go with you. After all, you're my guests here. And he follows me around."

I nodded. Logan muttered something I couldn't hear that made the muscles in Tom's jaw knot, but the jock kept his cool.

"We should probably do what we did last time. It worked like a charm." I said it to break whatever tension was growing between them.

"Tenth floor common room, then. I'll see you up there." He smiled again at me, then strode off toward the elevators.

"We'll wait until he's gone up and then take an elevator. We'll go into the common room and sit at a table away from him and wait for Dave to show up. I'll let you know if he does."

"And Logan," said Diego. "Keep your mouth shut around Prichard. You might not like him, but we have a job to do."

"Fine." That one word promised trouble, but I let it go for the present. Not the smartest move in the world, but I'm far from perfect.

The air was tense in the elevator as we ascended to the tenth floor. Everyone seemed lost in their thoughts about the job, and I believed that the seriousness of what we were doing had settled on them.

Ben, however, fidgeted and kept sneaking glances at me. At last, his thoughts blurted out in one quick stream.

"What's the ghost like? Does it look dead? If we see it, what will we see?"

I turned to look at him. "Those are good questions. When I saw him last, he looked like a college student. In fact, he resembled Tom a lot. He didn't look dead to me. But he'll be an eerie mist or something to you, if you can see him. Remember, almost nobody sees ghosts. This is a long shot."

"Oh. Okay." I don't think I made him feel any better because his face looked a little pale.

The elevator lurched to a halt, and the door slid open.

"Here we go," I said. "Are you all ready?"

Everyone nodded, and we exited the lift and made our way down the hall to the common room.

"Let's go in a few at a time, so we don't draw attention." I strolled in and took the same table I had taken the first time I went to this room. Rocks came with me, and he seated himself to my left. A few moments later, Logan and Tony entered and walked, hand in hand, to the table. Logan's eyes burned on Tom, who sat on the couch watching TV like last time. He did a good job of ignoring us. Ben entered last with Diego, and we were all seated together. We then took books out of our back-packs and pretended to work.

Dave Simons was not in the room. Of course, he had to play hard to get. I had been hoping to see him right away, let everyone get a good look at him, and then leave. But we had to wait for him to show up.

At some point, we switched to doing real homework. All except Logan, who sat glaring at Tom for most of an hour. Now and then, Tony put his hand on Logan's shoulder or whispered things to calm the guy down, but it never seemed to work for long.

After watching this for forty-five minutes, I leaned over and asked Tony, in a hushed tone, what Logan's deal was with Tom.

Logan's boyfriend shook his head and drew in a breath.

"Tom said some things about him in public. Insensitive things."

I thought back to my first experience with Tom Prichard. How he loudly called me Ghost Girl in front of everyone and made a spectacle of me in front of the class. Then I remembered how he opened up to me right after class, illustrating that he didn't mean to tease me but to ask for help. I frowned.

"Look, Tom's insecure, so he says things out loud and regrets it later. He did it to me when I first met him. But I had to look past that initial embarrassment to see that he cared underneath his bluster."

"Hey, let's not talk about this here," said Diego, also leaning forward. "Talking about it might set Logan off."

"I think Tom knows Logan's watching him," said Ben in a

near whisper.

"That's right!" Logan said aloud, rage dripping from each word. "He sees me. He knows what he did."

Tom flashed him a look that screamed "what the hell are you doing." I tried to give Tom one that said "Sorry. Just ignore him," but I don't think he got it. Still, the jock had the sense to turn his gaze back to the TV, if not his attention.

Tony took his partner's hand again. "Logan, remember the quest. Don't go berserk on us. Make your Wisdom save."

Logan shook his hand free without taking his eyes off Tom and sneered. "I'm not afraid of him," he snapped. "The guy's a stupid ass—"

"That's it!" Tom Prichard threw himself off the couch and stormed over toward our table. Logan leaped up and faced him, the two nose to nose.

The rest of the Dungeon Crawlers all groaned, but they got up and went to Logan.

I shoved myself between the two macho men and faced Logan. "Sit down and shut up!" I fumed. "You're ruining any chance we're going to have tonight, all because you can't keep yourself in line."

"Lexi!" Tony's voice cut through my rant. I glared at him, but his look of "you're making things worse" forced back my rebuke. "You see to Tom. I'll handle things here."

I backed away and bumped into something tall and unyielding. I turned around and found myself inches from Tom's face. He was enraged, but his anger fizzled out of him when our gazes met. We stood there for a moment in silence. His eyes were very blue.

"Um, sorry," he said and blinked. That made me blink, and we both tore our eyes from each other.

"It's okay." Only two words? When did I ever talk like that? And my voice was so soft I could barely hear it. I cleared my throat and tried to grin. "We're a little on edge. You know. Because of the ghost."

"Right." He let that word stretch a bit, then he stepped back from me. Was I disappointed? No. Of course I wasn't. He's not my type.

I glanced back at the others.

The Crawlers had Logan surrounded and were talking him down. It was working, and Ben flashed me a grin and a thumbs-up.

I scanned the room to see how the chaos affected everyone else.

And then I saw him.

Dave Simons stood in the doorway and stared at me, his eye unblinking as it met mine. And yes, I said "eye." A black hole existed where the other one should have been. This wasn't a real eye socket. It was a hole to some ghostly abyss, and I imagined I could throw a pencil through that hole and it would fly forever, looking for something to stick in.

My own eyes bulged in response. *Oh my god! What I did to him. It* stayed! *The damage didn't go away.*

The muscles of his jaw tightened, and then he sneered at me.

"You!" he cried, his tone accusing as though it was my fault he had lost it.

"He's here," I shouted and rose. I sidestepped Tom and positioned myself away from the others.

"Ignore them," I said to the ghost, who was already taking my advice. He kept his attention on me.

"I can't believe you came back," he spat. "Haven't you punished me enough?"

"What?" I said, incredulous.

"You came to punish me . . . for what I did to that boy. Now you're back to do it again? When will it end?"

"I never came here to punish you. And I'm not from the Ghost Police or anything. I'm a living woman who gets stuck every night in your world. I didn't ask for this, and I certainly have no big motives about you."

He frowned—an act that appeared painful to him because of the eye. "Then why did you come here before?"

"I told you. To leave Tom Prichard alone. I never wanted to hurt you. I only wanted to talk. And if I recall correctly, you attacked me. You gave me a concussion."

"And you did this to me!" He pointed at his empty eye socket. "Why won't it come back?"

Words failed me then. At last, the only sentence I could muster breathed out in a desperate whisper. "I don't know."

"You don't *know!*" He blasted the words at me, and for a moment, I thought I felt my hair move from it. "I'm disfigured! For eternity!" His rage boiled up, and he would explode if I didn't do something. This would take finesse to fix. Gentle words and a touch of kindness.

Unfortunately, I was too much into the moment to worry about any of that.

"Hey! I was defending myself. You were on top of me trying to kill me, and so I gouged your eye. You lunged at me on the stairs, so I stabbed you. Both times, I was already in a bad way because of the damned concussion. What the hell was I supposed to do?"

I stood glaring at the guy, and his face underwent a comical series of changes. First it jumped to surprise, where his mouth hung open and his brow furrowed in confusion. Then it bounced to sudden realization, where his eye went wide and the "O" of his mouth grew bigger. Then at last, he grew crestfallen and looked at me with concern.

"I did that? But I didn't mean to. Damn it! Damn it!" he fumed. But he didn't stop. He kept repeating those words with increasing tempo, like he was winding himself up.

"It's okay!" I said, my voice more pleading than I intended. "It's all—"

He leapt with a suddenness that surprised me, and he knocked over a nearby chair. Then he threw a fit, knocking over chairs and smacking a stack of books off the counter that lined the wall. That was exactly the type of power he demonstrated right before he rushed at me. "Damn it! God *fucking* damn it! I'm so stupid!" He shouted obscenities like that with every attack he made on inanimate objects.

"Um, Dave. You're losing your temper again!"

He spun around, anger etched in every line on his face. Then he took a deep breath and held it for a moment. His countenance eased, and he became normal Dead Dave again.

"Sorry."

"It's okay."

It was then that I noticed the silence in the room. I looked around and saw everyone staring from me to all the stuff that had been flung around the place in Dave's tirade. Their jaws hung open in shock. A few people had cameras going. Ben looked like an excited dog straining at the leash as he tried his hardest to remain calm.

"Look," I said to Dave. "Let's bury the hatchet. I never meant any harm to you. And I don't think you wanted to hurt me. Let's be cool, okay?"

He nodded. Then he suddenly stepped forward and held his hand out to me.

I had no choice at this point but to trust him. I took his hand, and he shook it. He had a firm grip, but there was no funny business. Relief flooded through his features when he released me.

"I'm sorry for everything, Lexi. I want to be friends."

"We are, Dave." I went to the table and gathered my books. "But I should go now. You kind of made a scene."

He scanned the room for the first time since his outburst. He grimaced.

"Will I see you again?"

"I assume you'd want someone to talk to."

Dave smiled. "Yeah. That would be great."

"Oh, and please leave Tom alone. I know you mean well, but it's messing with him."

Dave left and walked down the hall. And I noticed a spring in his step that had not been there before.

"You guys ready?" I asked.

That seemed to release the onlookers from their shock. At once, everyone in the room rushed over to me, questions about the ghost spewing from their lips in a steady stream of words. It was chaos. The Dungeon Crawlers formed a circle around me and tried their best to calm everyone down, but it was no use. The revelation that ghosts were real and that they just witnessed it was too much for the people who saw the deluge of books and furniture. More students had rushed into the room during Dave's freak-out to find out what was going on. A lot of people saw it firsthand.

WHAM!

A sudden crash rent the air so loud that it forced everyone into immediate silence. All heads turned toward the noise and saw Tom Prichard with his hand on an enormous book that he had slammed onto a table. He glared around at the horde of people who had been straining to talk to me.

"Leave this room." He didn't shout, but his voice carried throughout the place with the threat of pain to anyone who failed to comply. At first, nobody moved. Then he yelled, "NOW!" and the place erupted into action as everyone bustled out of the common room, crowding through the doorway and dispersing down the hall.

At last, only my friends and I remained. And Tom, of course. Ben and Diego looked like they were on the verge of retreating as well.

Tom joined us at our table. He seemed at ease now and even smiled a little as he came up to me.

"Sounds like you patched things up with him," he said.

I nodded. "He won't bother you anymore. He understands now."

Tony cleared his throat. "He didn't attack you?"

I shook my head. "Dave's not a monster. He just has a temper."

"I don't like him," said Tom. Everyone looked at him. He shrugged. "He hurt Lexi."

A lot of heads nodded in agreement to that. All but mine. But I wasn't about to argue the point. They were welcome to their opinions, and to be honest, it kind of made me feel good.

"Did anyone see the ghost?"

Ben and Logan shook their heads. The others shrugged.

Rocks was the only one who nodded. "Not really, but I *felt* it. It was more like the air got stuffier or heavier. I knew something was about to happen."

"Okay," I said. "This was a great test, then. We now know that none of you can see a ghost, but Rocks can sometimes feel one if it's strong enough. That's useful."

I turned to Tom. "Thanks for helping. I wasn't ready to deal with a crowd."

"No problem," he said.

The stories and videos of the event spread throughout campus at lightning speed. This changed people's opinions of me, from the crazy Ghost Girl who talks to herself to the amazing woman who talks to ghosts. The videos went viral on the internet, as well as making swift rounds through the college. I became a local celebrity. People hounded me everywhere with the stupidest questions about the ghost of Fenway Hall. I lost count of how many times I had to say, "No, it's not my boyfriend."

The Dungeon Crawlers and I sat in the Strout Hall common room around a table. Instead of character sheets and other gaming materials, I had spread out the pictures and descriptions of the banishing ritual. The group wanted to be involved, and I was all for it, since I needed the help. Detective Ross couldn't be seen doing anything weird like that.

"Okay," I said as the group stared at the picture of a big magical circle that was loaded with bizarre symbols around its edges and center. "This ritual works in two parts. I call the first part 'the trap.' The second part is 'the spell.'"

I gave everyone a second to absorb that before continuing. "The trap is the circle. We have to draw it on the ground in as much detail as we can. It should be big enough to fit the ghost and must be in increments of three feet."

"I'm a good artist," Tony said. "I'll draw the picture. Where do I need to do it?"

"It's got to be outside in the Quad," I said. "We know the ghost can move around there. The closer to the street, the better, but far enough back so that we don't get onlookers."

Tony frowned. "Then we're talking a three-foot circle, because we can only draw it on a walkway, and they aren't that big. I'll do some measurements as soon as we're done with this meeting."

I nodded. "Tony will draw the circle before we get started. We'll have to make sure nobody goes near it."

"Not a problem," said Logan.

"Yeah, you're the intimidating one," Ben said. "That's your job."

Logan grinned.

"Good," I said. "Now, Diego, Ben, and Rocks, you'll do the

ritual. You should make copies and study it."

"Lexi! I couldn't see the ghost, but I was aware of it. I think could be useful and do something more than just the ritual." Rocks looked from face to face after he said it. It had become obvious during the game that he enjoyed being the only other person to have seen the apparition.

I shrugged. "Good point. You and I will act as bait and lead the monster into the trap. The others will do the ritual."

There was a pause, where everyone stared at me in silence. I swear Rocks's face went white before my eyes.

Then I laughed.

"I'll be the bait. Rocks, you can look out for it and let everyone know that it's coming. Once I get it in the trap, you guys do your ritual."

"I can help with the ritual since I'll have nothing to do once the circle is drawn," said Tony.

"You should help Logan keep people away," said Diego. "The path will come from two directions, after all."

Everyone prepared for their part of the job. Tony focused on learning to draw the circle. He got some chalk and practiced outside in an out-of-the-way area. Logan studied the ritual just in case he was needed.

The spell wasn't too difficult, but it had to be done to the letter. And it included a circle of its own. But that circle didn't need to be right near the trap; only within sight of it. While everyone studied, I went outside to find the right spot for it.

My phone rang as I wandered around the Quad. It was Kai.

"Hey, how about Italian for dinner? My treat. I know a great place within walking distance."

I smiled. "Sounds great, but I'm busy tonight. How about tomorrow?"

"I suppose that'll work. What are you doing tonight?"

"Homework. Finishing an essay." I hated lying to him, but I didn't relish telling him I was doing ghost-related stuff with somebody else. There was always that chance the guy might get jealous, and I didn't want that. I also didn't want him showing up. That would create chaos.

"That's what you get for picking a major with lots of writing," he said in his usual cheery voice. "Maybe I'll see you tomorrow."

"Sounds good." I hung up. One bullet dodged. I wanted to spend time with him, and maybe do things that didn't involve ghosts. But I had to banish this thing before it killed another person, and introducing Kai to the Dungeon Crawlers at this stage was a bad idea.

19

With dusk approaching, we gathered our gear and set out to the Quad. I chose a point about halfway but a little closer to the pavement. This would put us as close to Boylston Street as possible without getting too close to the passersby. In fact, it was the walkway nearest the part of grass I had been crossing when I encountered Top Hat for the first time. So, I knew he could manage it.

Logan took up his position at one end of our area on the path to reroute people and to deal with questions. I did the same on the other side until Tony finished drawing the trap circle. Tony got to work right away, dropping to his hands and knees and scraping the chalk on the pavement. The rest of the

Crawlers went over the ritual and prepared as best as they could. They set up twenty feet from the trap and dressed in dark colors to be less visible to any passersby.

The student body took the whole security thing more seriously than I had expected. Kids would be kids, and not all of us were ready to trade in our irresponsible ways. But the threat of getting murdered worked its magic on them. We only got a handful of weird looks as students walked in pairs and groups farther in the Quad.

I stood on the path about ten feet away from the three as they set up for their ritual. The late September air had gotten colder, and the breezes from the ocean didn't help any. I had neglected to wear a jacket, and I regretted it as I rubbed my arms with my hands and shivered. So far, the temperature, though uncomfortable, was average. The occasional glance around the place showed no mist and no suspicious shadows.

At last, Tony finished drawing and put away his chalks. He then came to relieve me, and I went to see the others.

"Are you guys ready?" I asked.

"Ready as we can be," said Diego, his face grim. "This is going to be pretty intense, right?"

I nodded. "I won't sugarcoat it. If Top Hat shows up, the shit's going to get bad. Real bad. But I'll keep him from you and get him to the circle. Once he's there, he shouldn't be able to get out. Then, you get started."

"W-what if he *does* get out?" asked Ben. He looked pale and shook as he talked. It could have been the cold air, but I doubted it. Suddenly, I was concerned about our chances.

"Are you okay, Ben?" I asked. "If you're not ready, we can

do it tomorrow night."

Ben shook his head vigorously. "No. I've got this."

"Besides, Tony studied the ritual, too, just in case," said Rocks.

"Fine. To answer your question, Ben, I don't know. If it gets out of the circle, I'll give the word, and you'll all abandon your posts and get to Strout Hall together as a group. So I'll hold it off."

"But that's dangerous for you," said Diego. "We won't abandon you."

"You won't. I'll follow along, but I'll be covering you."

"I don't like it," said Rocks.

"Me either," said Diego.

"Yeah," said Ben.

"It's all we can do." I glanced around. Already, a mist had formed. "I think it's coming," I called out to the rest. "Get ready!"

I walked out onto the grass towards the spot where I had first seen Top Hat. Everyone was silent now and keeping low. In their dark clothes, I could hardly see them.

A definite spectral chill had crept in to accompany the fog, and now I looked from tree to tree, trying to see the shadows that always betrayed the ghost's approach. But no matter where I looked, I saw nothing.

It's here, I thought as I scanned the knee-high mist, decorative trees reaching up from it like the arms of the dead as they rose from the grave. *I can feel it.*

"I know you're here," I said out loud, and my voice seemed to die in the now-freezing air. "Come and get me!"

The mist swirled beside me with a sudden movement, and the shadowy form lunged upward and toward me.

I had only two seconds in which to act, and I spun around, swinging my arms in front of me. The intention was to knock the ghost's grasping arms out of the way and maybe send him off course beyond me.

This only partly worked. As planned, his arms missed their mark, and Top Hat did charge past me. But as he did, he grabbed my wrist and pulled me with him. This yanked me off my feet. I stumbled backward and fell into the cover of the mist.

I hit the ground and got a mouthful of grass as I took only a second or two to collect my thoughts.

This was a mistake. Top Hat came after me at once, crawling on all fours almost as fast as a German shepherd. I rolled quickly, slowing its approach, but I knew it would be on top of me in a matter of seconds.

I stopped my roll with my body on its side, facing my enemy as it hurtled toward me. As it leaped, its mouth twisted in a wicked grin, my fist flew out and struck it in the neck. I heard something crunch, and the monster dropped to the ground beside me, its hands going to its throat as it croaked and wheezed in agony.

I'd hurt it! But fighting it wasn't my plan. I leaped up and moved backward. Then I saw my next problem. The fog layer had covered the walkway. I couldn't see Tony's circle.

I looked first at the ritual group for help, but though they knew what I needed, they couldn't see it either. Ben stood on the edge of their circle, staring at me, his face wide with terror.

He was frozen in place. Useless. Tony was at his side, ignoring him and prepping to do his friend's part of the banishing.

A flashlight flared into existence and shone down at one spot about ten feet to my left. It was Logan, and he aimed the beam at the circle. I grinned at him, and he nodded and kept holding the light steady.

The rustling of feet on grass told me my opponent had risen, and I turned to face him. Top Hat stood there, only a few feet from me. It glared at me with pure hatred, and I returned the look with gusto.

"You and me," I said, taunting it. "NOW!"

Top Hat growled, and it came out hoarse but no less terrifying. It charged at me, its fingers now sharp as talons.

I ran straight for the spot where Logan's light fell. I didn't run at my full pace because I needed the ghost to keep following.

The light grew nearer. The footfalls came closer behind me.

Only three more steps. An icy breath blew on my neck.

Something struck me hard and threw me to one side. I tumbled, at first on the pavement and then onto soft grass. Then, at once, I leaped to my feet and took in the scene before me.

The Shadow Monster, which was now a more appropriate name for the ghost, stood only two feet from where I believed was the edge of the trap circle. In its hand was Logan's neck. The young man struggled in vain against the apparition's grip, which held him a couple of feet off the ground.

Tony cried to Logan and tried to break from their own circle to run to his love's aid. But the others held him back, shouting that he had a job to do. If I didn't do something now, Logan would be dead, and Tony would leave the circle and destroy all our chances of banishing the creature.

Logan dangled limply in the Shadow Monster's grip. Then, it opened its mouth wide for the fatal bite.

I charged the beast with all my speed, and when I slammed into it, we both tumbled the two remaining feet into the circle. Logan dropped like a rag doll to the ground.

As expected, the ghost fell across the line along with me into the trap but then stopped short of leaving the circle as though it had struck an invisible barrier. What I hadn't expected was that *I* hit the magical wall as well.

I was trapped inside the circle of banishment.

20

I stood as far from the monster as I could, one hand pressing against the vaguely warm edge of the circle's enclosing barrier. The ghost flung itself at the wall over and over again in a wild attempt to free itself.

I was trapped in a cage meant to hold a ghost. Was I a ghost? Had I died a long time ago and was now more spirit than human? Thoughts like those ran through my head as I stood there. I was only dimly aware of the monster's struggles and of my friends' frantic attempts to get me to leave the circle.

What would happen if they performed the ritual with me inside? Would I simply vanish and be gone like Top Hat? Would it cure me of my ghost ability? I suppose it depends on whether I'm alive or not.

"Lexi! What are you waiting for? Get out!"

My mind suddenly returned to the present, and I looked over at my friends. "I can't! I'm stuck in it!"

They all went silent for a moment, staring at me. Then they exchanged worried looks.

"What do we do?" Diego shouted.

Top Hat stopped fighting the barrier. Instead, it turned to consider me and my presence in the trap. A grin slowly spread across its hideous face.

"Do the ritual. Now! Before it kills me!"

That forced them into action. I could hear my friends' voices as they recited the words Professor Landry had translated. But my eyes were glued to the thing in the cage with me. We had a three-foot circle within which to fight. It for its lust of death, and me for my desire for life. Would it be enough?

The monster raised its hands and flexed the long, claw-like fingers. It thought it could take its time. Good!

"Do you remember Millicent?" I said suddenly.

It paused. The Shadow Monster cast me a curious look.

"That's right. Millicent. She's your friend. She talked to me, said you're not feeling well. Can I help you?"

A battle seemed to rage inside its ghostly mind, where the thing that turned it into a vile monster tried to subdue the dead man it once was. And for a few seconds, it looked like its original self was winning.

And then it keeled over in pain and anguish as the spell started to do its job. The monster inside him took control in one sudden push, and the ghost threw itself at me. Its hands reached desperately to tear at my face, its mouth wide open to bite anything it could get. I grabbed its wrists with both my hands and tried my best to hold it at bay, but I knew I was no match for it in a contest of strength. With as much force as I could, I shoved its arms to one side, then let go and ran around the circle to face it from behind. It turned to round on me once more, but this time I was ready.

I struck its knee with the full force of my side kick, and I heard the joint crack. It howled in pain and fury and threw itself at me again. I lunged forward past its claws so I could sink both of my thumbs into its eyes. I gouged them mercilessly, knowing I had to stop it before it could kill me.

It went into a frenzy at that moment. Its arms flew everywhere. The monster's body thrashed about like something was shaking it. Finally, one of its claws tore the skin across my neck.

Then it suddenly went stiff and silent. It stood staring at me, its mouth moving soundlessly as it tried to talk. The words "Be gone! Be gone! Be gone!" drifted on the wind, echoed in stereo by all my friends.

The ghost suddenly faded. It became a shadow that slowly dissolved. At last, I was left in the trap by myself. The entire time, I could feel a prickling sensation running throughout my body. It didn't hurt, and it never stopped me from fighting. Now, the feeling ebbed away, and all my warmth, energy, and consciousness went with it.

This is it, I thought as the blackness consumed me. *I'm banished from the world. I wonder where I'm going now?*

21

What clued me in? What was the thing that told me I still lived?

Pain.

Of course, it had to be pain. It couldn't be a soft caress, or a kind word, or a wonderful smell. It had to be fucking pain. But pain is real. It's physical. And it was the kind of sensation that required a body, with skin, nerves, and blood. My neck hurt.

The blackness that had been so complete ebbed away, replaced by light. But it was a pale, crappy kind of light. The kind that comes from fluorescent bulbs.

There were a lot of people I could have expected to see

when I opened my eyes in a hospital bed. Any combination of the Dungeon Crawlers would have been the obvious answer. Kai would also have made sense. Jenna, of course. But for some reason, I expected the figure that coalesced before me to be Tom Prichard.

But I was wrong with that, too.

Detective Ross stood beside the bed and looked down on me, his hard-as-rock expression softened with concern.

"It's all wrong," I said and was surprised at how weak I sounded.

His face creased with confusion. "What's all wrong?"

"Your face. It doesn't look right. You're supposed to be the hard-boiled detective, yet you look like you care."

He grinned at that, and it was the kind you get when a tough guy hears some witty sarcasm from another tough guy. That look kind of fit.

"That's better," I said.

"How are you feeling?" he asked. His voice was still gruff, but compassion was there, hiding in the background.

"Tired. What happened?" The most recent events were still a vague blur in my mind.

"From what I've been told, you tried something stupid."

The night's events came flooding back into my mind as though Ross had jimmied a stopper open.

"Oh, right. Yeah, I did do that. But I think it might have worked."

"Your friends said it did. Now, can you tell me what it was? They weren't clear. Something to do with ghosts."

"To be fair, I was planning on calling you if we were successful. Now I don't have to." I gave him a weak smile, then told him what we had done.

He walked to the window and looked out. Funny. As I spoke, I took in my surroundings. I lay in a hospital bed, in a room by myself. There was another bed, but it was currently empty. A tube was plugged into my arm, which was feeding me some clear fluid. A monitor wire ran from my other arm to a machine that beeped my heart rate at regular intervals. The window Ross now stood at was near my bed, with a chair and a nightstand between them. The nightstand held a bouquet of flowers in a vase. Those were probably from Jenna. I couldn't see much out the window at this angle, only the tops of a few buildings and a lot of gray. Water ran in little rivers down the glass.

"You thought you could banish the ghost. The one that's killed two people. And you thought you shouldn't tell me about it, because . . . why? You didn't think I'd believe you? I thought I had made my opinions quite clear on that matter. And then you decided to bring some friends along for fun."

As weak as I felt, I could still see where this was going, and it managed to piss me off. "No, I figured you'd believe. I know that much about you. I didn't call because I knew you couldn't do the ritual, being a cop and all. And I also knew that you would tell me not to do it. And no, I didn't bring my friends for 'fun,' as you called it. My friends volunteered. In fact, they wouldn't let me do it alone."

"At least they had some sense there," Ross muttered. "But they didn't understand what they were getting themselves into, did they?"

"I think they did. They knew this ghost had killed and could potentially kill them. But they also knew it was *going* to kill more people until we put an end to it. They understood that I needed help. Apparently, it worked. And nobody died."

"You almost did."

"One life to save many."

He whirled from the window to face me, his face red. The gruff, hard-boiled detective was back, and he was furious.

"That's bullshit, and you know it! Do you have a death wish or something? Do you *want* to die? Is this some ploy to end your nightly hauntings?"

The steady drone of my heart beeping from that damned machine increased in its pace.

"I don't want to die!" I shouted back. "But people were going to if I didn't do it. Lots of people."

"You can't say that for sure."

"Oh yeah? We both know that thing was going to keep killing until it was stopped. How long would it have taken you to think of using a ritual to kill it? How long, Detective? How many people would have died before you would have resorted to using my ritual?"

He didn't say anything at first. Instead, he glared at me, but the rage he had unleashed faded, and his sneer turned into a grimace. When he spoke next, it was quiet with a slight gravel to it.

"I set you up for this. I included you in this case, unofficially. It was because of me that you followed your line of research, and it was because of *me* that you tried this stupid, foolhardy stunt. You almost died, and that's on my head."

Ross grabbed his hat and coat from the chair and marched to the door. He paused after opening it.

"Call me when you get out of here. We need to debrief."

He closed the door gently when he left.

I knew Ross was upset because he felt responsible, and I understood that. But I'm my own person, and I didn't appreciate him chewing me out like that. I didn't work for him, and he was neither my teacher nor my guardian.

But I had little time to stew over Ross's words. A nurse came in and chatted with me, happy that I was awake. She took some readings and then left. Then a doctor came in. He couldn't find anything wrong with me. All he knew was that an ambulance brought me in unconscious. Nobody would tell him what happened, and he could never figure out what was wrong with me. They had given me stitches for the cuts on my neck, which were likely to leave me with scars, and he said they would keep me for the rest of the day to make sure that I didn't pass out like that again. Of course, I knew it wouldn't happen again, but I couldn't explain that to him.

My energy returned throughout the day, and when the Dungeon Crawlers arrived in the early afternoon, I felt a lot better. They stopped acting stiff and concerned as soon as I assured them I was fine. Then they went back to normal. Ben recounted the events of the night, with lots of pretend fighting and energetic reenactments. Rocks examined the medical equipment as though he knew how they worked. Tony sat at my bedside and tried to make me feel comfortable. Logan wandered the room with pent-up energy, like a caged animal.

Diego, in true Dungeon Master fashion, sat in a corner and watched everyone, an amused grin on his face.

Logan looked okay. Dark splotches on his neck showed bruising, but he gave it no mind as he stalked around the tiny room.

The fascinating part of all this was that every one of them saw the monster, though without the clarity that I had. I still had an edge on them regarding this special ghost, but it *was* solid in the living world. I hoped this was the last one, but I couldn't get past the notion that it wasn't over. Something had turned Luther Randolf into a monster. Could that happen again? I knew I would never feel comfortable until I understood what caused it.

"Okay, Lexi. I need to know what happened to you when you led the monster into the trap," said Rocks when he had finished studying the saline drip the doctor had removed from my arm. "You got trapped there, too, and that made no sense."

"I know," I said. "The details of the ritual never said that would happen."

"Could it be because you were in the Ghost World, too?" asked Diego.

Most of the others made motions to the affirmative, and I had to admit he was probably right.

"But what I want to know," said Tony, "is if the ritual banished Lexi's ability to enter the Ghost World."

I flashed him a look. *Could that have happened? Could I be free of that curse?* The big question I had at the time was if I wanted that to be true. I wasn't so sure. It had been a part of my life for so long that I couldn't grasp the concept of not having it anymore.

My look might have conveyed something akin to terror because Tony jumped up and started stammering.

"No! No! I don't think that's it! Really, I'm sure it's not the case!"

"It's okay!" I said, trying to sound calmer than I was. "It's fine. I know you were speaking hypothetically."

"Is there a way to test this theory?" asked Diego. "That is . . . a *safe* way?"

"I always feel it when it happens. And everything and everyone around me dims. It'd be pretty obvious to me."

"Hmm. I'd like more evidence, if possible," said Diego.

"I could find Professor Harrison, or I could talk to Dave Simons. We're on good terms now."

"Right," he said. "Then that should be our next goal. When do you leave here?"

I told them, and we agreed to test the theory that night. I would go to Grendel Hall with one of them and try to look for Professor Harrison. They all hung around a little longer, and we talked about happier things, like the game. I was good with that since it seemed clear to us that Top Hat was gone for good, and the ritual was a success.

Jenna visited me last that day. I called her as soon as the others had left. After I assured her I was fine, she promised to come as quickly as she could. She said she was suspicious when I wasn't around for breakfast, but since she didn't know what I had done that night, it hadn't occurred to her that there was trouble.

Jenna surprised me by showing up with Kai. They both looked worried and sat on either side of the bed.

"I told you I'm fine!" I said to Jenna after she noticed the bandage where the saline IV had been.

"You don't look fine," she insisted.

"Thanks. I appreciate that. But really, I'm good. They're going to let me out."

"Yeah, in a couple hours!"

"It's just observation. There's nothing wrong with me."

"I take it this is another ghost incident? I swear, every time you get hurt, there's a ghost behind it somewhere."

"Yes, it was a ghost incident." I flashed an apologetic look at Kai since I had ditched him last night. He looked surprised and interested.

"What kind of incident?" he asked.

"Hey!" Jenna cut in. "Don't encourage her! I know you had something to do with at least one of them."

"Jenna! I *am* a grown woman, you know. I choose to do these things."

My friend let out an exasperated breath. "I know. But I worry. You keep getting hurt. If you didn't get beaten up by these things, I wouldn't have a problem with it."

"You better get used to it. Ghosts are my thing. It'll happen no matter what I do."

"I'd like to know about this incident," said Kai. He eyed me with surprising intensity. I guess I didn't blame him. He must have expected to be a part of anything I did with ghosts.

"I fought a ghost that's been haunting the campus."

"You said you were working on an essay."

I cringed. "I'm sorry, Kai. It's just that I was doing the ghost hunt with some friends, and I knew that inviting you would cause a bit of chaos."

"Those gamer kids, right? I wouldn't have given them trouble. Are you saying they'd be jealous of me?"

"Do you think there'd be a reason for them to be jealous?" I eyed him with the hint of a smile.

He flashed that jaunty, confident grin I had learned to like. "Only if they want to go out with you."

A sudden intake of breath cut through the romantic tension, and the two of us turned to see Jenna, her hand covering her mouth, and her eyes opened wide.

"I'm sorry. I'll go out in the hall!"

She rose, but I grabbed her wrist.

"No. Stay here."

"Yeah, stay," said Kai. "We've got all semester to talk like that."

Jenna bit her lip but remained by my side.

Kai got up and walked around the room as the three of us talked about school and made plans to get me back there. Jenna had a car and would pick me up. I'd call with the discharge time.

Kai sniffed the flowers that were on my table. He lifted the card and stared at it for a couple of seconds, then put it back. Then he looked out the window.

"Looks like it stopped raining," he said.

"We should probably go," said Jenna. "Before it rains again."

We said our goodbyes, and Kai went out into the hall while

Jenna mothered me a bit more. When she finally went to the door, I called to her.

"Thanks for the flowers."

"Oh, they weren't from me. Kai and I barely found out you were here."

Once she left, I took the card and looked at it.

You've got to pick a safer hobby. You're driving me crazy! Get well soon. Tom.

22

My doctor released me at three o'clock, as my condition continued to improve throughout the day. Jenna came and drove me back to campus. As soon as we were in our room, I pulled out my phone to call Ben. Though I wanted to see Kai, my Ghost World condition was more important, and I wanted to test it out right away. But Jenna grabbed my phone away from me.

"Hey! I need that!" I said, annoyed.

"You're not calling your friends today."

"But I need to. There's something I have to check with them."

"You just got back from the hospital and have to take it

easy, like the doctor told you."

"You don't understand. Last night's ritual might have done something to my ability. It might be gone."

"Good. It was a bad thing, and you'd be way better off without it."

I froze, my next words unspoken. Until that point, Jenna had been a good friend and caring roommate. But right then, I wanted to punch her in the face. I mean, I understood her point of view, but that was not what I wanted to hear right then. I had to force down my emotions and pretend that what she said was fine.

"But it's a part of me, Jenna. How would you feel if something that was part of you suddenly vanished?"

"Why don't you stay here tonight and test it out. This is an old dorm. There should be ghosts around here somewhere."

"I haven't seen any," I said.

"That's because you spend so little time awake here at night. I'll bet if we wander around the place, you'll find something."

I looked at her, and our eyes met. "And you'll come with me? Looking for ghosts?"

"I won't see them, right? So, where's the harm?"

"Okay. I'll do it. Just the thought of you getting involved in my ghost life is worth it."

We ate dinner early so we could be ready when darkness fell.

The shadows of the sinking sun reached across our room from the window when we entered the hallways of Wembley Hall to look for ghosts.

"What's the plan?" Jenna said as we exited our room and padded down the well-lit passage in our socks. We weren't leaving the building, so we felt shoes were unnecessary.

"Since I don't know if this place is haunted, I guess we should make sure we're both seeing all the same people. When one of us sees someone, we point that person out. If three people are walking down the hall in front of us, say so. If what I see doesn't match what you see, then we found ourselves a ghost."

"Sounds simple enough."

We headed off on a tour of the building, first taking the elevator to the ground floor and walking around down there. The plan was to stroll around each floor and then take the stairs to the next level.

But we didn't get far.

We had walked down one hallway when I stumbled and fell against a wall. A dizziness spread through my body, making me unable to walk. I grabbed a telephone that hung on the wall to steady myself.

I took slow, careful breaths to avoid throwing up as the world spun around me. The crazy vortex of chaos continued, and I weathered it, keeping my eyes closed and my breath steady. At last, my body felt normal again. Carefully, I opened my eyes.

The corridor continued on, as it had before. The light gray carpeting felt good under my feet, and I stood up straight, releasing my grip on the telephone.

"I'm okay," I said to Jenna, then looked around.

What I saw made me step back, once again, to rest against

the wall.

Jenna stood before me, but she looked different than she had only a minute before. Her skin was pale and tinted with gray. All the colors of her body and clothing were muted, as in some of those artsy movies. She was bobble-heading, looking everywhere and calling my name, but I couldn't hear a word she said.

I touched Jenna on the arm, and she jumped, her head whipping around like mad, her mouth screaming in silence.

You can prepare your mind for any situation, work out all the things that could go wrong, and convince yourself that you can handle it, no matter what happens. Then you're taken completely off guard, and you're left standing in the hallway staring at your friend as she screams and wails and freaks out right in front of you. And there's nothing you can do to help her.

The world—my world—had changed. But somehow, that banishment spell had pushed me farther into the world of the dead, to a point where Jenna wasn't able to see me anymore, and everything to me looked dim and, well, wrong.

I turned back to the telephone that hung on the wall and stared at it for a moment. This dorm didn't have telephones. But I would bet it did a decade or two ago when there were no cell phones. My hand quivered in trepidation as I reached out and lifted the handset from the base and put it to my ear. A steady low tone droned from the speaker, and I knew it to be a dial tone. I typed out my phone number, the drone suddenly replaced with the beep for each press. Once I had finished, I waited. At first, I heard nothing, then a low hiss came across the line.

The screams of no less than a hundred people suddenly shot out from the speaker, and I dropped the phone, my own screams drowning those that now came from the handset that swayed from its line below the phone's base. I quickly grabbed it and slammed it back on its hook.

Jenna was punching buttons on her cell phone. She looked frantic like she might drop the device at any moment. Then, finally, the phone went to her ear. She waited a moment and then began talking fast at the poor person on the other end. I wasn't sure who it was, but I hoped it was Ben. I had once given her his number when I went to game with the Crawlers.

When she got off the phone, she stood on the spot and spoke in slow words. She tried to talk to me, but I was terrible at reading lips. So I studied her mouth and made out the words "coming to help." I nodded, then remembered she couldn't see me.

I reached out and touched her once on the shoulder. She jumped, then said "Lexi" in her soundless voice. I could read my name on her lips, at least. I poked her once. She stiffened, then her mouth worked into a determined grin.

She held up one finger and nodded. I understood. Another finger went up, and she shook her head. A third finger came with a shrug. "Got it?" she mouthed slowly.

I tapped her once. Still a nervous reaction, but she smiled.

Jenna said something, but I couldn't hear it. Three pats.

She brought up her phone and typed for a bit. Then she held it up in front of her. The words *Are you hurt?* glowed in the Notes app on her screen.

I rapped no on her shoulder.

Relief crossed her face, and she typed some more.

Going to the door to let Ben in. Stay here.

One touch.

She ran to the main entrance.

I was still alive because we could communicate. A ghost wouldn't have been able to touch her like that. Even Dave Simons couldn't, and he had more power than I had expected him to have. And I felt alive. Good. The vertigo I suffered when the change happened had vanished within seconds. Right now, I was fine. It all seemed like this was a different version of my usual ability. It was as though I had somehow slipped farther into the Ghost World, but I wasn't likely to be stuck there.

At least I hoped so.

Jenna came back shortly with Ben and Diego in tow. She held up her phone. *Are you still here?* showed in black letters.

I touched Jenna once on the shoulder, then, as an afterthought, I did the same to Ben and Diego. They both jumped, but Jenna was ready for it this time.

Jenna typed and showed the screen that said, *To our room.*

I gave her the affirmative, and the four of us went up to the sixth floor and then down the hall to our room. I could ride the elevator, which was an encouraging sign since ghosts never do. The three went down the hall, and I followed, close on their heels. As soon as Jenna opened the door, I shuffled past them into the room. They all seemed to notice my passing as they all looked around. I stood in one corner and waited for them to sit down. Since I needed to touch them to communicate, I had to stand in the middle of the room.

Each of them pulled out their phones and prepared to type.

Jenna went first. *Are you here?*

I let her know, and she told the others.

Ben typed away on his phone, then held it up. *What happened to you?*

Jenna started chewing him out, probably for his non-Boolean question. Diego typed and held up his phone.

Do you think you're still alive?

I tapped him once on the shoulder. He looked relieved and gave the others my answer.

There had to be a better way to do this. I looked around the room and saw a small whiteboard that Jenna and I had posted on the door to leave each other messages. I went and pulled it off the door and brought it over. Judging by their shocked reactions, they saw it.

I wrote, *I seem to be farther in the Ghost World than usual. Everything's dim. Can't hear you. But I feel fine.* I held it up, and they all read it.

Do you think it's permanent? asked Ben on his phone.

With some erasing and writing, I continued the conversation. *I hope not. I should be back to normal in the morning. We'll have to wait.*

Have you seen a ghost yet? said Diego.

I shook my head, then realized he couldn't see me. *No.*

I think you should try. The more you know about your powers, the better. Diego held up his phone.

Right. I'll be back. I set the whiteboard and pen down and went to the door. It was a simple thing, but it posed several questions to me. Opening it shouldn't be a problem since I could pick up the whiteboard. But could I go through it? After all, I was deeper than I had been before, so I might be able to pass through it.

I thought about walking through the door, telling myself that I would do it. Then I reached out my hand, repeating *I'll go right through* in my mind.

My hand passed into the wood of the door as though the barrier were not even there. I felt nothing. With a grin, I stepped through into the hallway. Being early in the night, the place was not empty. I avoided the people since it would freak them out to collide with someone they couldn't see.

I spent the next half hour wandering the halls in search of a ghost. This was easier to do than usual since only Ghost World objects, like the telephones, looked clear to me.

I found myself on the third floor, standing at the door to 312. Kai's room. He didn't know about the new turn of events in my ability. Of course, I never opened up to him about my normal gift. He didn't know that I could touch ghosts. An urge seized me to walk through his door and see him, but I resisted it. Even the idea of it felt creepy.

I stood there, thinking about it. As I did, words came through the door, and it grabbed my attention at once. Someone spoke in a low voice, and it took a rhythmic pattern. It also seemed to come from far away, as though down a long tunnel. At first, I thought he was singing, but no, this was more like a chant. And he wasn't speaking English. I didn't recognize the language, but it seemed old, like Latin.

Hey! I'm not supposed to hear a living person talking. But it was Kai's voice. I was sure of it.

Now I had to see. The urge to go through that door overwhelmed me. I lifted my foot to take that first step.

"You don't look the stalker type."

I whirled around. Before me in the hall stood a young woman. Another dead student. That made sense in a building that's always been a dormitory. She was about my height and maybe nineteen years old. At least, that was before she died. She wore loose, stonewashed jeans that looked brand new and a pink V-neck sweater that revealed a blue shirt underneath. The sweater's sleeves came down to the edge of her palms. The tight curls of her dirty-blond hair were long, bouncing around her shoulders. Or at least they tried to bounce. I suspected there was a lot of hair spray in there when she died. An 80s girl, fer sherr.

"Who are you?" I said. "I haven't seen you around."

"I'm Missy. Missy Baskins. You must have just died because you were alive when I saw you before."

"Nope. I didn't die."

"I didn't believe it either when it happened to me. But something's different about you. I'm not sure what it is." The girl came closer, and my mind tensed for a fight, even though she didn't seem threatening. Instead, I took one step backward.

She stopped, and her brow furrowed in concern. "You don't trust me."

"Should I?"

"We can't hurt each other. We're dead."

"I'm not dead."

The girl took a step back, then let out a long breath. Her expression softened as though she were about to console a terrified child. "This won't be easy," she said in a placating tone.

"But you need to learn. And the sooner you do, the easier it'll be for you in the long run."

"Look, I know the spiel. You're dead and stuck here as a ghost. I'm dead because we can talk to each other, and you can probably see me better than you can see everyone else. You think I must be dead because of all that. I hate to break it to you, but I'm alive. By day, I'm fully alive and in the world of the living. By night, I'm in your world. It's just that until tonight, I was only a little way into your world. I can't explain why it is, but it's a condition I've had all my life."

"You're full of it. That can't happen. People don't cross over unless they die."

"No offense, but how would you know that if you're stuck in here all the time?"

That stung her as she frowned and clenched her jaw. "I was alive once." The words hissed through her teeth.

Now it was my turn to sigh. "I'm sorry. I'm just tired of having to explain this to every ghost I meet. And trust me, I've explained it a lot."

Missy's frown eased, and she considered what I said.

"But how do you know that you're alive?"

"Because I'm enrolled in this school. My room is upstairs on the sixth floor. I have a roommate that I talked to just a few minutes ago. Granted, I had to draw on a whiteboard or touch her shoulder to communicate. But she watched me vanish when the sun went down, and as always, we'll see each other in the morning when I get up."

"What's a whiteboard?"

"You didn't have whiteboards?" I glanced down the hallway

and saw no whiteboards on people's doors, but a few memo pads had taken their place with pens dangling from them. I told her what they were.

"Oh. Okay. Look, you sound sure of yourself about this gift, but it took a long time for me to accept that I was dead."

I shrugged. This was going nowhere. "Okay, whatever. You'll believe me in time. It'll become obvious. But we can still be friends either way, right? I mean, whether I'm dead or alive, we can talk and hang out."

"True. I'd like that."

A smile played across Missy's face then, a mischievous, con-spiratorial grin that didn't look threatening. It resembled Jenna whenever she was about to gossip, which, despite her insistence to the contrary, she enjoyed.

"That boy's room. You were going to spy on him."

My eyes rolled. I didn't mean to do it. They have a mind of their own sometimes.

"I wasn't going to spy on him. I'm kind of seeing him."

"He's your boyfriend?" She gasped.

"Kind of. I think. It's complicated."

Her face twisted at the sad realization that our young love had been torn apart by my untimely demise. Egad, would she ever drop it?

"Don't worry. He and I are fine. Tell you what, maybe I'll try to prove it to you some night. Maybe tomorrow."

"Okay. That would be great." She didn't sound convinced that I could prove anything, but she did seem to want to see me again. That was fine.

23

This was the longest night I'd had in a long time. I couldn't sleep because I didn't know if I would wake in the morning.

Ben and Diego left an hour after I came back to the room, but Jenna stayed up with me. We chatted all night online since we couldn't speak to each other. At last, sunlight peeked around the buildings of Boston, and the two of us waited for me to reappear in the real world.

I was pacing from door to window when Jenna squealed with delight.

"YOU'RE BACK!"

She ran and threw herself at me, crushing me with her hug. "I was so afraid!" she said, tears streaming down her face.

"It scared the crap out of me. All those times you told me about your powers and I never believed it. But then you vanished before my eyes! And you *touched* me. It was so cold. I'm so sorry I never took it seriously. But really, how was I supposed to? We're all taught that those things could never happen in real life. Then it did. Oh, my god, I'm just glad you're back!"

I patted her awkwardly on her back. I was never an emotional person, and this kind of thing always threw me off.

"It's okay," I said. "I'm fine now. My ability just pushed me farther into the ghost realm than usual. I hope it doesn't stay that way, but if it does, I'll learn to live with it. As long as I have my days."

Jenna released her hold on me and stepped back. "How can you take this so easily? I mean, we couldn't see each other. We couldn't talk."

"I could see you, but you're right. Last night was terrible, and I'd be lying if I said I didn't mind. But you've got to understand that I've been living with this ability all my life. This change was, well, unexpected and sucky, but it was a slight change from what I'm already used to. And I don't think it will stay."

"Are you serious?" said Jenna, hope brightening her eyes. "How do you know?"

I shrugged. "It was something I felt last night. It didn't feel like it was going to last." That was a lie. In fact, I didn't know if this new ghost state was permanent or temporary. But it was a lie Jenna needed right then. Her rosy life was brutally broken by last night's events, and I wanted to mend it, even if it was with duct tape and staples.

"Good!" Jenna sighed. "What do you need now? Is there anything I can do?"

"Get me coffee."

"Coffee?"

"Yeah. Coffee. Tea. Anything hot. I'm cold."

I called Detective Ross as soon as Jenna and I split for our 8:00 a.m. classes. I didn't want to talk to him after the tongue-lashing he gave me in the hospital, but I knew I had to get it over with. To my relief, he said nothing bad when he answered. We made quick plans for dinner at the diner. Then he hung up. I couldn't tell if he was still mad since he always behaved like that.

My morning classes dragged, and I paid them no mind. My thoughts were on last night and my experiences deeper in the Ghost World. I had to admit, a part of me wanted to explore that realm in more depth, to understand the plight of ghosts even more than I already did. But I knew in my heart that going that far in was dangerous and threatened to hold me there forever.

And then there was Missy Baskins. She intrigued me. This ghost had seen me before, and either I had never noticed her or didn't think she was a ghost. Missy was convinced I was dead, and I wondered if I was. At least during the night. All my life, I assumed I remained alive even when I went into the Ghost World, but was that true? My physical body came with me every night. The concussion I got at Dave's hands attested to that. But what about last night? I had vanished from my friends' sight, and my surroundings became more of what the ghosts saw.

The more I thought about it, the more I knew I had to pull myself back from that abyss. And the thought came to me: could I control it? Could I pull myself back to my normal level of ghostliness? I would have to try.

I left campus at 5:00 p.m. to walk to the diner where I had met the detective before. The thoughts that dominated my morning abated somewhat now that I was walking in the semi-warmth of late September. Instead, I thought about Detective Ross and what he had said to me the other day.

Ross was mad. He had made that abundantly clear. Yet, he also cared about my welfare. He was pissed because I almost got myself killed. The detective's anger was all about him being a nice guy. Okay, so I wouldn't take the defensive and give him trouble. I'd just agree that I had been stupid and hope he'd move on from that.

The diner was busier than last time, but that was expected since it was dinner time. Detective Ross was waiting for me when I arrived. I took my seat across from him.

"You're looking better," he said. He already had his coffee. Another mug sat on the table, and he nodded toward it. "It's yours."

I took a tentative sip and then grinned. He remembered how I took it. Now, that was something they didn't have in TV cop shows.

"Look," I said, in my making-amends tone, "I should have called you before doing the ritual. The risk was high, and I should have taken as many precautions as possible. You were right."

He gave a quick nod. "So, what now? Is the case closed? I think we should at least stake out the Quad and make sure the ghost doesn't reappear."

"You don't believe the ritual worked?" I asked.

"I can't afford to when lives are at stake. We don't have a prisoner or a body, so he might come back. I need solid enough evidence that our killer is gone for good. If he's still around here and sees you in his stalking grounds, he'll go for you. You fought him once, so he won't miss the chance to go after you."

I took another sip of coffee to wash out the taste of irony in his words.

"Now, you want to use me as bait. Wouldn't that fit in the realm of 'doing something stupid'?"

"He becomes physical for all of us when he attacks. I'll be there to help."

"And how will that work? Guns don't hurt them."

"You said iron hurts them, right?"

"Yes, but iron weapons are a little scarce these days." I knew because I tried.

"I've got that covered. We'll go from here to the Quad and wait for it. If it comes, we'll send it back to the Ghost World for now, then work on Plan B. If it doesn't show, I'll sleep better. So we'll keep the alert on for now and then cancel it when he continues to not show."

"There's one snag in that plan," I said and then told him about the change in my ability. He took it well, all things considered.

"Is it going to stay that way?"

"I don't know. I hope not. My old condition was bad enough."

Detective Ross stared at me for a minute. I looked away under his scrutiny, glancing around the diner, then out the window. Shadows spread across the road as the sun made its final attempts at lighting the city.

"Maybe it's possible that you can control it."

Ross's words pulled my attention back to him. "What?" I said. Did my own thoughts just spew out of his mouth?

"Your powers. Think about it. All your life, you've let your ability control you. It was always something that happened, and it was always the same. Now, this ritual made it change. But what if you always could go that deep into the Ghost World, but you never tried?"

"That's crazy."

"Is it?"

"Yeah. Because I've tried hard to make my ability *not* happen, and I *never* succeeded."

"You might not be able to turn it off, but you might have control over how deep you go. This spell has shown you that you can go farther in than usual. It's something to think about."

"Okay," I said. "But right now, I'm about to vanish. I can draw on a whiteboard. I can type on a computer. But you won't see or hear me. If I touch you, you'll feel it."

"Right. Let's go. You go outside and wait for me while I pay the bill. I don't want you disappearing in here. If you're not there, I'll assume you are and I can't see you."

Without another word, I got up, grabbed my coat, and went as quick as I could out the door. I entered the Ghost World five seconds later.

24

Detective Ross got used to my invisibility quicker than my friends did last night. He paused when he stepped out on the sidewalk. He took a single glance around, then nodded.

"Let's go," he mouthed and walked up the road, retracing the steps I had taken to reach the diner. I tapped him twice on the shoulder. He shot a look at me, then made a curt nod and grimaced as he walked. I fell into step beside him, and we trudged through the cold Boston night together, Ross alive and me . . . Well, I guess I was somewhere in between.

This was my first time off campus after dark, aside from my ghost hunting trip with Kai. Ghosts came out of the woodwork around me. An awful lot of them seemed to be from long ago.

A woman stepped out of a second-floor door that wasn't there onto a non-existent balcony to shake a rug. Dirt and grit rained down on Ross and me. It bounced off me as though it were real, and I shook some of it out of my hair. The woman was an Echo, forever repeating that chore. I was glad her expression held no intelligence. I would hate to be stuck in a loop like that and be aware of it. The odd thing was that the debris she dropped would never have touched me before.

One man dressed in a suit and tie with a top hat on his head and a cane in his hand smiled pleasantly when our eyes met. He tipped his hat to me as he walked past. It was not the ghost we banished but another spirit from that same era.

This was all stuff I had seen before in other towns, only not in this quantity. What struck me as strange and filled me with dread was that the world itself had changed. Some buildings had features I knew didn't exist. I passed phone booths of varying styles, and I knew from my encounter in the dorm that I could pick one up. Carriages mingled with the cars on the streets. It was odd how they never collided but moved along as though they all existed in the same timeline. My newly modified condition had pushed me farther into the ghost realm, and it gave me the chills.

I stuck close to the detective as we rounded the corner and went up the road to Brent College.

The Quad looked like it always had, except dimmer. We crossed the grass in a straight line toward the scene of the murders. The police tape was no longer there, but I suspected cops still patrolled it.

Ross stopped at a bench near the center of the park. After

a casual glance around him, he sat down.

"I'll be bait," he said in a calm tone.

I tapped him once on his shoulder, and he gave a quick nod. Then I wandered out onto the grass, playing a different type of bait.

Time dragged by as the sky grew darker and the wind blew colder. I shivered. It was always raw this far into the Ghost World, but when it was cold for the living, it became damn near impossible to take. I grumbled about freezing to death as I paced back and forth across the length of Top Hat's stretch of grass. But the monster never showed. Now and then, I glanced at Detective Ross to see if he was preparing to call it quits, but he continued to sit there, playing on his phone and discreetly looking around. His countenance revealed nothing of his intentions; he was a skilled cop who knew how to conduct a trap like this. I hoped I never had to learn that skill.

Ross whipped his head suddenly to stare with mounting concern at Fenway Hall. I frowned because all was quiet, but then it hit me that I was deaf to all sounds in the living world. Following his line of sight, I saw flashing lights in the dorm's windows and lots of movement near the doors.

Detective Ross was on his feet and running toward the dorm, and I raced after him. The fire alarm was going off. That was obvious. But why? Was it real, or did someone just pull it for fun? Unfortunately, that happened a lot on college campuses. But Ross's expression was stern as he ran full tilt across the Quad.

It had to be something else.

We reached the entrance and saw people pouring out, some

calm, as though assuming it wasn't real, but others pushed hard at them, their faces twisted in terror. Ross grabbed one of them and shouted. The kid held a phone to the detective, and I looked over his shoulder at the lit screen.

Standing in a hallway was Dave Simons. But it wasn't the face I was used to. Instead, it was horribly disfigured. His mouth was inhumanly widened and full of razor-sharp teeth. His single eye glowed with red brilliance; the other remained a black hole.

Ross took a picture of the kid's screen with his own phone, then let him go. He then created a new text and typed, "Evacuating school. Can you stop it? Fourth floor." He held it up for me to see.

One tap on the shoulder gave him the affirmative, and I ran through the crowd and into the dorm. People didn't seem to notice that they were being pushed out of the way by nothing, and it was hard going, but I made it through and raced to the stairs.

I had no confidence in my ability to stop Dave. If he had become like Top Hat, he would be unstoppable, save by that spell. But how could this have happened to him? It made no sense. And after all these years of never seeing one, finding two in the same place within days of each other couldn't be a coincidence.

And after my adventure in the haunted house, I knew Top Hat wasn't feral. He was something else altogether. He had become a monster. And now Dave was.

I reached the landing on the fourth floor and paused. No sound filtered through the door, which meant everyone had already left. I took a moment to calm my nerves, which didn't work, and then pulled on the knob.

There's a certain expectation you get when you walk into a haunted house. Dim flickering lights and the musty odor of decay. But the sight that met my eyes was anything but. Emergency strobes flashed in the hallway, letting me know the fire alarm was still going. Thankfully, I couldn't hear it.

I roamed the halls. Since I was deaf to everything in our world, I had to rely on my vision alone. The first corridor showed no sign of activity. The second wing started out the same. It was empty, and nothing moved. I was halfway down and thinking of giving up when a sound broke the eerie silence.

A slow, slobbering growl came from farther down the hallway, and I noticed that the door to the common room was open. I padded to it and peeked in.

Dave Simons, curly blond hair, sports jersey, and all stood in the center of the place with his back to me. But his shoulders were raised and tense, and his head hung uncharacteristically forward. A sick growl came from him.

It looked like a tornado had hit. Tables were toppled over, creating plenty of space for the mass exodus that had undoubtedly occurred here. But one living person remained.

Tom Prichard stood by the far wall. His plain T-shirt was torn, and red glistened through the holes. A long slit ran down the leg of his gray sweatpants, which were now stained with blood. But the football player held his ground, his weight on the other leg. He raised a baseball bat before him like he was awaiting a pitch. Sweat poured down his cheeks, and his face was set in a grim stare as he waited for the ghost monster to make its move.

It was all I could do to hold back a gasp, but luck was with me, and the silence remained unbroken. I tried to catch Tom's attention with a tilt of my head, but of course, that didn't work, as I was invisible.

Dave tensed for a spring, and Tom raised his bat. The weapon barely shook, which impressed the hell out of me.

With three running strides, I crossed most of the distance between myself and the ghost and then launched myself in the air to perform a flying kick. My sensei taught me the maneuver to psyche out my opponent when sparring in a tournament. He said it had no tactical use. But I thought it might work well here. Exhilaration flowed through me as I hurtled toward my foe. Then my one extended foot struck Dave in the small of his back.

This threw him off his game. It interrupted his lunge, and his spine bent in a way it wasn't supposed to. He staggered forward and nearly fell.

I stopped in midair with a suddenness that surprised me, and I dropped like a rock, bouncing backward as I did. I slapped out, as all good karate students learn when falling, which saved my head from hitting the floor. But, damn, did my arms hurt!

I leaped to my feet at once into a guard stance, but then my jaw fell open.

Tom had wasted no time. He rushed in and whacked Dave repeatedly on the head with the bat. The wooden cudgel went up and down, and the dead jock could do nothing but raise its arms to block the attacks. Then, one arm snapped, and the creature howled in agony.

"Tom!" I shouted, but he ignored me and kept swinging as if his life depended on it, which I must admit, it did. So I stood there, staring at a total loss for what to do.

At last, Dave got his wits together and rolled backward, out of the way. Tom's final swing struck the floor in silence.

The monster was on his feet and turned to run from the room but paused when he saw me. We both stood in shock, each staring dumbly at the other. The drastic change in the dead boy's face shook me to my soul. It was still Dave, that was certain. But its eye was the black-in-red that Top Hat had, and the wide, dagger-filled mouth was there, too. It distorted the kid's usually friendly features in a macabre caricature of my ghost-friend.

Dave stared at me like I was food, but with a hint of recognition. Just a hint. A tear separated itself from the wet of my eye and ran for dear life down my cheek.

"Dave, it's me! Lexi! You know me. We're friends."

He cocked his head, confusion clouding his face. Finally, I was getting through to him.

I opened my mouth to talk to him but froze as movement behind him caught my attention.

Once more, Tom was not idle. He crept up to Dave and swung again.

The loud squishy crunch as Dave's skull collapsed to one side was both disgusting and bizarre. The baseball bat struck its target in total silence because it was in the living world. But I heard its effects on Dave. It was like hearing one half of a phone conversation that was all the sounds of a man dying.

But, of course, Dave wouldn't die. He lunged forward, his head lolling on a broken neck, and passed right by me to vanish around the corner in the hallway.

Tom rushed past me in pursuit, and I followed him. But we didn't get far. My living friend skidded to a halt, his head swiveling from side to side as he looked for the monster. I did as well.

Dave Simons had vanished. And he wouldn't return that night; I was sure of it. It was what Top Hat had done. Maybe he had limited energy to manifest in this way, so he would vanish once he used that power. I didn't know, and I didn't care. I was just glad he was gone.

But he'd be back. Dave Simons was the new feral ghost—no, not true. He was the new *monster* ghost. It was as though a monstrous baton had been passed to him when Top Hat was banished. It was Dave's turn to be the killer now.

I left Tom standing in the hallway. The danger had passed, and Tom wouldn't hear me, so it was time to call it a night.

Back outside, Ross was hard at work. Fire trucks crowded in front of the building, flashing red lights reflecting off every window. But the firefighters stood idly as Ross talked to a group of police officers.

I waited for him to finish. I couldn't sit since someone might trip over me. At last, he concluded, and the men left him alone. He exhaled and ran his fingers through his hair.

I tapped him on the shoulder.

He jumped. Then he looked around and pulled out his phone. He typed for a bit and held it up.

Is the ghost gone?

I poked him once.

For good?

One. Two. Nice and even so he would not misunderstand.

He grimaced. *You'll be back in the morning?*

Yes, I told his shoulder.

Then go to bed. I'll see you tomorrow.

I patted him one last time and walked to my dorm. Exhaustion flooded through my body, but I wasn't sure I could sleep.

Dave Simons was a monster now. And Top Hat used to be a normal ghost.

What the hell was going on at this school?

"They evacuated Fenway Hall!" Jenna said as soon as I got up. But the excitement drained from her face once I sat up. "Oh, my God," she added in a near whisper. "You look like a zombie."

I frowned. "What? Am I dropping skin?" As exhausted as I was, my sense of humor still had energy.

"Stop that!" My grin faded at the seriousness of her tone. "You don't look good."

"I'm tired. I didn't sleep well last night."

She shook her head and ran to fetch a hand mirror, which she shoved in front of my face.

A gasp escaped my mouth as I stared at an extra from a horror movie. My complexion was pale, and not the kind you get when you're sick, but a deathly pallor that made my skin look bleak and lifeless. One of my hands shot instinctively to my cheek to verify that it radiated heat.

But I didn't.

I felt neither cold nor warm, as though my body had no concept of temperature. The bloodshot eyes in the mirror went wide, and I turned away from it.

"What's happening to me?"

"I don't know," Jenna said.

We decided I should stay in my room and out of sight until we figured this out. Jenna ran to the cafeteria and returned with breakfast, complete with a cup of coffee. I drank the hot beverage, and it warmed my insides as it went down. But it had no effect on my outward appearance. I kept looking at the mirror, which was a bad idea, because more details came to my attention each time. Bags under my eyes made them resemble dark holes in a field of white, enhancing the ghostliness of my skin.

And that was it. It had to be. I was slipping farther into the Ghost World. Before long, I suspected I would fade from the living world altogether and live forever with people like Professor Harrison as friends.

"We have to do something!" I said.

"But what?" Jenna was on the verge of panic, with tears streaming down her face.

I called Rocks. He answered after five rings.

"Sorry if I woke you, but I've got a problem."

"You didn't wake me," he responded, and his tone was surprisingly serious. "In fact, we've been up all night trying to solve it."

"You know about it?" I asked, stunned.

There was a pause. "I was talking about you disappearing

every night. Is there another one?"

I told him, and again he hesitated. "Right. We're on our way." He hung up.

Our tiny room became crowded when Rocks, Ben, Tony, Diego, and Logan all joined us. They carried a stack of papers with them. They stared at me in shock for a bit, which made me uncomfortable. But one by one, they turned away and avoided looking at me. Ben's eyes were wet.

"Here's the thing," said Rocks. "We've been poring over the spell." He hefted the papers. "Diego thought there might be something there. Something that could, you know—"

"Oh, for Christ's sake, Rocks!" Logan burst out, as though he couldn't contain himself any longer. He turned to face me and thankfully didn't make a face at my appearance. "We've got to get the book this spell came from. It has the antidote to your condition."

"What?" I said. "How do you know?"

"Because of what it says at the end of the last page," said Ben. He brushed the tears from his face, which was now set with determination.

They were all trying to be strong for me. If I ever wondered what a genuine friend was like, I was staring at six of them.

Tony was the first to come near me. He switched from sitting on Jenna's bed to mine. "See, it tries to warn us of the danger of having a living person in the circle when the spell is cast. It talks about sending the victim to the realm of the dead. I guess for you, it pushed you farther in."

"And I'm still slipping," I added.

He nodded but remained silent.

"We need that book," said Logan. "But I don't think you should talk to your teacher. Not when looking like that. He'd refuse."

Three loud raps sounded on my door, and all seven of us jumped, then turned to stare at it.

"Quick, hide your face!" hissed Rocks.

Jenna shot him a dirty look and went to the door. She put an eye to the peephole and then looked at me, a confused frown twisting her face.

"It's an old man. Kinda creepy looking."

I grinned. "Trench coat? Maybe a suit underneath? Looks awkward?"

"That's him."

"Open it. He's okay."

With a disapproving shrug, Jenna opened the door to reveal Detective Ross standing there, his hands fidgeting with the hat in his hand. It figured he'd feel uncomfortable in a college dorm surrounded by students.

"Come on in, Detective," I called to him. "Join the party."

He took a few tentative steps in, his gaze flicking from face to face, as though sizing each one up as suspects. When his eyes rested on Lexi, they widened almost imperceptibly. Then the muscles in his jaw tightened and he looked away.

Great. He's getting used to these surprises. But I couldn't help thinking he might be blaming himself.

"Detective Ross, these are my friends. They helped me banish Top Hat. And Ross, we have another problem." I filled him in on everything, including what Tony had told me about the warning.

"Getting that book won't be an issue," Ross said once the story was over. "I'll talk to your teacher. He'll do it. But are you sure you can reverse this?"

Rocks shrugged. "There are no guarantees until we get that book."

"Then that's our priority. But I should tell you that Fenway Hall is closed off. Of course, the official reason is a gas leak that caused hallucinations. But we all know why. Top Hat is back."

A sudden bout of talking broke out, but I shushed them. "That wasn't Top Hat. It was Dave Simons, another Haunt. It was the one that sent me to the hospital."

Ross frowned. "I thought you told me that one was a normal ghost. People saw this one, and it looked a lot like your description of our killer in the Quad."

"What?" came several voices at once. "Is that what happened there last night?" asked Diego.

I nodded. "Yeah. We got rid of Top Hat, but now Dave is a monster like he was. It can't be a coincidence. Something is turning the ghosts on this campus into monsters, one at a time, and we need to figure out what it is and put a stop to it."

There was a stunned silence as the import of what I said sank into everyone's brains.

"Right." Ross stuck his hat on his head like it was a call to action. "But the first thing is to get you fixed. Now, tell me the name of that teacher of yours."

25

Professor Landry was in his office. It was a Wednesday, but he was between classes. He looked up when Ross and I entered. He frowned at me because I kept my face obscured under a hood.

"Lexi? Is that you?"

"Yes, it is. We need your help."

"Professor Landry, I'm Detective Ross from the Boston PD." He flashed his badge but held it out long enough for my teacher to read it. "Miss Downs here says you photocopied some pages of a book for her. An ancient and strange book."

The professor cast a concerned look from the detective to me and back again. "Yes. That's true. But there was nothing wrong with that. We broke no laws."

A wry grin cracked the corner of Ross's mouth. "You're not in trouble, Professor. But we need that book."

"You need . . ."

"Professor," I said, hoping to cut through his confusion and spur him into action. "There's some important information on the pages after what you gave me. I have to read it. So, if we can get it now before your next class, that would be great."

"Um. It's irreplaceable and somewhat delicate."

"We'll take good care of it, Professor," said Ross. "And I'll return it as soon as we're done with it. I promise."

"If the police need it. Okay." He stood up and led us from his office.

Our footsteps echoed off the walls of the old building as we went down the empty hallway. Closed doors on both sides encased classrooms full of students. We passed the room Professor Harrison and I had frequented. Another teacher was there, talking to the kids. I wondered if my ghostly friend could watch the class.

As we neared Professor Landry's room of artifacts, he broke into a run. "What the hell . . ."

With a quick exchange of looks, Ross and I jogged after him.

The door was open, its lock broken.

"Son of a bitch!" he said as we joined him. "I just replaced it!"

"Step aside," Ross hissed and pushed Professor Landry away from the entrance. He drew his revolver and nudged the door the rest of the way with his foot, the gun aimed inside.

"Stay here!" another hissed command, but he meant it for both of us this time. I was okay with that. This was his job, not mine.

The detective crept through the doorway, weapon in front, and searched with deliberate steps, ready to fire at any moment. When he left my line of sight, I kept my eyes glued to the inside of the room. If someone moved, I'd shout.

But he suddenly gave the signal. "Clear!"

Professor Landry swore under his breath as we entered.

I stopped and stared around the room, aghast. The rectangular room was always cramped, with long tables lining both walls. This left a narrow space to walk between them. The reliquary was always full of items and never looked tidy, but at least each of them sat erect and with its kin. But now, Landry and I had to tiptoe carefully over things that had been pulled from tables. The broken shards of an urn that I think had once been from a dig in Scotland lay scattered on the floor. But that was the only damaged relic I could see in the dim lighting. The professor flicked a switch, and the fluorescent lights overhead revealed the details of the carnage. It seemed that nothing was where it should be, and everything now lay on its side. Yet, nothing seemed intentionally broken.

I lifted a statuette of a long-horned animal and set it back on its feet.

"Oh, my god, Professor!" The words escaped my lips on their own. I had nothing to do with them.

My teacher was shaking his head in disbelief. "They've never ransacked the place before."

Ross spun his head toward Landry, surprised. "This has happened before?"

"Only about once a year," said the professor. "But it's never like this."

"You mean to say that people break in and take things from this room every year, and you *don't report it?*" Ross gaped at him.

"I didn't want any students to get in trouble. I've never lost anything important."

"Thieves are criminals, Professor. You're telling them it's acceptable to steal from the college."

"Hmm. I never considered that. Then I'm reporting it. Someone broke in here."

Ross's frown deepened. "Okay. Get me that book, and then you're going to itemize everything that was stolen, including what was lifted earlier this semester."

"Of course. I'll do that tonight, after classes."

"Good," said the detective. "Now, the book."

The professor made his way carefully down the center aisle and stood at a bookshelf lining the back wall. As he scanned it for our book, I cast my gaze across the tables. Ross was staring at them too, but he was also on his phone, calling in the crime.

There was something about the disaster before me that caught my eye. It was a pattern. I stepped up to the table and pretended to shove something to the side. My hand connected with a stack of scrolls that had fallen over. I did the same with my left hand, and my palm ended up on a toppled piece of pottery.

"What are you doing?" asked Ross, stuffing his phone in his coat pocket.

"This wasn't vandalism," I said. "Whoever did this was

look-ing for something. They were shoving things aside."

The detective nodded. "What were they after, I wonder?"

"I believe I can tell you that." Professor Landry tiptoed to us and handed me the book. "This was in my safe. When I saw how fragile it was, I thought I'd store it there for a while. Some-one tried to break it open. I can see the marks. And another thing." He glanced back at the bookshelf. "Its sister is gone. There was a second book that went with this one. I had kept it on that shelf. I know it was there because I went through it when we discovered the ritual Lexi needed. I think these two books were our thieves' targets."

"Do you remember what was in that book?" I asked.

My teacher shrugged. "More stuff about the dead. I didn't read it in detail."

"Thank you, Professor," I said as I stepped carefully to the door.

Ross stayed where he was. "Lexi, you go back to your room and get started with your research. I have to stand guard until reinforcements show. The lock here has been broken. Professor, you should start taking inventory."

"I have a class in ten minutes," he said. "It'll have to be after that."

"Okay. Just don't procrastinate."

"May I ask what's going on?" Landry said once we were out of earshot of Ross.

"You wouldn't believe me if I told you."

"Why do I have the feeling you cast that spell, and you think it worked?"

"Because you're smart. But it worked a little too good, and

now we have to fix things. I'd rather you not get involved, and I don't want to discuss it."

"Okay, but if these spells do work, be careful. I don't know how wholesome the people who wrote them were."

"I understand. You're pretty open-minded for a science teacher."

He chuckled. "I'm not saying I believe you. But there's a slim chance I'm wrong. So use that book at your own risk."

"You said there's only one key to the room?" I asked.

"That's right. It's my personal collection. The dean was nice enough to let me store it there, as long as I used the artifacts to aid my classes. Which, as you know, I do."

"And the school doesn't have one? Even though it's their room?"

"They never thought it needed to be locked. But after the first theft, I installed one. They approved, and so I had it done."

"How did the other break-ins happen if they never broke the lock before?"

"You know, it's that kind of logic that'll help you excel in school. The truth is, I sometimes forget to lock up. I don't like hoarding over my stuff. Mack keeps telling me I'm not careful enough with that room."

"Mr. MacNair? The janitor?"

"He used to study archeology, you know. So I've shown him around the place. He's a smart man. And he reminds me when I neglect it."

We stopped at the door to his office.

"Thanks for the book," I said. "I'll get it back to you as soon as possible."

"Okay. And be careful! Just in case it *does* work." Then, with a smile at his jest, he turned and disappeared through the door.

The Dungeon Crawlers were glad to see the entire book given into their waiting hands. They remained in my room despite the cramped conditions. They also skipped the rest of their classes without discussion.

Once we had settled into our work, my mind wandered to the events of last night. Dave Simons had become a monster ghost just like Top Hat, and there seemed to be no event that caused it. At least one night separated the banishing ritual from this. So, he turned into this demonic beast for no apparent reason.

And he hurt Tom.

The poor jock went to the hospital for his injuries. I didn't know if he was still there or not. The others were busy with the book, so I took out my phone and called him. He answered after only a few rings.

"Lexi! How are you? You weren't in class this morning."

"I'm a little under the weather, but I'm good. How are you? I was there last night. You couldn't see me, but I was in that room where the ghost had you cornered."

"Did you make him stumble? That was awesome! But why didn't I see you? That's not how it works, right?"

"It's a long story. But are you okay? I saw the blood."

"Oh, it's no big deal. I have a big gash on my leg and a few cuts. And a lot of bruises. But the doctor sewed me up and gave me something for the pain. I have to use a crutch to let the leg heal. The dorm's shut down. So the school shipped us over to a hotel two blocks away."

Relief issued from me in one long breath. "Good. I'm glad you're fine."

"What I want to know is: why could I see it? And why'd it look like a . . . well, like a monster?"

"That's a mystery yet to be solved," I said.

"It's not gone, is it? I didn't kill it?"

"You can't kill a ghost. But no, Dave's still there. He'll show up tonight, but he's stuck in the dorm, so we all should be safe for now."

"I'm not the only person you're doing ghost work for, am I?" He sounded nervous.

"Some friends are helping me figure out the mystery."

"That Logan kid?"

"He's one of them." Tom was acting strange, and I had no idea what he was getting at.

"Okay. Well. That's cool, I guess. Will you be back in class tomorrow?"

"Not sure. I hope so."

"Good. See you then."

"Yeah. And take care of that leg."

"You bet."

My smile faded at the stares from every face in the room. Nearly every face. Ross seemed determined not to stare at me. But Diego and Rocks had mild curiosity in their expressions. Tony flashed a knowing grin. Logan scowled. And Ben looked disappointed. Jenna, however, was beaming.

"What?"

Diego spoke up before anyone else could. "We figured it out."

That got Ross's attention. He jumped up and came over from his lonely corner. "What is it? A cure? What do we have to do?"

The others shifted their stares from me to Diego.

"It's a ritual, but not much of one. Kind of a cleansing thing. Modern-day witches do it. We'll need a private place where we can spread out and do it without being seen."

"There's nowhere like that on campus," Jenna said.

Silence descended on the group as we all tried to think of somewhere to cast the spell.

"I've got one," said Detective Ross.

"No offense, but you don't know the school at all," said Logan, suspicion etched on his face. "What place could you possibly know of?"

"Fenway Hall. I have access to it."

"Of course!" I exclaimed. "Dave will be dormant during the day. Can we do this thing before night?"

Diego nodded, and everyone got up. Even Jenna. When she saw me looking at her, she grabbed her coat and grinned. "I need to watch you get better. Besides, ignoring all your spooky stuff hasn't worked for me. So I might as well see what you guys do."

We must have looked pretty strange following Detective Ross across the campus to the dorm that was cordoned off with yellow tape and had cops stationed all around it. He flashed his badge and said a few words, and they let us through.

"How much space do you need?" Ross asked as we stood in

the lobby.

Diego glanced around. "We could do it here. But those cops out there would see us. How about a first-floor common room?"

We filed down a hallway and entered the first one we found. Right away, the guys spread out and moved the tables and chairs out of the way. Jenna helped. Me? Exhaustion had swept over me as we searched for a room. It seemed the longer the day went, the harder it was for me to function. I leaned against one wall as they worked.

Diego and Rocks drew a circle with thick sticks of chalk they had brought. Logan and Tony pulled candles out of a backpack. Before long, we were ready.

Diego had me stand in the center, which was getting harder to do. I wanted to lie down, but as it was necessary for the tiny circle they had drawn, I did as they said. They then began the ceremony.

To be honest, I paid little attention to it. I stood there while Diego and Rocks moved around me along its edge. They said things and chanted, but I didn't keep track of the words. Yet something was happening. A slight tingling rippled along the skin of my arms and then the rest of me. Warmth then spread through my body. It felt good. Life seemed to seep into my limbs and my mind. I smelled something nice. Incense. They swung censers as they circled me. I wondered why the fire alarm didn't go off.

At last, they had finished. Though still tired, I felt a lot better. Jenna rushed up to me and examined my face. She then held my hands and smiled.

"You look good, Lexi. You look *alive*. I think it worked!"

Everyone showered me with congratulations. But I had to admit, all I wanted was sleep. This time, it was a normal exhaustion, brought on by a night and a day of almost no rest. We went back to my dorm. Ross told me he'd return tomorrow and then left. Once we were in our room, the other Crawlers said their goodnights, and it was finally just Jenna and me. She tucked me in, which I didn't resist, and I fell into a comfortable slumber.

26

It was morning when I awoke, which meant I had slept through the rest of the day and the entire night. I didn't normally skip a night. One thing or another would always force me awake, yet I had made it through unscathed and un-waking. In fact, my body and mind were more energetic than they had been all semester.

It was beautiful outside. The sky had decided to be clear today, and the rising sun caused the wet grass to glisten like sparkling fairies. Though it was Thursday, Jenna convinced me to take the day off to recuperate. I could enjoy myself. Yay for me!

To be honest, I couldn't wait for that night. I wanted to see what happened. I no longer expected to vanish because Jenna had told me I hadn't overnight. But would I enter the Ghost World like I usually did, or did this ritual cure the condition that had been ailing me my entire life? The thought of losing that part of myself bothered me.

"The ghost is still there, right?" asked Jenna as we passed Fenway Hall. She said it so casually it could have been a question about a class.

"Since when are you interested in that stuff?"

"Since I started believing in it. You *literally* vanished that night. I can't rationalize that. You disappeared before my eyes but could still touch me. That went against everything I held to be true, but I saw it. If that could happen to you, I have to believe everything you told me about ghosts. So, now I'm curious. Is the ghost still around in that dorm?"

"Yes. Dave Simons is there, and something's wrong with him. He's become a monster, like the Haunt I told you about in the Quad."

"The one that killed those people?"

I nodded.

"But he can't leave the building, right?" she asked.

"He couldn't before, and that shouldn't have changed."

"At least everyone's safe."

"Yeah. But I'm sure Detective Ross can't keep the place closed off for long."

"He's going to use you, isn't he?"

"What do you mean?"

"That detective will try to send you in as a weapon to stop that ghost. And you'll let him."

"Dave has to be dealt with, and I'm the only one who can do it."

"I was right. Detective Ross will want to put you in danger, and you're all for it."

"It's not Ross, Jenna. I'll do it even if he doesn't want me to."

"Why? You don't owe it to that ghost. You didn't put him in that condition."

"How do you know? We banished the last monster Haunt, and now Dave becomes like him. It's as if it moved from one ghost to another."

We entered the cafeteria, grabbed trays, and went into the line.

"But how could that happen?" Jenna asked. "You make it sound like a parasite that jumps from host to host, but if that were the case, it would be a ghostly parasite, right? Then it would have been banished along with the Quad ghost."

I stopped short, causing everyone behind us to bump into each other. *Jenna's right,* I thought. We said nothing more while we found our seats. Once we had gotten settled and started eating, the chair across from me pulled out, and Kai Peters sat down in it.

He flashed Jenna a quick smile, then let it linger on me as he settled in.

"Pretty crazy what happened the other night?" he said.

Jenna shot him an unwelcoming look but said nothing since I smiled back at him.

"That sums it up." It seemed everyone wanted to talk about the Ghost of Fenway Hall. It made me less interested in doing so.

"We should go hunt it," Kai said between bites. "We kicked ass together the last time."

"You and I have different memories of that night. I seem to remember falling through a broken staircase and getting trapped in a basement full of ghosts."

Kai laughed. "But the dorm's in good condition. And there's only one ghost. And it's the one that hurt you." Those last words came out in a darker, more serious tone.

Jenna had been watching this exchange with interest and eyed me intently for my response to Kai's suggestion. I decided to take the easy way out.

"The cops would never let us in. And I wouldn't want to get caught breaking in."

Kai picked up his coffee and leaned back in his chair. A strange grin played across his face.

"It could be fun to watch the cops bungle the job. After all, they haven't got a clue about what they're dealing with."

I shrugged and ate my breakfast. Jenna grinned and followed suit.

Kai watched me eat for a bit and then sat forward and took a couple of bites before rising and collecting his gear.

"It looks like I interrupted a conversation, so I'll leave. Give me a buzz later, Lexi. I want to talk about the ghost at Fenway." And with that, he left.

"He's annoying," Jenna said after Kai was out of sight.

I grinned. "Only a little. But we have stuff in common."

"Ghosts? You now have a lot of eligible men that you have ghosts in common with. So you can afford to be picky."

"Kai's not my boyfriend. We spent some time together, and maybe we kissed, but—"

"You *kissed*? And you didn't tell me?"

"It was nothing," I said with a dismissive wave. It's funny how the subject of ghost fighting was preferable to me than romance.

"Then he's definitely not for you."

"Okay, let's drop it, shall we?"

We put our trays away and left the cafeteria to head back to our room. As we crossed the Quad again, Jenna changed her tack.

"What about that Tom you keep texting with? He seems nice."

I kept my mouth shut in part because I didn't want to answer her and because Detective Ross was walking from our dorm to us.

"There you are," he said in his traditionally gruff manner as we met him on the walkway. "How do you feel?"

"Aw, that's cute," said Jenna with a cheerful grin.

Ross flashed her a nasty look, but it just made my friend pout on cue.

"I'm fine. All better, in fact."

"Good. I need to go over some business with you, but first, there's a formality that needs to get out of the way. On behalf of the Boston Police Department, I would like to hire your services to deal with, er, trouble in Fenway Hall. This will be a consulting job. I brought a contract. Officially, I can't have you help if you don't sign it."

"What does it involve? What am I officially bound to do?"

I asked. This was above and beyond what I had ever done before, and I wasn't sure I wanted to be contracted to put my life
in danger.

A wry grin broke through the continual frown on his face.
"Nothing you wouldn't want to do. You'd be a consultant. That
means you'd only be required to advise and impart some of
your knowledge on the subject. Anything physical that could
put you in danger would be covered but not required. We'll
take care of you if you get hurt. It also means you can say no to
the rough stuff. I don't want you doing any more for us without
that protection."

"Again. Aw!" Jenna said and stuck out her tongue when
Ross flashed another look.

"So, all I'll need to do is talk about what I know and give
recommendations?"

"That's right."

"And I'll get paid?"

He nodded.

"Okay. Where do I sign?"

I ran into Kai on my way back to Wembley Hall after my
last class for the day. It was three o'clock, and the sun had wandered far to the west on its way down for the evening. The
ocean breezes felt good on my skin, and my smile was genuine
when Kai fell into step beside me.

"This is good timing," he said.

My smile deepened, but I said nothing.

"Are you done for the day?" he asked.

"Yup. What about you?"

He nodded. "Want to come to my room?"

The sidelong glance I cast him said everything I needed to say.

Kai jumped on the defensive. "Hey! I don't mean anything by it. It's just we usually talk about things that draw attention, and I thought it'd be nice to hang out in private for a change.

"Fine. But after dinner. I've got things to do." To be honest, I didn't think he would try anything. And if he did, I could handle him.

We chatted the rest of the way to the dorm. He left the elevator on the third floor while I continued to the sixth.

Of course, I couldn't tell him that I would meet with some cops about hunting ghosts. But he'd be better off not knowing that anyway.

If anyone had told me at the start of the semester that I would be at the Boston Police station, standing before rows of uniformed cops, I would have said they were crazy.

Yet here I was.

I stood beside Detective Ross, who gazed out at the ten men and women seated before us with grim satisfaction. My demeanor must have been far short of that because more than one cop gave me strange looks like they were wondering what I was doing there. But, to be honest, I did, too.

The door behind us opened, and a man entered. This guy was tall, ruggedly handsome, with his cropped short hair and cleft chin. He cast me an odd look. Sorry to be vague, but that was the only description I could give. It conveyed no emotion that came readily to mind, but it meant *something*. I just didn't know what it was. But it lasted only a second or two, and then he was beside Ross, whispering in his ear.

Ross acknowledged him without a word, and the man spun on his heels and left with an intensity that implied he had more important places to be. He shut the door behind him.

"Right," Ross said. "You've all been chosen to head up a new department, one that handles unorthodox cases."

Several people assembled nodded their agreement.

"How many of you have been told the nature of these cases?"

No hands raised, but one of them, a burly man in the front row whose shoulders and biceps threatened to tear his shirt, grinned as if to some joke.

Ross noticed. "Bronson? You heard something?"

"Yes, sir," he said. He had a powerful voice, and I wondered if it was for show. "I heard we're here to hunt spooks and monsters."

A ripple of muttered laughter ran through the room. I clutched the folder in my hands to my chest. It contained our notes on the banishing ritual we used on Top Hat. A lousy thought crept into my head, and I didn't want to be there anymore.

Ross chuckled, but it held no humor. "You heard right, Officer Bronson. This new team will respond to cases involving the occult and the supernatural."

The grin on Bronson's face faltered. "Are you kidding? Sir?"

"No joke. It's come to our attention that such things exist and can threaten public safety. We're the experts that get called in when cases like those arise."

Everyone stared at Ross in utter amazement, including me.

The barest hint of a grin tugged at a corner of his mouth. He was enjoying this. "This is your one chance to opt out. If you don't want to be involved in this department, you can leave right now. No judgments." He paused to let people leave. No one did.

"Sir?" a woman in the second row said. "I heard that any of us who stay will be promoted to detective. Is that true?"

"Yes, it is, *Officer* Lewis. If you join the team, you'll become a detective reporting directly to me. Any other questions?"

Nobody raised their hands, and none of them left. Silence fell on the group.

Ross nodded his satisfaction. "Good." He lifted a remote control from the podium he stood at and pressed a button. A TV hanging on a wall came to life, and the face of Dave Simons stared at me from its screen. But not the nice, friendly ghost of the jock, but the monstrous version I saw the other night. The picture was from a smartphone camera, and though it was a little blurry, the big mouth with its row of sharp teeth was still clear.

A couple of gasps came from the new detectives, but they all stared at the image with interest.

"This creature attacked students in a dorm at Brent College two nights ago. We've sealed off the building and put it under guard. This time, it failed to kill anyone, but a similar entity killed two pedestrians on Boylston Street. I believe some of you are familiar with that case?"

A couple of heads nodded, including that of Officer Lewis.

Detective Ross turned to face me. "This is Lexi Downs.

She's a student at Brent College. As well as being a witness to both creatures, she destroyed the first one, the one that *had* killed several people. Miss Downs, tell the team what you know about these creatures."

All eyes swiveled toward me, and I could feel the heat moving to my face. *Way to put me on the spot, Detective,* I thought, but knew better than to say it in front of the group.

I looked around the room and noticed something about these police officers that differed from those I had seen on TV shows. None of these people looked at me as though I was a joke. Instead, every one of them considered me with respect as they waited for the valuable information they expected to get. That somehow put me at ease. In fact, it made speaking to them easier than speaking in front of a class.

"Okay, first off, these aren't *creatures*, but ghosts," I said. Some raised eyebrows greeted me, but everyone wanted me to continue. *Sweet!*

"These things were once living people but are now spirits. But something happened to them that, well, turned them into that." I pointed a thumb at the screen.

A hand went up, and it was Officer Lewis.

"Yes?" I said.

"Ghosts can't touch anyone, can they?"

"Good point. No. At least, under normal circumstances, they can't. In fact, you also wouldn't be able to see them. The most sensitive of us usually only notice a mist or a vague shape. I'm different. They're visible to me every night. And they're *solid* to me, as though they're real. Don't ask me how this happened because I don't know. It just does, ever since I was little."

I paused and cleared my throat. Ross handed me a water bottle, which I thankfully popped open and took a sip from.

"But when these two ghosts got their monster mouths full of teeth, they became solid to everyone. At least at night. They still seem to disappear during the day. And they also don't stay that way for too long. Just long enough to kill, I suppose."

"They run out of energy," Bronson said. It wasn't a question. He was sure of himself.

"I think so," I replied. "But this creature's new to me. Until this semester, I wouldn't have sworn it could exist. So I don't know for sure."

"Okay," said another cop, this one a lanky man with strawberry hair cropped short. "How do we kill them?"

"You don't," I said. "Because ghosts are already dead. But you can banish them. It's done with a ritual. Yes, I'm talking about *magic*. It banishes the spirit, sending it back . . ." Where? I hadn't a clue. "Hopefully, they move on to where they're supposed to go."

"But you don't know," said Bronson.

My head shook almost without command.

"The plan is to do the ritual and send this ghost away," said Ross.

"Detective," I said, turning to face him, "I'm not sure if that's what we should do."

Ross frowned at me. *Uh-oh. He didn't like that.*

"Why not?" Good. He sounded calm.

"Because Dave Simons didn't get like that until after we banished Top Hat. One normal ghost becomes monstrous, and when it's sent away, another normal one takes its place soon after. On the same campus. It can't be a coincidence. And banishing Dave might only cause a different ghost to become a monster."

"But this ghost is dangerous, and if we know how to get rid of it, we should."

"Get rid of the monster we know to create a monster we don't know. We could do this forever, and people might die each time."

"Excuse me?" said another cop. This one was a short and stocky man with a grim face. "Ghosts are trapped in the place where they haunt, right? So, this Dave Simons won't be able to leave that dorm. This gives us the chance to study it."

There was some murmured agreement among the team.

"I'm with Detective Ross," said Bronson. "Kill the monster now while we have him."

Ross held up a hand to silence everyone, and it worked pretty well. The entire room fell silent.

"You've got a theory, Lexi. I can tell. What is it?"

"Something is changing these ghosts and turning them into monsters. We need to find out what's doing it so we can stop this for good."

"And how do you propose finding that out?"

I took a deep breath and let it out slowly. And here we came to it. The plan I didn't like but knew had to happen.

"I need to talk to Dave Simons."

Ross shook his head. "No chance. Too dangerous."

"I'm not saying I should go alone. After all, you've got a whole team. And I know now that iron hurts ghosts."

27

Missy Baskins was wandering around the third floor when I stepped out of the elevator. She saw me at once and ran toward me.

"You came to visit!" she cried.

"Oh, sorry. I'm here to see Kai."

"The boy in Room 312? Why? Don't tell me you want to spy on him again."

"That's right. You think I'm dead. I guess it's time to prove it. Let's go."

I strode down the hall, confident that my new ghost friend would be a believer at last. I knocked on the door to room 312 and, after a moment, it swung open.

Kai beamed when he saw me.

"I was wondering if you'd ever show up," he said.

Missy's jaw dropped at his reaction to my presence. *I told you so!* It felt good to gloat, even though I didn't say it out loud.

"Dinner went long. Jenna and I had a lot of schoolwork to talk about."

"At least you're here."

"For a little while. I have something I need to do tonight. But I can stay for an hour."

"That's better than nothing." He stepped aside. "Come on in!"

I winked at Missy, who stared at us aghast, and stepped inside. Kai shut the door, leaving the ghost standing alone in the hallway.

He pulled out his desk chair, the standard beige padded thing that all the rooms got, and sat down. I took a seat on the edge of his bed.

"So, you're busy tonight?" he asked.

"Studying," I lied. Then, when Kai looked suspicious, I added "Astronomy. I have to go look at stars with some other kids."

"Ah. I guess that's the only time to do it."

Now that we were sitting in his bedroom, the two of us found it hard to talk.

"Tell me about you," he blurted. "I've given you my back story about ghosts. Now, you tell me yours. How did this all start for you?"

I sat still for a moment as I tried to decide how much to reveal. Kai was right. He told me his drama, which was painful for him. I owed him something. But I didn't want to let him into my world. The others knew because they figured stuff out, and I accidentally blurted it. But with Kai, I was in control over the information, and I wanted to exercise caution. Still, we'd been through a lot together. That moment of silent thinking became a few moments, then a couple minutes. At last, I opened my mouth, and the words fell out.

"All my life, since I was little, I've been able to see ghosts. Always at night. They'd be walking down the street. Or looking out windows . . . sometimes over people's shoulders. Nobody else notices them. Only me. And they're all over the place. There was a girl from the 80s standing beside me when you let me in."

He shot a look at his door as though to see Missy there. Then he returned his gaze to me. He searched my face like he was trying to discern if I was lying. Finally, he seemed satisfied.

"You see them better than I do. The one on the stairs at the ghost house was just mist to me, but you saw more. You could tell what they looked like."

I nodded.

"Sometimes, they try to talk to me. And other times, they try to hurt me."

"Geez. That puts my little ghost stories to shame," Kai said.

"No. What you went through was hard. I wouldn't wish that on anyone."

He leaned forward in his seat and met my gaze. There was an intensity there that I hadn't noticed before. "You must hate them as much as I do. After all you've been through."

I broke away from his gaze and looked down at the floor.

He had bare feet.

"Hate isn't the right word," I said. "Pity is more like it. I feel bad for the dead. They didn't ask to be where they are, and most of them are just sad."

When I brought my gaze back to his face, his expression had changed. He was looking at me still, but I couldn't read him.

"Well, I *hate* them," he said in a quiet voice. "Every last one of them."

That was when I knew I could never reveal to him the full magnitude of my condition. In fact, I already said too much. I wanted to leave, but I didn't know how to do it without looking freaked out. And I felt that was important.

"I understand," I said.

"Do you? You don't hate them like I do. How can you understand?"

"I've had a rough time with some ghosts. Some, like the two in that house, are terrible. But I've seen good ones and those that are at least harmless. You've been a victim of a ghost all your life. It's all you know of them. So how you feel makes sense. I can't say I feel the way you do. But I get it."

He sat in silence for a moment as if considering what I said. Then he shrugged.

"You're right. I guess I hoped we had that in common, too. It would have made things better."

"We can still talk about ghosts. I don't have to agree with you on every point for us to have fun discussing it."

"I suppose," he said. He sounded defeated like he had been building up to something with our conversation and then realized that he couldn't go through with it. Apparently, we both had our secrets about the dead.

"When do you have to leave?" he asked.

"Soon."

"Okay."

We sat in awkward silence for a minute or two, and then I stood up. "I guess I should go now."

He nodded and went to the door. "Hey," he said as I exited into the hallway. "Sorry I brought things down. I wasn't in the right mood."

"It happens to everyone."

He flashed me a hopeful look and then smiled. "Good. I'd like to see you again. And we don't have to talk about ghosts."

"I'd like that," I said, but for the first time, I wasn't sure I meant it.

"I can't believe it!" Missy said as we went down the hallway. She fell into step beside me, oblivious to my lack of attention. "You're *alive*. I mean, I know you told me, but there's never been anyone like you. It's like you've got the best of both worlds. The best of *your* world. I guess it's a shame you're in mine at all. Still, I'm glad you are! There's so much we can talk about. I mean, all that's changed since when I was alive, I . . . What's wrong?"

The change of tone in her unending stream of words pulled me from my thoughts about Kai.

"What?" I said.

"Your talk with Kai didn't go well. Did he dump you?"

I shook my head. "Nothing like that. It's just . . . I discovered there's something we disagree on."

Missy laughed. "Is that all? Girl—wait a minute? What's your name?"

A slight smile broke the frown on my face. "Lexi Downs."

"Lexi," she said sagely. "You can't expect to agree with everything a boy says. I mean, it might pay to *say* you do, even if you don't believe it. Guys say lots of stuff you won't agree with. You've got to learn to let it slide."

"This is one thing I'm not sure I can."

She paused for a moment. I stopped at the elevator, then thought better of it and continued down the hall to the staircase. It would be rude to take the lift knowing that my ghost friend couldn't.

"So, it's a bad thing, huh? One of those things that are too important to ignore?"

When I nodded, she sighed. It still surprised me how some ghosts clung to their past lives so much that they seemed so real, so alive, even after decades of death.

"Damn. That blows," Missy said. "Are you going to dump him?"

"I don't want to."

"Then give yourself some time to think. Besides, giving a guy the cold shoulder drives them crazy." She grinned at me.

I opened the door and started up the stairs. Missy followed along as though skipping the elevator was normal.

"What makes me think you've done that before?" I asked, another smile tugging at my lips.

"It's my specialty. I mean, with this bod, I couldn't lose!" She posed for me and then burst into laughter. I joined her. After all, we were alone on the staircase.

When we came out on my floor, I had sobered up. After all, I needed to make appearances. I drew out my phone and put it to my ear. I laughed when Missy flashed me an odd look.

"Nobody can hear you," I said to her. "But they can hear me, so I'm making it look like I'm on the phone."

"Oh! That's right! So, those little things are telephones? Wicked!"

"That's why there aren't any phones in the building."

"Yeah, there are," Missy said, her brow creased in confusion. "There's one right there." She pointed to a bare section of the wall, and I remembered seeing them on my first night after getting stuck in that banishing ritual. That night, I was deeper into her world than I had ever been before, and I saw some of it. That made me wonder what her world looked like. Did this place resemble what it did in her day? Did it look like we were walking around in an 80s style dorm?

"Things have changed, Missy. I don't see the telephones. We should get together again and talk. I'd love to know more about you, and I could tell you more about what my life is like."

"That would be bitchin'."

It was five o'clock in the afternoon, an hour before sunset, and Detective Ross and I stood in the lobby of Fenway Hall. All the windows were shuttered, hiding us from nosy college onlookers. But, of course, nobody knew what we planned to do, so they had no reason to come peeping.

The rest of the team entered in pairs to avoid drawing attention. They showed up dressed to blend in with their personal gear stowed in backpacks and bags. Boxes of equipment had arrived throughout the day and were stacked with us in the lobby.

Bronson was first, along with a woman, Detective Elliot. Apparently, they had already received their promotions. Lewis came in through the front door ten minutes later with Detective Darren Holtz.

The team rummaged through the equipment and changed into gear that resembled SWAT armor, all black and bulky, with helmets and everything.

"What are you expecting?" I asked, frowning at them. "We're not here to do battle with Dave."

"Precautions," Ross said. "The Top Hat monster tore people's necks apart. Your friend's like him now. He'll try to do the same, and I'm not losing any of my men."

"*People*," I corrected. But I understood. Dave might come in for the attack before I could interview him. There was also a good chance that we wouldn't be able to talk to him at all. I hoped that at least a little of the old Dave Simons was still in him.

Once everyone had arrived and changed, Ross opened another container and pulled out strange items. One was long and narrow, with a sharpened point at its end. Another was a sickle-like blade curved back toward the wielder a few inches from the tip. There were others, all sharp and pointy. They all resembled makeshift swords, axes, and spears. Each detective selected one, hefting it and swinging it around experimentally.

Ross grinned at my confused expression. "We needed iron weapons. These were all I could come up with on short notice.

Luckily, we have someone on staff that doubles as a blacksmith at Medieval fairs in his free time. The fireplace pokers and shovels turned into pretty decent weapons, don't you think?"

I had to admit they were both impressive and clever.

"I'm hoping this case will justify a bigger budget for specialized gear. These might work on your feral ghosts, but they're toys compared with some threats that are out there."

"What do you expect to fight? Ogres?"

The raised eyebrow he shot me filled me with more questions, but they would have to wait. Ross called his team to attention, and they responded immediately, suddenly silent and turning to their leader.

"There is one feral ghost in this building. The sun's going down now, so it should appear soon. It'll probably hunt victims, and we're its only prey. We have weapons that should work against it, but we're not here to engage. The plan is to corner it and allow Miss Downs to speak to it."

Ross reached into the box and pulled out a flattened shovel sharpened into a blade. He nodded with satisfaction.

"But this creature won't want to stand and talk. If you must, defend yourselves. Your lives are more important than its. Besides, we probably can't kill it. Just send it away."

When everyone had shown their understanding, Ross continued.

"We'll split into three groups. I'll lead Group One with Bronson, Fitzpatrick, and Downs. Lewis, you'll head Group Two with Holtz, Baker, and Jones. Campbell, you take Group Three with Elliot, Yang, and Gordon. Group Three stays here in the lobby, guarding our escape if we need it. Groups One and Two will wander the halls in search of the ghost. If you find it, call it in, and we'll come. Don't engage unless you have to."

"And remember," I added. "It might not always be visible. It'll have to appear before attacking, and when it does, you can hit it. But it could show up suddenly. So, be on your guard."

"Right," said Ross. "Lewis, go take the upper floors, starting with the sixth. We'll start on the first and work our way up."

"Yes, sir!" Detective Lewis turned on a dime and led her group toward the stairs. At first, it surprised me that they avoided the elevators, but then it made sense. Four people would be sitting ducks in a cramped elevator car.

"Let's go," said Ross. As an afterthought, I grabbed a poker from the weapon bag and followed the detective. After all, I planned to encounter a ghost that meant to kill everyone it saw. Non-violence was the plan, but I wasn't about to be the only sheep among sheepdogs and wolves.

Each floor of the building was split into two wings that stretched out in opposite directions from the lobby. We chose the left way. This was not like the other times I went searching for a ghost. We moved slowly; our senses strained for any motion or sound.

To their credit, the cops were professional. They handled their improvised weapons as though they were standard issue. No one joked or grinned or even spoke. But they clearly didn't believe they would see a ghost. None of their faces reflected the right level of tension for the situation. Only Ross and I gave the job the respect it deserved.

The earpiece speaker crackled briefly. "Group Two here.

We have movement on the sixth floor."

We all came to a halt. "Do you have visual?" Ross asked into the microphone.

"Negative. We saw something duck down a side hallway. We're following."

"We're on our way," Ross said. He flicked off the mic and looked at me. "Nearest staircase?"

"End of the hall." I led the group. We moved faster but still showed caution since the other team didn't have visual confirmation of the ghost.

The staircase gave me pause. I had fallen here. After struggling with Dave, I had tumbled down a flight and received a concussion for my efforts. Ross cast me a concerned look, but I nodded and forged ahead. This was no time to be a baby, even though part of me wanted to curl up and cry.

Mounting the steps quickly was easier, knowing that a group of cops would catch me if I fell. Our footsteps echoed off the walls as we climbed the six flights.

"There's blood on the floor," said Lewis over the earpiece. "Tracks leading down the hallway. We might have a wounded student."

Without a word, we all sped up. My concern for the team rose with every slap of my shoes on the stairs. It's funny how you never hear sneakers unless you're trying to be quiet. Then, they make so much noise.

"They stop at a bedroom." Lewis's voice came in a near whisper. "We're going in."

"Negative!" blurted Ross. "Wait for us. We're almost there."

My breath gasped out when at last, I stopped at the door

to the sixth-floor hallway. We listened for a moment but heard nothing. Finally, Ross motioned to me, and I pulled the door open as he stood in a guard position, his flattened shovel raised before him.

The opening was empty, and he and I went through to stand in the hallway. As the rest of our team shuffled in, the two of us stared down the passage in stunned silence. Group Two was near the far end of the corridor. Lewis was in front of a door with a teammate on either side, all looking at it. The fourth cop, Baker, looked down the corridor with his back to us.

And a broad-shouldered young man in a football jersey crept up behind him, ready to strike.

"Watch out!" I shouted, but I was too late. The ghost lunged forward and sank its jaw into the neck of the unsuspecting cop.

The rest all happened in a blur. Baker swung around, desperately trying to dislodge the monster that now grabbed his shoulders and tried to force him to the ground. Lewis and the others searched for a clear path to attack. The two combatants were thrashing about, their arms flailing as Baker struggled to reach his attacker, but she couldn't find an opening.

Lewis saw her opportunity and swung her shovel-sword down in an arc that struck the ghost in his back.

Dave Simons released the cop, and an inhuman scream issued from its impossibly wide maw. The others backed off at once, clearly terrified by the monster.

But Lewis, encouraged by her successful attack, moved forward, her sword swinging before her. The ghost reversed down the hall toward us. Lewis's comrades recovered enough to follow suit. Even the injured cop, Baker, was still on his feet and taking the offensive.

Ross and I exchanged a quick glance, and then we advanced up the hallway, and as we did, an idea popped into my mind.

I tapped the microphone button. "Common room, halfway to us. Force it in there."

There was no telling if Lewis heard me or understood, but she continued to herd the creature down the hall, the common room coming ever closer. We ran to a point before the room's entrance. That's when Ross pushed me behind him, and Bronson stepped up to take my place.

At first, it pissed me off. But then, the idea of not engaging the ghost with the gaping maw full of teeth made me accept my fate as a tagalong. After all, I was there to talk to Dave, and fighting it wouldn't help in that at all.

Dave heard us and glanced back. The face I saw filled my head with doubt about our plan. There was no sign of the dead kid I knew in his one good eye. Only violence and murder.

What the hell happened to you?

Ross and Bronson threatened the ghost with their weapons, and Dave backed his way into the room. Bronson stepped forward and placed himself in front of the entrance as a human barricade.

"Now what?" Ross said to me.

"I go in and talk to him," I replied.

"No, you don't. It'll kill you." Lewis and the others nodded their agreement. Bronson was a statue, his eyes never leaving the ghost as it hissed at him.

"It's why we're here. Besides, you guys will come to the rescue if it goes south."

When Ross frowned at me, I continued, "Let's not waste the mission. We've come this far. We have to finish it."

"I don't like it," he said but moved aside.

I came up to Bronson. His stolid face was expressionless, but his eyes darted to me, and there was compassion there. He didn't want me to go in. But he moved enough for me to squeeze through.

Dave Simons backed up and tensed as I entered the room. My first order of business was to get away from the door so that reinforcements could enter if things went sideways. Two steps to my left did that.

Then I knelt and set my weapon on the floor. It's always the first step in negotiations, at least on TV.

Finally, I smiled at him. "Hi, Dave. It's me, Lexi. Let's talk."

It stared at me but stayed where it was. I said "it" because there was still no hint of intelligence in its eye or expression. Great.

"Do you remember me? We're friends. I'm here now to have a chat with you."

Still nothing. Yet, at least it hadn't attacked. So that was a good sign.

"Something has happened to you, Dave. You're not acting like yourself. Please, tell me what's going on."

Lips parted, exposing the teeth and letting a dull growl out. In the corner of my eye, Bronson tensed slightly. He did it so subtly that the ghost didn't notice. This was not the man's first negotiation.

"Dave Simons. I know you're in there. This entity has control right now, but you're there. And you're strong. I remember how powerful you were when you got mad at me. I don't blame you for what you did. In fact, I understand it. But you need to get mad now. This *thing* has taken over your body. *Your* body. Don't let that happen. Show it your strength. Teach it that you won't take it any longer. I know you can do it."

At first, nothing happened. The ghost stood there for a moment, its inhuman eye on me and its mouth still in that half growl. But now, no noise issued from it. It stood frozen, unmoving.

The eye changed first. It softened, and something familiar entered it. I was looking at Dave Simons again. Or at least a part of him.

The mouth opened, and it was clearly trying to form words, but all those teeth made it difficult. Then, at last, it croaked in broken English.

"It—it's strong, Lexi. S-so strong. I can't. I can't fight it."

"What is it, Dave?"

"Old. So old. And terrible. So much hate. It kills because that's—that's what it is. And it's so old."

The ghost shook its head violently and staggered. When it regained its composure, Dave was no longer there. The ancient beast within had suppressed him once more.

And it charged at me.

It rushed, with its body hunched forward and its claw-like hands outstretched, to grab at my neck or shoulders. I stepped to one side and swung my arms upward and around, guiding

Dave's body past me. I wasn't as strong as him, so I let his own momentum send him crashing into the wall behind me.

Bronson was in the room in an instant, shouting for me to get out. Which, of course, I did. I ran through the door, scooping up my weapon as I went by.

But it was unnecessary. The ghost had vanished in a swirl of black smoke. Then, like when the car hit Top Hat, it evaporated.

In the hallway, Holtz was trying to check Baker's wound, but he pushed him away.

"The survivor!" Baker said.

Ross put a hand on my shoulder. "Are you okay?"

I nodded.

"Did you get what you needed?"

"I think so." But I wasn't sure. At that moment, nothing was clear in my head.

"Will it come back tonight?"

"I doubt it. It used up its reserve of energy. But I can't be certain of that. It might recover."

"Then we'd better go."

We checked the door down the hall. It was a student, and he was still alive. But he had lost a lot of blood. Holtz was a medic, and he patched the kid up as best he could. Then the others carried him down the stairs to the first floor, where we rendezvoused with the rest of the team. We wasted no time in leaving. The boxes and gear bags stayed in the lobby, and we exited through the main entrance, the guards outside still in place.

"Go to bed," Ross said to me once we were out. "Then

think about what you learned. Call me in the morning."

I didn't argue and hobbled back to my dorm.

An ancient entity was hopping from ghost to ghost. There was still no apparent cause, but that was something. Hell, it was more than we've had to go on in a long time.

28

Friday dawned overcast and windy, and Jenna and I grabbed our umbrellas when we went to breakfast. She didn't ask me about last night's adventure. I think she was just happy I was unhurt.

Classes were back to normal, and Tom sat next to me in Literature class. He came in late with a limp and a crutch under one arm but grinned at me when he took his seat. "You're looking great! How are you feeling?"

"All better. Dave really did a number on you, huh?"

"It'll heal," Tom said. "Are you any nearer to solving the mystery?"

That forced a chuckle from me. "Getting closer, but we're

not there yet."

"Right. You and Logan Reyes."

"Me and my friends, you mean. But no. Me and the police. I'm consulting for them."

His eyes widened in surprise. They were remarkably blue. "They *hired* you?"

"Yup. They're on the case now."

"Good. They won't let you go in there after the ghost, so I'm fine with that."

I decided it would be easier to let him believe that.

We went our separate ways after class, and I continued my first normal Friday in some time.

The Dungeon Crawlers joined Jenna and me during dinner at the cafeteria.

"So, what's the deal with that cop?" asked Ben as soon as they had all taken their seats.

"He's working the case. First the Top Hat one, and now Fenway Hall. I'm helping him out."

"The guy was acting like your father or something."

"Of course he was. But it's obvious why, isn't it?" Jenna said.

We all stared at her. My coffee was halfway to my lips. Ben paused, a home fry half-chewed.

Jenna rolled her eyes. "Oh, come on. He blames himself for you getting hurt. This is *his* case, and you got injured because of it. Therefore, it's his fault."

"That's ridiculous!" I said. "Everything that happened was my doing, not his."

"You don't have to agree with him. But you're a kid, and

you were hurt when he was on the job."

"I'm not a kid."

"You are to him."

"Anyway," said Rocks. "Do you have any new info on the Fenway Ghost? I want to know why it went crazy, like Top Hat."

"Sure. Dave's being possessed by an ancient, evil entity. We don't know why, but that's what's going on." I told them about my conversation with Dave Simons but left out that the cops were involved.

"So, an evil spirit is jumping from ghost to ghost."

"And if we banish Dave, it'll jump into another one," I said. "We have to figure out how to eliminate the being without hurting the ghost."

"Of course, we don't know how to do that," said Rocks, setting his empty orange juice cup down as though for emphasis.

"Sounds like a research project," said Tony.

"I'm already overloaded with those," said Ben.

Logan shrugged as he chewed his burger. "I've got time."

"Me, too," said Tony.

"Yeah, we'll all work on it, as much as we can," added Rocks.

Diego had been quiet during this conversation, but now he set down his fork and cast a searching gaze around the table. Everyone hushed to let him speak. The Dungeon Master loved this kind of spectacle.

"Has anyone put thought into how this all started?"

Nobody answered right away, so Rocks eyed him with suspicion. "No, but I take it you have."

Diego paused for dramatic effect and then cleared his throat.

"I think somebody summoned the entity. And this same person sent it into the next ghost."

"Someone on campus?" asked Rocks.

Diego nodded.

My mind shot to the break-in at Professor Landry's lab. Now I couldn't wait to see the list of things that were stolen.

"Why would anybody do that?" Ben blurted out, incredulous. "It doesn't make sense. Why force a ghost to become a monster?"

"Maybe the perpetrators don't know what they're causing," said Diego. "Or they do and want to create chaos. Some people wouldn't mind seeing the world burn just to prove that they *can*."

"But that kind of person would be insane. So they should be easy to find."

"Not really," I countered. An important idea crept into my head. "Crazy people don't all look nuts. But I think you were onto something when you said *they*. If someone's making this happen, they will use a ritual, and that would definitely require more than one person."

"We're talking about a group of nutjobs," said Rocks.

"A cult?" said Logan.

"Wait a minute! Wait just a minute!" cried Ben. His gaze flitted from each of our faces with an almost manic expression. "You're all talking about a cult of evil magicians doing necromantic magic here on campus. Don't you hear how stupid that sounds? I can't believe I'm the one saying this, but this *isn't*

D&D. It's not a game. It's real life, and there are no real-life necromancers."

"Then how do you explain what's happening to the ghosts?" said Diego. His tone was calm, but his frown showed his annoyance at Ben's outburst.

"I don't know. None of us knows for sure. There's no evidence there's a cult or that anyone's casting spells except for us. And *we* didn't cause it."

"Actually, there might be evidence." All heads turned to me. Ben shook his head like he already had his mind set. "Someone broke into Professor Landry's lab. In fact, it was only a day or two before Dave went monstrous. Ross has him building a list of what they stole. And this wasn't the first time it happened. Landry told me near the start of the semester that someone had broken in and stolen a few things. Then Top Hat made his appearance. It can't be a coincidence. Someone *is* making it happen. We need to figure out who."

Silence fell on the group as we all considered what we knew about the situation. After a minute, Ben started eating again, then the others followed suit. I lost my appetite, but I sipped my coffee.

"I saw the police tape outside that room," said Rocks. "But I didn't know what it was about."

"I'd like to see that list," said Diego.

I was in my late-afternoon Calculus class when Detective Ross texted me. "Landry has the list. His office. 5:00 p.m."

That was good timing. After my discussion with the Crawlers, I had useful information for him. But as my class ended at 4:45, I had to go straight to the professor's office from class.

Puffy white clouds drifted slowly across the blue sky, pushed by the ever-present ocean breezes. The sun peeked out from its hiding place behind a skyscraper, and shadows already stretched toward me as I hurried to Grendel Hall. The heavy front door grunted as I hauled it open and stepped through into the comparative darkness of the old building. Mack was already there, and he tipped his head toward me in greeting. I returned the smile and continued on my way to the meeting.

I tried the professor's office door when I arrived, but it was locked. So, I sat down on the floor with my back against the wall and browsed on my phone. Footsteps echoed down the hall, but it was neither the professor nor Detective Ross. Instead, a student came around the corner. He wore a My Chemical Romance T-shirt and black cargo pants. His straight black hair hung down to partially obscure his eyes. The obligatory backpack looked out of place on him, but it reminded me he was a student.

It was one of the guys Kai hung out with. Owen? Damien? I couldn't remember. The guy glanced at Professor Landry's office and then at me, and then he smirked.

"Archeology student, eh?"

"Anthro, but yeah."

He nodded like he cared, but it was clear he didn't.

"Sucks what happened to him, right?" Again, the words implied empathy, but the tone betrayed them.

I feigned ignorance. "What happened?"

"Someone broke into his artifact collection. I hear they

stole stuff."

"Oh. You don't sound bothered by it."

He shrugged. "It's not like he uses any of it. He just hoards it away."

"Some call it studying."

A snort escaped his mouth. The first emotion he showed. I learned something about him.

"Looking at the artifacts and reading what others have written about them isn't studying."

"You've got a problem with his methods. Okay. That's fair."

"And you don't. You're a sheep. A follower. You take notes on what he says and accept it all as truth. But tell me, Kai's girl. Do you know *anything* about the stuff in that room? Before you answer that, consider this: can you know what something is for without trying to use it? Experimentation is an important part of science, but people like Landry don't touch the things they study. They just look and read. That's it."

"Well, Kai's friend, it's been real. But now it's time for you to wander off and leave me to my thoughts."

Another snort, this time with less animosity. "Think about what I said. Kai says you're smart. Prove him right." With that, the asshole walked down the hall and went through a door near the end.

It's sometimes funny watching hypocrisy walking around and talking, but this time, I found it tedious. He went on and on about Landry and being a blind follower, all while wearing the standard Emo uniform. That kid had become Suspect number one in the case of the stolen artifacts. After all, he showed disdain for Landry's "hoarding" of the relics, and talked up the importance of messing with things he didn't understand.

The professor came around the corner and smiled when he saw me. I grabbed my backpack and rose as he approached.

"Hope you weren't waiting long. I had to answer a lot of questions after class. You're not the only student interested in learning more." He pulled out his keys and unlocked the door.

He turned on the light as we entered and then went to his desk and sat down. I took a seat opposite him. He opened a drawer and pulled out a manila folder.

"Do you know a kid who dresses all Emo and is pretty outspoken about the way we study archeology?"

"Emo? Isn't that a musical style?"

"And a look." I described the guy.

"Ah, that would be Damien. He's not a big fan of the methods of modern archeology. Why do you ask?"

"I ran into him. He's a bit of an ass."

"That's not for me to judge."

"That's okay. I'll do it for both of us."

A knock came at the door, and Detective Ross's face filled its tiny window. Professor Landry waved him in, and the door opened.

Once the latch clicked shut behind him, Ross went down to business. "You got the list?"

"I do." Landry patted the folder that sat before him on the desk. "And I found it quite interesting."

"Why's that?" Ross asked. He must practice speaking with few words because he was a master at it.

"Everything that was stolen came from a single collection,

aside from that book. Nothing else was taken."

"They knew what they were after," said Ross.

"But that's where things get confusing. It's not a collection I've ever mentioned in class. It's rather obscure."

"What is it, Professor?" I asked.

"ME-1127."

I frowned. "That's its name? I've never heard of it."

"It doesn't have a name. It's never been associated with a specific culture. The artifacts were found in a solitary site in what is now Portland, Maine. But it didn't belong to the Algonquian-speaking people that lived there. It had a distinctly European look to the artwork while still retaining some Native American traits. Most scholars who inspected the collection believed it to be a hoax, but the carbon dating put it in the late 1200s. The common belief is that they were European relics of unknown origin that were planted there to create a sensational find."

"You don't believe that," I said. Something in his tone betrayed his skepticism.

"No, I don't. That theory wouldn't account for the Native American traits in the designs. If I didn't know how old they were, I would say it was a tribe that had included people who came across from Europe."

"Leif Erikson came to the New World before then," I said.

"Shortly before that, and he was the first. And he landed far away, probably in Newfoundland. The carbon dating contradicts my theory."

"So, it's a mystery," said Ross. "Why would someone steal them?"

"I don't know."

It was time to ask my question, and I wasn't sure how my teacher would take it. "Professor Landry, you know I've been interested in rites and rituals involving the dead. Can you tell me if the collection could have included something like that?"

The professor looked at me for a long moment before releasing an exasperated breath.

"I had a feeling you were going to ask that."

He opened the folder and turned it around to face me.

A photograph of a rectangular chuck of rock stared at me. On it were pictograms of people dancing in a circle around a man lying on a slab. And standing beside that slab was a person.

A person with a massive jaw full of sharp teeth.

I stared at the picture for a moment as the implications flooded my brain. *Diego was right! Someone was acting there on campus, casting rituals to create a monster. And we had no idea who it could be.*

When I broke from my shock-induced trance, I glanced at Ross. He was staring at it, too. But his features hardened as he did so. With a suddenness that made both Professor Landry and me jump, the detective grabbed the photo and folder, stuffed one into the other, and turned to face my teacher.

"Professor," he said. His tone was professional, but with a sheen of threat brushed over it with a heavy stroke. "You will tell nobody about what was stolen. Do you understand me?" When Professor Landry only stared back at him in surprise, he added, "*Nobody.* Got it?"

At last, the anthropologist nodded briskly. "Of course. I

won't tell anyone. Not even the dean, if she were to ask for it. I'll tell her to talk to you."

"Good. And if anyone asks about *this* subject"—he held up the folder with the photo tucked inside—"call me. I'll want to know who it is."

Professor Landry nodded. Apparently not well enough, because Ross leaned in and turned up the intimidation to eleven.

"This is important, Professor," his voice gritted out in a near whisper, but that only made it sound more threatening. "Someone is committing murder with that information, whether or not you want to believe it, and if you interfere with my investigation even a little, I'll throw the book at you. Do I make myself clear?"

Professor Landry looked terrified for a moment, then swallowed and straightened up. He frowned.

"Detective Ross," he said, his tone confident and professional, "I understand the gravity of the situation, and I know my duty. And I want the people caught as much as you. Ms. Downs is involved in your case, and these break-ins have put her life in danger. The safety and well-being of my students is of the utmost importance to me. You will have nothing but my full cooperation in this. I swear."

"And what if one of your other students is involved?"

"Then I turn him in to you. A criminal is a criminal, student or no. You taught me that."

Ross considered the professor for a moment, then nodded. "Good. You have my card."

29

"Don't you think you were a little hard on Professor Landry?" I said to Ross as we strolled down the road to get coffee at the diner. We were about to discuss the prospect of an unknown suspect on campus, so we felt more comfortable leaving the place behind.

"I had to impress upon him the gravity of the situation."

"Do you ever smile?" I asked, casting him a sidelong glance.

"Sure. All the time." His face contradicted that.

"I doubt it. You probably don't even smile at your cat."

He flashed me a quick look, then turned his eyes back to the sidewalk. So, he had a cat.

My attempts at levity fell flat, though I kept it up the entire walk to the restaurant. When we arrived, we took a corner booth. Ross ordered coffee, but I hadn't eaten. We sat in silence for a bit after placing our order.

"You ordered eggs?" It wasn't what I had expected him to say, but at least it was social.

"Sure. I'm starving."

"But breakfast for dinner?"

"Hey, if we're eating at a diner, you've got to get breakfast. It's like a law or something."

The slightest hint of a grin cracked the corner of his lips. I had seen that once or twice before. Maybe he'd upgrade to a half smile by the time we finished the case.

But I let him off easy and got down to work. "Hand me that folder."

He gave me a severe look.

"Hand me that folder, *please*."

It wasn't what he meant, but he pulled it from somewhere inside his coat and slid it across the table to me. I opened it and pored over the pictures. Something had caught my attention when we first saw them in Professor Landry's office. Besides the ghost monster, that is.

"I wish I had the book here," I muttered as I stared at the photocopies. There was a pattern to the bits of ritual we could see in the pictograms. Though they had little detail, they still resembled some of the drawings in the old tome.

"I think these pictures are related to our book."

"Really?" He leaned forward and examined the upside-down papers. "How do you know?"

I told him about the connection. He frowned.

"Our thieves figured it out," he said.

"And they stole one of the books."

"That's bad. We have to find these thieves. And fast!"

"Then you'll be happy to hear I have a suspect for you."

A single eyebrow raised on his face, then he nodded. "That Damien kid you mentioned? What's his story?"

I filled him in on our conversation outside Professor Landry's office, and he took notes. Yup, he even had one of those small wire-bound notebooks that flip open on the top.

"Doesn't sound like you have much on him," he said.

"Then call him a 'person of interest' or something. He was glad the place was broken into. If he didn't do it, he respects those who did. And he's all about messing with artifacts. 'Experimentation is an important part of science,' he said."

"Still circumstantial. Being sympathetic with the criminals doesn't make him one of them."

"He's involved. I'm sure of it. Call it a gut feeling."

The detective considered me for a moment then nodded. "I'll check him out."

"How do we go about finding the people who are doing the rituals?" I asked.

"We find clues, and then we follow them to see where they go," said Ross. "The problem is that I stand out on that campus, so there's not much I can do there."

"You want me to poke around?"

"I don't want you to."

"But you have no alternatives."

He didn't respond but continued to watch my face.

"Well, I'll do it. You *are* paying me, after all. It's my job."

"It's also dangerous. The people behind this won't appreciate your snooping. If they catch wind of what you're doing, they'll go after you."

"And they'll be in for a surprise. I'm no wimp."

"That you aren't. But you're not invincible, either. So, be careful. Let me know if you find out anything. And call me right away, at any hour."

"Yes, Dad," I chided. He gave me a weird look, and I decided I had crossed some kind of line. But he did sound a lot like my father, who was overprotective to a fault. Though with my special gift, it came with the territory.

"Sure, it can be dangerous. But I'm up to it. And if we want the perps caught and have this school get back to normal, we need to find these people and bring them in. I'm the best one for that job, and you know it."

"I keep thinking of you as a kid. That's something I've got to stop doing."

"You won't, but that's okay. I'll follow the lead I have on this Damien guy and keep you informed."

"Try not to give away what you're doing. It's important that nobody suspects you."

"Right."

"It could take a little time to run the background check on our suspect, but I'll text you when it comes in."

The main thought that went through my mind as I walked by myself back to my dorm was if Kai had something to do with creating the monsters. He was obsessed with ghosts, that was certain. But that didn't implicate him. He was friends with Damien, my current number one suspect. *Damn!* I had to talk to him. Try to find out what he knew.

I drew out my phone and texted him as I left the road and stepped into the comparative safety of the Brent College campus.

"You free? Let's meet up." I read it a few times before I hit Send. It was short and simple, and I didn't think it implied anything. But still, my finger hesitated over the button. *What if he* is *connected to it? What if he knows I've been working with the police? We hadn't made that a secret so far.*

At last, I tapped, and the text went on its merry way. If my new beau was bad, it was better to find out right away. Besides, he didn't act like his darkly pretentious friends. But then, the occult posters in his room came to my mind, and I cringed.

My phone beeped as I rounded the corner near Wembley Hall.

The reply popped up on the screen. "'Bout time. My room? Whenever."

"Be there soon," I replied.

I went to my room to drop off my bag. Then I was off again, heading to Kai's room.

Missy Baskins, the ghost of my dorm, joined me as I stepped off the elevator.

"Hi!" she said.

"Hey. How are you doing?"

"Bored. What's up?" A suspicious look crossed her face. "Are you coming to see Kai?"

"I am. Sorry. I do want to hang, though. It's just this is important right now."

We stopped at Kai's room. Missy smiled and bobbed on the tips of her toes. "I'll wait here for you. We can talk after."

I nodded, then knocked on the door, which opened at once. Kai stood before me, his smile infectious. His black hair was neat and straight and didn't cover any of his eyes. Ever. I mentally ticked off that one difference between him and Damien. His cheery disposition made another check on that list.

"Come on in."

His room was exactly as I had seen it before, right down to the occult-related posters. Now, some of them were bands, and I was okay with those. But others gave him a mark on a different list. Aleister Crowley's sinister mug glared at me from a prominent position in the middle of one wall. Posters of pentagrams, some of them upside down, decorated the room. He had several Satanic-looking ritual artifacts sitting on his desk and bureau.

"Interesting decor," I said.

"Comes with the territory. Ghosts are linked with the occult, you know."

"I'm not into this stuff, but I've been dealing with ghosts for my whole life."

"True. I guess it's the macabre aspect that grabs me. Horror movies, Lovecraft. It's all cool."

"Makes sense," I said with a nod.

Kai pulled two sodas from his mini fridge, and we sat down on his bed.

"What's up?" he asked. "Did you come over for a reason or

because you couldn't bear to be away from me any longer? I mean, you've been kind of brushing me off lately."

I flashed him a confused frown. Had I been? "I wasn't avoiding you. I've been swamped. That's all."

"Then this is a social visit? Cool!"

We talked a bit about school, and it felt awkward. It was strange because we had never felt like that before. Something was bothering one of us. Maybe both. I knew my concern, and I hoped Kai would tell me about his.

"I saw you talking with a cop a few days ago. A plainclothes one. What was that all about?"

And there it was. He tried his best to make it sound like idle chat, but this was it. This was the big thing on his mind. I wasn't about to tell him the whole truth. As much as I wanted to, I couldn't trust him.

"Remember those murders near the start of the semester? I witnessed one of them. Both of them, sort of. I saw the killer."

"You did?" This was not at all what he had expected, and he leaned forward, instantly excited. "What did it look like?"

It. Kai said "it" as though he knew it wasn't a living person. I didn't have any supernatural danger sense, but if I did, I bet it would be going off like crazy at that moment. The world seemed to collapse in on me, and all I wanted to do was escape. To get up and run from the room and never stop running.

Kai was involved with the monster and was excited about it attacking people. Kai. The guy I kissed.

Playing dumb was now imperative. There was no way I could tip my hand at him.

"He was weird, dressed in a tux and top hat. And he was

fast."

His brow wrinkled as though he was thinking about it. "That sounds like a ghost to me," he said at last.

"It couldn't be. He killed someone. Ghosts can't touch anyone."

"One touched me."

"You know what I mean. This man attacked his victim the way only a living person could. And I ran into him."

"You *what*?" That was genuine surprise.

"I charged into him, and he ran away. And I didn't use iron or anything." Of course, there were lies in my story, but I felt them necessary at this point.

His nod showed his understanding. "It was only a normal murderer."

"Is there such a thing?"

"Okay, a *living* murderer. I was hoping for something more. People from Fenway Hall say a ghost chased them out. So, the idea of the killer being a spirit was kind of cool."

Hmm. Could Kai be innocent, after all? Damn it! Why must you be so ambiguous?

"Sorry to burst your bubble."

"It's fine. But we should go out and find another haunted place to explore." Kai was giving me mixed signals. At first, he seemed like he knew the killer was a ghost, but now he even switched topics.

"Is that how you show a girl a good time?"

He flashed me a sudden look of surprise. Then he blushed. "That's right. You didn't want to talk about ghosts anymore. I could take you out to dinner again. Someplace different. A restaurant I've never been to." He cast me a knowing grin.

I laughed at that; I couldn't resist. It was funny and very Kai. But it left me more confused. So, I figured I had to roll with it and see where it went.

"That would be fun."

"Great! I'll work out the details."

A knock came at the door. Kai looked surprised. "Who could that be?"

He got up and peeked through the peephole. "It's Damien."

"Oh!" I stood up. "I can leave."

"I don't want you to. I'll get rid of him."

He cracked it open. "What's up?"

Damien's drab tone filtered through the gap. "We need to talk."

"Can't it wait?"

"No."

Kai hesitated, and I heard him exhale. Then he opened the door wide, and his asshole friend entered. When his eyes met mine, he stopped short.

I smiled at him. It took effort, but my love of making assholes uncomfortable fueled me onward.

"What's *she* doing here?"

"What does it matter to you?"

The Emo boy shrugged almost imperceptibly but said nothing.

"I'll let you boys talk," I said. When I came to the door and stood between them, I turned and kissed Kai on the cheek. "Call me when you have the details."

"Okay," was all he could say.

I felt like one of those sensuous dames in a noir movie as I stepped out into the hall. It was so unlike me, but it felt good knowing how Damien would react. He slammed the door shut.

Ha!

"Did he dump you, or did you dump him?" Missy Baskins waited in the hallway, leaning against the wall.

I turned my head back to the closed portal. "His friend slammed it. I'd love to know what they're talking about."

"Okay. Stay right here." Missy vanished through the door with a wink before I could stop her.

I stood staring after the ghost in disbelief. The Haunt was spying on Kai for me, and now I had to wait to hear what she found out since she was doing it for me. With a shrug, I walked down the hall and leaned against a wall, pretending to play on my phone. It lasted only a few minutes, but it seemed like an eternity. Catching up on social media took only about a minute, and I spent the rest of the time scrolling mindlessly through forums about ghosts. Of course, there was nothing useful, no tips to help me with my current situation.

At last, the ghost emerged from Kai's room and strolled past me. "I'd start walking if I were you."

Without a word, I fell into step beside her and waited for her to talk.

"It's time to look for a new boyfriend." She wasn't grinning like before. This was no joke. "There are other boys for you. I could point some out. And if you pick one in this dorm, I could check him out for you. But you've got to dump *this* guy."

"You know which guy I'm dating, right? Not the one with the hair in his eyes."

"Oh, he's worse! No, you're seeing Kai, and he's nasty enough to get far away from. Too bad you both live in the same building."

I opened the door to the stairs at the end of Kai's wing and went through. Missy followed.

"Are you going to tell me why I should break up with him?"

"It's not enough that he's obsessed with the dead?"

That earned her a look, and she shrugged. "Oh, yeah. So are you."

"What else about him?"

"The two of them have been doing crazy things. The other guy, Damien, said stuff about a ritual and figuring out how to perfect it. Kai says he doesn't want to do it, but it's obvious he does. He drooled about what Damien told him. Frankly, I don't know what you see in him. Aside from being alive, he's nothing special."

"What did Damien tell him?" It was like pulling teeth with this girl.

"Damien said they learned how to take control of ghosts. To make them do what they want. I think he's full of it. I mean, that can't be done, right?"

The look I gave Missy made her eyes widen a little. "No . . ." It came out in a terrified whisper.

"It might be true. Which means it's in your best interest to help me stop them. Did either of those guys say where they do the spell, or who else is involved?"

Missy shook her head vigorously. "Kai seemed to know everyone already, so neither of them said any names. And they didn't talk about places. Sorry."

"That's okay," I said. "You still got me a lot of information. And don't worry. Kai and I are over."

30

I'm a pragmatist. Even for affairs of the heart, I still temper it with logic. If Kai was involved with those who turned Dave Simons into a monster, then he was bad news, and I had to dump him. He might be handsome and dashing, but I draw the line at evil. Sure, Kai seemed to want out of the situation, but he was in on it, to begin with, and that killed it.

But dumping him now would look suspicious. So, avoidance was my new policy, at least until the culprits were caught and the case was closed. *Damn! How do cops do it?*

I told Jenna because she'd want to know and because he'd likely reach out to her to find me. She tried to console me, but I brushed her off.

"It's okay," I lied. "I didn't love him or anything." That part was true. It was totally a crush. I enjoyed seeing him. But Jenna had to stop. A sob-fest was not what I needed right then.

I stepped up my karate practice. The common room had plenty of space for rehearsing my katas. The katas weren't just shadow-boxing pretend people. Each imaginary opponent had Kai's face or that douchebag friend of his. Each strike hit them in the nose, in the solar plexus. Once, I imagined Kai doubling over from a vicious punch to his gut. At first, I felt triumphant.

Then I toppled to the ground.

Tears streamed from my eyes, and the sobs came unbidden. My chest heaved, and my jaw shuddered as my breath rattled out in ragged gasps. *Why? Why did it have to be him? Of all people, why was it the only man in this goddamned world that understood me? He was so sweet, so charming. We got along so well, and I was almost ready to open up to him and tell him everything.*

I'm so stupid! I screamed at myself. *He's fucking evil! He created a monster ghost that murders the living, and he was* excited *about it! You saw the look on his face when you told him about the killer.*

"Damn it, damn it, damn it, DAMN IT!" Those last thoughts came out in the real world and echoed around the empty common room.

Brenda, one of my dorm neighbors, appeared at the doorway. "Are you okay, Lexi?" Her face creased with concern.

My grief blew out in a puff of breath. Then I sniffled and wiped my nose on my sleeve. Finally, I rose and nodded with a broken smile. "Yeah. Just a little stressed."

Her smile was a lot more genuine than mine. "I get it.

Midterms suck. And you're doing Anthro, right? God, that's a hard major. I could never do that. If you ever need to vent, I'm next door."

"Thanks, Brenda." My grin was more convincing this time. I had to control myself. There was no use in pining over Kai. He made his choices. I had to make mine.

Then why did I still feel like there was a knife stuck in my back?

Saturday morning dawned dark and rainy. The wind blew across the Quad, sending the rain down in angled sheets to foil all attempts at staying dry. But Saturday was D&D day, and I wanted to discuss things with the gang. So, I stuffed my backpack into a plastic garbage bag, put on a raincoat and a wide-brimmed hat, and forced my way through the deluge.

My face was still dripping when I entered the common room where the Dungeon Crawlers assembled. Everyone was there, and they greeted me with grins and smiles. And snacks. Yet people wonder why I play the game.

Ben ran over and took my bag of books and worked to extract the valuable cargo, leaving me to peel off my wet hat and coat.

A quick glance around the room showed us we were alone. This was typical because our games could get pretty loud, and the rest of the students always found another room when we played. Today it was a blessing.

"I've got an update on the case," I said as I tossed my hat onto an unused table.

"Should you be telling us now that you're working for the

police?" asked Rocks.

That earned him a shrug. "I'm tasked with finding someone on campus, and I need help."

Everyone turned their heads to face me. Judging by the looks on their faces, it was as though I had invited them to a theme park.

"Who?" asked Diego.

"His name is Damien. I don't know his last name yet, but he's one of Kai's friends."

"I know him," said Tony. When we all cast him incredulous looks, he responded with his own expression of surprise. "What? It's not a big college. And if he was with your boyfriend when we saw him last weekend at Quincy Market, then yeah. You're talking about Damien Hull. Condescending asshole with the dark facade."

"That's him," I said while carefully draping my coat across a chair.

"He should be easy to find," said Tony. "I have a couple of classes with him."

I took my seat and thanked Ben for stacking my Player's Handbook and character sheet at my spot.

"The guy's a suspect. In fact, I know he's part of the group that's doing the rituals to turn ghosts into monsters. And I know Kai used to be in the group, but he quit. I, um, overheard them talking last night."

"You spied on your boyfriend?" asked Logan. He looked as though this had increased his respect for me.

"Kai's not my boyfriend. We were only dating, and that's over now."

"But you spied on him," he continued.

"Sort of. But the important thing is that Damien is part of the group. So we've got to follow him to find out where they meet and who else is with them."

The others nodded their agreement, and then they began plotting.

"We can't let him know we're following, or they'll disband or hide or something."

"Or go after us," said Ben.

"We'll take it in shifts," said Diego, taking the lead, as usual. "That way, he won't get suspicious seeing the same person around him all the time."

"Hey!" I cut in. "I can't ask you all to do that. My goal by bringing it up was to learn more about him and get an idea of where to find him. So *I* could tail him. But he and his group are dangerous, and I can't ask you to do that."

"We're not afraid, Lexi," said Logan. "Personally, I'd love a bit of action to make my days complete."

"This is important," Rocks said. "These guys have to be stopped, and to do that, their ritual place has to be found. You're our friend and fellow Dungeon Crawler. We won't send you on this quest alone."

"You're not *sending* me on this. Detective Ross is, and I would have volunteered if he didn't."

"Still, you're not doing it alone. End of discussion."

Having friends is a mixed bag. They're always there for you when you need them, but sometimes they'll do things that worry the hell out of you. But you've got to take the bad with the good. I just hoped they would be smart enough to not get caught.

"Now, with that mess out of the way," said Diego in his professional Dungeon Mastering tone, "we need a good plan. I think we should first find out what dorm he's in. Between all of us, we have every dorm covered. Whoever's in his dorm can keep an eye on him there and let us know, via our group chat, when he leaves at night. I'm assuming, of course, that they'll only do the rituals at night. Each of us can pick a different building to watch so that when he leaves his dorm, we can see where he goes."

We all liked the plan and started choosing buildings. I chose Grendel Hall since I knew it so well.

Balancing this case with my school workload grew difficult once we started tailing Damien. After only having begun an essay for Sociology class, a message was posted to the Crawlers' group. Damien was on the move, and he had a bag of goodies with him. I grabbed my umbrella and a dark jacket and ran from the room.

The rain came down hard, replacing the night's sounds with the steady drone of falling water. At least the wind had subsided, turning the storm from an insane deluge to a downpour. My feet splashed in the puddles that the walkways had become as I hurried to Grendel Hall. The message had come through only a couple minutes ago, and Damien was still in his dorm then. I was closer to the Anthropology building, making it likely that I'd show up first.

It was 8:45 when I slipped through the door and ducked into a darkened classroom near the front entrance. Damien had

Brad Younie

fifteen minutes to arrive before Mr. MacNair would lock the place up. I would wait until the janitor came and then come running, as though I had just been studying. It wouldn't be the first time, and old Mack was a nice guy.

I waited, and Damien didn't show. *He's not coming. It must be another building.*

The familiar click of the latch echoed down the hallway, and the huge front door opened at 8:58 and then closed seconds later. The wet squeaking of sneakers announced the approaching student. It also reminded me of the noise my shoes made when I first entered the place. I slipped out of them and picked them up in one hand. Damien strode purposefully past my hideout and continued down the main corridor.

I counted to ten and then peeked into the hall. He had opened the door to the staircase and gone through. As soon as it closed, Mr. MacNair came whistling around the corner and walked toward the entrance, his keys in hand.

Ducking back into the room before the janitor could notice me, I struggled with my newest problem. Mack was about to lock the building with me in it. At that point, I would be stranded in there overnight. But Damien would be too, which meant he *must* be up to something. And I had to see what it was.

With my eyes scrunched closed, I waited for the click, which happened almost immediately. Then Mack whistled his way back down the hallway.

Once the tune had dwindled into the distance, I padded to the stairs. I turned the doorknob gently and pulled the door open, stepping inside right away onto a landing. I could go up or down. Down led into the basement, while up went to the second floor. I listened for a long time, trying hard to hear Damien's footfalls, but there was nothing. All was quiet.

He had only gone one flight. But in which direction? I would choose up if I could because it was less creepy. The basement it was, then. If Damien were performing evil rituals, he'd go where nobody else wanted to.

My mouth worked in a silent mutter about being stupid and needing to work on my essay, but I descended to the dungeon level. Because, yeah—this felt like D&D. But in those games, we had a team of adventurers, and we were armed. I had nothing but my sneakers in one hand and my umbrella in the other. I had heard of a Victorian-era British martial art that used a cane as a weapon. *That would be good to learn*, I thought as I padded down the stairs.

The staircase ended on a concrete platform before a solitary door. A sign with the words EMPLOYEES ONLY emblazoned on it in bright yellow letters told me that what I was about to do could get me in big trouble. The fluorescent bulb above my head flickered annoyingly.

I took a moment to wipe the bottom of my shoes on my pants and then slip my feet back into them. Then, gripping the closed umbrella in my left hand, I opened the door and entered into a room bathed in almost complete darkness.

This was a boiler room. The ceaseless low rumble of a furnace set a background to the dark chamber with its concrete floor. My first thought was I had gone the wrong way, but a dim light that emanated from a solitary doorway told me to wait.

A voice drifted to me from that portal, and I knew this was the place. I approached carefully and almost stumbled over a stack of boxes. As I drew closer, I noticed no door on the opening, which explained why Damien left it open. I wanted to go up to it and listen, but that would have been too risky. So instead, the boxes would have to do.

"Everything's ready," came a voice from the other room. He sounded young, like a student. I'd never heard Kai's friends talk, so it could have been one of them.

"We're just waiting for him," said another.

"We're *always* waiting for him," whined a third person.

"This is his work," Damien snapped, and his words issued as a threat that sent a chill up my spine. "We're the acolytes. *He* is the true mage."

"Only because we let him. We can do this ourselves. Without him."

"Perhaps you should tell him, Shane," Damien spat. "Explain to our master that his services are no longer required. But don't mention my name because I'll have none of it."

A loud beep escaped my pocket, and I gasped. I yanked my phone out and silenced it. Then I knelt down as Damien's form silhouetted in the lit doorway. He wore a ceremonial robe, its hood obscuring his face. But I knew it was him. He had the broad shoulders and half-a-head height over me I had seen in Kai's room.

His gaze scanned the darkened place, finally coming to rest on the boxes I hid behind. I didn't dare duck, as any movement could give me away.

The door to the stairs opened, and someone entered. Unfortunately, the light from the stairwell framed the figure, so I couldn't see any details. The person was relatively short and stocky, but that was all I could make out. When he walked swiftly toward Damien, he vanished in the near-total darkness of the basement.

Apparently satisfied that the noise must have been the approaching cultist, Damien turned to the newcomer.

"We're ready, Master."

The master, whoever he was, said nothing but went past his acolyte to disappear into the room beyond. With one last glance around, Damien followed.

I lost no time getting out of there. I tip-toed to the door, then pulled it open as quietly as possible. It didn't squeak, which was a miracle. I slipped through and closed it gently. Then I went up the stairs, taking care to keep quiet.

That was when I ran into my next obstacle. Mack had indeed locked up, and I was sure the alarm was active. So, I was trapped in Grendel Hall with an evil cult doing rituals in the basement.

I stood there like an idiot, looking around wildly as though a way out would miraculously appear. I didn't relish searching the building for Mack with Damien and his crew lurking about.

"Lexi? Is that you?"

The way out, named Professor Landry, walked up the hallway, a messenger bag flopping lightly against his hip. A set of keys jingled in his hand.

"Professor, am I glad to see you!" I kept my voice down in case one of the evil people were to come upstairs, but my relief couldn't have been more evident.

"Locked in, eh? Some late studying?"

"Afraid so," I said with a grin. He didn't seem to notice my missing backpack.

"You were lucky I was working in my lab. The police released the room, so I was tidying up."

He went to a control panel in a corner and pressed a few buttons. Then he unlocked the front door, ushered me out into the rain, and followed behind. He then locked back up.

"Don't worry," he said with a casual grin. "You're not the first student to lose track of time. But most of them fell asleep. Somehow, I doubt that's what happened to you."

"Nope. I was wide awake. Thanks, Professor."

"Anytime."

We parted ways. Landry headed off to the nearest parking lot while I followed the wet walkway toward Wembley Hall. I messaged the group once I was safely in the dorm. Then I went to my room and called Detective Ross. I explained everything that happened, except for my friends' part in the search, and he said he'd look into it. He also told me not to return to the building that night. This was *his* job, and he didn't want anyone seeing us together.

"Isn't it a little late for that?" I asked.

"Nope. Just do as I say and stay away. Go to bed or study or something."

Well, I *did* have an essay to write.

31

My phone rang at 8:00 a.m. while I was finishing up my essay.

"The next time you do what you did, *don't* do what you did."

The frown that statement brought to my face lasted for only an instant. Ross's gruff manner had become predictable. "And good morning to you, too, Detective."

He grunted.

"Now, what are you talking about? Let me guess! You didn't want me to follow Damien and find the ritual room? You're welcome for that."

"Don't be so quick!" he replied. His tone reminded me of

when he shot down one of his men who was goofing around. But he paused before continuing, and when he did, he had lost that edge. "You're not a cop. You haven't been trained to do the things I've been asking you to do. So I can't blame you for your mistake."

A frown invaded my face. "What mistake?"

"You shouldn't have followed him. Staking out Grendel Hall was good. Watching him enter the building right as the place was about to close up gave us important information. But you tailed him to the basement and got caught. But, again, you didn't know better, so I'm not mad. I should have known you'd do something like that, and so it's on me."

"How was following Damien a mistake? I found concrete evidence that he's part of a cult doing rituals in that basement. In fact, I pointed you right to it!"

Ross paused before speaking. That was his second hesitation in this call. He was trying hard to keep his cool. Had I done the wrong thing?

"They saw you."

"No way. Trust me, if Damien had seen me, he'd have gone after me."

"Okay, then you tipped them off. Did you do anything, or did something happen that could have let the cultists know they were being watched, even though they didn't *see* you?"

The phone notification popped instantly into my head, and my eyes closed as a cringe replaced my frown. He was right, after all. I *had* screwed up.

"I get it. I made a noise, and Damien came out of the ritual room and looked around. But then his leader showed up, and

I thought Damien assumed it was him all along. I guess I was wrong."

"You were, but it's understandable. As a result, the cultists packed up and left. Probably right after you did. There were signs of activity. Dried candle wax on the floor in a circle. There were footprints but nothing substantial. We have enough to back up your claim that people were down there last night, but that's all."

"So, what *should* I have done?" I needed to know because we were back to square one, which was not my expertise.

"Do the stakeouts. Keep your eyes open on the kid. Then report to me when he does something interesting. You can send me texts. No matter how big or small. But if he goes into some dark, creepy place, *don't follow*! Message me and watch for him to leave."

I nodded my understanding, even though he couldn't see it. "Got it. Spy on the suspect from a distance and let you know what I find out. To be honest, it sounds a lot easier."

We started over. Once again, the Dungeon Crawlers began their mission to spy on Damien Hull and report to the group what he did. I thought of muting my notifications but decided against it in light of my new hands-off policy regarding the case.

Juggling classes, schoolwork, and tailing a bad guy turned out to be a challenging task. Of course, it was still Sunday when we started. Even so, as Damien seemed to do nothing interesting that day, the week began with a full load of spy work added to our everyday responsibilities.

My friends took it in stride. They were even cheerful about the concept of following our suspect around campus. However, Logan was a bit of a problem. He was itching to start trouble with the guy. But Tony knew how to rein his boyfriend in and keep him from ruining everything.

We didn't see any reason to change our original plan, as that part had worked flawlessly. So I went about my business until Tuesday night when I got a ping on the group chat that Damien was leaving the dorm with a loaded backpack. I dropped the pencil on my Calculus book and ran out to spy on Grendel Hall.

The weather was in my favor this time, being clear with stars speckling the sky. I hid among the bushes that lined the front of the building. If Damien went anywhere near the place, I would see him, and it was doubtful he'd notice me.

A few minutes after I was tucked snugly in my spot amid the foliage, Damien's sullen form became visible on the walkway, heading toward my position. Unfortunately, the moon hadn't risen far yet, so my only glimpses of him were as he passed underneath each lamp that illuminated the paved path. His face was set in a dour frown, which wasn't surprising since he always looked like that. But he glanced from side to side as he walked, as though checking if anyone was watching.

My muscles tensed in anticipation as he approached the stairs to the front door of Grendel Hall . . .

And then passed it.

Damien didn't even cast a glance at it as he strode by the steps and the bushes I crouched in.

Where the hell is he going? I thought and messaged my

friends that he was heading toward my dorm.

Then it struck me. *He's visiting Kai. Of course!*

As soon as it was safe, I climbed out of my hiding place and fell into step a good way behind him. Once I was sure Wembley was his destination, I'd tell the group, and Jenna would get into position to see him enter Kai's room.

But to my surprise, Damien turned off the main path and went down a walk that led to the street. It was a side lane that ran through a copse of decorative trees on its way to the side road I always took to go to the diner. He was leaving campus.

Shit!

I messaged Ross that he was heading off campus and told him the direction, then I turned to follow him. After all, this was still a public part of school grounds.

It didn't take long for me to notice that Damien was no longer on the path. I slowed my pace and scanned the trees that surrounded me.

A heavy object struck me from behind and sent me stumbling forward off the trail. Strong arms grabbed my shoulders, spun me around, and Damien, his face still rigid, shoved me up against a tree, his right hand holding my chest pinned to the narrow trunk.

This was one of the first holds you're taught to break in Karate class, and my body went to work on it before my mind could catch up.

I grabbed his hand as he held me against the trunk. I threw my other hand upward into his elbow, locking his arm out straight. I twisted, and Damien was forced to bend over forward. Now I had him under my control.

I opened my mouth to tell him not to move when he kicked my leg out from under me, and the two of us tumbled to the ground. This was a desperate act, as I could have broken his arm while falling.

But I didn't.

It took me by complete surprise, and I let go of him. We hit the pavement but were both in motion. I rose and ran, trying to break from the tree cover before he could catch me. If I did, we'd be in plain sight of anyone walking around on campus, including the cops that were still on guard at Fenway Hall.

And, of course, The Door watched the whole thing, standing like a sentinel between two trees. I bolted past it in my desperate dash for the Quad.

Damien thudded into me, and I fell sprawling on my face, my arms taking most of the scrapes from the impact.

He spun me roughly around and, once again, pinned me. But this time, he did so with all his weight. Though he was no body builder, he was bigger than me, and so I couldn't even squirm.

A thought flashed into my mind at that moment. It was a terrible fear from every movie where a woman was held helpless to a man.

But instead of going for my clothes, Damien punched me hard in the face.

Excruciating pain exploded from my nose to my chin, and I swear there were stars before my eyes.

Fists hit me first on my cheek and then on the side of my head. My noggin was battered back and forth like a punching bag. And I couldn't think straight, much less fight.

Then the attacks stopped. Damien's hands went to my shoulders, holding me down to the ground, and he leaned his face close to mine.

"Leave me alone, bitch!" he hissed. "You're going to keep your nose out of my business, or I'll do a lot more than mess up your pretty face. You'll wish—"

I never knew what I would wish because my head shot forward and struck him with a surprising amount of force. At once, I twisted my body, and he fell off me. I leaped to my feet, then, swinging my leg upward in an arc, I brought it down hard, heel first, onto his ugly mug. There was a crack and blood, and his hands went to his now-wrecked nose.

The fight was over, at least for me. With all my remaining strength, I darted toward campus, and this time, the asshole let me. I burst from the trees and stumbled into the Quad. People saw me and rushed to my aid. Before long, they surrounded me and helped me back to my dorm. A few kids ran down the path in search of my attacker, but it was doubtful Damien would be there.

The damage was minor. Damien didn't break my nose, and even though my head ached like a son of a bitch, I was sure there was no concussion. I was covered in bruises, and blood rivered from one nostril, but otherwise, I was okay.

A familiar face appeared before me as the group of four students helped me along. It was Tom Prichard.

"Who did this?" he said. His expression showed he intended to exact vengeance on my behalf with violence.

"I don't know," came my reply. Now was not the time to tell him, and Damien needed to remain free to lead us to the new ritual place.

"Describe him."

"Not here."

"Tell me now, before he gets away."

"He already has, so there's no rush. Let's go to my room, and we'll talk there. *Please.*" To emphasize things, my legs gave a fit of wobbling, and I nearly fell. Tom caught me and helped me along. The others ran ahead and ushered us through the entrance.

We made it home with no further trouble, and Jenna was beside herself when we opened the door. Once I was sitting on my bed with a steamy mug of cocoa that Jenna forced into my hands, the two waited for me to tell my story.

"Where's your crutch?" I said as I cradled the hot cup and gave it a sniff.

Tom looked around as though he had just noticed it was gone.

"I don't know. Must have left it outside."

"Don't you need it to walk?"

"I guess not," he said simply. He continued to watch me expectantly.

I realized at that moment, as Tom watched me with so much concern, that he needed to know what was going on. He had always been there for me throughout everything that happened. He listened to me when I described things that nobody in their right mind would believe. Looking at him now, I knew he was as close a friend as anyone could be.

I related what I understood of the cult casting spells to turn ghosts into monsters. And I told him about Top Hat. I explained it was what happened to his tagalong ghost, Dave Simons. Then, at last, I filled him in on Damien.

He sat there when my tale was over, considering it for some time. Jenna came over and dabbed at my face with a wet cloth. (I wouldn't let her do it while I was talking, no matter how much she tried).

"You don't want me to go after Damien, do you?" It was a question, but he knew the answer.

I shook my head. "We need to find where they meet. And that means we have to follow him."

"You won't. Not anymore." He was far less wordy when he was angry.

"I have to. I'm working for the police."

"No." The word assassinated my argument with its single, powerful syllable. Both Jenna and I jumped a little.

"You've been made. Damien knows you're following him, so he'll be looking for you. He'll never expect me. And I have a lot of friends. He won't be able to go anywhere without me knowing."

"No, no, no, no," I said, shaking my head vigorously. "We can't bring anyone else into this. Ross would kill me."

"Don't worry. My friends aren't going to know why we're watching him, and I'll only recruit those I trust. You have to let me do this because I'm right. If you try to follow him, he'll spot you, and his buddies will disappear."

As much as I wanted to disagree with him, I couldn't. I had to lie low, and someone had to take over for me. Besides, I had left him out of the entire case until now, so he would be the last person Damien would suspect.

"Okay. You convinced me. I'll add you to my friends' group chat. They're already following him. Now, if you'll leave, I'd like to get some much-needed rest."

He smiled and went to the door. "I'll check up on you later."

Jenna stood staring after him.

"Now, why aren't you seeing him?"

At that moment, I had no answer for her.

32

Over the next few days, Tom enacted his network of spies to watch Damien Hull's every move. The group chat was busy with people posting his location at all hours. The Dungeon Crawlers, of course, continued their vigil as well, but I think they switched their attention to Kai. Ben thought my old crush was dirty and set out to prove it. I had told him he was right but that following Kai wouldn't solve the case. Though he agreed, he still pursued his personal mission.

Tom became my bodyguard. He met me at the door to Wembley Hall when Jenna and I left for breakfast, and he'd join us. He then walked me to each class. This made him late to all of his classes, save Literature, which we had together, but he said nothing about that. I resented his insistence that I needed protection. Still, I enjoyed his company and decided it could have been worse.

Detective Ross was furious about my attack but wasn't about to change the plan. Damien was an adult now, and Ross gave me the impression he planned to throw the book at the guy. He also agreed with Tom's assessment that I should stay out of the stakeout. I told Ross about what Tom and his friends were doing. He didn't appreciate getting them involved but had to admit it was the best option.

Yet Damien refused to cooperate. Oh, we knew where he was, all right. At all times. He'd go to breakfast in the cafeteria, attend his classes, visit his pals in their dorm rooms, study in the Student Center, and then return to his room at night. At no time did our suspect do anything out of the ordinary. Of course, that, itself, was *out* of the ordinary. He must have known we were watching him or assumed we were. We continued as though it were the latter. "Eventually," Ross said, "he'll slip up."

It was eleven o'clock on Friday evening, and Tom and I left Strout Hall. We had a fun night of D&D. It was for me, anyway. Tom hung out and watched. He looked interested and joined in on our banter but refused to play, even when Diego offered him a character. Logan didn't like his presence at first, but he warmed up after Tom laughed at a few of his jokes and gave him as much respect as he did the others.

Tom's leg seemed better. He still limped a little, but he had given up the crutch.

The sky was clear, and the air warm—for a night in the

Ghost World, of course. Everything is relative to me. A light breeze blew in from Boston Harbor, coaxing my hair into a gentle dance.

"That was fun," Tom said as we strolled through the Quad.

"You sound surprised."

"I always thought it was, you know . . . nerd stuff."

"It is, but that doesn't mean it's not fun."

"I've got a lot to learn about you, don't I?"

"Yeah. But you can enjoy that, too. I'm not your average girl."

"You can say that again." He chuckled as he spoke, bringing a smile to my face.

"So, what's your deal?" I said to him. "You can't be defined by your sports shirts."

"And what if I am? Would that be a bad thing?"

I shrugged. There was a time when I would have said "yes," but now that seemed lame. For years, I'd had the preconception that jocks were big and tough and mindless. They were bullies, every single one of them, and they did it to make up for the fact they had no synapses to rub together. Yup. I had accepted the dumb jock stereotype, and now it made me feel dirty. He was a jock like I was a nerd, and we both had our misconceptions about the other's group. After all, I knew there was more to Tom than being a sports nut. He was kind, loyal, and even smart.

"No. That wouldn't be a bad thing at all. But I don't think it defines you any more than my gaming books define me."

"Does that mean you're not afraid to learn more about me?"

"Not afraid. Nervous, maybe. And very curious."

Tom grinned and opened his mouth to reply. But I never found out what he was going to say.

A wooden club came down on Tom's head from behind, and he dropped to the pavement with a groan. At the same moment, a hand appeared over my mouth, and an arm wrapped around my body, trying to force me to the ground.

I lifted my legs up to crouch in midair. My attacker hadn't expected that and fell forward. I landed on my feet and sprang with all my strength, out of his grip, and ran for help. There were too many enemies, and Tom was already down. So, escape was my best plan.

I'm a fast runner. Really, I am. But lately, it didn't seem that way, as both times I tried to run from an attack, someone tackled me from behind. This time, other people joined my tackler. Two of them pinned me to the ground on my stomach while the third stuck me with a needle. Then they held me in place until everything got wobbly. Of course, I struggled, but at that point, I was no match for three men who were stronger and heavier than me.

At last, blackness enveloped me, and I knew no more.

My head hurt, and I felt woozy. Then, slowly, my eyes opened. I didn't want them to because my mind screamed that stealth was imperative, but they wouldn't listen to me. The light was dim, but I could make out wooden beams with lots of dust and cobwebs hanging from them.

A basement ceiling.

The walk in the Quad came back to me with sudden clarity.

We were attacked. Tom went down. I was drugged. The cult had abducted me.

Oh, fucking great!

I moved my arm as slowly as possible and found it bound firmly to whatever I lay on. *Tied down. Okay.* I wanted to look around the place but didn't dare. It was likely to let them know I was awake. So instead, I used my other senses.

An odd odor hung heavy in the air. Incense, for sure, but there was something else. A stench, strong and unpleasant. Feet scuffled on dry concrete. Two, maybe three people. No one spoke.

Realization of my current plight dawned on me, and my body trembled of its own accord as terror took hold of my mind and heart.

I was to be sacrificed for a spell.

Okay, okay! I shouted in my head. *Calm down. Slow breaths. Don't give yourself away.*

"Ah, you're awake." Damien's voice came from my right. Though it was clear the jig was up, my eyes remained glued to the ceiling. Who said I had to make it easy for him?

"Stubborn as always, I see," he continued. A hint of triumph decorated his conversational tone as he approached me. I wanted to punch his face repeatedly until he couldn't talk anymore. "But you should look around. Someone who is as fascinated by the Ghost World as you should appreciate what we are doing here."

Pushing my fear as far back in my gut as I could manage, I rolled my eyes as though disinterested and turned my head to let the room into view.

And then I gasped, ruining the entire facade.

All this time, I had expected to see the standard Western magic tradition with a circle drawn on the ground and pentagrams everywhere. Instead, the sight before me was far more grotesque. Strings hung from the ceiling in places that were probably important to the ritual with body parts dangling suspended from them. They all swayed gently as the other three cultists worked to prepare. Though none of the bits dripped blood, each looked fresh, as if they had been carved off something that had been alive a day ago. In the dim lighting, I couldn't tell what they were from. I didn't want to know. Candles illuminated the place, their flickering flames casting everything in an eerie glow. The shadows moved in a macabre dance.

And on one wall stood The Door. The door in my mind that occasionally appeared when things were about to turn nasty for me in the Ghost World.

"How does this have anything to do with ghosts?" As much as I tried to keep my voice straight, it wavered some. His face lit up from it.

"With these rituals, we won't just summon spirits. We'll *control* them. Once we get it right, they'll do our bidding. It's a shame you will never see it, though. After all, you'll be dead by the time the spell is complete."

"So, I'm a sacrifice?"

"Fitting, isn't it? The girl who pretends to talk to ghosts is sacrificed to give us mastery over them."

"You think I pretend? That I make it all up?"

"Nobody can speak with spirits. Especially you. There's nothing exceptional about you in the least."

"What building is this?" I asked suddenly. An idea had snuck into my mind. It was desperate, and there were no guarantees it would work. But I had to try something.

"Don't worry, your phone's gone. We smashed it when we grabbed you so that your friends can't follow us."

"Still, what building are we in?"

He shrugged as though he decided the information couldn't hurt. "Grendel."

I snorted. "Grendel Hall? Where you were before?" Ross knew about this place. He'd come with his team if he tried to contact me and I didn't respond. My heart rose a little.

"Nobody will expect us to come back here. Cops are stupid."

"Yeah," I lied. "You're probably right."

Three more robed figures entered, bringing the group of cultists to seven. I had once read that it was a magic number. One of the new people joined Damien at the sacrificial altar, which I was tied to.

He removed his hood and, with yet another shock, Mack MacNair, the friendly janitor, smiled down at me.

"Hello there, Miss Downs. It's a shame you had to go and get nosy. I rather liked you. But you'll make a good sacrifice. They like 'em nice and young."

"Who? The ghosts?" Despite how terrible things looked, I still tried my best to be strong.

"That's right. They want fresh meat when they come a-callin'. And I couldn't pick anyone fresher than you. Goodbye now. It's time to get on with it."

At that moment, all the people in the room put their hoods

back up and took their places. Damien lifted an incense burner while Mack opened a book. It wasn't an old tome, but something he must have created himself. *Probably a translation of the text they stole,* I thought grimly.

If I'm going to try this, I've got to do it now.

The whole banishment debacle showed me that I might have abilities that I never knew existed. Some of my friends suggested as much. It was possible, though unlikely, I could contact other ghosts that haunt this building. And maybe they could help.

I couldn't run to The Door, but it wasn't a physical thing, anyway. Somehow, the portal was in my head, so maybe I didn't have to get up to open it.

I closed my eyes and thought about The Door. Its wooden frame was elegant, its knob made of brass and etched with strange symbols. Mentally, I reached out for that handle and was surprised when the touch of its cold metal came to my hand. *I don't know about this. That door is dangerous, and I've avoided it all my life. But right now, I'm desperate.*

I gripped it and pulled with my mind.

A frigid air washed over my body, and I shivered. The sounds of the ritual happening around me grew suddenly faint, as though a wall had descended between us. It was late at night, and I already had a foot inside the Ghost World, but now I had slid farther into that world. *Had I gone all the way in?* I thought. *Could the assholes even see me?*

I risked opening an eye and saw the robed cultists continuing their chanting and dancing. Everything looked dim and indistinct, more so than before. But I must still have been with the living, as one of them glanced at me and didn't react.

I had opened The Door in my mind, and things had happened. But what then? What could I do?

Mack came over and smiled down at me. He motioned to a hooded peon, who joined him at his side. Mack handed him a large ceremonial knife. It looked sharp.

"Put your hood down," he commanded his underling. The man obeyed, and I gasped.

Kai's black hair and handsome face were revealed before me. He didn't look as pleased as Mack. He frowned and avoided my gaze as he stood like a dummy, holding the knife.

Mack grinned. "I'm giving you the honors. But don't hesitate! Her despair will give us power." The villain now began chanting. By its tempo, the ritual was coming to its crescendo.

Kai gulped but raised the dagger above me. I tried to make eye contact, but he forced his eyes on my chest. Where my heart still beat. His mouth kept moving, and I think he was repeating the words *I'm sorry*.

"You don't have to do this," I said. In movies, the kid would respond with, "I have to." But Kai ignored me. He stopped mouthing and listened to Mack's chanting.

Motion erupted in the room. Several people had rushed in and attacked the robed men. One sped to the altar and began wrestling with Kai.

It was Tom.

The two wrestled over me for control of the knife. Tom was strong, and Kai seemed to have lost his nerve. The jock yanked the blade from his hand. But Mack grabbed Tom's arm, and they now fought for the weapon. Kai slipped back from the altar.

Coward!

Tearing my eyes from them, I looked around to see who else had joined the fight. I recognized Ben right away. He was swinging one of those mini baseball bats at a cultist, keeping him at bay. But his enemy was trying to find an opening. Ben was no fighter, and neither were the other Dungeon Crawlers, now engaged in battle. In D&D terms, they were all first level and squishy.

I had to do something quickly. Because those cultists planned to kill, and my friends were their immediate targets.

Once again, I squeezed my eyes shut and tried to probe the contents of The Door. There had to be something I could do to help.

Inside the portal, everything was mist, but shapes took form before me as I stared. Professor Harrison wandered around a hallway, glancing into the rooms he passed. Millicent, Top Hat's ghost friend, sat in a corner, sobbing morosely. Finally, Dave Simons came into focus, complete with his monstrous visage.

But as I looked at Dave, I could see he wasn't alone. A dark and nasty entity had pushed him aside in his own ghostly body. And it didn't belong there.

More ghosts wandered into view. The one Dave had mentioned, the Haunt of the Fenway Hall basement. Albert. I had never met him, but I felt sure it was him. Then Missy Baskins from Wembley Hall. She was following a group of girls down a hallway. She was trying to emulate their mannerisms. I had to remember to tell her not to. She was better the way she was.

I did something then. It wasn't a thing I intended to do, but my mind reached out and told the spirits to come. *Come and fight. Exact vengeance on my enemies, who are your enemies. End our pain and misery. And avenge Mr. Randolf, the ghost with the top hat.*

And they moved.

Through The Door, they emerged. From *me*, they spawned. Out into the room, ghosts appeared, and everyone there could see them. And the spirits were angry.

The fight had gone badly for my friends. Ben and Rocks and the other Dungeon Crawlers were now on the ground. Some still moved, but all were out for the count. Tom sat against a wall with a knife wound. Mack had once again turned to me and was about to thrust the bloody blade downward to my chest.

Then Dave Simons leaped, and Mack shrieked as the possessed ghost bit his throat out. Blood sprayed across my face. The evil man's scream transformed into a muted gurgle, and the janitor stared at his own creation with bulging eyes as the life poured from his gaping neck.

Professor Harrison threw himself at a cultist and pummeled him, driving him to the floor. Millicent gouged the eyes of another. Missy toyed with her foe. She let the man punch at her, and each hit did nothing to the ghost. It struck home, but she barely felt it because he was not as far in Missy's world as I was. Then the 80s girl, getting bored, started punching and scratching him. Her hairsprayed locks bounced gently with each strike. She didn't know how to fight, and it was almost comical. But her punches hurt him, and her opponent fell to the ground and lay still.

The fight was over in a couple of minutes. The ghosts who left them alone terrified my friends. The Crawlers remained transfixed by the horror of what they saw.

Tom, however, pulled himself painfully to his feet. He yanked the knife from Mack's corpse and staggered to the altar.

He smiled and said something to me, and I wished I could have heard him. Then he cut my bonds.

I reached out and grabbed the ghosts, one at a time, and sent them through The Door, back to where they had come from. I released them from their duty and let them return to their un-lives. Then I closed the portal.

The mist vanished from my eyes, and the room snapped into focus before me.

I sat up sweating, even though every inch of my body felt like I had just come in from a naked run in the Arctic.

"It's over," I said.

Tom nodded and toppled to the ground. The knife fell to clatter on the concrete.

Then sounds came from the outside, and Detective Ross entered, gun in hand, ready to deal justice, but it was too late. He and his teammates looked around in stunned silence. Then Ross ran to me.

"Are you all right?" he said, looking me over for injuries.

The words barely registered. My eyes scanned the bloody corpses of the robed men, desperate to find the one cultist I didn't want to see. But at last, I found him.

Kai lay on the floor beside the door. Scratches marred his perfect face. His mouth hung slack as blood oozed all over him.

Dead. My mind reeled. *Kai's dead. I killed him. I killed them all.*

Ross grabbed my head and forced me to look at him. His expression was soft as he examined me, but there was something in his eyes. Something I had never seen there before. Horror.

"I killed them," I said, but my voice sounded distant, as though it came from miles away. Everything was like that. The world had grown dim and muted.

Detective Holtz dropped to his knees beside Tom with a medical kit in his hands. *At least I hadn't murdered Tom,* I thought, then collapsed on the altar.

I was spent mentally, emotionally, and somehow, even physically. As soon as I hit the slab, I passed into a restless sleep filled with swirling mists, ravening ghosts, and people with their necks torn out.

33

The steady beep from a heart monitor droned in my head for several minutes before I realized I was awake. My eyes opened to a fluorescent light flickering annoyingly above me. But illumination from other lights made the place bright.

I should have been used to this sight by now, but it still surprised me.

I lay on a gurney in a little alcove in a large hospital reception room. Curtains formed two walls, and the third side was open to a wide area full of doctors and nurses going about their business. An extended counter was there, manned by people in blue scrubs.

Jenna Rand sat in a chair beside my makeshift bed, and she

beamed when she saw me turn my head.

"You're awake! How are you feeling?"

"A little tired. Why am I here? I mean, I never got stabbed or anything. So I should be okay."

"You were unconscious, and the doctors said your fluid levels were down. But they say you look healthy. So you'll come home today."

I glanced at my arm, where an IV ran up to a bag half-full of clear liquid. My heart monitor beeped a nice steady rhythm that sounded healthy to me.

"Good. Because I need to talk to Detective Ross. I have to find out what happened."

Jenna frowned. "You don't know? You were there."

"Don't worry!" I blurted as Jenna's face twisted in concern. "I don't have amnesia or anything. It was all a blur to me. Jenna, I tapped into more ghost-related abilities, and I think I killed people because of it."

"You did?" This was the first she'd heard of it. But of course, Ross would have kept it confidential. Police investigation and all.

I nodded. "I'll explain it later, but I need answers right now."

"You need rest," Jenna countered.

"But I've got too many questions."

Jenna gave me a look that my mother had given me unduly many times in my life. But then she shrugged. "I'll find someone to check if you're ready to go."

The doctor said I was. She took my temperature and checked a few other things. Then she disconnected me from the machines and let me get dressed. Jenna had brought me clean clothes. She was so practical.

We stopped by to see Tom because they rushed him there, too. He had an actual recovery room, unlike my little nook. I didn't envy him because it meant his injuries were a lot worse than mine.

My heart sank when I entered. Tom lay on the bed with various wires and tubes sticking out of him. I remembered him slumped in a corner with blood all over him. But he turned his head, and his face lit up when he saw me.

"Lexi! You're up and about! How are you doing?"

I went to his side. His complexion wasn't as pasty as I feared it would be. In fact, he looked pretty good. Jenna stepped away to look out the window. She wanted to give us time to talk. Unnecessary, but appreciated.

"I should ask you that question," I said with a smile.

"You first."

"There's nothing wrong with me. I guess the ghost stuff I did last night wore me out. Also, the cultists drugged me. So I slept and . . . apparently sweat too much? They let me sleep and gave me a saline drip. I'm good to go! Now you."

Tom grinned. "I got a knife wound on my side. Nicked my kidney. They did an exploratory procedure, but there was no actual damage. I lost a lot of blood, and I've got a big scar to show for it, but I'll heal."

"And your kidney's fine?"

"Yup. Scraped, but not cut open. So I have to take it easy for a while. And that'll be a piece of cake, now that everything's all over."

"So, it is? It's all done?"

"Yeah. Before the paramedics took me out of there, I saw all the robed guys down for the count. And there were a ton of cops dealing with them. It's over."

"What about my other friends?"

"The D&D nerds? They're fine. Some of them were getting up before I left, and the medics didn't seem worried about the others."

The breath that I had been unintentionally holding blew out at that moment, and a great weight lifted from my shoulders.

"That's good. That's really good."

"So, what's next?" He had a funny expression I couldn't fathom.

"Debriefing, I guess. I have to call Detective Ross and see what he needs from me. I don't know if anyone took your statement, but they will. Once that's done, your part is over."

"Same with you, right?"

"I was kind of working for the police as a consultant. So I expect I'll give my report and then sign a paper or something and get paid."

"Damn, I like yours better. I got nothing out of it but a pain in my side."

"I wouldn't say that. You made a lot of friends." I grinned. He grinned. It was good.

A moment of silence passed as we both shared awkward smiles. At last, I broke it.

"I guess I should call Ross. Get it all over with. I just want to be done with the whole affair."

"Yeah. You should do that."

"I'll be back to visit. Later today or tonight."

"I'm holding you to that. But I'll call you if the doctors let me leave early."

"Then I'd see you at your dorm."

"Hotel room. Evil monster ghost. Remember?"

"Oh, shit!" I said, and the weight of the world descended on me once again. It wasn't over after all. "I've got to fix that."

"Why must it be you?"

"Because who else will? I'm the expert."

He grimaced. "Then do it. But I still expect that visit."

"You'll get it. Don't worry."

I called Ross as we left the hospital. He said he was at "the scene" and would meet me at my dorm room in an hour.

Jenna went to visit friends when Ross showed up. He looked tired.

"Were you there all night?" I asked.

"No. I rested."

"What? Like an hour?"

"Two."

"Being exhausted all the time doesn't do anyone any good, you know."

"Tell that to my boss."

"I'm all better and ready to get to work," I said, getting straight to the point.

"What work? You're done. I just need your report. Tell me what happened, and we're all set."

"Nope. That's not all. I have to figure out how to cure Dave

Simons."

"Dave . . ." He broke off, then the bulb went on in his head. "The monster in Fenway Hall? You can fix him?"

"I have to. I was hoping to look at the books and notes the cultists had. They did this to him, so there might be a way to undo it without removing Dave."

"But wouldn't Dave want to move on?"

I shrugged. "I can't speak for him. And who knows what the banishing ritual really does to them. So let's focus on getting him back to normal."

"Okay, but first, I need to know what happened last night. Tell me the whole story. You weren't supposed to be nosing around."

"I wasn't. They kidnapped me." Then I launched into the tale, telling everything, including what I did with the spirits.

"The cultists' deaths are on me. *I* pulled the ghosts into the room and controlled them. I *made* them do it."

"No, you didn't. You sent them to fight the bad guys. You didn't make them kill anyone. Only one cultist died last night. Tavin MacNair. Your friend Dave killed him, and that monster did what he normally would. You couldn't control how they fought. To be honest, I bet the spooks all wanted to do what they did, considering what the cultists were doing to them."

He paused because of the slack-jawed, gaping stare I gave him. Only one died. Mack. But what about . . .

"Kai Peters?" I said, my voice barely audible.

"What's that? Kai Peters? Right." He opened up a folder and flipped through it. "He got beat up pretty bad. His face will never be the same, but he's okay. Why? He was wearing a robe, and a ghost took him down. According to him, it was, quote, 'a crazy bitch with big hair,' end-quote."

"He's okay? He'll live?"

"Yeah. But he'll live in jail. We're throwing the book at him like all the others. Why? Is there something I should know?"

I hesitated. Did I want him to go to jail? Part of me said "no," but the rest of me said he had to. Kai went to the ritual to do horrific things. He wore the robe, and he made an attempt. He might have chickened out in the end, but that didn't make him innocent. And I think he *was* about to kill me before Mack and Tom started fighting. As long as he was alive, I could be happy with him rotting in jail.

I shook my head.

"They're all going to jail?" I asked. "For what? Turning ghosts into monsters?"

Ross chuckled. "Did you see all those body parts hanging from the ceiling? They were from people. People they killed. And do you remember what they tried to do to you? That's attempted murder. Nope. We're putting them away for a long time."

Even Kai. But that's okay. I didn't really know him. I never did, and I don't think I ever will. Do I want to? I couldn't answer that question.

"Can I see their stuff? I need to get to work."

Fenway Hall looked the same as it did the night the team and I searched for Dave. It was quiet. The windows gave us no light, as we had waited until 9:00 p.m. to do the ritual. The power was on, of course, and I could hear the dull rumble of the furnace, but everything else remained still.

When I first woke up that morning, I had the weight of several deaths on my shoulders. Now, I had only one. And you could argue that Mack brought it on himself. After all, he turned Dave into the monster that killed him. To be honest, I didn't feel so bad anymore. The cultists deserved the beatings they got. I had no qualms about that. And Mack. Like I said. That was karma.

And I was ready to remove the entity possessing Dave Simons. It was my way to atone for using him as a weapon.

We stood in the lobby, myself and Detective Ross. He brought his entire team. All of them looked serious because they had all been there when Dave went on his rampage. They also were at last night's crime scene and saw the carnage Dave had done to Mack. They all believed in the supernatural now and would do their job to the best of their abilities.

"Okay. How are we going to do this?" said Ross.

"It's a ritual. We have to follow the instructions to the letter. You all have copies of it. Each of you has something to do. Some of you will perform the ritual. It takes three or seven people to do it. Those are magic numbers, so we have to use one of them. I'd recommend three. The rest of you can be ready in case things go bad."

Detective Lewis raised her hand. "It says here that the spirit must be present throughout the process. But this—entity is possessing Simons. Wouldn't it try to get away?"

"Right," I said. "My friends and I used another spell and circle that kept Top Hat trapped in one place, but it was hard getting the ghost into it. So I'll do what I did last night and summon him to us. I should be able to control him and hold him here as you do your part. In theory, it should be simple." But of course, I've found that nothing ever was.

The team set up. Baker, Lewis, and Elliot would perform the ritual, and everyone else would take up defensive positions. Holtz would be ready to help with any injuries. Ross planned to be my partner and ensure I was okay as I controlled Dave into position. There were so many variables, but they were professionals and did what they were supposed to.

Yes, this was crazy.

I walked over to The Door that had appeared on a wall. It looked as forbidding as ever. To be honest, I still didn't trust it and thought it would be better not to use it if I could help it. But Dave needed me. I grabbed the knob and pulled it open. Once again, everything changed for me. The sounds in the room shrank and became indistinct, as though they came through a wall. A gray mist swirled around inside the portal.

I scanned the contents of the fog, searching for Dave. It didn't take long to locate him. The ghosts that haunted my current location seemed the easiest to find. Once he was visible, I grabbed him and yanked him through the door, throwing him out into the lobby and commanding him to stay still.

Dave did what I said, but the creature within him struggled for control. It fought with me to free itself. It saw fresh meat and wanted to tear into them, and it was all I could do to keep it from doing that. I could see the beast before me, screaming and growling as it thrashed in vain against the mental bonds I had thrown around it. The three detectives began the ritual right away, wasting no time and forcing themselves to not look at the entity that strove to kill them. The others held their iron weapons ready, putting themselves between Dave and the spell-casters. Ross was at my side, his gaze shifting from me to his team, then back to me. His expression was grim.

Although I could control ghosts, the thing possessing him wasn't one. It was some other entity that didn't belong here or in the Ghost World. It was utterly alien. And that meant I had no dominion over it. Luckily, it couldn't leave Dave's spectral body, which I held still through force of will. But if it escaped . . .

The ritual began, and though I could see them moving and hear their voices, my concentration on the monster prevented me from knowing how well they did their job.

The entity became even more enraged when it recognized what the three detectives were doing. It thrust itself against Dave with enough fury to force the poor ghost to stumble. He took a few shambling steps closer to the line of cops blocking the ritual and then halted. Bronson and the others raised their weapons threateningly. Dave snarled and spat but remained in his new position.

But the attempt had taken a toll on me. Sweat poured down my face, and my consciousness slipped. I almost fainted. Dave would be freed if I did, and the creature would kill them all.

The beast grew passive for a moment, and I knew it was prepping for a redoubled attack. With all my concentration, I built up as much strength in my hold on Dave as I could, and I could feel the poor ghost shrieking in silence as his body twisted in agony.

Once again, the monster threw itself at the team. I screamed in misery as though the beast were physically mauling me.
But I remained firm. I couldn't fail. Hell, I couldn't weaken. If
my guard went down even a little, we'd all die. So, I pushed
everything I had into my defenses, preventing Dave from moving.

His arms reached outward, nearly touching Yang's face.
The man knew better than to strike at the monster while I was
holding it in place, and so he stood there, Dave's questing fingers an inch from his nose.

And then, with a deafening scream, the entity within Dave
vanished. The sensation was like playing tug-o-war when the
other team suddenly let go. I felt myself flung away from Dave,
and my force dropped. The ghost was free, but this time, he
didn't attack. Instead, he collapsed to the floor and cried. The
portal was still open. I had to return Dave to where he had
been. Even though he would remain in the building, it would
make him less corporeal. It would put things to right.

But not yet. The poor kid had gone through so much that,
in my pity, I let him rest. He lay there, curled in a ball, crying
his eye out, and we watched.

At last, his cries turned to sobs, and he looked up at me.

"Th-thank you," was all he could say. I cast him a weak
smile, then, with my mind, sent him gently through the door,
closing it behind him.

I wanted to sleep for days. Or, at least, to hide in my room
with the lights down low and have no interaction with anyone,
save maybe Jenna. But even then, in small doses.

There was something about tapping into my ghostly powers that I didn't like. Both times I opened The Door in my mind, it became easier to do it. Now, it was visible in my head every damn time I closed my eyes. You would think I would want bright lights and lots of activity to take that image from me. But I had developed a craving for darkness and solitude.

I hoped it was temporary.

Jenna forced me to visit the Crawlers and play some D&D. She said it would do me good. Of course, I told her about this change, and she didn't like it one bit. She packed my bag full of gaming gear, called my friends, and sent me out across the Quad to Strout Hall for a night of therapy.

She was right.

I walked casually down the paved path through the big grass lawn. It lost the eerie appearance it had taken when Top Hat first attacked. Instead, it was once again the nice, safe, happy Quad it had been at the start of the semester.

Fenway Hall had reopened, and students were everywhere, carrying their bags into the dorm. After tonight, the campus would be back to normal.

Tom returned from the hospital. I had visited him already, and he seemed better, except he wasn't supposed to move around much and would spend a fair amount of time in bed. Tom said his teachers were letting him attend remotely from his room. He didn't want to be a couch potato, but he agreed to do as he was told if I promised to visit him after each Literature class to go over the lecture.

On a whim, I stopped by Grendel Hall. The last place you'd expect me to visit after nearly dying there. But I needed to stop in on Professor Harrison. There were things I had to say to him.

He was in the classroom he liked to haunt.

The old teacher greeted me with a nod and a pained look.

"Hi, Professor. I wanted to see if you were okay. I honestly didn't want to do what I did the other night, and it's been eating me up inside. What I did was . . ." Words escaped me.

". . . was precisely what you needed to do." The professor turned to face me. "Of course, it was a terrible ordeal, yet I will get beyond it. But I think you misunderstood what you did. It seems you believe you controlled us. That you forced spirits on campus to fight those people. You did not."

I stared at him in shock, but he continued.

"You are a good person. Nobody else with your gift would waste their time chatting about anthropology with a stodgy old ghost professor like me. But you do, and you enjoy it, I think. When you brought me into that room—when you sent us all there—you told us to fight your enemies. But you bared your emotions when you did so, and I knew your thoughts. They rang clear in all our minds. You believed they were *our foes*, not just yours. And we learned then what they had done to Luther. You did this for all the trapped souls as much as for yourself and your friends. You had our well-being in mind. You can't force me to do things against my will. At least, you never exercised such a power. We fought because we *chose* to."

His words raced through my head, and although they made sense, there was something that wasn't right. "But I still told you to do it. Even if I couldn't make you do it, I thought I could. And I sent you there to attack them."

"But not to kill. You wanted us to fight, but I never felt an urge to do more than that. And that makes you a good person. Despite what they were going to do to you, you didn't want any of them to die."

Silence filled the room, and I stared at the Haunt. At last, I cleared my throat. "You aren't just a ghost to me. I've lived my life sharing my nights with the dead. At some point, I blurred that line. You're all friends. It doesn't matter if you're alive or not. I'm glad you're okay. And I'm happy you feel this way because I don't know what I would do if I lost you."

Professor Harrison beamed, and it radiated genuine affection. "And I you, Lexi. But you should go now. The new janitor is not as lenient as old Mack used to be. He'll lock you in."

I smiled and said goodbye, then ran out the door of Grendel Hall. But, of course, I would spend many more nights in that building, discussing theories and ideas with my favorite teacher.

I walked with a spring in my step as I finished my trek to Strout Hall. Things wouldn't go back to normal at Brent College. Sure, classes would continue, and jerks would still be jerks. But now, I had plenty of friends to help me weather the storm and whatever it brought.

And as for Tom Prichard, he was a big surprise. When the semester began, I had thought I knew him more than I cared to. Now, I couldn't wait to see him again. It's funny how that happens. How a simple course of events can change your attitude toward a person. Was he the right guy for me? I didn't know.

But I couldn't wait to find out.

About the Author

Brad Younie writes books mostly about magic in the real world because he thinks people need a little excitement in their lives. Being an eternal teenager in a man's body, he owns a collection of swords, wands, and spends way too much time studying these things. A man with many hobbies, he plays guitar, reads books, watches movies, and fences with lightsabers and swords that are a bit sharper. But most of all, he weaves tales of magic and mystery that chills to the bone as it makes the heart race.

CONTACT

BradYounie.com

 bradyounie